THE WEALTH OF SHADOWS

The WEALTH of SHADOWS

A Novel

GRAHAM MOORE

RANDOM HOUSE · NEW YORK

The Wealth of Shadows is a work of fiction. All incidents and dialogue, and all characters with the exception of some well-known historical figures, are products of the author's imagination and are not to be construed as real. Where real-life historical persons appear, the situations, incidents, and dialogues concerning those persons are entirely fictional and are not intended to depict actual events or to change the entirely fictional nature of the work. In all other respects, any resemblance to persons living or dead is entirely coincidental.

Published in the United States by Random House,
an imprint and division of
Penguin Random House LLC, New York.

RANDOM HOUSE and the HOUSE colophon are
registered trademarks of Penguin Random House LLC.

LIBRARY OF CONGRESS CATALOGING-IN-PUBLICATION DATA
NAMES: Moore, Graham, author.
TITLE: The Wealth of Shadows : a novel / Graham Moore.
DESCRIPTION: First Edition. | New York : Random House, 2024.
IDENTIFIERS: LCCN 2023038938 (print) | LCCN 2023038939 (ebook) |
ISBN 9780593731925 (Hardback) | ISBN 9780593731932 (Ebook)
SUBJECTS: LCGFT: Spy fiction. | Thrillers (Fiction) | Novels.
CLASSIFICATION: LCC PS3613.O5575 W43 2024 (print) |
LCC PS3613.O5575 (ebook) | DDC 823/.92—dc23/eng/20231011
LC record available at https://lccn.loc.gov/2023038938
LC ebook record available at https://lccn.loc.gov/2023038939

Printed in the United States of America on acid-free paper

randomhousebooks.com

2 4 6 8 9 7 5 3 1

FIRST EDITION

Title-page image from Adobe Stock
Book design by Barbara M. Bachman

For Hugo and Louis, gooses.

PART
I

VALUES

1

STRAPHANGER

"It might make sense just to get some [bitcoin]
in case it catches on.
If enough people think the same way,
that becomes a self fulfilling prophecy."

—SATOSHI NAKAMOTO,
THE PSEUDONYMOUS INVENTOR OF BITCOIN

August 23, 1939

Ansel Luxford was on his morning commute, his knees wobbling with
the routine swerves of the Marshall Avenue trolley, when he glanced
out at the banks of the Mississippi River and noticed a growing column of Nazis.

More than a hundred men descended in rows from the St. Paul side
of the bridge. They strode three by three. Neat and orderly, in matching corduroy pants, blue ties, and tin-colored shirts. Most of the men
had little red *L*'s sewn on their front shirt pockets. Probably hand-
stitched by their Nazi wives, Ansel reckoned, who were likely at home
that very moment raising their hordes of Nazi children.

The trolley slowed, then began its climb onto the bridge. The flour
mills of Minneapolis emerged in the distance. But Ansel barely heard
the shriek of the trolley wheels, he was so horrified by the sight of a
Silver Shirt march smack dab in the center of the Twin Cities.

Just that morning, he had sat at the breakfast table as Angela, papers
spread out in front of her like ramparts against the day, recited the
fresh, rotten news: Hitler had just sent a hundred thousand troops to
stand ready for invasion along the Polish border. The Soviets had given
tacit approval, agreeing the day before to appease the Germans with a

treaty of nonaggression. Britain and France were frantically seeking diplomatic solutions in the hopes of avoiding war. The United States was not seeking any sort of solution at all. She remained resolutely neutral in matters of European conflict. Angela carried the *Morning Standard* to the stovetop so that she could heat the baby's glass bottle while informing him of a new Elmo Roper poll: A mere twelve percent of Americans thought the United States should involve itself in any way in this European mess. The percentage who believed America should involve herself militarily? Two percent.

Angela spoke the digits with disgust. Who *were* these people? What loafer could be comfortable sitting by, guffawing to *Amos & Andy* every week, while the world went all to hell?

Only a fool could believe that the murderous fascists threatening civilization would remain an ocean away; they weren't even on the other side of the Mississippi.

The trolley shuddered as it ascended the bridge, toward the marching Nazis. Ansel was crushed against his fellow straphangers: working men and women in faded linen suits and sale-price Donaldson's dresses on their way to the Fourth Street banks and the Pillsbury mills. He collided into the shoulder of a woman who wordlessly adjusted her pillbox hat.

Then, for an instant, her eyes strayed from the Perry Mason novel in her gloved hand. She glanced outside. Surely when she saw the threat to civilization looming just beyond the windows she would exclaim in horror. Anticipating her scream, he prepared to soothe her.

She promptly returned to her reading.

He peered around the car. The commuters politely avoided one another's eyes, including his. If any of them were alarmed by what was happening, they gave no hint of it.

He felt a sudden urge to scream.

This wasn't even the first American Nazi rally he had seen in Minneapolis. But it was by far the biggest.

He couldn't make out the rear of the march. Row after row of uniformed men appeared at the bridge's apex before descending toward St. Paul. He figured they'd be headed to the Ark Lodge for what had become their monthly barn burner. Angela would read aloud their vile speeches from the next morning's paper. What of them she could stomach.

The men would no doubt be treated to high-toned dudgeon about the virtues of the "Hitler program" and how it might be applied, productively, to the Jews and Negroes of the United States. They would bask in the exaltation of dictatorship as the most advanced form of government. They would be urged to acquire shotguns and ammunition, though the details of their use would tactfully be left to each listener's imagination. The Silver Shirt leadership was clever enough always to leave their threats of violence implied, never precisely articulated. They knew better than to get arrested for incitement. At least not now, as their ranks swelled. As their rallies ripened: plump and anger-red. Something was going to burst.

The trolley rose to meet the marchers. The fascist front was no more than twenty feet away on the pedestrian pathway.

Ansel could very well picture what a man of principle would do in this situation: He would leap right off the trolley and run up to the biggest, blondest Nazi of the bunch. "Not here," he would proclaim. "You can have Germany, you can have Italy, but not here."

He picked out the very man he ought to say it to. He hadn't been in a fight since he was a schoolboy, but he could sure see himself getting into one today. The Silver Shirt would slug him first. Maybe Ansel's nose would break, maybe he'd fall as his blood dripped onto the pavement. But he'd stand back up and he'd hold his ground as the whole pack joined in, beating him raw. The thought of violence was energizing. Their fists striking his body, the soles of their shiny black boots crushing his spine. It wouldn't take them a minute to crack his skull.

For an instant, he even pictured a new headline in the morning paper: "Minnesotan Father Killed by Nazi Rally." A death like that might wake a few people up. It might become a tragic but noble fuel for a much-needed resistance. He imagined Angela's face, heartbroken. Then he wondered whether in his sacrifice he might finally become the man she'd always believed he could be. Their daughter, Angie, would be too young, he figured, to have memories of him. But he imagined her growing up with the nourishment of her mother's proud stories. She'd tell of his great deed to her friends, her classmates, one day to her husband.

He knew full well that the name Ansel Luxford was never going to grace a history book. But if he leapt off the trolley in that moment it might at least remain on the lips of his descendants. Uttered, in passing, on those occasions when conversation turned to the dark old days, and to those humble few who'd bravely faced the coming end of the world and done what little they could, yet *all* they could, to help.

Then, having pictured all of this with perfect clarity, Ansel did what everyone else was doing: nothing.

He harbored no illusions about the kind of man he was. A middle-aged tax attorney in a neatly knotted bow tie. A husband whose taste for Scotch whiskey was resulting in a slowly plumping waistline. A father who crawled out of bed most mornings with a lumbago around his middle so awful that he had to swallow two Cafaspirins before his coffee.

Once upon a when, maybe, he had been some kind of a boy wonder. After he'd fled his old man's Iowa farm, he'd set his sights higher than the endless blue sky: a top college, the best law school, a prestigious government position, eventually a partner in a lucrative private practice. Boxes he'd checked, one by one, with strangely diminishing satisfaction. Until he'd ended up right here, in the same place everybody does: the middle. The great yawning expanse of the middle that slowly, inexorably, devours the best and worst alike. Middle age. Middling success. Money but not wealth. Status but not stature. Good work, but not, if he was being honest, a legacy of Good Works.

He knew who he once was: a headstrong kid with nothing to lose but his shoelaces as he moxied his way ahead in the world. And he knew that nowadays he was a man with responsibilities, not least among them a wife and a daughter who depended on him not to get his skull cracked in on the way to the office.

The trolley rattled to the top of the bridge and then slowly rolled down the Minneapolis side. He turned to see the last of the Silver Shirts disappear behind the sloping apex.

He looked at his fellow nine-to-fivers blithely ignoring the evil amassing on American soil, then stared at the polish of his leather shoes. He knew that if he faced anyone's gaze, he would crumble with shame.

The trolley clanged into Minneapolis. One by one, the straphangers got off at their stops.

As it happened, Ansel Luxford's opportunity to change the course of human history would not arrive until the following Monday.

2

IF YOU ONLY KNOW
HOW TO READ THEM

"Price is what you pay. Value is what you get."

—WARREN BUFFETT

August 28, 1939

By six thirty the following Monday evening, the air inside the Old
Ebbitt Grill in Washington was thick with Camel smoke and the musk
of drunk civil servants. Down at one end, a party of pink-cheeked
bright boys slugged bottled beer. They'd just skipped over from the
White House, Ansel figured, from the way they peeped over each
other's shoulders searching for big-time connections. The tables by
the far wall, underneath the stag heads and crooked oil paintings, had
been settled by gray hairs. By the look of their colorful tie pins and
tumblers of Bénédictine, they were probably Commerce, working out
just how they were going to grab the attention of the Federal Reserve
this week.

Ansel found his own reflection in the backbar mirror. Boy, was he
ever a type himself: another stool-hunched boozer in a sweat-damp
suit, a banded fedora on his lap, a half-empty glass of half-brown sauce
in his mitts.

His plane had landed at Hoover two hours back and he'd barely had
a chance to drop his bag at the Carlton before rushing here. He wished
he'd had time to press his jacket.

A short, portly man hoisted himself onto the nearest stool.

Ansel gave him a once-over. Was this who he was waiting for? "Harry Dexter White?"

"You're Luxford?" White's voice was a nicotine growl. His tie was undone. His plump jowl hung over his shirt collar. His sleeves were rolled up beneath his suit jacket, giving his arms a strongman's bulge. He fished a Lucky Strike soft pack from his jacket, sucked out a cigarette, and lit it before Ansel had a chance to respond.

"Yes. Thank you for meeting with me."

"What can I do for you?" White blew smoke from his thick lips.

"I appreciate your seeing me on such short notice."

"What can I do for you?"

"It's a favor, and I'm—"

"I'd say it a third time, but I'd hate to be a bore."

Ansel hesitated. "You're busy. I'll get right to the point."

"It'd be a welcome change of pace."

It was in that moment that Ansel realized Harry Dexter White was an asshole. A fact that he could use to his advantage: You had to meet assholes head-on or they'd never take you seriously.

"I'd like to come work for you at the Treasury Department," Ansel said.

"You can send résumés to the personnel office."

"I'd like to come work for *you,* specifically, at the Treasury Department."

"Why?"

"Your sparkling personality."

White took a long drag from his Lucky. It was as if he were weighing whether it was worth the trouble to get offended.

Instead, he cracked a Cheshire grin. "Reginald," he called to the bartender. "An ice-cold martini, if you wouldn't mind."

"We don't serve 'em warm," the bartender answered.

Ansel tried to speak again, but White waved him off with a stubby finger. In one fluid motion, he put his cigarette to bed and then lit another. By the third silent puff, the bartender arrived with the martini. White took in an inch and two of the four olives with a single suck.

"It pays to be a regular," Ansel offered.

"Being a regular means I usually forget to pay. Look, John Pehle asked if I'd talk to you, and I rarely do what John asks, but he's doing me a solid right now on another matter, so here we are. I don't make decisions when I'm drunk, or even worse, when I'm sober. Whatever it is you want from me I'd say you got about a martini and a half to get it."

Ansel examined the contents of his own tumbler. The liquor was doing its work to calm his nerves, but he'd have to take care of the rest himself.

He downed what remained in the glass without a wince, then gestured to the bartender for another.

"I'm a Scotch man," he began.

"Whatever gets you through the night."

"Professionally, I mean. I'm an attorney. Taxes, estates, import/ export duties. I used to work at Treasury actually, right out of law school. I worked with John then. Before he worked for you. He was the one who told me about you."

"What exactly did John tell you?"

"That you're an acquired taste."

Ansel was sure he saw White hide a smile behind his next sip.

"I live in St. Paul. Mostly I do tax work for local businesses. Somebody dies, wants to pass along the hardware store to the cousins, that sort of thing. But one of my clients is a major Scotch importer. Most of the Johnnie Walker in Minnesota comes on their ships."

"Are there a lot of ships in Minnesota?"

"They've got trucks, too. My point: I know the Scotch business."

White didn't seem impressed.

"I used to drink here sometimes," Ansel continued. "This bar. A couple years back, when I was working at Treasury. You know what John and I paid for a finger of Scotch back then?"

"I have absolutely no idea."

"Eighty-five cents."

"You should be drinking better Scotch."

"Reginald," Ansel called out. "How much do I owe you?"

The bartender returned. "Leaving?"

"No, I just want to know how much this glass of Scotch costs."

"Seventy-five cents each," Reginald said. "You had two."

"Thank you. I'm sure Mr. White is ready for his second martini."

Reginald measured, poured, shook.

Ansel continued. "That bottle of Scotch cost the wholesaler about two dollars. The bar buys it for three. Twenty-four ounces divided into twelve two-ounce pours at seventy-five cents each is around eight fifty for the bottle."

White would not need a doctorate in economics, though Ansel knew he had one, to calculate the profit. "Sounds like I should open up a bar."

"Liquor is a good business. But why has the price of Scotch gone down?"

"The Federal Reserve is over on Constitution, if you're worried about deflation."

"The price of Scotch is going down here because in London the chancellor of the exchequer has dropped export tariffs on Scotch to nil."

"You're complaining?"

"I'm curious. So I did what I do when I get curious, which is to dig. You know what I found? It's not just Scotch. London has recently dropped export tariffs on certain pharmaceuticals, on a few high-end wool products . . . Even more curious! Why this very specific set of goods? And then it occurred to me: These are goods that happen to be purchased in great quantities by Americans. And we Americans pay for them in good old U.S. dollars."

A shadow darkened White's rosy complexion.

Perhaps Ansel was on the right track. "What a coincidence! If the Exchequer lowers export tariffs *only* on goods purchased by Americans, then the price to folks like us in bars like this drops. We buy more, we pay in dollars, and now a whole bunch of British exporters are sitting on mounds of American currency. What a terrible bother! They pay their workers and run their businesses in *sterling;* here they are up to their necks in *dollars.* Good thing they can get the sterling they need by trading all their dollars to . . . the Exchequer."

White glanced around the room. No one, it seemed, was listening to their conversation.

"Why is the British government stockpiling U.S. dollars, Mr. White?"

"Your guess is as good as mine."

"My guess is that they want to buy something. And they believe the only place they can buy it is America. For that, they're going to need dollars. So what is it?"

White leaned in, his voice at a whisper. "I'm thinking you ought to make plain what it is you want from me."

If Ansel was getting under White's skin, that meant that he was also getting somewhere. He had spent all summer building up this theory and had practiced delivering this speech so many times to his wife. Yet he found himself surprised to receive, in White's rudeness, confirmation that he was right on the money. "You like schnapps?"

"No."

Ansel raised his voice. "Reginald! Could I get a bit of schnapps on the side?"

The bartender shook his head. "Been out for a spell now."

"I wonder why that is." Ansel looked expectantly at White. "The Old Ebbitt is out of schnapps because Germany's liquor exports have gone down eighty percent. Interesting, isn't it? Either they're gulping down every last drop at home . . . or the Reichsbank is actively discouraging certain exports. Almost a perfect inverse of what the Exchequer is doing, isn't it? It's as if the German economists know that they will soon *not* need any dollars at all. I wonder: Why might Germany be preparing to sever herself economically from the U.S.?"

White blew smoke into Ansel's face. "Treasury has been lobbing sanctions against Germany since Kristallnacht. We poke them, they poke back. What a secret you've uncovered: Roosevelt dislikes Nazis."

"If the Germans cut liquor exports, what happens to the workers who'd been employed in the production of all that raspberry brandy? Well, it turns out the glass mills that made the schnapps bottles have been converted into steel mills. Where's all that steel going? It's hard to know exactly because the Nazis are, among their various sins, colossal liars. They say they're building Volkswagens, but most Germans don't own cars. Looking through the economic data I've been able to get my hands on—just the publicly available material—I was able to chart materials into the country, materials out of it. I have the tables back at the hotel, if you want to check my math. But it seems likely that all this extra steel is not being exported; it's going to the military. And the Wehrmacht are not building sedans, they're building single-engine Messerschmitts. Now, you see the problem with this, don't you?"

The smoke from White's cigarette appeared to darken. "Unless you really love raspberry brandy, no."

"The Ruhr valley bottle makers *were* getting paid by exports; the Ruhr valley fighter plane makers, not to mention the boys in the cockpits, are *now* getting paid by the government. So where's the government getting all this money?"

"You mean, where's the Reichsbank getting all these reichsmarks? So help me, if you start talking about monetary theory—John Maynard Keynes and all that insufferable navel-gazing—I will pass out where I sit. Let's cut to the quick and say that when the Reichsbank wants reichsmarks, it does exactly what the U.S. government does when it wants dollars: It prints some."

"Exactly. To pay for all this military spending, Hitler has to print new reichsmarks. And he has to print a lot of them. But he's not selling bonds on the international markets. Just the opposite: He's cutting Germany off from most foreign trade. Which means that one of three things is going to happen. One, Hitler will have to print so many new reichsmarks to satisfy the military payrolls that the ensuing inflation will make the Great Depression look like a dimple. Two, Hitler will pull back on military spending and the ensuing mass unemployment will make the Great Depression look like . . . I don't know, some kind of small pebble. Or three, Hitler will put all the Wehrmacht's new steel to use."

Ansel's voice became a grim whisper. "The Germans conquer new territory, and they expand their supply of both natural resources and, even better for them, taxable subjects."

He looked to the rows of alcohol behind the bar.

"You can tell the future of the world in those bottles," Ansel said. "If you only know how to read them."

"What're they telling you?"

"Germany is going to invade Poland."

White fished a stray bit of tobacco from his lower lip. "There are troops on the border. A lot of people think Hitler might pull the trigger."

"What I'm saying is that he already did. Two years ago, when he started letting go of Germany's dollar reserves. The moment he did that, the hammer started toward the pin. There's no stopping it. There's no turning back. Any moment now it's going to ignite the gunpowder and bullets are going to fly. The war has *already* started, Mr. White. The Brits are stockpiling dollars because the chancellor of the exchequer knows that to fight back they're going to need to buy American steel. American equipment, American oil, maybe even American weapons. *That's* what Britain can only pay for in dollars." Ansel leaned in close enough to smell White's charcoal breath. "But everything I just said? You already know it. You've done the same analysis I have. And even if Downing Street doesn't know it yet, even if the White House doesn't know it yet, the economists at the Exchequer and your men at Treasury know it's inevitable. And word is, you're the only one in Washington who's doing anything about it. So why am I here?"

Ansel finally paused long enough to take a cigarillo from his jacket pocket, snip the end, and fire it up.

"I want in."

3

THE ONLY SANE
PERSON LEFT

*"There are two kinds of forecasters: those who don't know,
and those who don't know they don't know."*

—JOHN KENNETH GALBRAITH

August 28, 1939 (cont'd)

White tapped his fingers against his martini glass.

"What is it you want to do for me?" he said at last. "Predict the future?"

"I can read the papers. Any sort of involvement in this European dispute would be hugely unpopular. The United States is, as a matter of law, neutral in any conflict between the UK, France, and Germany. Roosevelt can't do anything. The War Department, the Navy, the State Department—their hands are all tied."

"What is it you think that a Treasury Department division director can do?"

"That's what I came here to ask: What's your plan?"

White extracted the final cigarette from his pack. He crumpled the wrapper and took his time lighting up. "Sounds like John Pehle has been real chatty with you."

"He's a friend."

"If I had a plan to stop the Germans—not saying that I do—it would be pretty top secret, wouldn't it?"

"Right."

"The policy of the United States government is, as you so helpfully pointed out, neutrality."

"Yes."

"To do anything otherwise would be treasonous."

"Yes."

"If I had a plan, I couldn't even tell the White House, much less State, the military."

"Yes."

"If the FBI found out, me and whoever I might be working with would go to jail. Or worse."

"Yes."

"So if I had a plan so secret that I couldn't tell Roosevelt, Hull, or J. Edgar Hoover . . . why on earth would John Pehle tell a tax attorney from Minnesota?"

"John didn't tell me anything. I told *him* that I am a concerned citizen."

"It's the last word in that sentence that interests me."

"I told John that I am one of what seem to be precious few Americans who think that as bad as what these Nazis have already done, it's only the beginning. Tossing the Jews out of schools? Arresting thousands on bum charges and sending them to the concentration camps? Those work camps were supposed to have been built for POWs and now they're holding . . . who? Jewish shopkeepers, farmers, teachers? If *half* the stories you hear are true, the sooner the United States gets involved, the better."

"Your wife," White said. "She know you're here?"

An old drunk in the corner knocked over a chair as he tried to stand.

"What?" Ansel sputtered.

"Your wife. Angela."

Ansel failed to hide his surprise.

"You worked for the government," White said condescendingly. "We have files."

"What does my wife have to do with anything?"

White looked at Ansel's wedding ring. "Maybe you're bored of the snow. Maybe you're bored of the wife. So you flew here for one more shot at reclaiming your youthful glory."

"A shot at helping our country."

White rolled his eyes. "How does Angela feel about all that?"

"She understands as well as I do that there is a growing army of murderous fascists mounting all their resources to end civilization as we know it. And she believes, as I do, that we cannot just sit around doing nothing."

There were nights—more than he could count—where he felt like the entire world had gone mad and he was the only sane person left. Surely a man like Harry Dexter White must feel as he did! Surely he was in the presence of a like mind, no matter how gruff his manner.

White laughed. "You came all the way to D.C. to take a clandestine meeting with a man who maybe could get you into what you believed to be some kind of secret government program to fight Nazis using economics . . . and you told your wife?"

Ansel felt his face flush with embarrassment.

White looked satisfied at having his suspicions confirmed. "John Pehle told me a few things about you, too."

"What'd John say?"

"That you might be one of the smartest men he's ever met."

"Tell John thanks."

"A real storyteller, John said. Lots of men can read an import-export table; you can turn one into a sonnet. John said they used to hand you stacks of foreign-exchange charts and by the time you were done with them, they read like *Hamlet*."

"John is too kind."

"John said you're a real straight shooter, too. A man who's prudent in his profession, careful in his career, and honest with his wife."

"I fail to see the problem."

"The problem is that here you are, saying you want to join what you've imagined to be some hush-hush secret operation."

The bow tie around Ansel's neck felt suddenly constricting.

"A man like you, after achieving a comfortable, married middle age—how old is your daughter now, two?—suddenly you want to play secret agent? I don't buy it."

"You don't think I'm trustworthy?"

"Just the opposite. I think that you, Mr. Luxford, are a decent man. And me and my boys . . . Well, we ain't."

White stood. At full height, his eyes were dead even with Ansel's.

"But sadly, you've been misinformed," White said. "It is the policy of the United States government to maintain neutrality in this European conflict. Nobody at Treasury is up to anything regarding Germany."

"Hang on a minute—"

"Have a good trip back to Minnesota." White leaned in and whispered in Ansel's ear before marching away, "And tell your chickenshit friends at the FBI that if they want to take me out, they better send somebody who plays this game a lot better than you."

4

PAPER CLIPS

"Economists set themselves too easy, too useless a task if in tempestuous seasons they can only tell us that when the storm is past the ocean is flat again."

—JOHN MAYNARD KEYNES

August 28, 1939 (cont'd)

Ansel got himself crooked drunk before he undertook the harrowing two-block journey back to the Carlton. He paid no mind to the door-man's smug face as he stumbled inside. He ignored the spinning chandelier, the bronze lights swirling like a carnie ride. He only slipped once, at a lurch of the self-running elevator. His key took a bit of fussing to work into the lock of his single room.

He tossed his jacket and then his tie onto the twin bed.

He sat at the desk and telephoned home. He had to repeat the extension twice for the long-distance operator. Maybe on account of his slurring.

"This must be costing a fortune," were the first words out of Angela's mouth when she answered.

"Is she up?"

"I just put her down. How did it go?"

"I was hoping I could hear her voice."

"So not well, then?"

"Maybe you could bring her to the phone."

"You didn't get the job?"

Ansel didn't want to spend another minute talking about Harry

Dexter White. "The man said there wasn't a job. I'd been misinformed."

Angela didn't sound like she believed this any more than he did.
"What was he like?"

On the desk in front of Ansel sat a pile of research he'd brought
from St. Paul.

He idly opened the top folder, inside of which were pages of tidily
paper-clipped financial data. He didn't have access to any government
sources. Everything here had been right out in public: the financial
pages of *The New York Times*, *The Wall Street Journal*, some of the London papers, and even a few German and French ones. He knew only a
smattering of words in either language, but helpfully, numerical figures
didn't require translation. He'd assembled all of this on weeknights—
the baby asleep in her room; Angela downstairs listening to Sid Sil-
vers on the Twin Cities radio, the sound of her laughter bleeding up
through the floorboards to Ansel's study as he obsessed.

He shut the folder. What an idiot! If he had been dumb enough to
think that his amateur analysis was going to impress anybody, then he
didn't deserve the job that he wasn't going to get.

"Kind of an asshole," he told his wife.

In the silence, he could hear her choosing not to chide his language.
"We have plenty of those in St. Paul, in case you're feeling left out."

Ansel leaned over and tugged at his shoelace. The knot was tight,
his fingers imprecise.

"Any new words?"

"Hard to tell. Maybe *skunk*."

"Skunk?"

"We saw one, out by the trash. You should look when you're back."

"She knew what it was?"

"Could have just been, you know, '*sk-uuuuhhhh*.'"

He enjoyed imagining the sound of Angie's voice.

He leaned over farther for a better grip on his laces when he saw
something shiny on the dark carpet.

"You tie one on after?" Angela knew him well.

"I did."

He picked up the object: It was a paper clip.

"I support the maneuver."

How'd a paper clip get onto the floor?

Holding it in one hand, Ansel used the other to flip through the folders. It took a moment to find the paper clip's rightful place. "Lemons, lemonade, that kind of thing."

"Are there lemons in an old-fashioned?"

Here was where the errant paper clip belonged, holding together a set of sheets on German glass manufacturing.

How had it fallen off? These sheets had been right in the middle of the file. Inside the closed folder.

"Honey?" She sounded far away.

He slid the paper clip back into place. It fit so snuggly that doing so required effort.

It would have taken similar effort to pull it off.

So help him, that paper clip had been on those pages when he'd left this room a few hours ago. He'd intended on showing them to White the next day, once he'd awakened his interest. Ansel had prepared them thoroughly. *I*'s dotted, *t*'s crossed, everything just so.

Someone else must have searched through them.

He didn't feel drunk anymore.

"Ansel? You there?"

Someone had been in his room.

5

THE PRACTICAL
EFFICACY OF HOPE

"All money is a matter of belief."

—ADAM SMITH

August 31, 1939

Angela Luxford believed in Jesus Christ, Fred Allen, and Franklin Roosevelt, though not necessarily in that order. For as long as Ansel had known her, he'd been swept up by the gale force of her beliefs. She did not harbor mere preferences. When Angela believed in something, her commitment was absolute. She'd assure anyone who'd listen that the closest thing she'd ever heard to the sound of an angel's wings was the croon of Bing Crosby, and she had the record collection to prove it. The rosaries that she intoned nightly at the foot of her daughter's crib were the same ones she'd once said beside her baby brother's. She had missed exactly two meetings of the Catholic Daughters of the Americas in five years, both in the weeks after Angie was born. Fridays, without fail, she served fish. From the head of the table, she gave thanks first to God for hauling this country out of the darkest days of the Depression, but just behind Him she thanked FDR for being on hand to see the job through.

When Ansel first met her, she'd been leading a student group for Roosevelt at Catholic University. She hadn't minded that Ansel wasn't a Catholic—heck, that he wasn't a God-fearing man at all—so long as he voted for FDR. He helped her organize marches and manage donation campaigns. She was the one who'd suggested that they both go into government work after he'd graduated from law school. But where?

Since the early work of John Maynard Keynes had first scrambled his brain as an undergraduate, he'd harbored a passion for economics. "The dismal science," they called it, but it wasn't, not the way Keynes wrote about it: To understand how money flows through a society was to understand how blood brings life to the body of man. Ansel felt that in Keynes's treatises lay an explanation for everything: war, poverty, pestilence, or, if we only could get the numbers straight, the formula for an endless flourishing. But Ansel had no mind to spend his days in a classroom. His old man had been a schoolteacher and hated it. Ansel had gone to law school so he could put himself to use in the real world.

Angela found a secretarial position at the Justice Department, while Ansel got his foot in the door at Treasury.

"We're working for Roosevelt," she'd say, notwithstanding however many layers of bureaucracy stood between the president and two newly employed graduates. Back then it felt like every smart young Democrat in the country was headed to D.C. to help FDR turn things around. It was a hopeful time, and among Angela's fervent beliefs was a faith in the practical efficacy of hope.

And then, the slog. The wheels of government spun fast—but they mostly flecked up ditch mud. There wasn't a single thing Ansel worked on at Treasury that didn't end up caveated and compromised near to unrecognizable sludge by the time Congress got through with it. They were doing some good. But they were doing it slowly.

The hours grew and grew; the paychecks didn't. Neither of them was the type to complain, much less expect a life of luxury. But where, in their cramped one-bedroom, was the baby going to sleep?

When Ansel's old pal rang up and offered him a partnership in St. Paul, the timing seemed auspicious. The money sounded too good to pass up. He'd be making so much that Angela wouldn't have to worry about holding on to her job while holding on to an infant.

They'd assured each other that they were only being practical, making sound long-term decisions for their growing family, as they'd carried their few boxes up the wraparound porch of a Victorian two-story nestled into a beech-lined cul-de-sac.

Since they'd arrived, Angela had directed her political energies toward writing letters to the editors of nearly every daily in Minnesota. When she opened her morning *Tribune* and discovered an imprecise headline, she wrote a letter. When she read an article in the *Dispatch* that failed to include relevant context, she wrote a letter. When she read the *Pioneer Press* approvingly, making it front to back without correction, she would write a letter anyway, suggesting potential future stories. Nearly every month one or another of the papers would print one of her missives. Ansel had tried cutting out the clippings once, but Angela didn't see the point in saving them for posterity. She wasn't doing it for the glory of seeing her name in newsprint. She was making sure her fellow citizens were as informed as they could be about the world around them. Over the last few years, this meant seeing that they were as alarmed as possible about the mounting threat to global peace and prosperity coming from Germany. If Angela had anything to say about it—and based on the quantity of her letters to the editor, she had quite a bit—one could not be too informed. Or too alarmed.

She wasn't the type to stop moving, not even in St. Paul. So while the baby napped, she took up an interest in all things Chinese. She started dropping into each of the two Chinese restaurants in town and asking if she might observe their kitchens. Apparently the chefs got a real kick out of seeing this raven-haired American lady, a hint of her father's Sicily still in her accent, pursuing an interest in their Shanghai cuisine. She was working on getting the noodles right at home.

The night after Ansel returned from Washington, dinner was something she called "lo mein." It was like some of the pastas that her Italian mother used to crank out, she said.

After they put the baby to bed, she took the fold-up writing desk into the sitting room and unsheathed her Underwood portable. From the kitchen, as he cleaned dried sauce off the dishes, he could hear her putting the world to rights with its insistent, thunderous clatter.

She hadn't shown any disappointment about his failure to get the job with Harry Dexter White, but his defeat must have been eating at her. How could it not? She'd married a fellow in the cause, an idealist who used to wake up before his alarm rang every morning because working for his country was an honorable thing. Now he spent his time helping rich people avoid import taxes so that his daughter could grow up in a house with a mahogany balustrade.

He'd donate more to the Benson campaign, he told himself as he scrubbed a serving fork. That was something he could do.

Who was he kidding? His life had amounted to little; all that promising optimism had fallen to the banalities of middle age. He had a sudden urge to tell Angela he was sorry. He'd promised her more than creature comforts. She'd once believed in him. And he was grateful for it, even if this time her faith had been misplaced.

The sound of the doorbell was so loud that Ansel instinctively looked to the ceiling, hoping it hadn't woken the baby.

Angela appeared in the kitchen doorway. "It's nearly ten."

"I'll see who it is."

On the front porch he found a lanky teenager from Western Union. "Ansel Luxford?" the boy said.

Ansel nodded. The boy handed him a telegram and was already gone by the time he'd torn it open.

The telegram read: "Still interested? Hotel Lowry. 10:30 P.M."

It was signed: "White."

6

HOW FAR ARE YOU WILLING TO GO?

*"From the saintly and single-minded idealist
to the fanatic is often but a step."*

—FRIEDRICH AUGUST VON HAYEK

August 31, 1939 (cont'd)

The lobby of the Lowry was apportioned in nineteenth-century opulence: Ornate chandeliers hung from a vaulted ceiling and plush armchairs sank into violet carpets. Ansel entered at 10:34 P.M., according to his wristwatch, and found no one waiting for him.

Not wanting to seem conspicuous, he went to the radio room and took a seat on the davenport. Previous occupants had left the Philco running. A brass band played tinnily from the speakers.

He'd smoked half a ten-cent cigarillo when he heard a man's voice over the radio. Ansel wasn't really listening, not until a few words poked out at him.

"Bombing . . . Warsaw . . . Ports blockaded . . ."

His spine stiffened. He went to the lacquered Philco and turned up the volume.

". . . reports that complete mobilization has been ordered in Britain, as Parliament meets to discuss its commitment to fulfill its obligations to the people of Poland. Paris reports that the Nazi invasion began near Danzig, after—"

There was a knock. Ansel turned to find the night porter rapping his knuckles on the molded doorframe.

"You Luxford?" The porter did not hide his indifference.

Ansel nodded while trying to make out the words coming from the radio.

"There's a call for you. A long-distance line from Washington, D.C. Man said you'd want to take it in the back office."

Ansel saved the remaining cigarillo and followed the man through a rear hallway. They came to a door whose sign read MANAGER.

Inside, the night porter gestured to a telephone on the messy desk. "Your friend said you needed some privacy."

With that, he was gone.

Ansel lifted the receiver. "Hello?"

"It's White."

"I just heard . . . I think I heard . . ." Before he realized he was saying it, he blurted out, "I'm not working for the FBI."

White's laugh came across the line like a burst of static. "You're probably not. But a time like this, it's a risk I've got to take."

"They really did it? They invaded Poland?"

A crackle on the line. Ansel pictured smoke swirling around White's head. "Past two days, anyone loitering in your rearview?"

"What?"

"Giving you the tail. If somebody's had their eyes on you—if anybody's been a little too curious about our conversation—you hang up this instant. Good night, goodbye. What I do, I can't do if we got looky-loos."

Ansel thought of the displaced paper clip in his hotel room. He didn't know for sure that someone had been looking through his papers. The maid might have knocked them over; he might have dropped them himself without remembering. Was he really going to miss out on what might be the biggest opportunity of his life—a chance to be of real service to the anti-fascist cause—because one night he'd gotten himself sauced and found an errant paper clip?

"Not of which I'm aware." Ansel was a lawyer through and through.

"You sure?"

"I can't claim to be an expert on tails. Or even a novice." He would keep his eyes peeled. If he saw further evidence that he was being followed, he'd tell White straightaway. He wasn't being deceitful, he was being careful not to jump to far-fetched conclusions without any evidence.

White took his time. Perhaps he was pondering Ansel's judicious response. "You told me you want to fight these Nazis."

"I do."

"You think they're rotten to the core, and you want to help stop them?"

"That's right."

"Then my next question to you is: How far are you willing to go?"

Ansel wasn't sure how to answer.

"I'm offering you this job," White continued. "And I'll need a response from you now on whether or not you want it. One answer, zero equivocation. You say to me a single word. If that word is no, then we never speak again, and you will live a long, happy life about which I couldn't give two shits. But if that word is yes, then I'll see you in Washington. Monday morning, eight A.M."

That's in four days.

"You say yes and there's no going back. Maybe at the end of this we get world peace and you and me, we're heroes. Or maybe at the end there's an electric chair. Or maybe one night we just disappear . . . and your wife, your little girl, they never know what happened. I need to spell this out so you can't say I didn't warn you. If you come work for me, I'm going to ask you to do things that are not legal. I'm going to ask you to do things that are not moral. Our enemies? They are bad people. Make no mistake: So am I."

Ansel realized he was gripping the receiver so tightly that his knuckles hurt.

"Now." The hiss traveling across the line sounded like a pit of slithering snakes. "What'll it be, Mr. Luxford?"

7

SETTING SAIL

"The time to buy is when there's blood on the streets,
even if the blood is your own."

—APOCRYPHALLY ATTRIBUTED TO
BARON NATHAN ROTHSCHILD

September 1, 1939

"Yes," Angela said the next morning. "One hundred percent. Let's go." She held the baby in the crook of one arm, resting the warm bottle on her shoulder so Angie could drink; with her other arm she unfolded an early edition. The headlines were printed as thick as mortar shells, a gloomy storm of hell-black ink.

The bright morning light warmed the kitchen. Ansel was still in his soft, thick pajamas. Not that he'd slept the night before.

"We'd have to leave the day after tomorrow," he said.

She didn't hesitate. "Ethel's husband is a realtor. From down the street? I can talk to him about putting the house up for sale."

"Officially, I'd be joining the Treasury's Research Department. Background work on the unfolding European crisis, how it might affect American business."

"And in reality?"

He shook his head. He didn't know. Whatever White was up to, he was keeping it close to the chest. "If I say yes to this, there will be things I can't talk about at home. A lot of things, probably. It's a top secret position. I know that might be . . . I don't know, hard for you."

The baby finished the bottle and Angela set her down, making sure her wobbly legs were steady. "*If* you say yes? Didn't you already?"

She sure had his number.

"I had to make a decision in the moment and I reckoned you'd—"

"You were right."

"The money will be terrible."

She laughed.

"I mean it. Really terrible."

"We can stay with my parents for a spell. While we look for a new place."

She'd grown up in the D.C. area. Most of her family was still there. For her, this was going home.

"If the money turns into a problem," she added, "I could always go back to work."

She said it in a way that made it sound as if he'd been the one who told her to quit her job. But she'd been carrying and they'd been moving; he didn't remember it being much of a debate.

He nodded, and then turned their conversation toward the great many practicalities that would need ironing out.

The banalities of moving consumed their day and continued well into the night. They should have been exhausted, as they barely had time to sit, much less eat or rest, and yet Ansel felt they both whirred with a newfound energy. Like they were young again, at the prime of their lives, setting sail for a grand adventure.

A few times over the course of the day he caught a certain look on Angela's face, this curious gleam in her eye. He was filling a leather suitcase with stuffed animals when he saw it first, as she stared at him from the doorway. He returned home from the dealership with a newly purchased trailer and caught a flash of it as she watched him hitch it to the back of the family's Ford. It had been so long since he'd seen this look that he didn't even recognize it right away. It was only well after dark, as he wearily took his boots off for what would be another fruitless attempt at sleep, that he realized what it was.

She was proud of him.

8

BLACKOUT
OF PEACE

"When goods do not cross borders, soldiers will."

—FRÉDÉRIC BASTIAT,
NINETEENTH-CENTURY FRENCH ECONOMIST

September 3, 1939

The voice of Franklin Delano Roosevelt thumped from the Ford's radio as it sped through a barren stretch of northern Ohio. "Let no man or woman falsely talk of America sending its armies to European fields. At this moment there is being prepared a proclamation of neutrality."

The radio shrieked a high electric buzz and then crackled into nothing. There was only the rhythmic thump of the tires against the highway, the whoosh of the wind, and a few scattered bursts of static. Outside was black, a sky bereft of stars. The sedan's headlights seemed to expose only a few feet of oncoming pavement.

Angela slept in the passenger seat. Angie was restless, wiggling on a pile of blankets in the back. Most of the family's possessions, certainly everything of any value, were hitched to the bumper. Every time Ansel pushed the car past fifty, the clunky trailer threatened to topple.

It'd been a long drive, but Pennsylvania wasn't too far now.

The president's voice thudded back into the car. "Most of us in the United States believe in spiritual values."

Angela stirred.

"Most of us, regardless of what church we belong to, believe in the spirit of the New Testament. A great teaching which opposes itself to the use of force, of armed force, of marching armies and falling bombs. The overwhelming masses of our people seek peace."

On Saturday, a German bomb had killed twenty-one civilians when it landed on a Warsaw apartment house. This morning, Britain and France had simultaneously declared war on Germany. Hours later, British ships had blockaded the Baltic Sea near Skagerrak, and in response the Germans had torpedoed a British passenger liner on its way to Scotland. The radio had said that fourteen hundred passengers had been aboard. Including 292 Americans. When she heard the news, Angela had closed her eyes and made the sign of the cross.

"I hope the United States will keep out of this war. I believe that it will. And I give you assurance and reassurance that every effort of your government will be directed toward that end."

Did the president know of the plots developing within his own administration? Was he aware that what he was saying was, strictly speaking, untrue?

"As long as it remains within my power to prevent, there will be no blackout of peace in the United States."

He turned to his wife in the passenger seat. He watched her listen to the soft patter of the president's falsehoods. She seemed to be deliberating.

"If he knows," she proclaimed finally, "then he's saying what he needs to, for the country. If he doesn't know, then he's sure got the right people working for him. Either way . . ."

She bowed her head, as if silently thanking her lord for the blessing of FDR.

Ansel inched his foot down on the gas. The sedan rattled as it careened ahead into the dark.

9

ECONOMIC WARFARE

"Teach a parrot the words supply *and* demand
and you've got an economist."

—APOCRYPHALLY ATTRIBUTED
TO THOMAS CARLYLE

September 4, 1939

The stool-and-counter on Constitution Avenue had a twenty-cent
ham-and-egg special, but Ansel was too hopped up on coffee and
nerves to be hungry. He was sipping from his third cup when a friendly
face came through the door.

John Pehle's patrician demeanor had barely changed since Ansel had
worked alongside him nearly a decade before, though his slicked-back
hair had receded more aggressively from his scalp. After handshakes
and warm words of welcome, Pehle sat across from Ansel in the window booth and draped a paper napkin over his tan suit. Ansel was reminded that Pehle was bred from a family that had as much money as
Ansel's had none. Pehle had been to all the best schools, read all the au
courant novels that formed the basis of cocktail chatter, took his kids
to the family's house in Connecticut every summer. And yet somehow
the moment he and Ansel had met, carefully tucking away their umbrellas beneath the hallway hat rack on the Treasury's ground floor,
before either of them even had offices, they'd become fast friends.
They discovered they were lawyers among economists; practical men
amid theoreticians; and they both had a mind to keep the floor from
getting slick on a wet day.

"So John," Ansel said after the waitress brought fresh coffees, "what's going on?"

It turned out that Pehle had little idea.

A month prior, Pehle said, Harry Dexter White had come into his office and told him to dig up some new office space. Something nearby that nobody would pay much mind to. The W&J Sloane building on Twelfth Street, three blocks from Treasury, turned out to have an un-used fifth-floor storeroom. The furniture store had never been all that fashionable—that "gauche faux Versailles nonsense," as Pehle put it, had thankfully never found favor in Washington—but as they sold even fewer of their Louis XV line of cane settee window benches than they'd anticipated, they'd started renting out their unneeded upper floors to the government. The Bureau of Internal Revenue had taken over the fourth, for storage. When Pehle came around on behalf of Treasury and inquired about temporarily renting out the top floor to house a team of researchers, the manager cut him a swell deal.

"A team of researchers?" Ansel asked.

Pehle sipped from coffee the color of khaki. "That's all Harry said. What we are to be researching, or who exactly constitutes this team, went unmentioned. Such is Harry's way." He consulted his gold Rolex. It was time to go. "Ours is not to reason why. Ours is but to . . . Well, you know."

Ansel didn't, but let it drop.

"You'll get used to it."

———

AN HOUR LATER, ANSEL sat beside Pehle in a makeshift conference room on the fifth floor of the unpopular furniture shop. Price tags still hung from the wing-backed walnut chairs. Despite the ornate styling, Ansel was sure he'd built sturdier ones with his own hands back in Iowa when he was a teenager.

Around the oval table sat a handful of men, fewer than Ansel had expected. They'd exchanged names and handshakes quickly.

At one end was Joe DuBois. Disheveled and floppy-haired, he reminded Ansel of a graduate student who'd stayed up all night preparing for a colloquium. He was a lawyer, evidently, though one with a curious expertise: gold. He told Ansel that he'd first come to Treasury to help confiscate gold bullion, which was still being hoarded by some no-good rich louses in this country despite the caps on ownership that Roosevelt had instituted after the Depression. He'd even worked with the Secret Service to prosecute a few hoarders. He looked like a dopey academic, but the way he spoke of throwing rich people in jail, he sounded like a Communist, a firebrand, or both.

Beside him was James Saxon, who didn't look old enough even to have graduated from college. But Pehle, who apparently knew Saxon, whispered to Ansel that the kid had gotten his undergraduate degree in the spring. Saxon had been White's summer assistant and had evidently earned a promotion. He claimed, as Ansel shook his hand, to be their resident statistician.

Herman Oliphant appeared to be their adult supervision, and he already looked stressed at the prospect. Frighteningly thin, he was by far the oldest of the group, with dignified gray hair and a pitch-black three-piece suit, despite the heat. He reminded Ansel of an undertaker. He was the Treasury Department's general counsel, Ansel would learn. He'd be back and forth each day from his official duties in the main Treasury building and his clandestine duties here. On paper, at least, Oliphant would be Ansel's direct boss.

There was a woman sitting nearest the door. Mabel Newcomer, Pehle had said was her name. She had a small frame and a smaller face, which was buried in a notebook. She was probably near fifty, her white hair clumped up in a frizzy bun. If there was going to be only one secretary for the lot of them, then this really was a top secret operation.

Harry Dexter White finally entered in a huff. He slammed the door behind him and checked his pocket watch. The antique timepiece suggested an old-fashioned streak that cut against his ill-fitting suit— a note of moneyed refinement amid his salt-of-the-earth demeanor. He addressed the assembled as one: "Welcome to the goddamn Research Department."

He took his seat at the head of the table. "I'm guessing most of you are wondering what our mission is. I hope a few of you might already have put it together."

Ansel hadn't. He looked at the others: Were they all a step ahead of him?

"You're here," White continued, "because you believe that the Nazi threat is real and you want to do something about it. We are physically here, in this building, because the Research Department is to be so insignificant and little noticed that even though some of you have positions elsewhere in Treasury, the rest of the department will leave us be. And I am here because my friend and boss, Secretary Morgenthau, is a good friend of the president. And Secretary Morgenthau—Henry—went to *his* friend and boss and said that he had some men who had a mind to stop playing possum when it came to the Nazis. Would it be all right if Henry's friends got up to something? Quietly, behind the scenes, no press, hush-hush. What did the president say? He did not say a word. And I'm told that with a smile, he made quite clear that the conversation never occurred."

White took a long moment to stare the group in the eyes one by one. "What the president does not know cannot hurt him. And what he does not care to know, we will make sure he does not know, is that clear? Because if he does come to know what we are doing here, then he cannot claim ignorance of what we are doing here."

Ansel looked at the bookish lot around him: They didn't seem any better trained for clandestine activities than he was.

"We have no official support," White continued. "No War Department, no State Department, no Navy. We have no weapons. We have no ships. We have no badges. What do we have? We have the greatest economic minds of our generation."

It felt as if everyone were taking the opportunity to take in everyone else. Was this motley assembly really so august as all that?

"I don't, err, well . . ." James Saxon spoke first, his childlike voice quivering. "You should know that I don't actually have an economics degree."

"That's fine," White said.

"Mine is in the law," Pehle said. "I suppose I had a minor in economics."

"I'm a tax attorney." Ansel added his confession to the chorus.

"I chose each of you for a good reason." White sounded annoyed. "But if anybody is concerned about not having enough titles or degrees or pieces of paper with little gold stars on them, rest assured that the Professor here has a doctorate in economics from Stanford."

Ansel considered the dignified Herman Oliphant. Who shrugged.

"Columbia," said Mabel Newcomer. "My master's was from Stanford."

All eyes turned to the mousy woman.

"I stand corrected," said White. "And now Professor Newcomer teaches the subject at Vassar."

Ansel felt like a jackass.

"Well," she added sheepishly, "just the first-year girls."

"Still," said White.

"And I do have to teach those classes—I told you that, Mr. White—so actually I'm only here part-time."

"Secretary Morgenthau," White boasted, "recommended the Professor personally."

"His daughter Jane was in my class," she explained.

"Look." White took control. "In a sense, you're collectively making my point for me: We're all there is."

"All there is for what?" Joe DuBois asked, speaking for the group.

"The United States cannot engage in military warfare against the Germans. So we are here to wage the only kind of belligerence we can: economic warfare." White lit the first of the day's many Lucky Strikes. "We're going to crash the German economy."

10

THE DARK WIZARD OF GLOBAL FINANCE

"Someone's sitting in the shade today because someone planted a tree a long time ago."

—WARREN BUFFETT

September 4, 1939 (cont'd)

Even the driest factual accounting of the size of the German war machine would have produced awe in Ansel and his new colleagues, but hearing it described by way of Harry Dexter White's salty verbiage inspired a special kind of terror. Ansel already knew the gist of this data—the trend lines, the sloping curves—and yet as he listened to the grim details delivered between furious puffs of a seemingly bottomless pack of cigarettes, he could feel the apocalypse drawing near.

The German military was 3.7 million men strong. The aerial Luftwaffe alone boasted over 400,000 souls who could fly 4,200 operational aircraft. The land-bound Wehrmacht had at its disposal 7,300 freshly armored tanks, organized in six independent divisions. The German steel plants were at present engaged in the manufacture of three million howitzer shells . . . *every month.*

"For the record," White said, "does anybody here know how many military aircraft we got in the United States?"

The mostly amateur economists did not.

"Twelve hundred." White spoke the number with evident distaste. It sounded hauntingly meager.

"And to be honest, more than half of them don't even fly anymore. How about the UK?"

They at least turned out to possess 3,500 operational aircraft . . . but many dated from the Great War. Their army held a mere 890,000 men.

The army of the United States? A laughable 170,000 soldiers.

The French numbers were similarly dire.

"The collective democratic states," said White, "are outmanned, outgunned, and outmuscled in every way."

There was a long moment of silent smoking.

"Anyone in the mood for a silver lining?" White rubbed his hands together like he was about to dive into a ribeye.

"Last few years, Simon Kuznets over in Commerce—I'm sure a few of you know him—has been all over everybody about this new idea: gross national product."

Ansel hadn't heard of it. By their looks, Pehle and DuBois, fellow lawyers, hadn't either. Saxon frowned, as if trying to recall something he'd skimmed over while studying for his finals last year. Only Oliphant, who must have been at Treasury long enough to know every economist in D.C., nodded at the mention of Kuznets's name.

"Professor, you want to help educate the boys?"

When she spoke, her voice had the sweet chirp of summer birds. "Is there something called 'the economy'? If so, can we measure, precisely, its size? These are the questions that have led Kuznets and his colleagues to create a statistic named 'gross national product.' It's causing quite the stir. It is, in short, the sum total value of all of the goods and services produced by a nation in a given year."

Ansel tried to wrap his mind around how one might even begin calculating a figure like that. The others appeared engaged in similar head-scratching.

The Professor seemed sympathetic. "It is, of course, astoundingly difficult to measure. And the irony, for our purposes, is that the people most equipped to do so live in Berlin."

"The Reich Statistical Office," said Ansel. He'd seen some of their work in his research. And for the first time that morning, he felt himself on solid ground.

"That's correct." She smiled at him as if he were the only student about to receive decent marks. "The most thorough, detailed, and complex economic statistics in the world are right now being produced along the Mühlenstraße, just over the river from Brandenburg. The German economists therein have over the past decade invented whole fields of statistical measurement. I've never seen anything like it. Kuznets and his colleagues haven't either. Harry was just discussing the size of the German military—well, I would suggest that it's nothing compared to their army of world-class statisticians."

Ansel couldn't help but glance at James Saxon. The Research Department's own statistician had only recently learned to shave.

"They have more data, which they are slicing, dicing, conjoining, and parsing in more novel mathematical methods than anyone else on earth. It was in fact all of their data, and their ingenious analytical devices, that inspired our friends at Commerce to have a go at this GNP problem."

Professor Newcomer looked around at the unsold furniture. "The Reich Statistical Office was given every resource they could ask for. To get all of this data, of course they would need to take an active interest in the private financial lives of their citizens. Bank ledgers, tax returns, bills of sale. As per their commission, the SS was instructed to provide them everything they might ever want."

Ansel pictured an army of statisticians with a division of SS officers at their beck and call. The Bureau of Internal Revenue had enough problems getting accurate tax returns out of Americans. If they'd had armed secret police working for them . . .

And yet this left him with a question.

"Why is the SS working for the economists?" he asked. "I mean, you said commissioned—by whom?"

As soon as he'd spoken, he feared that he might already know the answer.

The Professor turned to White. Something cold and dreadful passed between them, daring each other to speak aloud a name they both knew.

"Hjalmar Schacht," White whispered, as if the mere invocation might raise a malevolent spirit.

A respectful silence fell across the table, as it would in any room of economists anywhere in the world.

"I'm sure you've heard the nicknames," White went on. "What the Brits call him. 'The Dark Wizard of Global Finance.'"

Ansel had. Hjalmar Schacht had for years been the head of the German Reichsbank. By most accounts, Schacht had single-handedly led the German economy out of the Depression. He'd arranged for the financing of the autobahn, a public-works project of such magnitude that Roosevelt had used it as inspiration for his own post-Depression efforts. Schacht was one of the most powerful officials in the Third Reich, and he was also considered the smartest.

"The financing of the German war machine was designed and executed by Hjalmar Schacht. Personally. But helpfully, the Reich Statistical Office he built has also provided us with a means of defeating him. If you'll follow me."

White led them from the conference room to a wide bay of tables. On each were dozens of banker's boxes, stacked to the ceiling. There were hundreds in total. Filled to the brim, Ansel realized, with statistical tables. In German.

"They make all of this available to just anyone?" Pehle asked.

"No," White says. "But they make it available to enough people that I had a way of getting to some of them and borrowing copies. How? That's not your business. Your business is figuring out what on earth Schacht has done and how in the hell he's done it."

The stacks of boxes blocked most of the light from the windows, so the room, even at midmorning, was dim.

"Our friends at Commerce were able to use some of these data—the bits they themselves borrowed—to calculate their GNPs. Professor?"

"Composing contemporaneous figures is dreadfully hard," she said, showing her notebook to White. "These numbers are mere approximations, especially when trying to standardize across countries—"

"Last year," White declared, blowing past her caveats, "the GNP of the United States was seventy-seven billion dollars. The GNP of Germany? Thirty-three billion dollars."

While Germany was obviously smaller than the United States, the number was still shockingly low.

"I promised you a silver lining. Here it is: They have the guns, but we have the money. Moreover, there is a clear target for our inquiries. Twenty years ago, these bastards lost a war, tanked their currency, and got saddled with a reparations bill so large that it bankrupted the nation. Germany has since endured two decades of crushing poverty. Their economy is roughly the size of Britain's and less than half the size of ours. So by what unholy sorcery did Hjalmar Schacht build the largest war operation in the world out of . . . nothing?

"Our job is to figure out how the Dark Wizard casts his spells. He has conjured into being some financial miracle oil that powers the German military machine. We're going to learn how it works. And then we're going to light the son of a bitch on fire."

11

WILLIAM SHAKESPEARE VS. ADAM SMITH

"No matter how great the talent or efforts,
some things just take time. You can't produce a baby
in one month by getting nine women pregnant."

—WARREN BUFFETT

September 16, 1939

All the economists Ansel had known fell into one of two camps: numbers crunchers or philosophers. This group turned out to be no exception.

Professor Newcomer fell squarely in the philosophical camp. She had another degree in sociology, Ansel learned, and her response to the impenetrable cloud of financial data before them was to investigate its sources as well as its interpretations. Where did these numbers come from? Did they really mean what this chart, despite the pleasing certainty of its *x*- and *y-axes* claimed? Regarding the unfathomably large growth of the German military, she seemed more frightened by the whys than by the hows. Why were the Nazis committed to wreaking such death and destruction upon the world? Could they even consider the Nazi economy to be composed of rational actors making calculated bets, as Adam Smith might have suggested? Or was this an orgy of mass delusion, a psychosis of murderous intent rendered banal by the routine exchange of currency?

She took the overnight sleeper down from Vassar after her Monday classes, which meant that she arrived on Tuesday mornings. She would march in, bleary from the station, and work straight through Saturday, then take the sleeper back. She stayed at a hotel, and so far as Ansel could tell she spent her rare free hours on long hikes through the Virginia woods. Unmarried, she'd evidently come from a line of academics. She was the family outdoorswoman.

The Professor had a troublesome habit of talking down to the younger men in their unit, especially James Saxon and Joe DuBois. She spoke to them like they were her students, Ansel sensed, which needn't necessarily have been such an issue but for the fact that they were getting poor marks.

James Saxon looked ready to drop her course. He was a computation wiz. He did not burden himself with rumination. But if they needed two sets of data replotted using common terms? He was all over it. More than once Ansel arrived at the office in the morning to find that Saxon hadn't left the night before. Be it breakfast or neckties or fascism, he didn't seem to think about anything too deeply. The boy would stay up all night tabulating figures, down half a pot of coffee from the Childs down the street, and then, as if he were returning from a long and restful vacation, get right back to it. Ansel didn't think he'd ever had so much energy, not even when *he* was twenty-three.

All this propulsive pep drove the Professor batty. She started marking Saxon's pages with red pen: "Why?" she would scribble on top of his dutifully composed charts. "What does it mean?" He'd roll his eyes as soon as she left and then, with a wordless shrug, go straight into the next one.

Saxon responded to the occasional chatty inquiry about weekend plans with the mention of a young woman he was seeing. However, Ansel was pretty sure that her details kept changing. One week Saxon was picking her up from a dormitory at GWU. The next he was visiting her at Georgetown. Either the kid was making up this girlfriend, or else he had more than one. Ansel found both possibilities to be equally plausible.

Joe DuBois seemed perfectly comfortable without much companionship. He came from a devout Quaker family in New Jersey. He didn't drink, didn't smoke, and didn't believe in war. He conducted his work here on purely pacifist grounds. The Nazis were warmongers and must be stopped, but he could not condone the taking up of arms to stop them. Crashing their economy, he assured Ansel, was not the same as waging war: It was just business.

He also happened to be some kind of prodigy. He flipped through documents with the speed of butterfly wings and yet managed to retain all he'd read. He might have even had a photographic memory. He'd gotten his undergraduate degree from the University of Pennsylvania at eighteen, and then his law degree by twenty-one. Now at the ripe old age of twenty-six, he was White's chief legal adviser on this project, transferred over from the main Treasury office to help the Research Department maneuver their way through the U.S. legal system. It wasn't so much that what they were going to do needed to be legal, as White helpfully explained. It was more that whatever they were going to do, they needed to be able to claim that they thought it was legal when they did it.

Breaking—or smartly bending—the laws of the United States didn't seem to bother DuBois at all. He'd made his oaths to God, and those he took as serious as a grave. But ingeniously conspiring to find methods of breaking the law in spirit, while not quite in letter? That was chess. And he seemed awfully good at it.

Intellectually, he was as philosophically minded as the Professor, but that shared instinct failed to develop into much of a working relationship. Among DuBois's many eccentricities: He came and went at odd hours. He never said hello or goodbye and equally freed himself of most other daily social niceties. He wore a strange homburg hat made of thick fawn felt, and he often left it on while he worked. Ansel got the impression that he hadn't socialized much outside of his Quaker community.

John Pehle, on the other hand, was the sort of gentleman who could socialize with anyone, anywhere—a skill of great potential use. He was connected, in D.C. and New York and probably everywhere else. Whatever the Research Department was going to do would likely require pulling various levers within the grand contraption that was the U.S. government. Pehle knew whose hands gripped which sticks, and he might just be able to convince them to tug.

Seemingly the only person he could not befriend was Joe DuBois. Pehle was the product of generations of good breeding. He exuded old-world class. He did not appreciate hats worn indoors or how-do-you-dos unanswered. There was a way of doing things. Pehle hadn't made the rules, nor did he care where they'd come from. But he followed them because one couldn't save civilization without being civilized.

Herman Oliphant only made it over to the Research Department every other day or so, and when he did, he seemed instantly itching to return to his real office down the street. Technically, he was the highest-ranking member of their team, but the idea of actual management, in the sense of organizing a staff of workers toward a common pursuit, he seemed to find tedious. He'd been Henry Morgenthau's trusted adviser for decades and had arrived with the Treasury secretary in the early days of the administration. Oliphant's allegiance, it became clear, was not to White, nor to Treasury, nor even necessarily to the United States. He served his old friend Henry. And since Morgenthau had blessed this operation, it fell to Oliphant to make certain that White and his new recruits did not do anything that might get the secretary indicted.

Oliphant kept a copy of the U.S. criminal code on his desk. He found no need to open it: The Research Department was getting nowhere.

In the first weeks of the department's existence, the Nazis marched through Poland in an unbroken line of battlefield victories while Ansel and his colleagues failed to peer behind the smoke and figure out how on earth they were managing it.

German financial charts soon filled their impromptu offices, and among the many things they lacked were an effective filing system and a dictionary. Of course, Ansel thought, they wouldn't have more than a smattering of German between them.

It occurred to Ansel that if White had been *trying* to staff this unit with the least-prestigious economists in the country, he couldn't have done much better. But then, what choice did he have? Their work was top secret; their mission was unpopular. If asked, anyone reputable would have had to think at least twice before signing on. And how would White have been able to ask? He couldn't well have run through the halls of the Ivy Leagues asking if anyone might want a job in clandestine service.

The days were long and unseasonably hot. The fifth floor of the W&J Sloane building grew dangerously overheated, and yet the researchers didn't feel safe opening the windows. Who knew who might be looking in? The curtains had to remain drawn.

Harry Dexter White came and went as he pleased, and his visits were marked largely by his displeasures. The group was not working fast enough. They had made insufficient progress. Honestly, had they made any progress at all? Hjalmar Schacht might very well be a genius who had built an exquisite machine—Germany was a brand-new sports car, a Mercedes-Benz luxury W150, a masterpiece of engineering— but it should not take an equal genius, White told them, to tear the thing apart and work out how it runs.

One late afternoon, White actually brought over a photograph from *The New York Times* of Hitler himself riding such an automobile.

"I'm going to cut the brakes and watch Hitler drive this thing over a cliff. All you need to do is tell me where the damned cord is."

Ansel found the metaphor to be evocative. But it didn't help them work out how German military spending could keep rising, year on year, even as tax revenues and inflation remained mysteriously constant. Pehle was offended by White's hectoring; Saxon was indifferent; DuBois winced at the language, especially in front of Professor Newcomer; Oliphant was seldom there.

As the last member recruited, Ansel was technically the lowest man on the totem pole. As a tax attorney by trade, he was also the one with the least obvious role.

His strengths were not mathematical. Nor theoretical, governmental, or even, truth be told, economic. Ansel was a storyteller.

For him, the practice of economics was not a numerical science; it was a narrative art. He had met people who assumed that economics was the study of money. But for him, it was the study of decisions. An economy was a collection of many millions of individual decisions, made by each person inside it.

The Research Department had more numbers than they knew what to do with. The trick of it was, to the Professor's point, not the *what* but the *why*. Showing that the bank savings rate among German citizens had risen dramatically in the past five years was easy; Saxon had put it together right here, on table six of memorandum A-19. The question was what had caused it to do so? What else was rising (or falling) at the same time, on the same scale? How could cause be separated from effect? How could unrelated phenomena—the subpar German potato harvest of 1935, the slight rise in automobile prices—be winnowed away? Or were these developments not so unrelated after all? What story might connect the burgeoning of bank savings, the dearth of potatoes, and a murderous assault on the Jews of Europe?

Ansel wasn't much for literature, but sometimes he suspected that Shakespeare was a better chronicler of economic behavior than Adam Smith. All people—most certainly including the members of the Research Department—were whirling vortexes of motivations and cravings. To attribute singular causes to their complex and contradictory behaviors would be to render them as simple as the characters in a fairy tale. And yet simplicity—the clarity by which this begets that—was precisely what the Research Department required. Shakespeare could paint his characters' inscrutability; the Research Department was tasked with crafting a story in which motives were unambiguous.

Ansel's job was not long division. It was storytelling. It should fall to him, Pehle suggested, to describe their findings to White. And then, White ordered, to spin them into a tale that Secretary Morgenthau might act on.

Pen in hand, Ansel needed no reminding that the ink in which he scribbled told of real blood.

The front pages Angela read aloud each morning practically dripped with tragedy. Their ritual at the breakfast table had grown more crowded since they were now staying at her parents' two-story in Bloomingdale. Ansel and Angela slept in her childhood bedroom, while Angie slept in the bedroom that had once held all four of Angela's younger brothers. In the morning, they would sit with her parents, and she would intone the previous day's atrocities, just like they were still in Minnesota. But instead of tut-tutting sympathetically, Angela's father seemed to find the ritual morbid. He distracted himself with the sports pages.

Last week, the German bombing of Poland extended from Warsaw to the small open towns to its south. The following day, the Germans captured eighty thousand prisoners as the city of Gdynia fell following a thirteen-day siege. By the weekend, the Soviet army readied for an eastward march. Rumors were that Stalin was sharpening his knives and contemplating the map of Poland, preparing to cleave off his own share. He hadn't stood in the Nazis' way; they'd promised not to attack the Soviet Union; and now he might be able to claim nearly a third of Poland for himself. As if a piñata had shattered and any child present might grab for a handful of sweets.

The British navy was well into an obvious and depressing defeat on the seas. When the British admiralty put out a statement, reprinted dutifully across the globe, that they had sunk "a number" of German U-boats, it only served to accentuate the direness of their loss. "What number might that be?" White said when the afternoon edition arrived. "Two?"

Ansel started taking a bromo each night so he could sleep. It helped for a few hours, but he'd still wake up well before dawn, his heart racing. He rarely saw Angie, but it couldn't be helped. He was out of the house most mornings before she was up, and there was no way he could be back in time for her bath. Angela had her mother to help, but he was the one who didn't get to hear the new words his daughter was learning day by day. He reminded himself that he was doing all of this for her. He was making sacrifices so that she could come of age in a world in which the Nazis had not been allowed to control half of Europe. Or all of the United States. Ansel was working to secure his daughter's future, even if it meant giving up this time with her in the present.

He told himself it was worth it.

12

POLITICS
AT CHURCH

"SOVIET TROOPS MARCHED INTO POLAND AT 11 P.M.;
NAZIS DEMAND WARSAW GIVE UP OR BE SHELLED;
FIERCE BATTLE IS RAGING ON WESTERN FRONT"

—*THE NEW YORK TIMES* FRONT-PAGE HEADLINE,
SEPTEMBER 17, 1939

September 17, 1939

The Nazi flag unfurled in the wind above Massachusetts Avenue, snapping as loud and sharp as a gunshot. It must have been thirty feet long. Looming high up on the flagpole, it blocked the autumn sunlight, casting a faded shadow onto the street.

From the back of Angela's father's Buick, Ansel stared up in horror at the swastika menacing above the Gothic German embassy. The building looked like a medieval castle—like something that belonged in the mountains outside Berlin. The embassy was busy for late on a Sunday morning. Nazis in black uniforms marched in and out, a spring in their step.

Angie was on Ansel's lap. Instinctively, he moved her so she didn't have to see the flag flying only a mile from the White House. Of course the symbol wouldn't mean anything to her. But still: No American child should see this.

"Mussolini this, Mussolini that," said Angela's father, Dominick, as he turned off Massachusetts heading back toward Bloomingdale. "Your cousins over there say he's not so big a deal. He's cleaning the place up. They like the man, and they are there every day. Not like these boys from the newspapers. They come, they see a parade, they go. What do they know?" He found less traffic on Sixteenth Street. "You don't have to worry so much."

Angela, sitting beside Ansel in the back seat, ground her teeth. Her father was getting her goat, and Ansel's attempts at diffusing their mounting argument had thus far been ineffective.

"He's aligned with Hitler," Angela said.

Dominick pressed on the gas. "It's a hard world."

Angela's mother, Lucretia, sat in the front, tactfully silent.

Ansel wasn't going into the office until noon so that he could first accompany the family to church. He never went with Angela back in Minnesota—she knew where he stood on all that—but now that he was sleeping under Dominick's roof, he felt it best to be respectful.

It wasn't much use. Dominick had never liked him, and given that Ansel had abruptly moved Angela back to D.C. so that he could take a lower-paying job and they could stay in her childhood bedroom, he didn't think he was going to get on the man's good side anytime soon.

"What the Germans are doing to their Jewish citizens—not to mention to the Polish—is well beyond hard," Angela said. "People being rounded up by the thousands. Tossed into concentration camps."

Dominick removed both hands from the wheel so he could shrug. "The Jews are not citizens anymore in Germany. Correct? So when a Jew is arrested in Germany, they don't go to jail, they go to the camps like any other prisoner of a war. The British have concentration camps for the war prisoners in Africa. Don't the Soviets have them too?"

Angela turned to Ansel, requesting backup. He tried to strike a middle ground: "You won't find me defending what the British did to the Boers. But at least that was a proper war. Germany, on the other hand, seems to be convicting scores of Jews within its borders—people who *had been* citizens up until Hitler promptly changed the laws—on what sound like imagined seditions. And in such huge numbers . . . Plus, these German camps, who knows what's going on inside them?" He hoped Angie wasn't following what the adults were on about.

"The stories that have leaked out," Angela added, "are beyond horrific. I know you've heard them."

"Sure."

"They don't concern you?"

Ansel couldn't see Dominick's face, but he didn't sound too concerned.

"Still so hot out," Lucretia offered to no one in particular.

"Papa," Angela said, ignoring the entreaty. "We can't turn a blind eye to this."

"You're too young to remember the Great War," Dominick said. "But there was a lot of this nonsense going around then, too. At the shop, I would hear the gentlemen telling stories. German soldiers going village by village in France, slaughtering the little babes."

"I remember that!" Lucretia added brightly. "Those were in the papers."

Dominick turned toward the back seat. "Not everything in these papers is the truth."

"Just because the French government put out a lot of shaky anti-German propaganda during the Great War," Ansel ventured, "doesn't mean that the current stories are necessarily untrue."

Now Angela shot an annoyed look toward Ansel. "Not necessarily untrue?"

Dominick smiled. "You married a lawyer."

"And my husband knows that when it comes to fascism—when it comes to the Nazis—there are principles involved."

"Principles? Every time somebody in the world does something you don't like, we should invade? All these horror stories you read—any of them mention what the British have done in India? Or the French in Indochina? Maybe we should civilize Paris and London after Berlin."

"Don't forget Rome." Angela winced after she'd said it, as if realizing she'd gone too far. Dominick was touchy about the country of his birth.

Lucretia shook her head. "No politics in church. That was your *nonna*'s rule."

"We're not at the church yet," Angela said.

For the first time, Lucretia swiveled her head toward the back seat.

It required only a single raised eyebrow to let Angela know that if she was reduced to pleading technicalities, then she'd already lost the argument.

––––

INSIDE ST. MARTIN'S, ANSEL politely sat for the service and then, when it was all over, he shook the hands of a great many family members and friends. He was separated from Angela in the crowd for a while, talking to her younger brother Tom and his pals about the Dodgers' winning streak and the new Plymouths.

"Lower to the ground," Tom said approvingly, giving Ansel a nudge. "Easier for a kid to climb into. Or kids?"

"The Soviets invaded Poland yesterday," Ansel said to the group. "Can you believe they did it so soon?"

Tom and his pals wore blank looks, like he was telling them about the latest episode of a radio serial they'd never picked up.

Tom put a hand on his shoulder while addressing the others. "Ansel's a bit of a worrier."

It occurred to him that from the neighborhood's Sunday morning conversations, one would have no idea that there was a war on. He caught mention of Roosevelt's name here and there—this was Washington, after all—but did not hear Hitler's even once. The congregation seemed utterly free of the anxieties that darkened Ansel's and Angela's every dream.

Ansel realized that he'd spent the past weeks locked away with his Research Department alongside likeminded Cassandras all fearful of the coming apocalypse. They bickered incessantly, but they did so because they shared the same fears. Returning to the civilian world and finding himself surrounded by such indifference was a shock. Didn't these people care what was happening an ocean away? Or far closer than that: Nazis thronged the streets of St. Paul. Their flag hung proudly above Logan Circle. And not even the pious seemed to notice. Or worse, if they did, they simply didn't care.

When Angela appeared again, she bounded up to him buoyantly. "Good news!"

Smiling wide, she led him away from the others. "You remember Margaret? From school?"

Ansel didn't, but nodded anyway.

"She says her friend's office is scrounging for typists. As many as they can find. She says she can get me a job."

She was looking into his face with such excitement that he knew he couldn't allow himself to wince. "A job?"

"With the government." There was, for her, no higher calling. "Margaret says there's a typewriter shortage. Any girl who can bring her own is hired on the spot."

"Do you feel you need a job? I know my salary isn't what it used to be, but . . ."

He caught his error instantly by the look on her face: This had nothing to do with money. This was about doing something to help their common cause.

She stepped back. "I can't just sit at home doing nothing."

From the corner of his eye, Ansel caught Dominick and Lucretia chatting with a pack of their neighbors. This was just what Ansel needed: Dominick blaming him for sending his wife off to type up another man's correspondence. It wasn't that Ansel minded having a working wife, not exactly. It was that he knew what other people would think: that he hadn't lived up to his responsibilities as a husband and a father. He could already hear the gossip in his ear: *Ansel Luxford should probably worry a little less about what's happening in Europe and a little more about what's going on in his own home.*

"You don't want me to go back to work." She said it ruefully, like she half blamed herself for not having anticipated his reaction.

"I didn't say that."

"You didn't say much of anything."

He dropped his voice to a warm whisper. "Why don't we talk about this later?"

She looked around like they were in the middle of an empty field and not smack dab among a hundred parishioners. "Would you rather I stay home and teach Angie to speak German?"

"Come on."

"I'm not a naïf. I know that my typing up a few letters in a government office is not going to mean the difference between democracy and fascism. But if I can do something—anything—to help, then I'm going to do it. Wherever I might be useful."

"Wherever?"

She took a moment. It seemed that regarding this next part, she had in fact anticipated difficulty. "The job is at the FBI."

13

THE AVERAGE
AMERICAN MARRIAGE

*"The root problem with conventional currency is
all the trust that's required to make it work."*

—SATOSHI NAKAMOTO

September 17, 1939 (cont'd)

Ansel and Angela stayed up late that night, tucked under the blankets
as they talked about walls.

Angela said she thought he didn't like the idea of her working
on account of his old man. He didn't see what that had to do with it.
But she asked him to tell her again about the stone wall near the
edge of the farm, back in Iowa, where he would hide when the old
man started in on the gin. That wall must have been there a hundred
years, placed by some ancient settler. The rocks were uneven, ele-
mental. Full of crags and holes where the wind had knocked out
black stones. The earth nearby had a slope to it, and if Ansel hid behind one particular part of the wall, the old man couldn't see him
from the porch. Some nights he'd stay out there till well after it got
dark, after the dewy chill settled onto the hard earth. He'd count
the stones until he was sure the old man had passed out. Then he'd
tiptoe back in, trying not to wake him. Most of the time, Ansel succeeded.

He hadn't been home to Iowa since he was seventeen. He exchanged
letters with his two sisters, both married, both still in Harlan. Angela
made him send 4x6 glossies when Angie was born. But Ansel hadn't

exchanged a single solitary word with the old man, not since he'd left—nor had he any intention of doing so.

Occasionally he wondered how long the wall would last. Eventually the old man's heart would give out; his sisters would sell the land; a new family would move in and knock the wall down so they could lay another row of corn. No walls last forever.

Ansel didn't see what any of that had to do with his crummy reaction to the thought of his wife's answering another man's telephone.

She said that it was because of his family that he had these bourgeois notions. He'd grown up poor, the son of a schoolteacher who barely grew anything on their dusty land and resented the brats he was forced to babysit. Maybe the old man had resented children in general and took it out on his own. But Ansel wasn't poor any longer, he'd made sure of that. Angela suggested that he couldn't bear the thought of anyone thinking otherwise.

"You want me to tell you how much we lost selling the house in St. Paul?" he whispered. The baby was right in the next room. The walls were thin. "We're not here because of money."

"No," she whispered back. "We're here because there are no old walls to protect this country from the Nazis. There's just us to do the Lord's work. And the president's."

Ansel didn't need to remind her that the unit he was working for was top secret. Harry Dexter White was sure that the FBI was looking into them; he seemed convinced that Hoover had a personal grudge against him. If the FBI found out what the Research Department was doing, Ansel and his colleagues would be in the kind of trouble that meant jail time.

Thus the wall that Ansel and Angela would have to erect would be between them. They'd both already passed background checks when they'd first taken government jobs. Since she wouldn't need a new one, no one would ask her, initially, about her husband's work at Treasury. There would be no one to lie to. But the less she knew about his work, from here on out, the less she'd have to keep from her new bosses. And the less trouble she'd find herself in if the Research Department's clandestine operation ever blew up.

Likewise, she'd be sure to come across information at the FBI that she couldn't share with him. They agreed that when she did, she should remain silent.

"How many husbands really tell their wives the whole truth about what they do all day?" she whispered.

Ansel couldn't speak with authority about the state of the average American marriage. But he hadn't gotten the impression that it was something he wanted to emulate.

"I don't like the thought of lying to each other," he said.

"It won't be lying. It'll just be not talking."

Now *that,* though he didn't say it, sounded like an average American marriage.

"This is what we've always wanted," she said. "Service. Let's not lose our nerve now that we've gotten here."

He went to the sink and downed two bromos. The next morning, he had to brief Secretary Morgenthau on the unit's progress for the first time. He was going to need at least a couple hours' sleep.

"Let's see how it goes tomorrow," he whispered when he returned to bed. "When you speak to the FBI. Then we can work out more of a plan."

He was making it sound like she hadn't decided to take the job the moment she'd heard about its existence. But of course she'd already chosen, just like he'd done when White had finally offered him a spot.

"Yes, that's fine." It was nice of her to pretend likewise.

"I should sleep."

"Big day tomorrow?"

He nodded, eager to tell her all about it. Henry Morgenthau was not just Roosevelt's right-hand man—he was the president's oldest friend. Their families famously owned neighboring estates in East Fishkill on which their wives enjoyed long walks together through their adjacent apple orchards. When FDR became governor, he appointed Morgenthau to the agricultural commission. When he was elected president, he brought his friend to the Federal Farm Board. The Republicans had sure raised hackles when he asked Morgenthau to be the secretary of the Treasury. And they had a point, seeing as Morgenthau had no economic training or education of any kind. But who better to safeguard the financial security of the New Deal than the president's closest confidant? Staff could handle the grunt work. Staff like Harry Dexter White. Staff like Ansel.

Word around G Street was that White was as close to Morgenthau as Morgenthau was to the president. And first thing in the morning, Ansel was to be at the secretary's side. It would be practically like meeting with FDR himself.

But Ansel stopped himself before he said any of this to Angela. Per the understanding that was now to constitute their marriage, he reminded himself not to speak a word.

14

SHADOW CURRENCY

"I would never read a book. . . . I don't want to say no book is ever worth reading, but I actually do believe something pretty close to that. I think, if you wrote a book . . . it should have been a six-paragraph blog post."

—SAM BANKMAN-FRIED

September 18, 1939

"Don't get too technical with him," White cautioned as he led Ansel across Fifteenth Street to the main Treasury building. "Simple and snappy."

Ansel hurried to keep pace while avoiding oncoming traffic. "Got it."

"And for God's sake, don't start reeling off a bunch of numbers."

"Right."

"Secretary Morgenthau can't stand that stuff."

"Numbers?"

"Excess detail."

They both entered then showed identification before ascending the staircase to the third floor, where they navigated a slalom of secretaries and frenetic aides.

"Remember," White said over the clack of what sounded like a thousand typewriters banging away in unison. "He's not an economist."

"Neither am I."

White stopped. "None of that either."

"None of what?"

"Getting cute."

White led Ansel to the closed door of Morgenthau's corner office. He didn't have to announce himself to the secretary's secretary: They were expected.

When the doors swung open, Ansel found the room inside large and wood-paneled, decorated with the oil portraits of men Ansel guessed were previous holders of the office. High windows loomed along the far wall, through which Ansel could see the West Wing. A door to a private toilet was half open behind the heavy desk. The bar cart in the corner boasted what looked like real crystal tumblers.

Henry Morgenthau was reclining on his davenport, reading the morning's *Post*. He stood for his guests.

"Harry. And you're . . ." Morgenthau was well over six feet, bald on the top of his scalp, with large wire-rimmed glasses that curved around the sides of his head. The jacket of his gray three-piece suit was draped over a chair. He seemed unembarrassed to receive visitors in his shirtsleeves.

"I'm Ansel Luxford."

Morgenthau extended a hand. Ansel gave it a proper shake.

From a dirt farm in Harlan to a private audience with FDR's closest confidant. Ansel imagined the look on his sisters' faces: If they could see where he was now! And then he reminded himself that he could never tell anyone that he'd been here. Much less why.

"Bar open?" White gestured to the whiskey.

"Things must be really dire," Morgenthau said. "You're asking for permission instead of simply helping yourself."

White did just that. "Mr. Luxford is our house raconteur. He's going to tell you how the Nazi economy works."

Morgenthau looked expectantly to Ansel.

Ansel looked enviously to the liquor.

"Okay," he began. "From our analysis—and to the naked eye—it's quite clear that Hjalmar Schacht has for the last five years taken on truly unprecedented levels of both surveillance and control of the German economy. Our question: What's he actually doing? Germany is nominally a capitalist country, but true to their name, the Nationalsozialistische Deutsche Arbeiterpartei—that is, National Socialist, or Nazi Party, for short—claims to have created a socialist economy in their homeland. I would argue that neither is true, and that what Schacht has built there—ingeniously—is a near perfect autarky."

Morgenthau stared at him blankly.

White finally handed over a drink while silently cautioning with a look: Cut the technical claptrap.

"What I mean is, in a nutshell, that the German economy is self-sufficient. Like a perpetual motion machine, as the physicists might say. Only this machine has an output: war. Every aspect of the German economy has been tweaked, shifted, or reimagined to produce as much war as possible."

"How?" White guided him along.

"Okay, so, let's say that you own a farm. A real *volk* kind of existence—let's say it's a pig farm. I will pause to note that if you happen to need extra land for your farm, the government will be happy to steal you some. They've been confiscating the farms of Jewish land-owners for years on various legal pretexts."

The secretary leaned thoughtfully against his desk. "Are there a lot of Jewish German pork farmers?"

It took Ansel a moment to realize that he had a sense of humor. "Maybe that's a poor example. But you see the point. We want to know how Germany is paying for its military power? Step one is confiscation. They are simply looting as much cash, gold, jewelry, and, most importantly, land as they can from their Jewish population. And now they're taking all of the above from the Polish as well."

"That's a lot of land," White added.

"And a lot of stolen gold." Ansel was building up steam. "Why is the gold important? We'll get back to that. But so, you're this pig farmer working on land the government confiscated for you. The Wehrmacht needs food for its soldiers, so it's going to buy some meat from you. In fact, the army is growing, so the Wehrmacht will pay you extra so you can expand. Things are going pretty well for you. For your whole family actually. You've got this son, but instead of toiling away on the family farm, the government is going to offer him an even

better job opportunity. Just like they're paying you, the farmer, to expand, they're paying IG Farben, the world's largest chemical company,
to open new factories because they need the chemicals for the expanding Wehrmacht. Bombs, bullets, guns, and so forth. In fact, IG Farben
is building a huge new plant as we speak, just down the road from your
pig farm—in an out-of-the-way town called Auschwitz."

Morgenthau frowned. He would certainly have heard the stories
about Jewish "criminals" convicted by the state for "sedition" being
sent to the big work camp at the Auschwitz chemical factory.

Ansel continued: "So in summary, the government subsidizes jobs
not only in the Wehrmacht but effectively at private companies like
IG Farben—who are making a pretty penny, err, a pretty reichsmark—
and depend on an unpaid slave class of 'criminals' to cheaply power
their production."

"Where are all the reichsmarks coming from?" White asked.

"That's the question exactly. It *should* take a tremendous amount of
reichsmarks to make all this happen. In a way, it's like something
Keynes would propose: There are people in Germany out of work. So
the government is offering them work to do and paying them to do it.
Keynes would urge the government to spend as much as it needed, so
long as there remained jobs to fill, and to run up its debts as necessary.
Only . . . the Germans aren't."

White crooked his head. "They're not running up government
debt?"

Ansel shrugged. "They are, but not nearly enough to account for
the size of the war machine they're building. Moreover, according to
their budgets, they're barely even running up military *expenses*."

Now the secretary looked lost.

"That doesn't make a lick of sense," White said. "How can they
make all these fighter planes and tanks without . . . spending money?"

"And now we arrive at the hellish genius of Hjalmar Schacht. Let's
go back to our pig farmer. The Wehrmacht is paying him well for his
pork, and they are paying him in reichsmarks. He takes those reichsmarks and deposits them into a . . ." Ansel paused for emphasis.

Neither White nor Morgenthau responded.

"A bank!" Ansel said.

"Ansel," White growled, "get to the goddamned point."

"That *is* the point! Look, the bank takes all of these reichsmarks on deposit and with them it purchases government bonds. A special kind of government bond that Schacht has created, called Mefo bills. And here's the thing: The bank *has* to buy them."

"And what is a Mefo bill?"

"Five years ago—that's how long they've been planning this—the government created a private corporation called M.E.F.O. It stands for something extremely long and German. It's technically a private company, so it isn't on the government ledger. But the Nazi high command jump-started the Mefo company with a secret loan of a million reichsmarks."

At the word *secret,* Morgenthau shot a glance at White. Ansel got the impression that the secretary did not know where White got all of his information and preferred it that way.

"Then," Ansel continued, "Mefo went to the banks and promised them a guaranteed four percent annual return from their bonds. Awfully sweet for a corporate bond, especially when German government bonds paid less. The banks started buying up the Mefo bonds— colloquially called Mefo bills—and everybody knew, so far as we can tell, that Hitler and Schacht were behind the company. It's all handshake deals. The banks knew that buying the bills curried favor with Hitler. They bought the bonds with all of their newly deposited reichsmarks, and Mefo sent the reichsmarks right to the Wehrmacht. Now the military has an off-book source of funding: The Mefo money—which pays for all those planes and tanks and such—doesn't show up on government budgets because it comes from a private company. The German military budget is much, much higher than it appears to be, because they're not paying for it with reichsmarks—they're paying for it with Mefo bills."

White did not appear impressed. "This sounds like a Ponzi scheme."

"Not quite. Because I know what you're going to ask next. What happens when Mefo has to pay back the bond holders? Answer: They don't."

"You mean, exactly like in a Ponzi scheme?"

"It's smarter than that. The Mefo company, under a legal pretext crafted by Schacht's attorneys, keeps extending the terms of the bonds. Six months, then twelve months, then five years. And since the banks know who's behind it, they let it happen. What are they going to do, call Hitler a crook? We've seen what happens to seditionists. Plus, Mefo keeps reporting that the bonds are returning four percent every year. The banks receive statements saying as much, and that Mefo is automatically reinvesting the profits . . . in more Mefo bills. The banks return those profits to their customers, whose savings accounts are similarly showing great returns."

"What about inflation?" The secretary was following along, thank goodness. "All that extra money—Mefo or otherwise—sloshing around the economy . . ."

"Well, first, the Nazis use price controls. The government just sets the price of eggs and bread and most everyday goods, so the prices cannot legally rise. And then, second, customers cannot withdraw their Mefo profits from their bank accounts. There are legal limits, enforced by the SS. If people can't spend the money, it can't go chasing up the price of things and starting an inflationary spiral. And honestly: Why would they even *want* to withdraw their money? On paper, they're profiting handsomely. What's to complain about?"

Morgenthau found a gold cigarette case in his jacket pocket and took his time lighting one. Ansel had trouble reading his expression. Was he beginning to grasp the vile ingenuity of what Schacht had constructed?

"The thing to complain about," White said, lighting up himself, "is that the money isn't real."

"Isn't it? The Mefo bills are effectively an alternate form of German currency. The government makes reichsmarks and gives them to citizens. The citizens deposit the reichsmarks into banks, which convert the reichsmarks into Mefo bills. The Mefo bills produce steady returns, which show up on the citizens' bank books as interest on their deposits. People's accounts keep growing—on paper. Everyone believes that they're making money hand over fist. Last year, the German government issued nineteen billion reichsmarks' worth of normal bonds. Plus another twelve billion reichsmarks' worth of Mefo bills."

"Which are essentially a fiction." Morgenthau ashed into a tray on his desk.

Ansel turned pensive. "I ask again: Are they?"

White took a swig from his glass and a smoke from his Lucky. "I know a scam when I see one."

"On the one hand, it is. Over a third of the German money supply is essentially in the form of a newly imagined currency that is backed, such as it is, by a fake company that doesn't even make anything. On the other hand . . . it works."

White did not appear impressed.

"There's a concept that's recently appeared in the economic literature," Ansel continued. "Shadow currency."

"Shadow currency?"

"There's a real currency, and then there's another one underneath it. As real as a shadow is to the object that casts it. Germany doesn't have one economy running on one currency: It has two. Its economic power is virtually doubled. Schacht uses this shadow currency to build real tanks, real warplanes, real bullets. Those bullets are, as we speak, killing real people. What I'm saying is, when it comes to currency . . . what's real? What's fake? Because there are a bunch of Polish soldiers lying dead in a ditch outside Warsaw right now, and they had families, mothers, children, friends . . . Sounds pretty goddamned real to me."

Even Ansel was shocked by the force of his outburst. He'd been so long engaged in the technical minutiae that he'd forgotten that the point of it all was a tragedy.

Morgenthau seemed to appreciate Ansel's unexpected passion. "How do we stop it?"

Ansel finished his drink. "The good news is, we don't have to. It'll collapse on its own. Eventually, people will need to buy real goods and services with their Mefo money. They will not content themselves forever to be rich only on paper; one day, enough folks will actually want new homes or new automobiles or new kitchen knives. Then the government will be forced to do one of two things. One, they can default on the bonds. They can simply not pay out the reichsmarks promised on their balance sheets. This will, of course, obliterate any faith in the creditworthiness of the German government. All German bonds will instantly be worthless. Which will crash the economy. Or two, the government can announce that its citizens may finally convert their Mefo bills into reichsmarks. This will explode the quantity of reichsmarks, and all the inflation they'd kept at bay up until that point would burst forth like an exploding dam. Which will crash the economy. Either way, the system cannot last forever. Self-destruction is wired into its design."

"Excellent news," Morgenthau said. "When will that crash occur?"

Ansel sighed. "That's the bad news. The crash will occur when enough Germans want—or need—to use their Mefo money to buy real things in the real world. When will they do that? When they don't have enough. Now, Germany produces many things. What Germany cannot produce, it can to some degree buy—but it can't trade Mefo bills for francs or dollars or sterling, because Mefo bills are only legal tender, so to speak, inside Germany. Technically they're not even that. The Nazis have some gold reserves they can use for foreign trade, but not enough. So how is the country getting all of the things it needs? Right now, it's stealing them. Food, minerals, labor . . . It's getting the materials from Poland and Czechoslovakia. It's getting slave labor from the Jews. The system is powered by war. The economy runs on a fuel of brute conquest. It requires, by design, a constant supply of new land, new theft, new slaves. The system will collapse . . . when Germany has no more lands to conquer."

No one said anything for a long moment.

"If Germany wins," Ansel offered, "and the whole world falls under their control, the German economic machine will eventually collapse. But until then, they can't stop expanding, even if they want to."

"Poland is just the beginning," White said.

"France. Britain. The USSR. If Stalin thinks that Hitler will remain true to their nonaggression pact, he hasn't looked at this data. If economics is destiny, then Germany must continue to take new territory. Their shadow currency will grow larger than their supposedly 'real' currency, but no problem. The balance sheets of the banks, the big companies, they'll all take in record profits. And then, when every inch of the earth and every man, woman, and child who breathes are under Nazi control, the dam will break: There will be a financial crash."

"Let's say," Morgenthau suggested, "that we wanted to put a stop to the Nazis somewhat sooner than that."

Ansel peered into his empty glass. "The best idea we've had so far is to go after their gold. It's not a grand slam, but it's something that could hurt them. Or at least slow them down."

"You want to go after Germany's supply of gold?" Morgenthau asked, casting a strange look toward White.

White gestured toward Ansel. Who got the distinct impression that the senior men knew something he did not.

"There are a few things Germany can neither make nor steal," he continued, trying not to let this derail him. "Iron ore, cotton, gasoline, corn. It buys those things on the global market, and for them it has to pay in gold, seeing as how they've preemptively cut themselves off from dollar-denominated trade. But the German government, as well as plenty of large German corporations, keeps gold reserves in U.S. banks. Hell, they've even got a bit of gold stored for safekeeping under the New York Federal Reserve."

"Every country in Europe stores gold in New York," Morgenthau said. "We're bankers to the world."

"So we confiscate the German gold."

"Wouldn't that be illegal?"

Ansel turned up his palms. "We can take a page from Schacht's book and write up some law to make it legal. Hitler will whine and moan, but what's he going to do about it? Invade Poland?"

White went over to Morgenthau's ashtray. The secretary leaned in and whispered just loud enough for Ansel to hear: "You didn't tell him?"

"I'm not in the business of telling people things they don't need to know."

"If this is your group's plan . . . You didn't tell any of them?"

"I wanted you to hear what I was hearing."

In the silence, it seemed the two men were conducting a debate in an unspoken language. Ansel looked back and forth between them, awaiting a translation. "What didn't you tell us?"

After another long moment, it was Morgenthau who finally spoke: "We tried that already."

15

HOW WOULD IT LOOK?

"The basic feature of our economic theory is
that we have no theory at all."

—ADOLF HITLER

Ansel struggled to make sense of what Secretary Morgenthau had just told him. "When did you try confiscating German gold?"

"Last spring," Morgenthau said. "After the *St. Louis* incident."

Ansel remembered following the story from St. Paul with a mounting horror. Nine hundred Jewish refugees had managed, against all odds, to escape from Germany in a crowded ship called the *St. Louis*. It had sailed to Cuba, but because the Reich insisted that the passengers' flight out of the country had been illegal, it hadn't been allowed to dock. It then sailed to New York . . . where the State Department had, in an act of gracious diplomacy toward Germany, likewise denied the ship entry.

Within a few weeks the *St. Louis* had failed to find a port that would take it anywhere on the Atlantic. So it sailed back to Europe. No one knew what happened to the passengers upon their return. But most likely they'd been sent to one of the German concentration camps.

Morgenthau went to the windows. Ansel could not see his face as he gazed out toward the White House. Against the darkening sky, the building looked quiet and cold.

"I went to the Oval Office myself," Morgenthau said into the glass.

"Harry had told me the gold idea, something he'd cooked up with Oliphant. State wanted to appease Hitler by refusing the *St. Louis* a port? Fine. 'I don't work for State,' is what I told the president. 'I work for you.' Here we are, politely holding millions of dollars' worth of Nazi gold, keeping it cool and dry for them? Let's grab it. We could fight back without firing a single shot."

The secretary was silent for a long moment. As if mourning what might have been.

"Someone at State nixed it. Or had it nixed. I was told that confiscating the gold would constitute a *provocation*."

"As if invading Czechoslovakia wasn't a provocation," White grumbled.

"Somebody at State?" Ansel felt two steps behind. "Who? Why?"

"We don't know who it was," Morgenthau said. "We don't know how they got the ears of the White House. And we sure as hell don't know why they were so interested in protecting Germany's gold. But it must have been somebody experienced. Connected. He knew how to work the president's senior staff, and he knew how to do it without leaving fingerprints. I've been pulling strings over there for years, and whoever pulled these was a fellow with a light touch."

Ansel thought about his misplaced paper clip. There were dark currents flowing through the government, and they ran deep under the surface.

"I'm Jewish." Morgenthau blurted it out so suddenly that Ansel first thought he'd misheard. "Did you know that?"

Morgenthau still faced the windows, but Ansel gathered the question was directed at him. "I did."

"'How would it look?' That's what I got back from the White House. 'How would it look if we allowed our sole Jewish cabinet member to pursue a personal vendetta against the Germans?'" The gentleness in Morgenthau's voice seemed to barely cover a buried anger. "Perhaps if I were a Christian, I would not be so easily constrained. Politics is full of cruel ironies, I suppose, but this is particularly galling. The Jews of Europe might well be better served if the secretary of the U.S. Treasury were *not* one of them."

It occurred to Ansel that Morgenthau might be the first Jew with whom he'd discussed Nazis. He had no Jewish friends. He had no Jewish neighbors or colleagues—not of which he was aware. He'd met Jews before, to be sure. Among his clients in Minnesota and among some of the other recruits when he'd first joined Treasury. But there were certainly no Jews in Harlan when he was young, nor at Catholic University when he was in law school.

Ansel studied the unreadable back of the secretary's head framed by the fading light from the windows. Here was Morgenthau, one of the most powerful men in America. He hosted famous clambakes every summer for the editors of *The New York Times* and shared fresh-picked apples with the president. He could spike—or crash—the markets with a single phrase. Meanwhile, his kin labored in horrific conditions in the Auschwitz work camp.

Morgenthau suddenly spun on his heels, no longer concealing his anger. "Somebody has convinced the White House that it would be poor public relations to heed the advice of their Jewish cabinet secretary. Rest assured: I am going to figure out who the hell it was."

Ansel did not doubt it.

Morgenthau addressed White. "Meanwhile, your new team has been working for how many weeks now, and the only idea you've brought me is something we already thought of six months ago?"

White rubbed out the last of his Lucky. "Give them time."

Morgenthau checked his watch. He was measuring time in minutes, not weeks. "I can't keep them secret forever."

White turned to Ansel: "You need to come up with something that doesn't violate the Neutrality Act. Something that State cannot even *argue* violates the Neutrality Act. Whatever it is, we have to knock the legs out from underneath the German economy without giving the appearance that we're picking sides."

"Bring me something soon." Following White, Morgenthau directed his rebuke at Ansel. "Something better than *that*. Or go back to wherever Harry found you."

Warm with humiliation, Ansel lowered his eyes and offered a small nod.

White had known for days that what they were bringing to Morgenthau was lacking, hadn't he? And yet he'd asked Ansel to give this presentation anyway.

He hadn't needed his house raconteur to tell a story. He'd needed a body to take the blame.

16

ANOTHER DINNER PARTY RUINED BY COMMUNISM

*"Capitalism is the extraordinary belief that
the nastiest of men, for the nastiest of reasons,
will somehow work for the benefit of us all."*

—JOHN MAYNARD KEYNES

September 20, 1939

Like every other idea birthed by the Research Department that month, the notion of an office dinner party was wet-nursed by their failure. Perhaps they might break bread, John Pehle suggested, so they did not break one another's spirits. Perhaps they might even be sociable enough to bring their wives?

Joe DuBois declined instantly. And being Joe, he didn't offer a reason. The Professor protested that when she was stuck in Washington, away from home, she preferred to spend her evenings more productively. James Saxon at least claimed to have preexisting plans. A date, he said, with an unspecified girlfriend. Herman Oliphant wasn't present to receive the invitation, so was spared having to contrive an excuse.

But given the tremendous lack of progress the team had made, it was White, of all people, who put his foot down and demanded collegiality. Dinner would be at his house that Wednesday. It was not so much an invitation as an order.

Angela was tickled at the prospect of finally meeting Ansel's colleagues. She wasn't set to start at the FBI for a few more days, and he was still working out when—or if—he should bring his wife's new job to his boss's attention. On the drive to Bethesda, he reminded her that he'd told her far more about what the Research Department was really doing than he was supposed to. "Officially we're engaged in research on the economies of Europe. That's all."

"Not to put too fine a point on it," she replied, "but isn't that all you've done anyhow?"

He wished she was wrong.

She promised that she'd have no trouble finding plenty of other topics to discuss with his colleagues besides economics.

"With this group?" Ansel said, exiting Route 614 onto a quiet, hickory-lined street. "Good luck."

The idea of a man as unfinished as Harry Dexter White possessing any kind of home life seemed about as incongruous as a fresh lilac growing out of a crumpled pack of cigarettes. So when Ansel and Angela pulled up outside a two-story colonial, positively picturesque in its graceful normalcy, he triple-checked the address. Harry Dexter White lived . . . here?

He did. And when Ansel knocked, a tall, handsome woman opened the door. Her short hair was a natural gray, and she wore reading glasses around her neck.

"You must be the Luxfords," she said with a hint of European accent, perhaps the East. "Oh, daisies!" She saw the flowers in Angela's hand. "My favorite. How ever did you know?"

"You must be Mrs. White," Angela said, and handed her the bouquet. "An educated guess."

"Anne Terry. And it does seem like it's going to be just such an evening." She led the Luxfords inside. "An educated one."

They found her husband mixing up a pitcher of martinis in the sitting room while a pair of dark-haired little girls played a spritely rag duet on the grand piano. Not only were the White daughters skilled, but they were unembarrassed about playing on cue for guests. Ansel watched Angela take them in, even joining them at the bench for a tune. By the look on her face, he feared that she might demand his assistance in producing a sister for Angie before the night was done.

In the presence of his family, Harry acted like a real live human being. Not once did he bark rudely. Not for a moment did he seem itching to be anywhere else. Even his smoking was down to a breezy single pack for the evening. As if all his cantankerousness were merely a stiff jacket he wore to the office, and at home he was free to slip it off and don something softer.

John Pehle arrived with his wife, Francha. Willowy and elegant, she was as consummate a guest as Ansel remembered her having been a host. It turned out that the Pehles lived only a few miles from the Whites, though the two families had never before socialized. Francha said she was intent on correcting the lapse.

James Saxon arrived with a striking brunette who looked to have come straight from the hairdresser. "Finally," Saxon said, "you'll get to meet the girl you've all heard so much about!"

She blushed at hearing that he'd spoken of her with his colleagues. Ansel asked about her classes at the university, taking care not to mention which one, since he was pretty sure he'd heard Saxon mention a few.

She responded with confusion. "I work the notions counter at Woodward & Lothrop. Perhaps you're thinking of someone else?"

She addressed the question pointedly toward Saxon. Who then fired an angry look at Ansel.

"Bernice and I met when I went in to buy some items for my aunt," Saxon said. "Surely you remember?"

"Of course," Ansel lied. The mystery of Saxon's personal life became, if anything, murkier. He was grateful when Angela approached with fresh martinis and Bernice asked how the Luxfords had met.

Ansel felt the two of them fall into a pleasant, practiced banter as they took turns filling in the story. They hadn't performed this ritual in some time. Ansel realized that he'd missed the recitation. Marriages, like all alliances, required their foundational myths.

The Luxfords remembered the story of their meeting differently. Or perhaps, he thought, they enjoyed the routine of remembering it differently. There was a pleasure to be found in interrupting each other every few sentences, unfurling their tale in overlapping fits and starts.

Ansel offered that he'd met his wife in law school. She'd been working for the dean. "You make it sound like *you* were my professor!" he
chided her, as usual.

"I worked for your professor," she shot back, as she had many times
before. "I was technically your superior."

Father Sheehy not only taught torts, he ran the debate club, of
which Ansel was a member. He'd found himself hanging around the
hall most days to make chitchat while Angela straightened up after a
session. She had teased him about his straw hat, calling him a country
mouse. She had made fun of his Midwestern sincerity. The only thing
on which she'd commended him had been his work ethic. It was lucky
he had one, she'd said, on account of his lack of natural aptitude.

Francha laughed at that line.

Ansel hadn't gotten up the nerve to ask Angela on a date until the
second-to-last week of the spring semester. "You almost let me slip
right through your fingers," she said.

Father Sheehy had married the Luxfords at the end of the following
summer. Angela's large family had been in attendance, her parents and
all four brothers. Ansel had no one on his side of the aisle. But there
wasn't any point in mentioning these details over cocktails.

Joe DuBois and the Professor arrived together, and they were ex-
ceedingly late. The Whites' daughters had already vanished upstairs to
baths and bedtimes. The adults downstairs were on their third pitcher
of martinis. Apparently the Professor didn't keep a car in Washington,
so DuBois had been enlisted to give her a ride out to Bethesda. During
which she discovered that she did not care for his light touch behind
the wheel.

When the group sat at the dining table, Anne Terry had to physically
remove the felt hat from DuBois's head. The seating was traditional,
which was helpful in that it split up DuBois and the Professor, who'd
already spent more than enough time together for one night. But it
was unhelpful in that Ansel ended up beside Bernice. He struggled to
find questions to ask that would not betray his utter ignorance about
her existence.

All in all, things went pretty well, considering. This was largely on account of Anne Terry's conversational acumen. It turned out that she was a published author, which all the ladies found fascinating. She had her own study in the back of the house, separate from her husband's, in which she wrote children's books: retellings of Shakespeare's plays, crafted for youthful readers. It was never too early, she felt, to introduce children to proper literature.

Ansel would have been content to spend the evening discussing how to render Macbeth palatable to a six-year-old, but sometime after the roast beef was served, he heard a disquietude developing from the far end of the table. The topic, he was unhappy to discern, was communism.

"Stalin's nonaggression pact with Hitler is an error of tactics," DuBois was saying. "Not an error of ideology. Comrade Stalin isn't perfect, but you can't go blaming communism because one man made one boneheaded mistake."

"There are a few other things for which I'm happy to blame communism," Saxon said in return.

"Widespread prosperity? Civil peace? Is that what you don't like?"

Pehle made a sour face. "Did you call Stalin your comrade?"

"And why not? Aren't we all brothers?"

"Are you a communist?" Bernice asked DuBois with shocked incredulity. She made it sound like she'd never met one before. Perhaps the notions counter at Woodward & Lothrop was not so full of revolutionaries. Or at least not ones so open on the subject of class warfare.

DuBois looked around the table for support. "We're all Democrats here, aren't we? We can speak forthrightly about the need to pursue the common, *collective* good of man?"

"We can," White said.

"My dad voted for Hoover," Bernice said.

Angela scoffed audibly.

Ansel thought it best to interrupt before his wife could jump to the defense of the president. "We all support Roosevelt. But I think Stalin's choice to align with the fascists in Germany and Italy does not speak well of the Soviet Union."

"The Soviets," Anne Terry interjected with surprising force, "are not a colonial power. Unlike the British, they don't seek an empire. Unlike the French, they don't sail halfway around the world 'civilizing natives.' Unlike us Americans, they don't keep an entire racial class in legal subservience. One may have a bone to pick with Stalin, but clearly one can see that communism itself is a noble enterprise."

"One may," Pehle suggested, "though one should not." He addressed DuBois. "You're a Christian man. You don't worry for your fellow believers under godless collectivism?"

"Less than I do for the poor of our country, be they believers or otherwise. In your neck of the woods, you may have been spared the sight of your neighbors tossed out of their homes and left starving on the streets during the Depression. We weren't."

"I'm proud to say we gave to every itinerant we saw back then," Francha said. "There were so many on the road to our summer house."

"So hang on here, *you're* a communist too?" Bernice said to Anne Terry, lagging a few steps behind in the conversation.

"Don't think of it like a switch," DuBois said, "on or off."

"If centrally planned economies are machines," the Professor said, speaking for the first time in a while, "then I fear they're defective."

"Aren't you in the employ of the U.S. government to do just that?" DuBois countered. "Plan our economy?"

"We study how the Nazis planned theirs. We don't think it's something to emulate."

"Maybe that's why they're winning and we're losing."

Ansel felt it best to steer this conversation away from the details of their clandestine work. "We're humble researchers. And good Democrats. No one here is a communist."

"I am." Anne Terry set down her silverware and stared defiantly at her guests. She spoke like a woman with nothing to hide. "Because communism works."

Bernice used a fork to push a slice of beef away from her across her plate, as if it were tainted.

Saxon reached over and plucked the slice off his date's plate, downing it in one gulp. "Capitalism works pretty well, too."

"I do feel there's a difference of a few famines between the one and the other," Pehle said. "When the first million starve, it might be a mistake. But by the time the third million do, it begins to feel like a design flaw."

"Oh, you don't believe those stories, do you?" Anne Terry sounded to Ansel like his father-in-law speaking about Germans. "The Depression was brutal throughout the world, and the *Times* proved that those Soviet famine stories were wildly exaggerated."

White stepped in, offering branches of peace in all directions. "I think my wife's point is that it's fashionable these days, thanks to the Republicans"—he addressed Angela—"to draw a sharp line between capitalists and communists, Americans and Soviets. But really we're on the same spectrum. The government spends more money, they spend less, workers get more rights, they get fewer." He addressed Professor Newcomer. "It's not night and day. Maybe we could learn a thing or two from them." He addressed DuBois. "And maybe they could learn a thing or two from us."

Ansel was more surprised by his boss's sudden geniality than by his hostess's Stalinist sympathies.

"Let's not have another dinner party ruined by communism," Saxon said wistfully.

"Another?" Angela said. "You're all government employees. I'm not sure that making a habit of expressing communist sympathies at dinner parties is such a smart idea."

"Not all of us work for the government," Anne Terry said. "You and I—and Bernice and Francha—may speak our politics freely."

"I do," Angela said.

"Speak freely?" Francha asked.

"No. I work for the government . . ."

Ansel reached out a hand to stop her, but he wasn't fast enough.

"I work for the FBI," Angela continued.

The acronym landed like a munition. The silence that followed felt louder to Ansel than if the table had burst in an explosion.

Ansel looked at his wife, who also clearly felt she had little to hide. He then turned to White, who appeared puzzled.

"You work for the FBI?" he asked her. "And Ansel didn't mention it until now?"

If Angela realized that she'd brought their precarious situation up prematurely, she didn't show it. She was proud of doing her part in Roosevelt's government. "Well, I'm only typing up correspondence. And I don't start till Monday."

"I was going to mention it tomorrow," Ansel offered lamely. He looked around the room at his colleagues. Even the Professor wore a tense expression. The lot of them were like lambs who'd suddenly discovered a wolf in their midst. The wrong word and they might be devoured.

But White didn't appear worried. He seemed amused. "Imagine if J. Edgar Hoover heard about our colleagues' communist leanings."

"Sympathies," DuBois softened.

Bernice perked up. "So it's true? What my father was saying? That the FBI is going through the government, rooting out communists?"

"Seems Angela would know," Anne Terry said. It sounded like a challenge.

"I don't start till Monday."

"Then you'll have to keep us posted."

"The Soviets are on Hitler's side," the Professor said. "At least for the moment. Anything sent to Moscow might just as easily end up on its way to Berlin. If there really are communists in the federal government . . . Well, I should most certainly *hope* the FBI is working to find them."

"I'm sure the FBI is hunting for all sorts of things," White said pointedly in Ansel's direction. Since their first meeting, Ansel was well aware that White was concerned about the FBI's looking into the true nature of their clandestine unit. They might not be hiding communists, but they were certainly hiding something.

And now, evidently, White would need to be concerned about hiding it from Angela Luxford.

Ansel wondered whether he'd be fired before morning.

He looked his boss right in the eye. "The government's a big place.

Takes all kinds. And all kinds of secrets. Who knows which of them, if any, the FBI are interested in?"

"It's a nice thing," Francha offered genteelly. "A husband and wife, both doing government work."

Ansel felt a sting. Had Francha judged him for having a wife who worked? Was there condescension beneath her impeccable manners?

"Perhaps you can ride to work together," Pehle said. "Like neighbors."

Ansel's insides churned.

"Neighbors," he said in White's direction, "with strong fences between them."

"No man is an island," Anne Terry said.

"Certainly not a married one," Pehle said.

"And who would want to be . . ." Ansel began, and then stopped. He suddenly felt his mind at the lip of some great precipice.

"Ansel?" Angela turned to her suddenly mute husband.

"Sorry . . . I . . . An island . . . No man . . . Neighbors . . ." The idea that was forming in Ansel's brain was so laughably obvious that it left him feeling like a fool.

He looked up to find them all staring at him. "I need to get back to the office."

"Now?" Angela asked.

Ansel nodded and stood. White looked up at him with curiosity. His role thus far had not been to provide the big ideas. But clearly White could see that Ansel had one, and perhaps he wanted to find out where it might lead. "I'll drive you."

"Was the roast really so overcooked?" Anne Terry said, confronting the premature end of her dinner party.

Pehle rose to his feet. "The roast was divine. If only I could stay for seconds."

"I'll come too." The Professor was not going to let whatever was happening at the office go uninspected.

And as soon as she'd spoken, Saxon stood as well. "I'm sure," he said to Bernice, "that Mrs. Pehle won't mind driving you back to Edgewood?"

Perhaps he wanted to ace the Professor's class more than he let on.

Bernice frowned. "I live in Chevy Chase."

DuBois said nothing as he went straight for his hat in the cloak room.

Ansel held his wife's hand. "Do you mind?"

In her eyes, he could see that she knew that whatever was happening was too important for him to discuss aloud. She shook her head and squeezed his hand in return.

"You want to tell us what this is about?" White asked as the slightly drunk, largely hungry members of the Research Department followed Ansel out the door.

"No one is an island," Ansel said. "No matter how much one might try to be."

17

A BETTER OFFER

*"And it will often happen that a man with wealth in the
form of coined money will not have enough to eat;
and what a ridiculous kind of wealth is that which even in
abundance will not save you from dying with hunger!"*

—ARISTOTLE

September 20, 1939 (cont'd)

"What if we've been looking at the problem from the wrong way around?" Ansel said to the others after they'd rushed up the stairwells of the darkened furniture store to their office. Pehle poured glasses of whiskey for everyone, making sure their late-night work would not be hindered by unexpected sobriety.

Ansel tore through reams of financial data looking for one sheet in particular. He knew he'd have to put in a request for more from the NBER when they opened in the morning. Until then, the plan forming in his mind would have to remain frothy, invigorating conjecture.

"How ought we look at it?" Pehle distributed tumblers.

"We're trying to strand the Germans on an island of their own making by confiscating their gold."

"We'd like to." White found a trove of cigarettes in Herman Oliphant's temporary desk. "But we can't."

"We don't have to," Ansel offered. "If we stop the trade from the other end."

"Which end would that be?" Saxon said.

"Who are Germany's largest trading partners?"

"Italy," the Professor answered from memory. "Japan. Argentina. Brazil."

"Italy has made her allegiances clear. So have Japan and Argentina. But Brazil . . ." Ansel found the sheet he was looking for. He showed the others the breakdown Saxon had prepared weeks ago on German-Brazilian trade. "Brazil is not a natural ally for Germany. Just an avid trading partner. They sell the Germans huge quantities of coffee."

"Something tells me," Pehle said, "that we're not going to defeat the Nazis by cutting off their coffee supply."

"The Wehrmacht," White added, "is perfectly capable of rampaging through the rest of Europe even if they feel a touch sluggish in the mornings."

"I agree." Ansel gestured to the sheet. "But we might get the job done by cutting off their supply of iron and cotton."

"Brazil's other major exports to Germany." The Professor didn't have to look.

"You can't build tanks without iron. And you can't put soldiers inside them if they've got nothing to wear."

"You propose that we strike a deadly blow at the Nazis' sense of fashion?" White asked.

"I propose that the Northern European winter is a cold one. And that soldiers can only wage war if they manage not to first die of hypothermia."

DuBois wasn't sold. "The Germans pay the Brazilians handsomely for their iron and cotton. They pay in gold. Of which Berlin has, I'm sorry to say, just enough."

"And they're acquiring more." Saxon held up the previous day's *Post*. The German military march across Poland was as quick as it was brutal. Warsaw, they all knew, would have plenty of lucre for the plundering.

"If you're suggesting we try to crash the global market for gold . . ." DuBois said. "That might cause more widespread misery than if we let the Nazis win."

"Again, I agree," Ansel said. "But you're still thinking about this in terms of stopping Germany's ability to pay. I'm saying: What if we stop Brazil's ability to sell?"

For the first time, White looked at Ansel like he was impressed. Maybe he saw where Ansel was headed before the others did. Or maybe he merely saw that Ansel's plan would be devious. And deviousness was the quality that White valued most.

"How are we to deter the Brazilians from selling to a flush customer?" Pehle asked.

"We don't. I'm not suggesting that we *deter* Brazil from anything. All I'm suggesting is that we make them a better offer."

———

THE PLAN THAT ANSEL sketched out was shocking in its simplicity. The Germans were buying all the iron and cotton they could from the Brazilians. But if the U.S. Treasury went to the Brazilian government, as well as to the private companies manufacturing and mining the stuff, they could simply outbid the Germans. Surely the Brazilians would be happy to take their payment in dollars! It was convertible to gold, practically the same thing.

"What is the United States supposed to do with all this iron and cotton that you'd have us buy?" the Professor asked.

Saxon answered before Ansel could. "Who cares?"

"Exactly," Ansel said. "The point is that the Germans won't have it. The Brazilians aren't ideological fascists. They want only to sell their wares to the highest bidder."

"How much," DuBois asked, "do you think it'll cost to outbid Germany?"

It wouldn't be cheap, of that they could be assured.

"It will be difficult," Pehle said, "convincing Congress to requisition us some spare cash to buy a ton of cotton that we don't need."

"Many tons," Saxon corrected.

"I was being metaphorical. And the senators from our Southern states may not react favorably to such a proposal. You know, turning America into a net *importer* of their signature commodity."

Ansel had to admit that getting the money from Congress would be a problem. He hadn't yet arrived at a solution.

A quiet gloom quickly settled over them.

near the cockpit, but he couldn't be sure. The men from War were the fit ones in scuffed shoes, the sort who hadn't let their desk jobs bulge their waistlines. Ansel figured he and White blended in well with the assorted others—anonymous government men in light linen suits and dark ties. This was their goal: not to draw attention.

Even as the cargo plane landed and the thirty or so Americans streamed into a fleet of black cars, they said little. Only one of the men, a debonair-looking sort with hair so slicked that it burned hot in the sun, and a tight little mustache so trim that it unfortunately resembled Hitler's, acknowledged White. His name turned out to be Sumner Welles, and he joined Ansel and White in their car.

"Thank Christ," Welles said as soon as the doors were closed. The driver appeared to be a Panamanian civilian, in a cap and uniform, but Welles either didn't notice or didn't care enough to let it seal his lips. "I'm lucky you're here to save me from those snakes." Presumably he meant his fellow diplomats. "What are you doing here, Harry, by the way?"

White looked right at Welles when he answered. "The Treasury Department wants to be sure that our relationships with our long-time trading partners in South America are not disturbed by this nasty European business."

Welles's expression indicated that he did not for a single second believe this.

White's expression, in return, dared his countryman to say so out loud.

Welles finally laughed. He rolled down the window and blew fresh cigarette smoke into the humid afternoon air. Tall palm trees loomed over the road into the city, and beyond them Ansel could see miles of canopy. It didn't take long for the heart of Panama City to appear up ahead: a bright flag of yellow, red, and green buildings backed by the lush Ancon Hills.

"Who are you?" Welles got around to inquiring of Ansel. "Never seen Harry travel with a pal before."

"Mr. Luxford," White said, "is my attorney."

Welles shook his head. "Best of luck with that."

Ansel gave his name and offered a shake. He tried making conversation in order to work out how White and Welles knew each other, but White only barked in annoyance and Welles only provided sly jokes.

"Over at State, we like to pride ourselves on our ability to prevent armed conflict. Seems we've had better months."

Ansel remembered Morgenthau's suspicion that someone within State was working to sabotage Treasury's anti-German efforts. Might such a person be acting out of pacifism, rather than fascism? Ansel had a mind to point out that the war had started years ago and Treasury was simply doing its damnedest to catch up. But then he decided it was best not to speak a single unnecessary word.

"Ever been to Panama City?" Welles asked.

"I've never been outside of America before," Ansel admitted.

"You still haven't," White said. He explained that this was all still part of legally unincorporated U.S. territory. The Canal Zone wasn't Panama, it was America. Sort of. For the Panamanians' protection.

It sounded like a racket.

The Hotel Centrale was right in the heart of Casco Antiguo, across the busy road from the Plaza de la Independencia. It was of French-style construction, four stories with ornate balconies and a row of shops at the base: a pharmacy, a newspaper stand, and a cigar store with signs in English.

Welles bid them goodbye and asked the driver to carry him on to a nearby hotel. "See you in the morning? Or is the Treasury Department not attending the conference formally?"

White stepped out of the car. Ansel followed, handing his single bag to a porter. He could see the lobby through the open double doors. It was a gilded touch of Versailles not four hundred feet from the Atlantic. Not ten miles from the mouth of the untamed jungle.

"I'll see you soon," White said to Welles through the car window, avoiding the question. "But you never mentioned: What exactly is *State* hoping to get out of this?"

Welles's grin was as thin as his mustache. "Peace. Prosperity. Good-will. What else?"

September 23, 1939

The conference was at the National Institute, a university complex a few miles from the Hotel Centrale. When Ansel arrived the following morning, he thought it looked more like a Roman villa than a university, ancient and imposing, even with the bright yellow paint that covered the entire exterior.

Thick stone columns held up the main entrance. Inside, hundreds of chairs were set up in rows, with tables and a lectern at the front of what seemed once to have been a ballroom. It all appeared appropriately photogenic. So much so that it took Ansel no more than a minute to deduce that the real work would be done in the hallways.

Thousands of men and hundreds of women from dozens of nations were making side deals all around him. Every time Ansel turned a corner he was greeted with a cacophony of whispers. He spoke no Spanish, so he was useless at uncovering the duplicities that coursed through the building.

The night before, White had set up a private meeting with Jacome Baggi de Berenger César, a Brazilian government emissary who had a specialty in international finance. The morning was barely underway when Ansel and White met him in a university courtyard lined with camoruco trees. Jacome wore a thick beard, lightly salted, and stared at Ansel with piercing black eyes that never seemed to blink.

He introduced himself in perfect English. He had an aide with him, a small woman carrying an armful of folders, who spoke only to Jacome, and only in Portuguese.

By the standards of diplomats, White was not exactly charming. "Hot here," were his first words to Jacome. "I'm coming to you with a proposition."

Jacome gazed up at the buildings surrounding them, each one full of conniving men with offers of their own. In the windows, Ansel could see people huddled together in hushed conversations. It was all one big, leafy, humid, smoke-filled backroom.

"Ansel," White said. "Time to talk turkey with the man."

Jacome frowned, as if worried his English were failing him.

"It means money," Ansel said.

Jacome looked reassured: They were all speaking the same language.

Ansel detailed the offer: The U.S. government wanted to buy, and incentivize private American companies to buy, as much Brazilian cotton and iron ore as they possibly could. To secure the kind of volume they had in mind, it would only be fair that they offer to pay above the current market rate. Whatever price Jacome's government thought was fair.

"You cannot make cotton in America?" Jacome asked curiously.

"We want more," Ansel said simply. "And we can pay you in a form you'll be hard-pressed to get anywhere else: American dollars."

Jacome's face betrayed nothing of his thoughts. He conferred with his aide in a dense fog of half-whispered Portuguese. He didn't seem concerned that Ansel or White would be able to translate, and in this he was correct.

He finally turned back to the Americans. "The Germans purchase quite a bit of those exact products from our biggest export companies."

"Sounds like Herr Hitler and I have the same taste in fabrics," White said.

Jacome rubbed his hands together as if American dollars were already between his palms. "I strongly doubt that. There are some colleagues from our central bank I would like to speak with. They may have some questions for you as well."

"If I were them," Ansel said, "I'd have more than a few."

"The Balboa Yacht Club, off the Calzada del Almador, has the best rum selection in town. I will be there with some colleagues this evening. After ten."

"What a coincidence," White said. "So will we."

Jacome nodded. Then glanced to his aide, who appeared to confirm that their business was, for the moment, concluded.

"You know, I don't mind Herr Hitler so much as most," Jacome said as he turned back toward the conference. "But the one thing nobody has ever accused him of having is taste."

———

THE HOUSE SPECIALTY AT the Balboa Yacht Club was a mojito made with an obscure local rum. It was delicious, though Ansel couldn't claim to have the most developed taste in rums. He and White sipped their cold drinks at a window table. The club was crowded with locals who talked over the jazz quintet. The music was up-tempo but Ansel didn't see anyone dancing. Between numbers, he could hear the gentle rhythm of the ocean surf coming through the open windows. He could smell the salt water.

Ansel had spent most of the morning sitting through various public addresses in the official conference hall. They all had the same unavoidable theme: neutrality. The nations of South America had sent emissaries to Panama to proclaim their neutrality into as many microphones as they could find. The U.S. emissaries announced all they were doing to *assist* the Chileans and Argentineans and Venezuelans and most especially the Brazilians in their principled neutralities. To hear the diplomats speak, one would think that what was happening in Europe was an unfortunate tragedy without culprits or heroes. The nations present here vowed, in an act of mutual interdependence previously unseen on such a global scale, to remain uninvolved.

White didn't stay for the speeches. Nor did he tell Ansel where he was going when he left the conference. Not telling Ansel any more than he needed to know, and frequently not even so much as that, was apparently White's modus operandi.

Ansel's boss was a hard sort to get a handle on. Even more so after the glimpse of his charmed homelife. He was never warm, that was for sure, but sometimes he did make Ansel feel pleasantly depended upon. That was, when he wasn't making sure that Ansel was blamed for their collective failures. He couldn't have been more than a decade Ansel's senior. But he nonetheless reminded Ansel of his old man—distant and inscrutable except in clarifying moments of anger. There was never much pleasing Ansel's old man, and Ansel's childhood had improved dramatically when he'd stopped trying. His mother could try to read the tea leaves of the old man's shifting moods if she really wanted to. Ansel found it best to take his lumps and move along.

He'd been sitting in amiable silence with White for a while when they looked up to see Jacome and his aide making their way through the yacht club. The aide carried another stack of documents, though she'd changed into a dress fit for the evening.

Before arriving at his chair, Jacome greeted their waiter with a nod, sending the young man off to fetch his usual. "You like the rum here?"

"Sure," White said. "You ready to make a deal?"

Jacome paused. Clearly small talk was not in White's repertoire.

"I have some questions," Jacome said.

"Let's hear."

Jacome's aide took a blank sheet from her stack and prepared to take notes.

"What are the intentions of the United States," Jacome asked, "in terms of helping its allies in Britain and France?"

"I have absolutely no idea."

"You're here, aren't you, on behalf of the United States?"

"We're here on behalf of the Treasury. What the White House intends, much less the departments of State or War, are above my pay grade."

"Aren't you the ones who pay them?"

Jacome spent the next half hour politely grilling White on all avenues of U.S. government policy regarding the war in the Atlantic. Trade routes for both countries ran through waters filling up with warships: Which paths to Europe remained safe? His aide kept scribbling on her pages, though Ansel could not conceive of what she was writing down since White did not disclose a single piece of real information. Ansel wasn't sure if that was because White was such a good liar, or because he simply didn't know anything. But Ansel got the distinct impression that Jacome thought the U.S. government was much more unified and organized in its policies than it actually was.

Eventually White had withstood enough. "Look, do you want our money or not? My colleague is prepared to get into the details of our offer."

"It won't be necessary," Jacome frowned. "I'm afraid we're not able to alter our trade arrangements at the moment."

Ansel didn't flinch.

White paused. "You think that when the naval war in the Atlantic grows hotter, that'll be a better time?"

Jacome shook his head. "We have other factors to consider."

"The Germans are paying you well. But their dollar and sterling reserves are virtually depleted, so they can only pay you in gold."

"You don't like gold?"

"I like dollars. So do you. I don't mind a little hardball, but let's get on with the negotiations."

Jacome looked to the ceiling as if in silent prayer. "We have *other* factors to consider. Other trade partners. You haven't approached our friends in Argentina or Chile with similar offers, have you?"

If White was flustered to find that Jacome was ahead of him, he didn't show it. "They have deeper economic ties to Germany than you do."

"We're the 'weak link'? Is that your expression?"

"It's not my expression."

"I consulted with our bankers. And they consulted with their colleagues in Argentina."

"This deal was offered to you."

"It's a complicated deal. And like I said, we have a lot to consider. Our friends in Argentina are taking payment for their exports in reichsmarks."

For the first time, Ansel caught a flash of fear on White's face. "You wouldn't."

"We haven't."

"You sure as hell better goddamn not." White was losing his cool. "For your own sake: When the war is over, all those reichsmarks are going to be worth nothing."

"If the Germans lose, that's right. But what if they win?"

"They won't."

"If the Germans win . . . what use will we have for dollars?"

White fumed. The tautology was maddening: Only the victor's currency would have value after the war. But to win the war, each side needed to assure the world that its currency had value.

This was not a war of armies: It was a war of currencies. Did the future belong to dollars, sterling, and francs? Or reichsmarks, lira, and yen?

Jacome stood. "We're not following the path of our Argentinean friends. We will honor our trade agreements with Germany and we will take payment only in gold. And thus, we will remain neutral."

"You think sending iron ore to Germany so they can turn it into tanks is neutral?"

"I think it's the best we can do." Jacome shared a look with his silent aide. Their business here was concluded. She folded up her notes.

White stayed seated, glowering from his deep chair. "This isn't the last you're going to hear from us."

"Life is long. So is war." Jacome walked away, charting a course for himself through the crowded club.

His aide, however, remained in place. She shot a quick glance toward her boss.

While his back was to her, she extended a hand to Ansel.

"Till next time." Her English was exquisite.

Ansel didn't know what to do besides shake her hand. "Till next time."

As their fingers touched, he felt her slide something into his palm.

She dropped his hand and left quickly, catching up with Jacome near the door before he'd even noticed she'd tarried.

Ansel looked down at his palm, discovering a scrap of folded paper.

White's glower transformed into a curious frown as Ansel unfolded it and together they read a few hastily scribbled words:

"Argentina did not kill deal. He was <u>American</u>."

19

EVERYONE IS LYING ABOUT EVERYTHING

"A man generally has two reasons for doing a thing.
One that sounds good, and a real one."

—J. P. MORGAN

September 23, 1939 (cont'd)

White did not speak to Ansel as they bolted out of the yacht club. Nor did he speak on the cab ride back to the Casco Antiguo, or on their walk through the lobby of the Hotel Centrale. Once they'd locked themselves inside White's room, he seemed ready to finally say something and then stopped himself. He glanced around the ornately decorated suite: so many nooks and crannies in which to hide a radio transmitter. Rather than say anything, he held a finger to his lips, and then tapped his right ear: *Someone might be listening.*

White did not say a single word to Ansel until, at last, they found refuge in the lobby bar. Amid the midnight bustle, the density of the crowd provided its own measure of privacy. The first words that came from White were angry: "Who'd you tell?"

"That we're here?" Ansel asked defensively. "No one. I told Angela we had to take a trip but I couldn't say where. She doesn't even know I'm out of the country."

"You're not. Technically." White scrounged for a dish of peanuts on the bar and stuffed a handful into his mouth.

"Why would an American want to kill the deal?" Ansel asked.

White didn't offer an answer.

"Could it have been someone at State?" Ansel asked. "Like before? Your friend Welles . . ."

White chewed forcefully. "It wasn't Welles. And as for somebody else at State, how the hell could anyone have known what we're doing here?"

"I found a paper clip." Ansel couldn't stop from saying it any longer. If he was being followed, and whoever was following him had somehow made it all the way to Panama . . . Ansel couldn't risk being responsible for another disaster.

"A paper clip?"

Ansel explained.

When he'd finished, White stared at him for a long moment. "You found a paper clip on the floor of your hotel room."

"Yes." Ansel felt unburdened by the confession. "I didn't tell you before because I wasn't sure what it meant. But now . . ."

White removed his handkerchief and wiped his brow, as if cleansing himself of Ansel's incompetence. "Somebody just sabotaged a trade deal that could have turned the tide of this war and you're talking to me about a paper clip?"

Ansel had a hard time explaining why, in context, the event had felt quite sinister.

"What are you going to do?" he asked, giving up.

"What am I going to do?" White leaned back on his stool. "Buddy, we've been had. Either it was a mysterious American who had us, or else Jacome wants us to believe it was. Either way, he was never going to make a deal. That whole meeting was arranged so that he could pump us for information. Because I'm not a goddamned idiot, he failed. But until I prove otherwise, what I'm going to do is assume that every goddamned one is lying about every goddamned thing."

White grabbed another palmful of peanuts. "Including you."

September 26, 1939

Ansel stewed around Panama City for a few more days while White failed to smoke out a single clue as to who'd betrayed them. White had always struck Ansel as suspicious, but the knowledge that some-one close by may have been conspiring against him spun his paranoia into high gear. Where he went on those days, and whom he spoke with, remained a mystery. Ansel was left to wander the conference and listen to the same milquetoast speech about the moral necessity of neutrality delivered, with scant variation, in language after lan-guage.

They finally flew home commercially, retreating from the Cris-tobal airport on Tuesday in a Pan Am seaplane bound for Miami. From there, another plane delivered the two men, who'd exchanged all of a dozen words with each other since Panama City, to Washington. It was late when they landed, and they each slunk into separate taxis with the bare minimum of farewells.

Ansel felt depleted. He was out of smart ideas. He was out of any sort of ideas at all.

He hadn't told Angela when he'd be back, so the house was dark when he arrived in Bloomingdale. He tried to be as quiet as he could getting his key in the lock and entering Angela's childhood bedroom.

He was certain he'd barely made a noise when the bedside lamp flicked on. There was Angela, sitting up in bed, her pale face suddenly illuminated.

He gave a start. "Geeze! Sorry. I didn't mean to wake you."

"You didn't."

Ansel checked his wristwatch. "Is something wrong?"

She bit her lip nervously.

He undid his bow tie. "I'm sorry I couldn't tell you when I'd be home."

"It's not that."

"What is it?"

"I just started. At the FBI. Yesterday. I didn't imagine I'd see any-thing . . . I just started!" She shook her head in disbelief. "But since I'd typed at Justice before, they said I didn't need any training or any mess-ing around with the introductory forms. Right away, they put me on the desk of an agent who . . . Well, no reason to tell you his name. It doesn't matter."

She was silent for a long moment. She seemed to be mulling a difficult decision.

Ansel sat beside her on the creaky old mattress.

"We made an agreement," she said after a while. "Didn't we? Not to share the details of our work?"

He nodded.

"But what if I heard something . . . something you'd *need* to know?"

"What would I need to know?"

"I suppose that's the question." She looked pained.

Ansel knew that his wife was a woman who took her vows seriously. She'd made one to her husband standing at the altar of her church. She'd made many to her Lord. And she'd felt herself making one implicitly when she went to work for the government. Though to whom, Ansel wasn't sure: Her president? Her country? The law?

Which of her vows should take precedence now?

"The agent . . . The desk I'm at . . . He's hunting for Soviet spies in the U.S. government."

"It's no secret that Hoover is spooked about that."

"I'll say. They've just formed a whole division devoted solely to rooting them out. Hoover's people are convinced that there are Soviet agents in senior government positions."

"What makes them so sure?"

Angela doled out her words with care. "This morning I was taking dictation. In a meeting. They were talking about a defector. A Soviet spy who'd switched sides. This person gave up the identities of a half-dozen Soviet agents in Washington."

Ansel toyed with his unknotted bow tie. "They think this defector is credible?"

"They seem to. And *nobody* seems to have a clue how far Stalin is going to take his deal with Hitler. Does 'nonaggression' mean he's sharing intelligence with the Germans?"

"They have to assume a Soviet spy is effectively a German spy."

"Exactly. This defector said that over the years, a number of Americans agreed to work for Moscow. But then Moscow's deal with Berlin took them all by surprise. Who are they working for now? Maybe they're not even sure themselves."

Angela rubbed her shoulder under the straps of her nightgown. "Imagine me sitting there, these men chatting away like I'm not even a fly on their wall. I'm typing as fast as I can and the keys seem so loud, but it's like my typewriter and I don't even exist. Laughing and joking away about their old ladies and their clubs and the Giants and this defector. And one of them says that the defector mentioned another Soviet agent. Well, the defector didn't know the name of this agent. No identifying details. Man or woman, young or old, nothing. All the defector knew was that this Soviet spy just got a new position. Only weeks ago. A position in Treasury. In the Research Department."

20

IDEALISTS

*"I was not sympathetic to the assumption that criminals had
radically different motivations from everyone else."*

—GARY BECKER,
NOBEL PRIZE—WINNING AMERICAN ECONOMIST

September 26, 1939 (cont'd)

Ansel had a lot of questions. For that matter, so did Angela.

To begin with: Who could it be? The defector, if the FBI gossip
she'd transcribed was accurate, claimed not to know. Was the defector
certain that such an agent even existed? Yes, and the defector claimed
to have recently seen carbon copies of documents smuggled out of the
Research Department and sent, via unspecified channels, to Moscow.
The documents concerned Brazilian foreign exchange reserves and the
South American cotton trade.

"That doesn't sound too important, does it?" Angela said. "But it
sounds specific."

It sure did: Ansel thought he knew exactly which documents the
defector must be referring to. He'd typed them up himself.

He failed to hide his reaction from his wife.

"So that rings a bell?" she asked. "The defector is right?"

Only Ansel's colleagues in the Research Department had seen those
documents. And only they would have understood why they were important enough to pass along.

Ansel felt sick to think that his work might have landed in Berlin
before he'd even arrived in Panama.

"The subject matter," Angela said, "sounds pretty esoteric to the FBI men. So they don't think that unmasking this particular spy is of the highest priority. Not when they have bigger rats to trap."

The thought of any of Ansel's colleagues moonlighting as a Soviet agent seemed absurd. Sure, DuBois had expressed some communist leanings over dinner. So had Anne Terry White. But that didn't make them traitors. . . .

It occurred to Ansel that if he was a Soviet agent, the last thing he'd do at a party would be express pro-Soviet sentiments. If he was secretly working for Moscow, he'd tell everyone who'd listen how much he couldn't stand the Soviets. He'd behave, in other words, like the Professor had at that dinner. She'd defended American capitalism forcefully; so had Pehle. But if John Pehle was a double agent, Ansel would eat his hat. He'd known the man for over a decade!

Perhaps a spy would behave like Herman Oliphant. He'd avoid socializing with his colleagues at all.

One phrase spun round and round in Ansel's head like a drop of blood circling a porcelain drain: *"He was American."*

Had it been someone in the Research Department, not someone at State, who'd sabotaged their deal with the Brazilians? None of the others could have flown down to Panama without being discovered. But the double agent would have had plenty of time to tell his handlers in Soviet intelligence what Ansel and White were plotting. The Soviets, of course, wouldn't have much reason to nix an American–Brazilian trade deal. But if Soviet intelligence had wanted to demonstrate either their usefulness or their bonhomie to German intelligence . . . well, the Germans had quite a few reasons to kill the deal, and they must have had other agents in position in Panama to bury the knife.

Ansel recalled White's suspicions: *Was* the saboteur an American? Or did Jacome just want White and Ansel to believe that he had been?

Ansel's suspicions spun like a top, furiously pointing in new directions only to end up back at the same uncertain place.

If the question of "who?" was disconcerting to ponder, the matter of "why?" was even darker.

Communism? Money? Something stranger?

Ansel had known communists his whole life. Most of them, like Joe DuBois, admitted their ideological commitments freely. Especially in the years after the Depression, the Soviets had seemed as much a natural ally to America as Britain or France. Perhaps the double agent was simply trying to foster cooperation between the United States and the USSR, and found himself poorly used by Soviet intelligence, aiding the Germans without realizing it.

But if so, did that make the spy a patsy? Or a fool? Ansel's colleagues had many flaws. None were fools.

As for the question of money, well, the irony was plain. No one Ansel had met at the Treasury Department seemed in the least bit motivated by money.

The questions faced by Ansel and Angela only multiplied as the hours wore on. But the most difficult one was the question that required an immediate answer: What were *they* going to do about this?

Whatever it might be, they would have to do it together.

By the time the dawn light started to intrude from beneath the shades, their most unsettling thought was that they would both soon have to go to work.

21

RUM TOO STRONG
FOR YOU?

*"The curious task of economics is to demonstrate to men how little
they really know about what they imagine they can design."*

—FRIEDRICH AUGUST VON HAYEK

September 27, 1939

For once Ansel was nearly the last one in the office. They were all surprised to see him, as neither he nor White had yet informed the group of their trip's failure, or of their early return.

The Professor saw Ansel slink in first: Shouldn't he still be in Panama?

Saxon had apparently slept at his desk overnight and smelled like it. DuBois had separated himself away in a far corner with a large stack of documents and a bottle of milk. He seemed to be in a trance of calculation. Oliphant examined the work Saxon had completed the night before. The only member of the Research Department who wasn't there was White.

On the plane, they'd made the decision to be forthcoming with the entire team about being outplayed in Panama. Their logic was simple: If someone outside the Research Department had sabotaged the deal with the Argentineans, then learning the details might help someone within it figure out who'd done the deed. Alternatively, if the Judas was here among them, then Ansel would only be telling the culprit something he already knew.

But now, surveying the faces of his colleagues, Ansel hesitated.

Another wrinkle, unknown to White or himself when they'd made this plan—another spy, this one Soviet. Or were the rats one and the same? Would everything he was about to say end up being reported back to Moscow? Or, heaven forbid, Berlin?

"Rum too strong for you?" Pehle said as soon as Ansel removed his hat.

Ansel informed the group about their unfruitful meetings with Jacome; but he did not speak a word about Angela's defector. He couldn't risk letting the Soviet agent know that the FBI was on to him—or her. Moreover, if the FBI ever learned that Angela had leaked their classified secrets to her husband, the Luxfords' problems would become distinctly more proximate.

Just as he'd made an agreement with White on the plane in regard to one possible spy, he'd made an agreement with Angela at dawn concerning the other: Wait. Watch. Listen. If one of them figured out who the traitor was, they would act. Until then, silence was their most useful tool.

So Ansel measured his words. His colleagues each focused on different elements of the bad news. DuBois simply couldn't understand why the Brazilians would side with the Germans over the Americans.

The Professor was most interested in Jacome and his aide: Who were these people? Were they definitely acting on behalf of their government?

Saxon responded with a shrug. You win some, you lose some. He'd been more upset when the Tigers lost to the Yankees last week 10–3.

Oliphant consumed two entire Hershey's bars while the group digested the information. He didn't speak, which was probably for the best. The room could not contain any more ambient anxiety.

Pehle tried his best to put on a brave face. "Well, what now?"

"What has everyone been working on while we were gone?" Ansel asked with his best attempt at normalcy.

Going by DuBois's expression, all he'd done was rub salt in a fresh wound.

"Joe and I made a few discoveries," Pehle said. He didn't make it sound like good news. "Joe? How would you feel about taking Ansel through those sheets?"

DuBois felt fine about it, and over the next hour he showed Ansel what they'd found: U.S. bank accounts held by private German citizens were being emptied at an alarming rate. Curiously, those citizens predominantly had Jewish surnames.

At first Ansel didn't understand. But DuBois explained: Many German Jews, and Polish ones as well, had kept some of their savings in American banks over the past decade. It had seemed safer than keeping it in German banks, given the tenor of things over there. Clearly they'd been right. But since '34, Hjalmar Schacht's army of statisticians had been compiling records of all the German Jewish money hidden around the world. Especially in America. How? They'd passed a law requiring all Germans to register transfers they made to or from U.S. banks with the government. They knew where all the money was. . . . And now they were confiscating it.

"How are they confiscating it?"

"We can only guess," Pehle said.

"I would guess," Saxon interrupted, "that they send the SS into somebody's house, arrest him for 'sedition' or whatever nonsense. Put a gun to his head. 'Sign over the checks.' Remember how after Kristallnacht, the German government collectively fined the Jews of their country a billion reichsmarks in damages? Reimbursement for the riot? All the Jews within German territory are, by German law, in debt to the Reich."

"I remember this," Ansel said. "An even billion. Like somebody in high command just picked the biggest number they could think up."

"The Reich," DuBois continued, "gave itself the legal right to confiscate any private Jewish holdings. In response, the Jews started—or in many cases continued—to hide money in dollars. In American banks. So now the Reich is finding those caches and confiscating those dollars."

"But the make-believe debts aren't enforceable in the U.S.," Ansel said. "Why would the U.S. banks send the dollars back?"

"Oh, it's worse than that. Our banks are letting the Reich use the dollars in those accounts to buy goods all over the world. Japan, Italy, Spain, now China—it's hard for the Reich to move gold around. Lots of international companies are still wary of reichsmarks, and Mefo bills are an exclusively Germanic fever dream. But U.S. dollars, privately transferred from U.S. banks . . ."

Ansel didn't say anything as a hideous gloom descended.

"They're *banks*." DuBois spoke the word with more disgust than he used when describing the Nazis. "Moving money around is what they do. To them, it's a matter of business as usual."

Of course there was an obvious solution to the problem DuBois described. They could simply order the American banks not to transfer dollars to Germany, or to any other country if they thought the transfer was happening at the behest of the Reich. Ansel could write up the legislation in an afternoon.

But they couldn't do it, and DuBois and Pehle and the others already knew why. "Any action we take," he said out loud, "has to be neutral toward Germany."

Pehle stretched. "We can't take a position on the legality of the German 'debts.' The Nazis say they're owed; who are we to say otherwise? We can't issue a policy regarding German accounts that doesn't apply equally to British and French accounts."

Oliphant wandered over. "Something tells me that now would *not* be a good time to sever French businesses from American markets."

For the same reason they couldn't confiscate German gold beneath the New York Federal Reserve, they couldn't prevent the Germans from looting the dollar savings of Jews. And of course, Ansel reasoned, the Reich wouldn't stop with Jews. When they needed to, they'd fine Polish citizens for something and snatch their dollars, too. Czech dollars, eventually Belgian dollars.

The Professor sighed. "If we cannot take their gold, and we cannot take their dollars, and we cannot block their trading . . . I'm not sure what we're going to be able to do to crash the German economy."

"At this point," Pehle said, "I'd settle for merely hobbling it a bit."

"If only that were the extent of your problems."

They all turned when they heard a grumble coming from the doorway. It belonged to White.

He entered scowl first. "You got weightier concerns."

"Weightier than our failure to put even so much as a dent in the German economic machine?" Pehle said. "Isn't that what you brought us here to do?"

"I just came from Morgenthau's office. And he just came from a long morning walk with the president."

Now that he had their attention, White took a moment to remove his coat and light a cigarette. "The president wants to supply weapons to our allies in Britain and France."

"All right!" Saxon looked like a kid who'd gotten a new comic book.

"Yes," Ansel said, "it's about time." He was instantly invigorated. For weeks, if not months, he'd hoped that Roosevelt would have the nerve to do something just like this.

But White did not appear to share in their enthusiasm. "They're the poor bastards fighting this war, and we've got weapons they can use. Roosevelt wants to put the guns in the hands of men who can pull the trigger."

"Pardon," Pehle said, "but to my ears you're reporting a positive development as if it's a setback. Have I missed something?"

"The problem is . . ." White waited, testing them. Who would figure out the problem first?

"We can't," Oliphant said wearily. "Due to the Neutrality Act, the U.S. can't simply give armaments to the British."

White nodded.

"What if we sell them?" DuBois said.

"That is exactly what Morgenthau suggested to the president."

"And?"

White didn't answer.

"Even that," Pehle said with a sigh, "is too much. Isn't it?"

"It is," White confirmed.

Ansel understood the cause of White's sour demeanor. "We can't offer to sell weapons only to Britain and France. Anything we do—any offer we make—we have to make to all parties. Neutrally."

White nodded again. "So that's it. The president is looking for a legal way to provide weaponry to Britain and France without violating the Neutrality Act. Oh, and it needs to be able to pass Congress."

There passed another moment of silence.

White looked annoyed. "Maybe I should have mentioned off the bat. The president wants this to happen. Morgenthau wants this to happen. I want it to happen. The British and French need it to happen. I came down here because you lot? Your job is to figure out how on earth to make it happen."

22

TWO ECONOMISTS WALK INTO AN AUTOMOBILE DEALERSHIP

"Most economic fallacies derive from the tendency to assume that there is a fixed pie, that one party can gain only at the expense of another."

—MILTON FRIEDMAN

October 1, 1939

The only conclusion reached by the Research Department over the following week was that Professor Newcomer desperately needed a car. For the past month, each of them had been enlisted at various times to drive her around Washington. She relied on taxicabs to ferry her for short distances, but when she needed to go farther than Union Station she'd ask one of her colleagues for a lift. When she wanted to go hiking in Rock Creek, Pehle had to drop her off on his way home to Bethesda. Not that it was on the way. Saxon had been cajoled into taking her to an old friend's house in Silver Spring; Oliphant drove her to the Brentano's in Falls Church. Only White had the gumption to flat-out refuse.

So in the face of increasingly suggestive comments from the team, the Professor agreed to purchase a used vehicle. She could store it in a garage on Twelfth Street when she was back at Vassar.

"I'll go on Sunday," she announced at last. "But the research is quite clear. A single woman walking into a used car dealership is a target for getting ripped off. I know what I want and I know what I should pay. So I'll need one of you men to stand beside me and not say a word."

For reasons that never became clear to him, Ansel was elected to perform the duty. This was met with some pushback from Angela. He was missing church with her parents so that he could accompany a woman from work on a personal errand?

Ansel assured his wife that nothing untoward was going on.

"I'm not worried about your having an affair," Angela replied. "I'm worried that when you and Mabel negotiate against a crew of experienced car dealers, they're going to end up owning this house."

Still, Ansel picked the Professor up from her hotel on Sunday morning, and together they ventured to a dealership she'd selected on Bladensburg Road.

"So what make of automobile has caught your eye?" Ansel said as he drove.

The Professor removed a notebook from her large purse and perused her notes. "I've been reading up on Pareto optimality."

It was then that Ansel realized why the others had so adamantly insisted he be the one to take her. "I see."

"A used car market is the textbook definition of a constrained Pareto optimality." She laughed to herself. "I have used this very example with my girls!"

Ansel vaguely recalled something about Vilfredo Pareto in school. Italian, wasn't he? "It's a statistics thing? The 80/20 rule?"

"The 80/20 rule is about how within a given system, twenty percent of the causes will tend to produce about eighty percent of the effects. If you own a shop, about twenty percent of your customers will tend to produce about eighty percent of your profits. If you're building a car, about twenty percent of the parts will cause around eighty percent of your breakdowns."

"You'll want to be sure you buy a car that doesn't break down."

"Yes, but that's where Pareto optimality comes in. We tend to think of any negotiation as antagonistic. Dog-eat-dog. But if you're designing a marketplace, like one for used cars, you don't actually want pure competition."

"Let me stop you right there." Ansel addressed her with Angela's voice in his ear. "If you don't think what's about to happen when we walk into this dealership is competitive, we need to rethink your strategy. Every dollar you pay is one less for you and one more for them."

The Professor shook her head. "A Pareto optimal system benefits all parties. That's the whole point. In any system of distributions, with multiple parties and multiple items of value being distributed—in our case, primarily automobiles and money—a distribution can be said to be 'Pareto optimal' when no party's position can be improved without harming another party's position."

Ansel did not think any of this would help them score a plum deal. "Right."

"If I were to pay an extra dollar in price, but in exchange the dealer gave me something that had a value to him of less than a dollar—an extra floor mat, perhaps, or a window cleaning—then the distribution would be *more* Pareto optimal. Neither of us lost; rather, we both gained."

Ansel pulled his Ford into the dealership's parking lot. A line of sedans sparkled in the morning sun. The paint jobs were fresh. The tires were buffed. As to the condition underneath their hoods, he could only guess.

Professor Newcomer seemed to have arrived at a similar place. "The constraint on Pareto optimality inherent in a used car dealership is that the dealer knows a lot more about the condition of the car than we do."

Ansel turned off his engine. He could see a salesman approaching, a smartly dressed man with a thin face and a wide grin. "I can peek under the hood for you, but without days of examination, there's no way to be sure we aren't buying you a lemon."

The Professor opened her door. "It's only a lemon if I pay more for it than the value I derive from it. The key to crafting Pareto optimality, in a constrained system, is to realize that information itself has a value. As do plenty of things that don't ride around on four wheels."

———

THE DEALER'S NAME WAS Buckland, and he spoke slowly, with a gentle Southern drawl. Everything about him was unhurried: his gait, his speech, his salesmanship.

The Professor was prepared. She wanted a Ford because they were the most popular cars on the road, which meant that she knew the most about their resale value. She wanted a three-window coupe because they were among the least expensive models. She wanted one from '35 or '36, for reasons Ansel did not learn.

Buckland had four on the lot. Two in blue, one in black, one in green. The Professor informed him that she would not derive value from the color of its paint.

Buckland took his time, and then made the Professor an offer. "I'll give you that blue one for 220 dollars."

"I'll take it," the Professor said.

Ansel had not yet spoken a word.

Buckland looked shocked, though he did a good job of hiding it. Ansel figured this was probably the fastest sale he'd ever made.

"Fine," he said, "just fine." He reached out and shook her hand. "I'll go draw up the paperwork."

"Let's speak about that first."

"The paperwork?"

"For *230* dollars, I'll want a one-year warranty. Anything breaks, for any reason, you repair it. Free of charge."

Buckland spoke sweetly. "Oh no ma'am, perhaps your husband here can explain. We don't do that."

"Repairs?"

"Warranties. We have no way of knowing what you do with the vehicle once it leaves this lot."

"Precisely! I have no way of knowing what the previous owner has done with the vehicle before it arrived here. Hence the warranty. I'm working to even out our informational imbalance."

Buckland stared blankly. Then turned to Ansel.

Ansel shrugged. This was the Professor's negotiation, and he was under strict instructions to keep his mouth shut.

"I need to speak with my manager," Buckland said after a moment.

"No you don't," the Professor responded. "Tell you what: 240 dollars."

Buckland gave a start. "240 dollars?"

"For a one-year warranty with no limitations, I'll pay 240 dollars. I'm not buying an automobile from you. I'm buying information about the history of the automobile. What repairs do *you* think will be required in the next year? I don't know how much longer I'll need the machine, but probably not more than a year before I sell it. So what I want to purchase from you is what you know about what doesn't work in that vehicle. The more likely you think it'll be to break, the more you'll charge me for the warranty."

"It's in fine condition," he said.

"You're paid a commission of the sale price. Are you not?"

He seemed so flummoxed by her that he couldn't keep himself from nodding.

"So it's in your interest to increase the sale price, and in my interest to acquire assurance about the automobile's condition. You get more dollars. I get more thorough fine print on the contract." She smiled. "We profit, together, optimally."

In the end, the Professor bought the blue three-window coupe for $248 and a contract complicated enough that Ansel's law degree actually came in handy. The thing was nearly six pages long, and Ansel worked the language out with the manager, who turned out to be so fascinated by this whole production that by the end of the day he asked the Professor out to dinner.

She declined.

After signing the documents and writing the check, she walked Ansel back to his car. "Thank you for the ride. And the company."

"You'd think," he said, "that as a lawyer I'd know more about the value of the fine print."

"The devil is in the details. Maybe all the money is, too."

He opened the door and turned to bid her good afternoon. Only he found her stopped a few paces behind him, frozen in place. She wore the strangest expression.

"Professor?"

"The fine print . . ." She looked straight at him. "Instead of going home, may we hop in our fine automobiles and meet at the office?"

"You have an idea?"

She nodded. "What Mr. White was talking about. Selling arms to our allies. I think . . ." Her mind seemed to spin furiously. "I have an idea about how we might do it."

"Sell arms to the British and French without selling to the Germans?"

"No." She started backing away, moving quickly toward her new car. "I think we should offer weapons to the Germans, too."

Ansel was more confused than ever. "You want to sell weapons to the Nazis?"

She turned away, speaking hurriedly into the wind. "I want to take a very hard look at the fine print."

23

THE FINE PRINT

*"When the law and morality contradict each other,
the citizen has the cruel alternative of either
losing his moral sense or losing his respect for the law."*

—FRÉDÉRIC BASTIAT

October 4, 1939

They stood at the windows in Morgenthau's office, their backs to the White House, as Ansel made an announcement: "We have a plan to turn this country into the largest arms dealership in history."

The secretary leaned against his desk, scratching at his chin. Then he glanced at White, who reclined casually on the dark leather sofa.

White had heard all this before, and in his silent look he seemed to advise Morgenthau to listen awhile longer before passing judgment.

The Professor, standing beside Ansel, seemed unsure of how to act in the presence of the secretary. So Ansel continued.

"Airplanes, armored cars, tanks, munitions, explosives, bullets—the United States has them all. And we can make more. We've got industrial capacity greater than any nation in Europe. And our factories can be put to anyone's use. We build to order."

The morning sun reflected off Morgenthau's round glasses. "You suggest that we become bespoke arms dealers?"

Ansel nodded. "To any nation that can pay. And quality, such as we produce here, doesn't come cheap."

Morgenthau did not appear to like the sound of this.

"Just wait," White advised him.

"Our friends at Boeing, Ford, General Motors, and Remington will see record profits. As will our War Department, which has not hitherto been known for generating profits at all."

"You remember that Ansel is a lawyer," White said to Morgenthau, "not an economist, when he uses words like *hitherto*."

"I only wish a lawyer had come up with this," Ansel said. "But the Professor—our best economist—deserves the credit."

She seemed uncomfortable with compliments.

"You wanted a bill that we could get through Congress," Ansel continued. "I'm not sure how many congressmen can vote against a policy that will generate record profits for the government, and for so many important American corporations. Who happen to have factories in Kansas, Connecticut, Michigan, Maryland, New York, and Washington State. I'm sure you can count the jobs, and the votes, yourself."

Morgenthau certainly could. But there remained one not-insignificant problem. "What about neutrality? If we open up the U.S. as a great big weapons dealership, what do we do when the Germans want to buy?"

"Simple," Ansel said. "We sell to them."

Morgenthau turned to White. Had he misheard?

He hadn't.

"If the Germans want to buy from us," Ansel said, "they are more than welcome. The United States does not discriminate."

Morgenthau rubbed at his neck. "If your big trick here is that we just sell more weapons to the British than the Germans, it won't fly. The Germans have more gold."

"Oh, we won't be accepting payment in gold. So the Germans will learn when they receive the contract." Ansel turned to the Professor. "Would you like to describe the fine print for the secretary?"

She cleared her throat. "Like any seller, we write the fine print on the deal. Not unreasonably, we have conditions. Two of them. One, we only accept payment in our own currency—U.S. dollars."

"Funny," White added. "The coincidence—Britain has of late been stockpiling lots of dollars. I'm sure they'd be happy to start spending them."

"That's not bad," Morgenthau cautioned. "Japan trades in gold. So does Italy. But if what your reports have said these past few days is true, then Germany can acquire dollars by seizure. Not as much as the UK, but enough to buy our arms. And let me make this very clear: I am not willing to sell a single munition to Adolf Hitler."

Ansel understood. "That's where the second condition comes in. We don't offer delivery."

Morgenthau frowned. "What?"

"When you buy a car," the Professor said, "you don't expect Ford to deliver it to your home. You have to pick it up from the dealership. Same situation here. We'll sell a B-17 bomber to any nation on earth. But they have to pay in U.S. dollars, and they have to come pick it up themselves."

Morgenthau began pacing across his office. "How would the Germans be able to get a transport ship across the Atlantic? They'd have to pass right through the British naval areas."

Ansel shrugged. "That's not our problem."

Morgenthau finally smiled. "The only two countries on earth who have both the dollars to pay and the clear shipping routes to handle transportation are Britain and France."

Ansel nodded. Morgenthau would need to sell this idea to Roosevelt, who would then have the harder job of selling it to a wary public. They would need convincing that this move was a purely mercenary one, and that America was in no way picking sides in the war. Publicly, the deal could be about one thing only: money.

Surely that was an end on which all Americans could agree.

Ansel stayed quiet as Morgenthau worked through the operation looking for holes. Of course a few enterprising Republican legislators would realize what Roosevelt was really doing. The isolationists in the opposition party were wrong, but they weren't idiots. And they had plenty of allies among isolationist Democrats, whose loyalty to the president would assuredly be tested by any policy that smacked of anything as catastrophically unpopular as engagement in this European mess. So the "fine print" would need to give the White House quite a lot of political cover as the president claimed to be enacting a neutral policy to create jobs in the American heartland. Helpfully he would not be lying.

"I suppose you already have proposed language for this?" Morgenthau said.

From his briefcase, White produced two sheets. The bill was shorter than the Professor's automobile purchase agreement, so merciless was its simplicity.

Morgenthau read it over twice before he spoke again. "We'll need to find a friendly congressman to sponsor this. It can't appear to come from the White House."

White stood. He gestured toward Ansel and the Professor to follow him out. "I got a feeling the White House won't have too much trouble finding a congressman from Kansas, Connecticut, Michigan, Maryland, New York, or Washington who wants to bring a host of jobs home to his district."

Ansel and Professor Newcomer had nearly arrived at the door when they heard Morgenthau's voice.

"Where'd you find her?" he asked White.

"She teaches your daughter's freshman economics class."

Morgenthau looked up at Professor Newcomer. "How's she doing?"

"C plus."

Morgenthau's laughter was deeper than Ansel had imagined. He went behind his desk and pressed the button for the intercom. "Miss Klootz," he said into the device, "I'd like to speak with the president."

24

CASH AND CARRY

*"No one would remember the Good Samaritan if he'd
only had good intentions; he had money as well."*

—MARGARET THATCHER

October 9, 1939

On Friday, Senator Key Pittman, Democrat of Nevada, gave a rousing
speech in the Capitol Building in which he proposed an amendment to
the long-standing Neutrality Act. Nevada held few factories, but the
White House evidently felt that Pittman, as president pro tempore of
the Senate, would have the clout to muscle this new bill through. Over
the next few days, it seemed that they were correct. Roosevelt's political team dubbed the new policy "Cash and Carry," which played well
on the evening news hour. It was brief, it was catchy, and it made in-
tuitive sense. It sounded like the American government was a humble
fishmonger: Customers had to pay in cash, and they had to do the
carrying. The Democrats were largely on board, and the Republicans
were caught without a good narrative to fight it.

The War Department began conversations with their British and
French counterparts regarding precisely what weapons would be most
appreciated—an endless variety of specific guns, mortars, bombs,
trucks, tanks, and planes. The Germans didn't bother inquiring into
their own purchases—they surely saw what was really going on here,
and Ansel imagined that somewhere, Hjalmar Schacht was tipping
his hat to the ingenuity. Treasury began negotiations with the British

Exchequer and the French Trésor public about how exactly they intended on paying for all of this matériel. The president was selling
Cash and Carry to the American people on the promise that it would
turn a profit. It needed to do just that.

On which point, the chancellor of the exchequer sent word of one
important detail: Britain was flat broke.

The Exchequer sent the Research Department reams upon reams of
official government data to prove their penury. Ansel and his colleagues spent days poring over the suspiciously incomprehensible documentation. They appreciated that the British were angling for a
deal—who wouldn't be?—but for the UK to claim that they possessed
few dollars within their banks was a bit much. Surely the empire must
have a few pennies saved under the mattress for a rainy day, especially
given the storm clouds looming on the horizon.

Morgenthau dispatched White to London to get to the bottom of
this payments mess. "Flight leaves in the morning," he informed the
Research Department. He must want legal counsel with him, Ansel
thought, as he had in Panama.

Ansel wondered whether he ought to tell Angela where he was
headed. He was now concealing so many different pieces of information from so many different parties that he was having a hard time
keeping them all straight.

Which part was his wife in the dark about, again?

Then White said, "Joe?"

DuBois looked surprised. "Yes?"

"I'd like you to accompany me as counsel."

25

POACHED LOBSTER
AT TWENTY
THOUSAND FEET

"The best things in life are free.
The second best are very, very expensive."

—COCO CHANEL

October 9, 1939 (cont'd)

Ansel had to take a walk. He found a third of a cigarillo in his tin and smoked the remainder as he made circles around H Street.

White's attention was like the sun, rising hot all of a sudden and then vanishing just as quickly. His employees basked in the warmth of his interest and enthusiasm, only to be left in the cold when his focus flitted elsewhere. To be at the center of his attentions could be sweltering, but it was better than the indeterminate darkness of his indifference.

Why had White chosen DuBois? It didn't matter. Ansel wasn't offended; he was understandably concerned. If a Soviet spy whose dispatches might be bound eventually for Berlin ended up at the very center of negotiations for the supply of American arms to the UK, that wouldn't constitute mere economic espionage—that'd be a proper military crisis. Which kinds of tanks, and in what numbers, did the British require? And according to what timetable? The Research Department did not have access to that information, thank goodness. But such details would likely be passed around the conference tables in London.

Was DuBois the double agent? Ansel found himself pondering the odds: Was it fifteen percent? Thirty percent? There was simply no way to know for sure. And even a one percent chance of such sensitive documents falling into German hands was unacceptable.

Ansel considered asking White if he could go along instead, but he could picture his boss's gruff reaction: He'd choose his own damned counsel his own damned self, thank you very much. There was no way a man like White would respond favorably to a request from a subordinate that would reek, however it was presented, of personal ambition.

Which, the more Ansel thought about it, suggested a story he might be able to tell.

He found Oliphant that day at lunch in the main Treasury building. Ansel had extra pickle slices that had come with his sandwich, he said. He thought Oliphant might appreciate them.

"Funny business," Ansel said as Oliphant munched. "Harry taking Joe with him to London. Aren't you senior counsel?"

"You know Harry."

"That's the issue. I feel like we're about to send an American bull into an English tea shop."

Oliphant removed his glasses for a moment and scratched his nose. Surely his concern would be for his friend Morgenthau: How much trouble was White going to get into in London that would blow back on the secretary?

"After the disaster in Panama," Ansel continued, "I just wonder whether we wouldn't be better served in London by the presence of somebody who can remember to take his hat off indoors."

Ansel didn't have to say much more before Oliphant himself suggested that he would go see Harry that very afternoon, and make clear that he should be the lawyer to go along. Oliphant outranked both White and DuBois, didn't he?

Ansel was able to finagle a private moment with DuBois as soon as he returned to the Research Department. "Can you help me with some of the French documentation tomorrow? I don't speak a word, and you do a bit, don't you?"

DuBois shook his head. "I'm supposed to go to London with Harry tomorrow."

Ansel adopted a look of confusion. "I thought Herman was going instead? That's what he told me. Harry changed his mind. Wanted someone with more experience in sterling exchange rates."

"I wrote my undergraduate thesis on sterling. I know much more about it than Herman." There was no trace of arrogance in DuBois's voice. It was a simple statement of fact.

Ansel shrugged as nonchalantly as he could. "Maybe Harry forgot."

And that was all it took.

The evening sun was still visible when White marched by Ansel's desk. "Go home and pack. Plane to London leaves early."

Ansel figured that if he tried to feign surprise, he'd overdo it. Best to simply not react at all. "Sure. But what about—"

"Joe is too damned annoying to travel with, and Herman is worse."

That night, Ansel tossed tooth powder, a toothbrush, razor blades, and a full bottle of bicarbonate into an old sponge bag as he told Angela he'd be home soon.

She didn't ask where he was going.

Every single commercial steamer bearing a U.S. flag had been tucked away in a Nassau County port since early September, when the naval war between Britain and Germany erupted. So a single daily flight aboard the Yankee Clipper was the only route to London. The flight from New York to Southampton, a small port city nestled along the English Channel, would last nearly twenty-seven hours, the woman from Imperial Airways informed Ansel after he confessed that this would be his first trip out of the country. She reassured him that private sleeping quarters would be provided, though he and White would have to share a day cabin. Ansel instantly pictured the Orient Express. Having failed to hide his surprise at the luxurious accommodations, he learned from the airline woman that Winston Churchill himself—finally reappointed to the admiralty last week—had flown on the very same bird back in June, as a private citizen. He loathed the sea, she reported knowingly. The Clipper he'd found to his liking.

White said all of six words to Ansel in the entirety of their first night and morning aboard, even as they made a brief refueling stop in Newfoundland. White led the way in retiring to their separate toilets and sleeping quarters. But even back in their shared day cabin the following morning, White spent the hours silently paging through documents that had classified seals from the War Department on their cover. Whatever they were, Ansel wasn't cleared to know.

It was at lunch on their second day of travel, as the Clipper flew somewhere over the Arctic toward another refueling stop in Ireland, that White suddenly appeared at Ansel's table with a keen interest in conversation. The dining cabin stewards wore coats with matching gloves as they served butter-poached lobster on porcelain plates. The scent of fried garlic wafted through the cabin at twenty-thousand feet. Ansel had never dined so well in his life. With a war on, a six-course lunch bracketed by escargots and mille-feuille, complete with port pairings, was so decadent as to feel sinful.

"So." White lifted his champagne flute. "How bad is it?"

Ansel had spent most of the flight trawling through the latest financial records they'd received from the Exchequer. "It is extremely bad."

"What are they claiming?"

Ansel gazed out the window at one of the bluest skies he'd ever seen. He thought the gray and white shapes below were likely masses of ice. "If these numbers are correct, then the British, given the volume of aircraft and munitions they're requesting, will run out of dollars to pay us in approximately three months."

White tore a chunk of freshly baked bread with his fingers. "If they think they can defeat Germany by January, I wish them Godspeed. But since that sounds unlikely, what do they propose instead?"

"They have not actually proposed anything. The White House offered to help, Downing Street accepted with gratitude, and now the Exchequer is pleading poverty."

"You think Downing Street and the Exchequer aren't seeing eye to eye?"

Ansel shrugged. "It might not be the most shocking thing, different parts of the same government working for opposite ends."

"What do you think the Exchequer wants?"

"They're not telling."

"Something about all this feels extremely English." White groaned. "I mean that as an insult."

"I gathered." Ansel had gotten the impression that White's previous dealings with the Exchequer had not gone any better than this one. "But the thing is, unless all this data is pure fiction, they're not wrong to plead penury. Given the financial resources they've already committed, and the unbelievable volume of the military expansion required of them to keep up with Germany, they really are hard up."

White signaled to the steward that his glass was in need of refreshment. "You see what you've done wrong there?"

"What?"

"You believed a single word out of their mouths."

26

THE MOST
LOATHSOME MAN
IN BRITAIN

"One man's opportunism is another man's statesmanship."

—MILTON FRIEDMAN

October 11, 1939

Approaching in the dark of night, London looked like a moonlit mausoleum. Not a single electrical lamp was on, by order of the government. The bombing they were anticipating hadn't started yet, but already it looked like someone—something—had died.

Ansel and White had landed near the coast around sunset and begun the hours-long drive through the countryside into the capital. The experience was increasingly eerie. What few cars were on the road drove without lights. They inched forward at half speed into the foggy darkness up Great Chertsey Road toward the city.

Not three weeks earlier, the government had evacuated a million children from London. A great and horrible attack was to come, and all Chamberlain could do was ready the shelters. Driving in, Ansel could already feel that the waiting must be the hardest part. What would it be like to live here realizing that the world as you'd known it was gone? That something was soon to fall, at a time you could not predict, and in a manner you could only dread? A nightmare loomed above the mansard roofs.

They drove past house after house, each one emptied of children, each one dark as a grave and holding on to inhabitants who had stayed because they could afford, given their years, to die.

Ansel imagined sending Angie off into the countryside. But then, where could she go that would remain safe? There was no hiding his daughter from what was coming, he reminded himself. There was only allowing her to sleep soundly in the dark while she still could. Meanwhile, all he could do was roam through the night, an armorer in a cotton bow tie polishing his paper weapons.

————

SO WHY WOULDN'T THE British hurry up and take them?

Ansel had spent the bulk of his professional career in Washington, but until he arrived in London he'd never experienced so many politely ineffectual bureaucrats in one place. He had trouble fathoming that there existed so many in the entire world, much less within the damp, gray palaces of Whitehall. Each government building he went to—and he and White went to many—felt like a recently excavated tomb to a different forgotten monarch. Each official meeting was announced with a lengthy and pointless ceremony of titles and commitments to the friendships between great nations. The ratio of words uttered to substance communicated rose, minute by minute, to unfathomable levels.

All he and White wanted to do was negotiate an exchange of money for weapons. And yet it was confoundingly unclear with whom they were to do the negotiating. Every man was there to help, but no man seemed to possess the authority to do much of anything.

White had the force of sheer rudeness on his side, and he seemed to have no qualms about deploying it wantonly. He practically brayed at some minor Exchequer subsecretary: "Say a number, for God's sake, so I can say a higher one and we can start arguing."

He never got the pleasure.

At the close of their first day in London, a black car deposited them back at their hotel, equal parts bedraggled and bewildered.

"What on earth was that?" Ansel said at last.

"That," White said, making his way straight through the lobby to the cubby holes of house telephones, "was the runaround."

"Don't they want our help?"

"Some of them do. And some of them . . ." White trailed off. "God-damn it, I know who's behind this."

He took hold of a telephone receiver, then turned to Ansel.

"Of course it's him," White said. "I should have known. Not a damned thing around here without his setting it all up."

"Who?"

"He's like a hateful spider, and this entire country is his web. He rubs his legs together and the whole thing shakes. That vain, pompous little prick—this deal wasn't his idea, so he's going to torch the whole thing out of spite."

"Who?"

"The most vile, loathsome son of a bitch in Britain."

27

TILTON HOUSE, SUSSEX

"In economics you cannot convict your opponent of error.
You can only convince him of it."

—JOHN MAYNARD KEYNES

October 14, 1939

Despite—or perhaps because—John Maynard Keynes happened to be the most well-known economist in the world, he was also a hard man to find. White spent the following day sending cantankerous telegrams through the most hallowed halls in London in order that he might "smoke the bastard out." The only public intellectual who might be more famous than Keynes was Albert Einstein, though his company was certainly in less demand. Einstein was a once-in-a-century genius—not that Ansel knew much about him, physics being outside of his interests—but Keynes? If one read the exuberant global headlines that greeted his every utterance, he sounded like *fun*.

His early life bore all the dutiful hallmarks of a certain sliver of English society: Eton, Cambridge, civil service in the India office. But then, so the stories went, Keynes got bored. He found his way back to Cambridge and became a fellow at King's College when he was only twenty-six. He lectured on economics, which was noteworthy for two reasons. First, he didn't have any formal training in economics; and second, he didn't have any kind of graduate-level education at all. The papers sometimes said he was "self-taught," though Ansel felt that this obscured the issue: Maynard Keynes hadn't needed to learn the modern field of economics because until he came around, it hadn't been invented.

His arguments were complex, varied, free of both technical jargon and any mathematics whatsoever. He was a theorist's theorist, but his writing was so evocative that he found a popular audience. He was of the political left, unquestionably, but he was unencumbered by the shadow of Marx. No socialist, he simply wanted the government to make life somewhat better for its citizens. His theories concerned just how they might go about doing it—and, most crucially, how they might go about paying for it.

It was Ansel's first reading of Keynes's work as an undergraduate that inspired his own lifelong passion for economic study. He owed Keynes, he felt, his entire life. He imagined that at that very moment, the Professor was likely teaching the man's early work to Morgenthau's daughter.

Keynes had published his first papers in 1909 and his first book, on the financial landscape of India, in 1913. By the time of the Great War, his theories—and his reputation—had grown so influential that the government assigned him a high-ranking position at the Exchequer. There he successfully managed Britain's economy through the war such that not only did she avoid the economic collapse that plagued every other European participant, but somehow—and only Keynes really knew how—Britain left the war in better shape economically than when she started.

All manner of titles and medals greeted him at the end of the fighting. Which perhaps said something about England, as opposed to the United States: The former was a place where an academic could become one of the nation's leading war heroes.

And then?

He thumbed his nose at the whole thing.

Sent to Paris to help negotiate what would become the Treaty of Versailles on behalf of the UK, he was so incensed by the deal he watched being formed that, rather than endorse the thing, he quit. With great fanfare, he renounced his government position because he believed that the conditions the UK was demanding were punitive to the point of mutual destruction: He argued that the financial penalties with which Germany would be saddled would doom the country to decades of financial ruin, which would then cause a deflationary crisis in its currency, and that this crisis would inevitably lead to a dark turn in German politics, causing the rise of some manner of violent populist dictatorship.

He wrote this in 1919.

The diplomats told him he was insane.

So he returned to his Bloomsbury mansion and in mere weeks wrote a book-length diatribe against the treaty. His dear friend Henry Macmillan published the quickly sketched pamphlet as a favor.

They sold one hundred thousand copies in the first week.

"The Economic Consequences of the Peace" became one of the biggest-selling titles of the decade on both sides of the Atlantic.

The following years served not only to vindicate Keynes's predictions—with horrible, sickening accuracy—they also magnified his popularity, and, as a result, his wealth. He wrote a weekly column syndicated in newspapers around the world. He made early financial investments in Virginia Woolf's writing career (he let her stay at his London home rent-free) and Picasso's painting (he personally bought a set of sketches early on), and was rumored to have earned untold fortunes playing the currency markets. Then, when Lydia Lopokova, the prima ballerina of the Moscow ballet, found herself entangled in a messy split from her fiancé, Igor Stravinsky, Keynes swooped in and promptly married her.

So where was he now, this fabulous and wealthy Nostradamus with the possibly even more fabulous ballerina wife? He had no official government post or academic position. He did not, as far as White could discern, occupy himself with anything so common as a job.

Keynes was not in Whitehall, they learned, though he did sometimes "consult" with the prime minister—Downing Street's word, not White's—on important matters. Neither was Keynes elsewhere in London, they discovered, not even at his row of houses on Gordon

Square. Nor was he in Cambridge, though the staff at King's mentioned that he did retain some kind of murky title and so, they boasted, was known to frequent its libraries.

They finally located him in Sussex. Despite the outbreak of war, he was spending the month in his country estate nestled beneath the hills.

Having confirmed his location, White did not require—much less request—an invitation. He demanded a car and driver from the embassy, and as soon as a harried young GI arrived in a topless Bentley saloon, he sent a brief message to Tilton House informing Keynes that he was on the way.

White practically dragged Ansel into the automobile to begin the slow three-hour drive. Ansel understood his frustration, if not quite his festering personal antipathy for Keynes.

Despite the high regard Ansel felt for Keynes, he figured it was best not to argue the point with his boss. But Ansel could not believe that he'd soon be in the company of such a legend. He cautioned himself not to act starstruck.

Finally, the GI pulled their car off the highway. Miles of dirt road led them to a pastoral farm flanked by orchards of greengage trees and a full stable of noisy pigs. Green fields dotted with purple berry bushes went on for countless acres in every direction. The nearby village, which they'd driven past on the highway, housed the farm's laborers, and was, so their tour guide helpfully informed them, also part of Keynes's holdings.

The Bentley pulled up to Tilton House, an earthy eighteenth-century farm given new life by its new owner. In the driveway, a trio of laborers polished the wheels of a shiny silver Rolls-Royce.

White took one look at it and snorted. "*This* is what he's like," he said, though Ansel wasn't quite sure what that was supposed to mean.

The butler arrived to greet them.

White gave his name. "Tell him I'm here and tell him to hurry the hell up."

Unruffled, the butler asked if they might wait inside while he delivered the message. They followed him under the stone archway and through a central corridor lined with impressionist paintings. Ansel wasn't an avid admirer of art, but he was fairly certain he recognized more than one of the pieces on the wall.

"Is that . . . ?" He gestured to one of them, a still life of orange-yellow apples.

The butler didn't slow his walk. "The Cézanne," he informed the visitors, "is one of Mr. Keynes's favorites."

White issued a guttural *humph.*

In the sunroom they were greeted by another member of the household staff, who suggested that they might be more comfortable in the library. They followed him through an Italianate loggia lined with fig trees and crawling with grapevines. The courtyard smelled of fresh fruit, even in October.

The library ceilings must have been thirty feet high. Curved windows let in warm light from the south downs in the distance, giving a gentle glow to the shelves of books that went all the way around, from the floor to the ceiling. The shelves contained thousands of volumes easily. It smelled faintly of nighttime fires from the granite fireplace in the center of the far wall.

"I can't imagine why he needs to bother with the Cambridge libraries," Ansel said as he gazed up at the books, "when he's got this place right here."

White snorted. "To be seen in Cambridge, I'll bet. You know how this type likes keeping up appearances."

Ansel did not know anyone of Keynes's type.

He perused the shelves. Almost immediately, he found what appeared to be a first edition of Isaac Newton's *Principia*. He looked more closely, reminding himself not to touch anything, as he scanned early printings of Descartes and Leibniz, Rousseau and Bentham, Spinoza and Hume.

White plopped himself onto a priceless-looking antique chair, lit up a Lucky Strike, and flicked his ash on the Persian rug.

Minutes later the door opened and a tall, frail man hobbled in. He didn't quite limp, but he didn't quite walk upright either. His white mustache was bushy and unkempt, his balding head overrun with wisps of gray hair. His flannel suit was baggy, and his tie must have been left on the hanger.

Ansel struggled to recall Keynes's age. Wasn't he at most in his late fifties? The man walking toward him appeared decades older.

"Mr. White. I wasn't expecting you."

White stood. "Mr. Keynes. This is my attorney, Mr. Luxford."

Keynes looked back and forth between White and Ansel. "Oh you Americans. You never can go anywhere, can you, without your attorneys?" He sounded like he was joking, but not entirely.

Ansel figured that it was only once in his life that he'd get to shake the hand of John Maynard Keynes. As he did, he found himself thinking that if this moment was all that came of the trip—hell, if this was all that came of his stint in the Research Department—it would not have been time wasted.

Keynes called for tea, and as he carefully lowered himself into a seat, Ansel complimented him on his collection.

Keynes smiled. "I saw you by the philosophers when I came in. Do you read much of the humanists?"

"No, he doesn't," White answered on his behalf.

Keynes addressed his response directly to White. "Pity. The point of a place like this is not collecting. It's reading. That bunch of volumes I purchased from the estate of Lord Gibbon after his passing. Do you know, a few still have his pencil marks in the margins from when he was writing his great big tome about the Romans. Remind me, Mr. Luxford, to show you later. If such things interest you."

The implication, Ansel gathered, was that such weighty matters were not of interest to White. Unless he was mistaken, the grave dislike between them went in both directions. It seemed a cruel irony: Here were two men with similar expertise, with nearly identical purviews, with sympathetic political leanings, allies in what would likely become the greatest challenge of their lives. And yet merely to stand between them, as Ansel presently did, was to be caught in a tense crossfire.

"Thank you," Ansel said to Keynes. "That's kind." He got the impression that right now, the best thing he could do to serve the anti-Nazi cause was to play middleman.

"Why are you jamming us up?" White asked, flicking at his cigarette.

Keynes noticed. "There's an ashtray on the table. And I'm not sure to what you are referring."

"We got the runaround from all your sharp little lemmings in Whitehall. Gum in the gears of this deal. Why? You want our help, or do you want us to let the Germans bomb you back into Anglo-Saxon times?"

Keynes was pale, Ansel noticed. Was he sick?

"That's an evocative analogy," Keynes said. His voice was high, his diction immaculate, the product of a thousand years of perfect breeding. Yet his spine slouched. His lungs emitted a sickly wheeze. He seemed like an ancient castle whose grand façade was perfectly maintained but whose inside was corroded with rainwater and mold. "You know that I don't currently occupy a government post. I'm sorry you've found the workings of our Exchequer slower than would be to your liking, but I'm not sure what it is you believe that I can do about it."

White rolled his eyes. "Suck eggs."

"Pardon?"

"None of those goons shoots a fart without first asking you for permission. Government job or no."

"An even more evocative analogy."

"Your country needs planes. Tanks. Weapons. We are happy to make them for you. Let's cut through all the crap. We can make a deal right here, right now."

A servant arrived with the tea. Keynes took the opportunity for silence—perhaps to gather strength—and did not speak again until he was alone with his American visitors.

"You're right as always, Harry. My friends in Whitehall have shared with me your proposals. Cash and Carry, that's what Mr. Roosevelt calls it? The good souls at Number 10 asked for my opinion, and I told them flat out: It's a bad deal."

"For the Nazis? It sure as hell is."

"For Britain."

"You want a discount? The U.S. government is not the sale rack at Claridge's."

"Firstly, Claridge's doesn't offer a sale rack. And secondly, I've no interest in haggling with you about money."

"So what's your beef?"

"With 'Cash and Carry?' I've two. Cash. And carry."

White spat stray tobacco into the ashtray. "When the Luftwaffe comes, I hope they come here first."

Ansel reasoned that this was an opportune moment to step in. "Mr. Keynes, if I may . . . Our government, our country, is trying to be of assistance to yours."

Keynes looked to Ansel hopefully. "And for your friendship, not to mention your good intentions, I can say on behalf of my countrymen that we are all grateful."

"So what don't you like about the deal we've offered you?"

"As I said: I don't believe that Britain should pay in cash, as your president puts it. And I don't believe that our resources should be devoted to doing the carrying."

Ansel felt as if he were watching a drowning man eloquently refuse a life preserver.

White looked like he was about to leap right at Keynes's throat, so Ansel tried asking the obvious question before he could. "Do you have another proposal?"

"I do." Keynes took a long sip of tea. "I think it would be best if you simply gifted us these armaments. As a sign of our enduring partnership. And I think we'd all be best off if the U.S. military brought these machines to our shores. It'll be more efficient that way."

Ansel thought of all the work he and his colleagues had put into crafting this deal. Surely a man as brilliant as Keynes must appreciate the ingenuity of its design!

Keynes regarded him the way he looked at Angie when she handed him a Crayola sketch: What a terrific . . . cat? Or is this a pigeon? Why don't you tell me all about it?

"If we do not help you," White growled, "the Germans will win."

Keynes nodded. "I couldn't agree more. Which is precisely why you should hand over the weapons."

Ansel ignored his bruised pride. "Not to be rude, but you're the ones asking for *our* help."

"I don't recall asking."

"If you don't get it," White said, "the Nazis will take control of Europe."

"Indeed. You Americans are lucky that you have us to do the fighting for you."

"Damn it. We have all the leverage."

Keynes spoke in a familiar tone: A cat, is it? What a *creative* choice you've made, my dear, to give it wings. "As you said, if we don't receive your help, then the Nazis will take Europe. They will take France, and then they will take the Soviet Union, and eventually they will, alas, take the British Isles. Italy will take Spain, Japan will ravage through China, and then, what chance does the United States have?"

Keynes plucked his cup from its saucer. "Sounds to me as if we have all the leverage in the world."

28

A LASTING PEACE

"In a conflict, the middle ground is least likely to be correct."

—NASSIM NICHOLAS TALEB

October 14, 1939 (cont'd)

The situation deteriorated from there.

Keynes continued politely declining any sort of financial agreement between the two countries while White veered back and forth between accusing Keynes of villainy and accusing him of stupidity. Neither Ansel nor White could comprehend that after all the trouble they'd gone to—that Roosevelt himself had gone to!—in order to help the British, they might simply turn around and say "no thank you." White eventually rose to his feet and did his yelling from a standing position.

Keynes remained reclined on the sofa, sipping his fortifying tea, as he reminded the Americans that there was more than one way by which Britain might be destroyed. The Luftwaffe were one possibility, to be sure—but so was cutting a bad deal with the United States.

"We cannot give you dollars that we do not have," Keynes explained. "If we make a deal with you to win the war that leaves us so impoverished after that we might just as well have lost . . . What would be the point?"

White wasn't having it. "You've been stockpiling dollars for two years, as Mr. Luxford here can attest. He's getting quite a deal on Scotch."

Keynes raised a bushy eyebrow in Ansel's direction.

Ansel summarized his barroom analysis. "You must have ample dollar reserves by now. In banks here and, even more helpfully, in New York."

Keynes did not appear impressed. "What meager dollar reserves we possess will assuredly be required for other purposes."

"What the hell is more important than buying armaments to fight the Germans?" White said.

"We have crucial trading partners all over the globe. We need dollars, sometimes, to make these trades. And before you offer to take your pound of flesh in gold, we can't afford to part with any of that either."

"I wasn't about to offer any such thing."

Keynes looked wistfully at the dregs of his tea. "It's quite a predicament."

White muttered a quick series of unintelligible insults. Keynes waited politely until the sotto voce outburst had concluded. Keynes gave Ansel a look that requested sympathy: See what he has to put up with?

But Ansel was firmly on White's side, despite expressing himself in more temperate language. "Surely we can find a way to make a deal together such that both of our nations survive the Nazis."

"A decent reminder," Keynes said, "that we share the same goal."

"We'll need to pay Mr. Ford, and all his workers, in something, in exchange for making you all these arms."

"I agree."

"The United States is officially neutral in the war. No one in this room thinks we should be, but we are, and that's the law."

"You yourselves would fight if you could, of course. I understand."

Finally Ansel was making headway. "Exactly. And for the same reason, we cannot legally budget our own dollars to make your arms."

Keynes lit up as if suddenly taken with a marvelous new idea. "What about receiving your payment in sterling?"

"How dare you!" White could no longer contain himself.

"Harry," Ansel cautioned, not quite following why this proposal had so offended his boss's sensibilities. "We can take that idea back to Washington," he said to Keynes while simultaneously trying to work out how such a proposal might be pitched as neutral.

"Absolutely not." White was adamant. He spoke as if he'd finally uncovered the secret trick in Keynes's dastardly game. "Maynard here thinks that he can use this crisis to expand his sterling bloc."

Keynes quietly sipped the last of his tea.

"Dozens of nations peg their currencies to sterling," White explained to Ansel, who was grateful for the assistance. "Of course India does, as do other members of the empire. But Egypt, too, basks in the stability that pegging provides: Why risk trying to convince the world of the value of the Egyptian pound when one might simply declare that it is always worth precisely one pound sixpence sterling? Sterling goes up, Egyptian pounds go up. Sterling goes down . . . Et cetera. Their local exporters rest easy knowing what rates their goods will fetch on the international markets. Norway, Sweden, Portugal, Iraq . . . The list of countries that peg to sterling is long. Bad news for Maynard: The list is shrinking."

Keynes didn't appear perturbed. "Oh dear, we've lost Sweden. How ever will we go on?"

"Britain will go on just fine. But sterling's dominant position in international trade will not. What you want is for your Exchequer to set monetary policy for the entire globe. By controlling all that currency, you can control the world economy. The nation that pegs its currency to yours must follow your lead—they can't very well make more of theirs willy-nilly, can they, without exploding the peg? So when they need money, they must come ask Father for their allowance." White raised his hands as if asking a giant for pennies. "As much territory as your empire has covered with soldiers and diplomats, your sterling bloc has covered substantially more with its money. The sun technically does set on the British Empire. It does not set on pounds sterling."

Keynes flicked a stray tea leaf back into the cup.

White continued. "If we allowed you to pay us for these weapons in sterling, we'd saddle our Treasury with massive sterling reserves.

We'd have no choice but to spend them in South America. Then in Asia. Even in Europe. What a surprise: The world would be flush with sterling-denominated trade."

"Would that be such a bad thing?"

"Yes. Because if you borrow from us using money that you create— the value of which you control—then you can use your bulbous sterling bloc to sneakily devalue the loans later."

"I can't believe you think we'd try to pull some sort of trick on you."

"You're pulling one right now! And I won't have it. You want our weapons? You buy with our money."

"We don't have enough."

"Go get some! I'm so sorry that surviving this war will require sacrifice. It's a pity. But there is simply no way that you can both pay us for these armaments and simultaneously expand the kingdom of sterling. There's only so much money in the world."

Keynes smiled, as if at a joke he needn't bother speaking aloud. "I suppose it depends on whose money we're talking about."

White appeared ready to pop. "London is as grim as the reaper's right hand, and you're using this as just another opportunity to pull one over on us."

"No, Harry. I'm thinking further ahead than breakfast. Which I might suggest you try as well. The seeds of this war were planted at the end of the last one. I'm trying to make quite certain that we never have to go through anything like this ever again. We do not achieve a lasting peace by turning Great Britain into a vassal state of America's."

"Nor do we achieve a 'lasting peace' at all by turning America back into a colony of Great Britain's."

"Then you agree: Our real task here is more than merely to win the war. It's to win the peace that follows."

"Eh," White said, "*merely* winning the war does seem kind of important."

"Winning the peace?" Ansel asked. He'd spent so much time dreading this war; he'd never once thought of what might come after. The best he'd even hoped for was a vague survival.

But evidently Keynes had set his sights higher. "What we do now— the deals we make or do not make today—will have consequences. Not just in this war, but in the many years to come if, Lord willing, we prevail. I'm not being peevish for the sake of King and country. I'm being prudent so that your children— and how are the girls, Harry, I'm remiss in not having asked—will never face a war of global proportions again in their lives."

White raised an eyebrow disdainfully. "Never? Oh, that's all you're after? Using the payment particulars in the fine print of an arms deal to somehow stop the next great war?"

Keynes took this in as if gauging the accuracy of each word separately. At last he said, "Yes. That is exactly what I'm doing."

White huffed. "With typical modesty."

Ansel had no clue what to make of this.

"How," he asked, "do you intend to stop this hypothetical future war?" Even just saying the words felt absurd.

But Keynes regarded him hopefully. He seemed pleased to have found a guest with whom he might at last discuss something of genuine import.

"With money," Keynes said earnestly. "What else?"

29

THE FUTURE OF
MONEY

*"Our standard account of monetary history is precisely
backwards. We did not begin with barter, discover money, and then
eventually develop credit systems. It happened precisely the other
way around. What we now call virtual money came first."*

—DAVID GRAEBER

October 14, 1939 (cont'd)

There was a moment of silence before one of Keynes's servants coughed
politely from the doorway, letting him know that he was required elsewhere.

"If you'll excuse me, gentlemen," he said to his American guests.
"It's been such an invigorating, if unexpected, visit."

He did not appear to feel any need to explain himself further.

"We're going to sell you these weapons," White called as Keynes
made his way to the door. "And then we are going to send you the largest bill you've ever seen." White gazed up to the antique editions on the
top shelves, their faithfully preserved spines rising to the heavenly glow
from the dormer windows. "Something tells me you can afford it."

By the time Ansel and White reached the front of Tilton House,
their GI was nowhere to be found. A member of the staff was dispatched to locate him. Getting the sense that the wait might be lengthy,
Ansel ventured back inside for a toilet.

A servant sent him in the direction of the library, but it didn't take
more than a minute for Ansel to find himself lost.

He still felt lightheaded after his minutes swimming in the currents of Keynes's grand visions and merciless intellect. He was grateful

for a few moments in which, if he opened his mouth, he needn't fear saying something impossibly stupid.

He came to a closed door at the end of a long hallway of open ones. He wasn't snooping, he would later reassure himself. He was merely disoriented when he chose to turn the brass knob, positive that he'd arrived back at the courtyard.

What he found instead was something stranger.

The square, two-story room before him held in its center a set of glass cabinets, of the kind one might find in a museum. Afternoon light from the high windows illuminated the relics inside. Ansel stepped closer and found in the nearest cabinets a set of clay tablets. They looked ancient. They were fractured and incomplete, with what appeared to be some sort of writing etched into them.

Looking around, he saw that the cabinets encircling the room contained smaller artifacts, some resting on stone blocks, others affixed to paper. The papers held small circles of precious metals—hundreds of them, perhaps thousands. They were coins. Aged ones, from nations and empires that Ansel did not recognize. Beyond the coins were small clay pots with their own symbols and signs. Among the pots, Ansel saw arrowheads. Colorful necklaces of beads. Sharp shards of whale bone tied together with leather strings.

Ansel found himself drawing closer to these objects as if in the throes of mesmerism. A few of the coins were imprinted with words that looked very much like Old English. Most were etched with symbols from eras before any history of which he was familiar. What were all of these things?

"Money," came a nasal wheeze from the doorway.

Ansel turned, startled.

It was Keynes. Who had apparently read his mind.

Ansel looked at the worn, cracked clay pots beside him. This was money?

"Isaac Newton was an alchemist." Keynes approached. "Did you know that? The greatest scientist in our history, he was fascinated by one of our deepest mysteries: how to convert silver into gold. There were, he found, two ways. The first was mythical alchemy, on which he spent decades conducting subterranean experiments. Without, I gather, much success. Virgin's blood and hair of newt will only take one so far. But the second way? Newton found it much easier. One slaps a few symbols on a silver coin, courtesy of the Royal Mint. And abracadabra—it's now worth more than its weight in gold."

Ansel peered inside the nearest cabinet. He found an inch-wide silver coin imprinted with the face of what looked like an ancient king. On its reverse, a figure seemed to be performing a dance, or perhaps casting a spell.

"That's from the Greco-Bactrian Kingdom," Keynes said in answer to the question Ansel hadn't yet asked. "The face you see? That's Menander the First. Around 100 B.C., if I'm remembering correctly. He ruled over what is now Afghanistan, stretching into India. Old Menander was Greek, but late in his life he converted to Buddhism. So his currency was designed for trade in both the political realm and the spiritual. Look: On one side, that's Menander. On the other? A Greek god performing the Buddhist *vitarka mudra*."

Ansel stared at the image of a Western god conducting Eastern magic.

"What is this worth?" Keynes asked. "Once, it was worth twenty staters, I believe. Which in Menander's time would have bought you a set of new horseshoes. And now? Nothing? A fortune? What is a currency worth when there no longer lives anyone who believes in its power?"

Ansel wasn't sure how to respond.

"People believed that coin was worth twenty staters because they believed in Zeus or the Buddha or Menander. The nickels and dimes in your own pocket . . . What must you believe in, I wonder, to grant them their power?"

Ansel instinctively reached his hand into his jacket pocket. There were indeed a few coins inside. But never before had they felt to him like magical talismans.

Ansel glanced to the large clay tablet at the center of the chamber.

"That's from Mesopotamia," Keynes said, following Ansel's eyes. "The city of Uruk, in what is now Iraq. That writing is something called cuneiform. The tablet is hard to date precisely, but the world's greatest experts happen to be just down the road in Cambridge. They tell me that it predates the birth of Jesus by about three thousand years."

Ansel inched closer. "This huge tablet is . . . money?"

Keynes laughed. "Exactly. That is the real question. What is money? Where did it come from?"

Ansel vaguely recalled reading something from Adam Smith on the subject—probably back in college—but he'd never given it much thought. "Your hobby is the history of money?"

"If you want to know where money is going, you have to know whence it came."

Ansel gestured toward the ancient cuneiform tablet. "You're saying that it came from this?"

Keynes took in Ansel's evident interest. "How long have you known Harry?"

Ansel could not claim that it had been long.

"Do you trust his judgment?"

"Yes."

"Because you seem genuinely thoughtful about the big picture. And in all the years I've known Harry, he's never once considered anything besides the dirt pile right in front of him that he's working so hard to step over."

"He hired me. He brought me into this." Sure, they'd had their disagreements. But White was his boss and his countryman. Keynes, on the other hand . . . Well, what exactly was he?

"So," Keynes said, "I suppose he's done at least one thing right."

Ansel tried not to let himself be swayed by the compliment. If Keynes hoped to create daylight between his American guests, he would not find Ansel so easily isolated.

Ansel looked back at the strange objects inside the glass cases.

Keynes seemed grateful to be able to expound upon his favorite subject. "What is the alchemy that turns an object—a coin, a piece of paper—into money?"

Ansel could not claim to be an economist of Keynes's stature—or to be an economist at all—but there was one subject he just so happened to know a lot about: "Taxes."

Keynes looked pleased by this answer. "Taxes? Why?"

"Anyone can make a coin. What turns that coin into money is when the government says that it's the only thing you can use to pay your taxes. Put it another way: The words that matter most on a dollar bill are not *one* or *dollar,* but rather *This note is legal tender for all debts public and private.* Money is whatever the government says it accepts as payment for taxes."

Keynes turned to a cabinet of wooden coins with numbers etched into them. "These wood pieces are from the sixteenth century. They were made only a few miles from here, a little pub down the road. Working men would come in for their pints; sometimes they had the appropriate coin of the realm, sometimes they did not. The men, I understand, were always buying one another rounds. So the pub started minting these wooden pieces: their own currency. Each one was worth a pint of ale. That one there was worth four. It's actually one of the first coinage systems ever used in England. The 'central bank,' as it were, was the barman."

Ansel looked at the pieces. "But they aren't money. They were legal tender only inside the pub. You couldn't trade them elsewhere."

"Of course you could. If I wanted to trade you a bushel of grain for this coin and you were willing to accept, who's to stop us? It was just that one could only redeem the coins for ale at the pub."

"You can't pay your taxes with ale. Though I imagine some have tried."

Keynes laughed. "There's more to life than ale and taxes."

"You're saying that money needn't be created by governments?"

"I'm saying it was never 'created' at all."

Ansel made no attempt to hide his surprise.

"Have you read George Knapp? The chartalist theory?"

Ansel admitted that he had not even heard of such a thing.

"Nineteenth century. A response . . . no, a complete and total *refutation* of Adam Smith on monetary history. Your notions about the importance of taxation are intellectual descendants of Knapp, in a way, though I'd argue the most important point has been lost."

"The most important point is . . . ?"

"In Smith and Knapp, we find two different narratives about the origins of money. Two fundamentally incompatible ways of thinking about what money is and how we as a society ought to manage it. One is very popular and forms the basis of all contemporary economics. And the other . . . the other one is right."

Keynes stared at a jar of what appeared to be some kind of preserved grain. "Our first tale comes from the great raconteur Adam Smith. It is the story of barter. Before the invention of money, there lived a pig farmer who lacked shoes. So he set off to find a cobbler who would trade him for a pig. He couldn't find just any cobbler, though. He had to find a cobbler who happened to want a pig at the exact same time that our farmer wanted new shoes. Smith called this difficulty the 'double coincidence of wants.' And then, luckily, our farmer finds such a cobbler! The men began to barter. How many shoes was this pig worth? A difficult problem to solve. This system of barter was inconvenient and cumbersome. So one day some bright fellow comes up with this thing he calls 'money.' Wood chips or rare rocks or other objects that can represent value. The lives of the farmer and the cobbler improve as the economy of the land blooms, because trade is made simpler and more efficient."

"Yes." Ansel felt himself on solid footing. "This is how I'd always understood it."

"The only trouble is, according to Knapp and his followers, this story holds no logic or sense. Where and when, precisely, is it supposed to occur? It doesn't sound much like ancient Mesopotamia, even though they had money millennia ago. No, this sounds vaguely medieval. Then, how do our two characters relate to each other? Are they kin? Friends? Do they worship the same god, kneel in the same church? If this is a medieval village, are they bound to the same feudal lord? If so, wouldn't the lord's men be involved in managing the exchange? The story seems to exist in the land of Aesop's fables, not in any actual place or time. This is the root problem with Smith and with the generations of economists he spawned: Everyone in his stories seems exactly like him. An unmarried, friendless Scot with no ties to culture or society."

"Did Adam Smith really not have any friends?"

"Could you imagine being friends with Adam Smith?" Keynes shuddered. "Knapp's story, and the one told by the chartalist economic underground ever since, is not so neat and tidy. The chartalist theory is that money was never invented. It is instead a fundamental element of human society. Money predates any of the objects that we use to count it, or any of the written symbols that we use to describe it. Money existed before paper, before coins with symbols etched onto them, before parchment and ink and tablets carved from stone. Before *language*. In the beginning, there was money. . . . Since Adam and Eve first frolicked in their garden, humans have exchanged things for each other. Not according to bills of sale, but according to cultural, legal, and religious rules." Keynes pointed to a necklace made of red shells. "There exist a people in the Papua Islands who use those necklaces for their trade. But the colored shells are not currency. They're part of a long, difficult-to-comprehend set of religious rituals that allow the people to share their harvests." He went again toward the cuneiform tablet. "This recorded debts. The symbols etched into the stone are money. All money is, really, is value. And as long as there have been human beings, those human beings have had values."

Ansel thought again of the dollars in his pocket: What values was he upholding by his belief that those papers were money and that a necklace of shells was not? *In God We Trust*, that's what the money said. In what did Ansel trust?

Keynes continued: "Your argument about taxation descends from Knapp in that it suggests that *markets* did not create money—*governments* did. I'm saying money was never created at all. It has always been."

"You said earlier that you had a plan to stop the next great war from occurring. This is part of it?"

Keynes ran his fingers along the glass cabinets. "I was in Versailles back in '19. I watched them concoct a peace agreement that, for a number of reasons, not only failed to prevent the war we're presently engulfed in but in fact assured its occurrence. I told them! I told *all* of them. They failed to listen. And so here we are." Keynes hunched over like a man decades his senior. "I will not let this happen again."

Ansel thought of his own pain and frustration over the last year as he'd watched the world tumble heedlessly into a preventable tragedy. Keynes had been living the madness of Cassandra for twenty years.

"Harry believes that I am cynically conspiring to elevate sterling's role around the world. Our friends in Whitehall and at Number 10 believe similarly, in fact. They're all wrong. I believe that what the world needs is something new."

"A new currency?"

"Yes!" Keynes's words tumbled out with urgency. "Not fresh etching on ancient coins—not different portraits upon the same old slips of paper—but something *fundamentally* new. We, for the first time in five thousand years, at this exact and fateful moment, have the sole opportunity to fundamentally change what money can be."

Ansel didn't understand. "How?"

"A global currency."

What should one say to something like that?

"We can build a new currency that is not bound to any nation. Not a British currency or an American one, not a German or a Japanese. One that isn't controlled by venal politicians or fickle gods. A currency outside the dominion of both Menander and the Buddha."

"If there existed a global currency . . ." Ansel struggled even to imagine such a thing.

"If there existed a global currency," Keynes went on, "we could use it to knit together all the economies of the world. We could tie the economic bonds so tight that even the idea of going to war with another nation, much less actually financing such a thing, would be impossible."

Ansel tried thinking it through. "People who use the same currency do not go to war with one another?"

"There will be other Hitlers. Other Goebbels. Other Schachts. The body of man will never be free of such germs. But money is the blood that animates the limbs, and if we can swap out this old and rancid plasma for something naturally resistant to such infections . . . The best cure, after all, is never to get sick in the first place.

"Even if we win this war, the world will be in tatters. Entire continents will be reduced to rubble. Rebuilding will be the work of generations. And we will have an opportunity to start from scratch. Reconstituting a ravaged world will require a simply unfathomable amount of money. The question we—me, and you, and Harry—need to answer right now, before the bombs start falling over London and Yunnan province, is this: What money will we use to bring this desiccated corpse back to life?"

Ansel struggled to fathom the scale of Keynes's project. "Who would administer this new global currency? Print it, manage it, set laws around it, enforce them . . ."

"Ah! Now, Mr. Luxford, you're asking the right questions."

Ansel looked around at the cabinets full of rusted medallions and chipped animal teeth. Tokens from once vast civilizations whose citizens believed themselves to be at the vanguard of human progress, only to find their existences unremembered, their precious monies turned to fragile relics.

"You said *if* we win this war," Ansel asked. "What happens if we lose?"

A cloud covered Keynes's face. "If we lose, then you and I, my friend, will both be dead. And the Nazis can create a world built on whatever money they like."

A car horn blared. Disoriented, it took Ansel a moment to realize it had come from the front driveway.

"That must be Harry," Keynes said. The spell of his enthusiasm was broken. The tiredness returned to his haunch. "You shouldn't keep him waiting."

The horn blared again. Ansel took his time going to the door, relishing his last moments with these strange items.

"You tell your boss . . ." Keynes said as Ansel crossed the threshold.

"You know? I don't care what you tell him. But you strike me as the more thoughtful one. So between us?"

Keynes gestured around his chamber of ancient monies so removed from use as to make them worthless, and yet so precious and antique as to make their true value immeasurable. "It's time to start thinking bigger."

30

A HARDWARE STORE NEAR BOSTON AND A CHURCH NEAR MONTMIRAIL

"Money is . . . the apogee of human tolerance. . . .
Thanks to money, even people who don't know each other and
don't trust each other can nevertheless cooperate effectively."

—YUVAL NOAH HARARI

October 14, 1939 (cont'd)

"What pretentious bull crap," White said as they drove back through the downs. "He's going to prevent a third great war thanks to some old pub tokens he keeps in his private museum? I'll bet you Maynard has never stepped foot in a pub in his life."

Ansel admitted that he hadn't quite learned all the details of how, precisely, Keynes's new world currency would work, nor the manner by which it would prevent a future war. But Keynes's convictions certainly seemed noble.

White offered a few brief obscenities. "I have known that man for a long time. Trust me: All of his highfalutin 'make the world a grand and wonderful place' talk is a sham. I'm sure his cockamamie scheme for this, that, and what-have-you looks swell on paper. But out in the real world, Maynard has never once done something that did not serve, in the end, to benefit exactly one person and one person alone: Maynard."

White returned to one of his quiet, stewing phases. He spoke little on the long ride back to London, or during the longer wait until the next flight of the Yankee Clipper. He seemed lost to his own angry thoughts.

He didn't say much to Ansel again until the Clipper was somewhere over Greenland. Ansel was awoken from a nap by a knock at his cabin door. He hadn't realized that he'd dozed off; he was still wearing his suit and tie.

He found White waiting in the corridor. "Let's have a drink."

They went to the dining cabin and ordered.

"You think I'm a crum-bum," White said after the glasses arrived.

Ansel could feel cold arctic air whipping past the airplane windows. "I don't know what you mean."

"You think that I'm a jerk. Rude, blunt, ornery."

Ansel wasn't sure whether he ought to reassure his boss or whether he should just be honest. "Warmth can be overrated."

"You also think Maynard Keynes is the elegant peak of sophistication."

"Why do you hate him so much?" Ansel hadn't intended the question to come out so bluntly.

"I don't," he said. "Not really. I hate what he represents. The old guard. The ancestral lords." White tapped at the window. "I hate the assholes who lounge on transcontinental flights while they graciously work out the fates of everyone down below."

White laughed to himself, perhaps wondering whether anyone was immune from becoming the very thing they most despised. "My dad owned a hardware store. In a little town near Boston. I worked there as a kid. Then again after I dropped out of college. I was flunking, had the good sense to quit before they expelled me. If you'd asked me when I was twenty-five if I'd ever be sitting here with you, flying around the world and trying to save civilization from fascism, I'd have said you were nuts. It's not modesty: I really truly thought I was going to spend the rest of my life managing the hardware store."

This was already more personal detail than Ansel had ever gotten from his boss.

"I ran that hardware store great after my dad passed. We expanded.

A second location. We were looking at a third. I had it all worked out. I met Anne Terry. We got married. And then the Great War. I volunteered for the infantry." White sipped his gin. "I spent most of the war in Boston training the younger men. By the time I made it to France with my unit, the fighting was long over. We were just wandering around, nothing to do. Patrolling for stragglers, cleaning up. We went into a village one day. Beneath the Montmirail mountains. This old church. I thought the place had been abandoned. I went in first, alone. I mean, I wasn't worried. Obviously no one else could be there. No one alive."

He finished the rest of his drink in one long gulp. "The women had been raped before they were killed. And the kids were . . . Some were babies, you know, just babies. By the time I saw the bodies, they must have been lying there for weeks." He looked down. His voice was so quiet that Ansel could barely hear it over the sound of the engine. "I left pretty quick. Found the other troops, told them there was nobody in the church. 'Let's move out.' We did. I never told anybody what I saw in there, except for Anne Terry. But after that day I knew I was going to spend the rest of my life making damn sure nothing like that was ever going to happen again.

"I got my college diploma a year after I got back. I was going to work in the government, I'd decided, so I applied to Harvard. Got my doctorate at the promising young age of thirty-eight. Been working my way up the ladder at Treasury ever since. A lot of economists, they might be real swell with their multiplication tables. But if they've never managed inventory for a small chain of suburban hardware stores? They don't know squat about the look a man gives you when you put a paycheck in his hand. Or when you cut him a break on a spokeshave he can't quite afford. It's an irony, I suppose. Maynard talking about the Great War, 'not again,' all that nonsense. You know where Maynard spent the war? In some posh London office sliding pieces of paper around, making sure that both he and his country could leave the war in exactly the same position as they'd entered it. His own position at the top of the food chain: That's what he fought to preserve then, and it's what he's conniving to preserve now. Ancestral inheritances, afternoon tea, cricket on the lawns, priceless art on the walls. I don't think he cares one bit about the fate of the world so long as he's the one running it. What he calls altruism is, at best, noblesse oblige. More likely it's the impeccably bred assurance that the only person on earth who's smart enough to rule the world is him. Ten to one, I promise you, when you get to the bottom of whatever scheme he's cooked up, the end result will somehow miraculously involve his dictating the fate of the universe by the stroke of his pen."

White stood. He stretched his arms, allowing his plump belly to extend over the table. "But I'm grateful to Maynard for one thing: the reminder that we ought, on occasion, to look at things from the vantage point of twenty thousand feet in the air. And from up here, our greatest challenge is not winning this war. It's doing so in a way that allows us to stop the next one. And the one after that."

White removed the last Lucky from his pack, lit it, and then dropped the crumpled paper onto the tablecloth. "First thing when we get home, I want you to set up a meeting with the team."

"Which ones?"

"All of them. All hands on deck, ASAP. We're behind."

"Behind?" Ansel watched White's smoke drift through the cabin.

"Keynes has his plans to set the future of the global economy? It's high time we had our own."

31

MR. LUXFORD GOES TO BETHESDA

*"Hollywood is a place where they'll pay you a thousand dollars
for a kiss and fifty cents for your soul."*

—MARILYN MONROE

October 17, 1939

Even though Jimmy Stewart stood nearly a foot taller than the angry
senators encircling him, he still seemed in over his head. Anyone who
was anyone in Washington—and many who weren't—had donned
their best evening wear and pressed themselves into Constitution Hall
for the premiere of the star's new picture. Ansel couldn't remember
ever hearing of a movie premiere in the District before. Apparently
neither had anyone else. The guest list, he was told, was four thousand
names long. Morgenthau and family declined the invitation on account of their being at their estate in New York. White and family
declined on account of there being nothing that he wanted to do less
on a Tuesday than subject himself to some crummy Hollywood spec-
tacle. Which meant that the Research Department inherited four tickets. Ansel snapped up two so he could take Angela, leaving Saxon and
DuBois to come along stag.

Angela scoffed audibly through most of *Mr. Smith Goes to Washington* and delivered her verdict over cocktails in the rotunda loudly
enough that Frank Capra himself probably heard: "It's unconsciona-
ble."

"It makes our government out to be nothing but a rat's nest of snakes and charlatans," she continued. "It's bad for FDR and it's a poor reflection of our country."

Ansel watched the mob of the people's representatives run roughshod over Jimmy Stewart. The poor guy looked like a deer in their headlights. Evidently the senators hadn't liked the picture any more than Angela had.

"He wins in the end," Ansel protested. "They pass the bill." He'd found the picture charming.

Angela turned to DuBois. Surely he'd be on her side.

"Is this what all the pictures are like?" DuBois said, holding a small plate in each hand. One was full of boiled shrimp, the other red dipping sauce. He struggled to dip a shrimp into the sauce and eat it without the use of a third hand.

Ansel frowned, putting together the implication. "You've never seen a movie before?"

DuBois twisted himself into knots trying to get a shrimp into his mouth. "We went to church instead when we were kids. Lots of good stories in the Bible."

This left Angela more flummoxed than the movie had. "Our family always managed to do both."

DuBois shrugged. Based on what he'd just seen, he didn't seem to think he'd been deprived of much.

Across the rotunda, a pair of tanned Hollywood men arrived at Jimmy Stewart's side. Cavalry, it seemed, to mediate between their star and their government.

Angela saw the same thing. "Can you imagine if they show this picture in Europe? They shouldn't release this. It makes the American government look venal and self-serving."

"Except for Jimmy!" Ansel had been a fan since that *Thin Man* picture.

"Who's Jimmy?" DuBois asked.

"That's my point," Angela said, ignoring DuBois. "This is practically Nazi propaganda. Hitler will love it."

"I think that's overstating the case," Ansel said.

DuBois turned to Angela. "Does Hitler see a lot of pictures?"

"Not American ones," Ansel offered.

Angela gestured to a bald man giving the Hollywood boys what looked to be a piece of his mind. "That's the president's appointment secretary, isn't it? He looks like he's about to garrote those men with a cocktail napkin."

"Mason, yes." Ansel couldn't believe that the White House—or their Democratic allies in the Senate—were really so up in arms about a picture.

"Ansel?" Saxon appeared out of nowhere. "Can I ask a favor?"

Ansel had lost track of him in the crowd after the picture ended. "Where have you been?"

Saxon gestured to a brunette by the windows. She held two flutes of champagne. "Sally knows an after-hours spot. I was going to go with her."

Angela took in the brunette and nodded appreciatively. "She seems like quite a conversationalist."

Saxon removed an envelope from his jacket pocket. "Harry is supposed to go to New York tomorrow to see Morgenthau. He left his tickets on my desk. I said I'd drop them in his mail slot tonight, but . . ." He raised an eyebrow in the direction of his new friend. "She's going downtown. You know Harry's all the way out in Bethesda."

Ansel saw where this was headed. "So *I* should drive out there in the middle of the night?"

Saxon placed a hand on his shoulder. "C'mon. Please. Just this once."

Angela gestured toward the girl. "Is that what you plan on saying to her?"

Saxon laughed. He seemed to enjoy the ribbing. "Do me a favor. You were young once, weren't you?"

Angela grimaced at the implication.

"I'll tell you one currency more durable than dollars," Ansel said. "Favors. If I say yes, you owe me a big one."

"Do favors qualify as currency?" DuBois said with perfect seriousness. "What's the old economists' line? For something to function as a currency, it must be first a store of value—that is, it must have some intrinsic, stable worth. Second, it must be a unit of account—that is, measurable and quantifiable. Third, it must be a medium of exchange—you can trade it."

The team's first meeting on postwar planning wasn't scheduled to begin for a few days, but evidently DuBois was already deep into it. Perhaps as a pacifist there could be no higher use of his days than putting a stop to a war before it had even occurred.

Saxon's concerns seemed more in the here and now as he pressed the tickets into Ansel's hand. "Value? Account? Exchange? Sounds like we've got it all."

Ansel clutched the tickets. "Fine."

"You have my deepest thanks." Saxon left to join his waiting brunette.

"I don't want your thanks!" Ansel said to his back. "I want a favor!"

Angela sighed. "Such is love."

DuBois finished his shrimp. "Such is currency."

———

ANSEL DROPPED ANGELA OFF at her parents' place before driving out to Bethesda. The highway was dark. The wide suburban streets and their rows of well-kept lawns were only slightly more lit, thanks to the sparsely placed streetlamps. Ansel pulled to a stop across the street from White's home and cut his engine. The house was black with quiet slumber save for a single light blooming somewhere deep inside.

This was Ansel's first surprise. What was White doing up past one in the morning? Didn't he have an early train to catch?

The second surprise arrived moments later in the form of a green DeSoto. Ansel heard it before he saw it, rumbling down the desolate road and then coming to a stop right in front of the house. The car remained eerily still. From across the street, Ansel couldn't make out its driver. But whoever it was, he left his engine running and his headlights blazing bright into the wet night air.

Ansel was immobilized by the strangeness of the sight. He couldn't say why, precisely—surely there were a thousand reasonable explanations for what he was witnessing—and yet the situation seemed odd enough that Ansel kept his distance. He slumped down in his darkened car, unobserved, it appeared, by the DeSoto's driver.

White emerged from the house wearing a robe and slippers. He tugged the cloth tight against the chill. He dashed straight to the DeSoto and got in.

The car kicked into gear and drove to the corner, gently pulling a right under the yellow pool of a swan-necked streetlamp. Ansel could see White speaking in the passenger seat but couldn't see past him to the driver. He listened to the car receding into the distance.

He remained still as he reassured himself that whatever he'd just seen, it was no excuse for paranoia. Angela's talk of spies had rubbed off on him. The proper thing to do would be to drop the tickets in the mailbox and go home.

Only, something even odder then occurred: Ansel heard an engine approaching from down the street, on the other side of the house. It crept closer and Ansel discovered that it was the same green DeSoto. It must have circled around the block.

The car then went right past the house, to the corner with the swan-necked lamp, before turning right once again.

It took less than a minute, going by Ansel's watch, for the car to make the same loop another time.

White and his driver were circling the block again and again.

The car made seven loops before finally stopping in the very spot from which it started. White got out and shut the passenger door behind him gingerly.

As he hurried back into his dark home, Ansel could see that he was carrying something: a brown leather briefcase.

He hadn't been holding anything when he'd left.

Once White was inside, the DeSoto rumbled into motion, driving one final time underneath the streetlight. At last, Ansel could see the driver.

It took only a second for Ansel to recognize his face.

32

THE INSIDE MAN

"There is only one difference between a bad economist and a good one: The bad economist confines himself to the visible effect; the good economist takes into account both the effect that can be seen and those effects that must be foreseen."

—FRÉDÉRIC BASTIAT

October 17, 1939 (cont'd)

Ansel hadn't seen Sumner Welles since their commute through Panama City. Welles and White had seemed friendly enough on their drive, but agreeableness did not go far in explaining why the two men had taken a clandestine meeting in the middle of the night. Or why Welles had just passed White a mysterious briefcase.

Ansel sat in his parked car on the moonlit suburban street as the pieces began clicking into place. At first he wished he were more sober so he could think faster. After a moment, he wished he were drunker so he might better handle the truth.

If Jacome's aide was being honest, then an American had gotten the better of them in Panama. That American had to have known that Ansel and White were in Panama City; and he had to have known whom they were meeting with, and for what. The only two people who Ansel knew for a fact had all of that information were himself and White.

If Morgenthau had been correct that someone at State had been secretly working to undermine the efforts of Treasury for the past year, then a likely suspect was Sumner Welles. He'd been in Panama.

He'd been up to *something*. Only, when Ansel had previously voiced suspicions about Welles, he'd been shot down: by White.

If the chatter Angela had overheard at the FBI was correct, then the Soviets had a man on the inside at Treasury who was leaking classified information to Moscow, and perhaps even all the way to Berlin. Anyone in the Research Department *might* have done it; but of course, the member most capable of betraying their team would be the person who'd assembled it. White would know exactly what he could get away with and how he might get away with it: He'd been the one to design their security protocols.

Ansel remembered the misplaced paper clip, his very first indication that not all was as it seemed. Who else had known that he was staying in that hotel? Besides White?

And yet the Research Department had been White's idea. He'd staffed it, personally. Why would he do all this if he was secretly working against his own government on behalf of the Soviets? Or worse?

But then Ansel found himself thinking about this point from another angle. Like an optical illusion, of the kind you'd find in a puzzle book. From one angle, the drawing looks like a turtle. From another, all the same lines reveal the animal to be a hawk.

White had put together a "secret" group that Morgenthau knew about, and that Roosevelt clearly knew existed in some form, to advance the anti-Nazi agenda they favored privately but could not advocate for in public. And yet what had the group actually managed to accomplish? White had staffed it with quite possibly the least-prestigious group of economists he could find. At every task they'd been given, they'd failed. Thanks to White, they couldn't even make a deal with their own allies in Britain, much less the neutral nations of South America. If Ansel's Research Department had been created purely so that it might fail . . . what exactly would be different from how it presently functioned?

Ansel felt like the most gullible fool in Washington. He'd been nothing but a puppet. He hadn't been chosen for his abilities; he'd been chosen for his incompetence. And goodness, had he ever demonstrated it in spades.

Not anymore. It was time to make things right. And it was time to get even.

If the leather briefcase contained instructions from Welles and White's Soviet masters, the contents would be proof of their conspiracy. If Ansel got hold of it, he could take it to Morgenthau. Or higher.

He got out of his car and knelt beside one of the wheels. He always carried a fountain pen with him, tucked into the inside pocket of his jacket, but he'd never before put it to such a purpose. With all his strength he jammed the pen into the tire. The rubber emitted a high wheeze.

He knocked on the front door of White's home. He heard stirring. Suddenly the light in the vestibule burst to life and the door swung open. White was wearing the same robe. He had a sleepy look on his face. "Do you know what time it is?"

Ansel handed him the tickets. "From Joe. He made a new friend at the premiere."

"How was the picture?"

"FDR's people seemed up in arms about it. Anti-American propaganda. I liked it." Ansel gestured back to his Ford. "I just got a flat coming up the street. You mind if I borrow your telephone? Call AAA?"

White looked toward the car. Hopefully he saw the front tire sagging. "You don't have a spare?"

Ansel shook his head. "It'll only take a minute."

"I can lend you mine."

"I pay my dues every year. Might as well get some value for it."

"My car is right there."

"I don't want to put you out any more than I already have, showing up like this. If I could use your phone, I'll be out of your hair in a jiffy."

White gave him a long look. With weary annoyance, he led Ansel inside.

From the foyer, Ansel could see a light coming from the study. That must have been where White had taken the briefcase.

White started toward the kitchen, but Ansel broke away and went straight to the study. "Thank you, I see a telephone this way."

White seemed irritated as he followed. "There's another . . ." But Ansel was already in the book-lined study. On a central desk sat a few piles of paper, a typewriter, an art deco lamp, and the telephone. He saw the brown leather briefcase resting on one of the built-in bookshelves.

He turned to find White staring at him from the doorway. Even if White was suspicious that he'd seen something, he'd have no way to test Ansel's position without revealing his own.

Ansel picked up the receiver and asked the operator for the number. While the call connected, Ansel turned back to White. "Could I trouble you for a glass of water? It was a long drive."

"A glass of water?"

"If it's not too much bother."

White stood still for another long moment. Then he went to the kitchen.

Ansel heard a woman from AAA answer the line as he set the receiver down and went right for the briefcase. Popping the latches, he discovered a folder of documents inside.

He could hear White's footsteps approaching. He looked at the folder. Would White notice if a few pages went missing?

He grabbed a handful and stuffed them into his jacket pocket.

White reached the doorway as Ansel slammed the case shut and strode back to the telephone. He had the receiver in his hand as White appeared with a glass of water.

"Hello? Are you there?" came the woman's voice from the end of the line. Ansel pressed it close against his ear, muffling the sound.

"One moment, please," he said into the telephone before taking the glass from White. "Thank you."

Ansel dutifully reported his flat tire to the woman from AAA. She assured him that a car would be on the way within minutes.

"You get what you needed?" White said after Ansel had set the receiver back into its cradle.

"They're on the way. I can't thank you enough." Glancing down, he saw that the bulge of papers in his pocket didn't protrude too much. "I've put you out too much already. I'll wait in the car."

White said little as he ushered Ansel to the door. Ansel felt a dizzying rush as the cool night air hit his cheeks. He realized he'd been sweating.

"This is ridiculous," White said.

"What is?"

"You're not waiting around in the cold all night for some kid to show up with a patch. I'll give you a ride."

"You don't have to—"

But before Ansel could protest further, White disappeared into the house. A few moments later, he returned with shoes on his feet, a jacket on his shoulders, and car keys in his hand.

"I'll leave a note for AAA. Let's go." White marched toward his own car. Ansel had no choice but to follow.

Once they were both in, White turned the engine and slid the heater knob all the way to the right. He flicked on the radio. The thrum of Glenn Miller's "Moonlight Serenade" washed through the car.

"Thanks," Ansel said. "This is more than kind."

"Don't mention it."

"Oh, before I forget . . ." White fished around in his jacket pocket. After a moment, he removed a small silver pistol.

"You mind if I grab the papers you stole from my briefcase?"

PART
II

ACCOUNTS

33

MOONLIGHT SERENADE

"The whole financial history of the world is about moving from currencies of distrust to currencies of trust. If you look at grain, which was the original currency in ancient Mesopotamia, it required very little trust. You can eat it. You don't need to trust anybody that it's valuable. As you move to gold and paper and digital currency, there is more and more trust. Blockchain is an attempt to go back. . . . As a historian, I'm skeptical."

—YUVAL NOAH HARARI

October 17, 1939 (cont'd)

White held the pistol just above his lap. "What's going to happen now is going to happen slowly, quietly, and peaceably. My aim is not to hurt you. But if someone were to be hurt, it won't be me. You understand?"

Ansel indicated that he did with as little movement as possible.

"You're going to come around and take the wheel. I'll take your place over there. Then you're going to drive."

"Where?"

"Wherever I goddamn tell you. Let's go."

It was three in the morning when Ansel followed instructions to pull off the highway into Forest Heights. The country they drove past was rural, a smattering of old farms and acres of gentle hills.

"Turn right." White held his pistol casually in his lap. He'd made his point. Ansel tried to work out the math in his head: If White wasn't out to kill him, where were they headed? But if White did mean to kill him . . . ? Well, if their positions were reversed and Ansel was the one with the pistol, he'd aim to pull its trigger as far away from human ears as possible. He'd drive out to a place just like this.

They rolled through a small town, past a post office and a police station nestled beside each other on the moonlit main street. Then they went through a patch of forest. But just as Ansel braced himself for the worst, they arrived at a clearing. He saw a grand estate ahead. A ten-foot-high masonry wall formed a perimeter around a massive property. A heavy black gate was already open for their arrival. Ansel drove them inside. He saw a manor house: two stories of red Flemish brick gleaming devilishly under the light of the crescent moon. From the main building extended at least two neo-Georgian wings surrounded by formal European gardens. The grandeur of the Old World, the style of the new.

Lights were on inside. Standing under the milky-white transom of the grand entrance, lit by the headlights of the approaching car, was Sumner Welles.

He wore purple silk pajamas, and he did not seem happy to be receiving visitors at this hour.

Ansel wordlessly followed White into the palatial home. When Welles saw the squat pistol in White's hand, he sighed. "Are we being a touch dramatic?"

White evidently didn't think so. He delivered a flurry of whispers into Welles's ear. Welles kept his eyes on Ansel as he took in whatever White was telling him. Then he suggested that they all sit down in a nearby sunroom.

Through the skylight, Ansel could see a multitude of stars. The furnishings seemed decades old, of sturdy turn-of-the-century stock. Welles clearly had money, lots of it, and if this place was his, then the money had been accumulated generations ago.

The house looked like somewhere Keynes might live.

Ansel sat in a wingback wooden chair. When White told him to produce the documents he'd stolen, he did. Welles gave them a quick once-over. Then handed them back to White, who did the same.

White set his pistol down on a nearby coffee table, within arm's reach. "You're working for Long?"

Ansel was genuinely confused. "Long? I don't know who that is."

Welles and White exchanged a look.

"I hired you," White said to Ansel. "Getting you involved in this was my screwup. So I'll take responsibility for fixing it. You tell us how Long found you, how he put you up to this—and why the hell you agreed. You tell me that, and I can work out a way for all of us to make it through in one piece."

Ansel was incensed. "I'd ask you the same thing. Why are you selling out your country?"

White and Welles exchanged another look.

Now Welles appeared confused too. "Mr. Luxford, it's nice to see you again. Harry has told me so much about you. Now, what do you think we're doing?"

Ansel did not have the patience to be coy. "You might be Soviet agents, but you're doing Berlin's bidding whether you know it or not."

They both stared at him for a long moment.

And then Welles laughed.

White was unamused. "I don't trust him," he said to Welles.

Welles waved a hand in the air, the loose sleeves of his purple pajamas swaying. "Oh come on. This guy? He's soft as they come. Just look at him. He has no idea what's really going on here."

Ansel was beginning to fear that Welles was right.

White did not seem inclined to give Ansel the benefit of the doubt. "You're going to tell me exactly how you came to be snooping through my things."

Ansel's best move, he figured, was to tell them the truth. Well, most of it. He told them about the Soviet defector who'd provided evidence to the FBI of a spy in the Research Department. But he took care to minimize Angela's role in the story and to make clear that while he and his wife had discussed sensitive matters, the information had flowed in only one direction.

White took it all in without reaction.

Welles at first received Ansel's tale with bemusement. But by the end of the story, his smile had faded, and in its place was a pale visage of worry.

"Could be the FBI set this up," Welles said to White. "Made sure Mr. Luxford's wife overheard something she was bound to repeat to him."

"You think Hoover's people are that smart?" White seemed to be piecing together an extremely intricate puzzle. "No, I suspect that the FBI, bless them, are dumb enough to have bought the story she told her husband."

Welles took this with a serious nod.

Ansel had more pressing concerns. "Can you put that pistol away? Unless you plan on killing me, in which case, let's get on with it."

"Harry? Let's not be rude."

White handed Ansel the pistol. "Check it."

It felt light. He flipped the cylinder. Sure enough, it was unloaded.

"I needed to know if you were working for Long," White said. "I'm starting to think you're not."

"Who's Long?" Ansel asked. "What's really going on?"

White stood, apparently struggling with a decision. Finally, he plopped himself beside Welles on the sofa. "You got cigarettes?"

Welles slid a silver case across the coffee table.

White lit up before speaking again. "There's no Soviet spy in the Research Department. That's a ruse concocted by, I'm willing to bet my life, a man named Breckinridge Long. Either the FBI's 'defector' is a plant, or maybe the defector is real, but Long fed him bum information about what was going on inside Treasury. Long could have gotten our files any number of ways. He's at the State Department. Pretty senior. He was on that trip to Panama City, and I suspect that he was the American who nixed our deal with Jacome."

Ansel turned to Welles. "He works with you?"

"He used to," Welles said. "They fired me last week."

"They fired *you*? Why?"

Welles turned to White. "What level of transparency would you recommend on this matter?"

"Your secrets. Your decision."

Welles took his time considering. "I'm a married man. Two children. They're at our cottage in Maine for the week, thankfully." He gestured around at his empty manor. "My wife and I have an under-standing in our marriage, but what she may forgive—what she even encourages—would not read well if printed in the papers. You under-stand?"

Ansel felt that on this point, at least, he got the idea. "The FBI fired you for . . . indiscretions? With women who were not your wife?"

"Men. And I can assure you, I was quite discreet."

Ansel had no idea what to say.

Welles did not appear to require a response. It was his life, and in the privacy of his gilded world he could do as he pleased. But Washington, Ansel knew, was not so gilded as this place.

"Despite that discretion, however," White added, "Long has held evidence of this for a while. Last week, he decided he should deploy it. He told the FBI, and within hours Welles was out."

"Why last week?"

"Because," Welles said, "I discovered something. A batch of cables from Warsaw."

"Cables?"

"I was able to snatch a few carbons before they sacked me. That's what was in the briefcase I gave to Harry earlier. Once I'd found them, Long needed to get rid of me as quickly as possible; and he was, as usual, prepared with a pretext." Welles shook his head, as if respecting the skill with which his opponent played his cards.

"What was in the cables?"

White raised a hand. All in good time.

"I gave them to Harry," Welles continued, "because I need his help to prove what Long and his rotten buddies are up to."

"What are they up to?"

White exhaled a cloud of thick smoke before answering. "You know how we got a secretive group at Treasury so we can do things without anybody—especially anybody in the White House—needing to know?"

"I'm aware."

"Well, Long has one at State."

Ansel evidently failed to hide his surprise.

"What?" asked Welles. "You thought you were the only ones?"

Ansel had, as usual, been naive.

"Long's group has been a step ahead of us this entire time," White went on. "Ten to one, it was the FBI who broke into your hotel room in D.C. Thanks to Long, they've been tapping my telephone for months. Seems he found a way to get to Jacome before I could close the deal in Panama City. I'm still not sure what he promised the Brazilians on behalf of State in exchange for rejecting Treasury's offer, but we'll find out. You remember the *St. Louis*? That ship of Jewish refugees that couldn't dock in America, had to go back to Germany?"

Ansel sure did. He'd been as horrified about it as Morgenthau was.

"Who do you think it was who stopped the *St. Louis* from finding a port in New York? Long's group at State. Who nixed our plan to confiscate German accounts in American banks, to cut off Germany's dollar supply? Morgenthau was sure somebody at State was working in secret against us, wasn't he? Thanks to Sumner here, I know now that it was Long and his team. They've been cleaning our clocks for the last year, and if what Sumner has uncovered is true—and I'm afraid that it is—then they have even bigger villainies on their minds."

"I don't understand," Ansel said. "What was in the cables? And why would Long and his group want to foil our plans to stop the Germans? Aren't we all on the same side?"

White flicked his ash into Welles's marble tray. "Maybe I should have mentioned at the top. Long and his group? They're fascists."

34

CABLE 631

*"He who is unfit to serve his fellow citizens
wants to rule them."*

—LUDWIG VON MISES

October 17, 1939 (cont'd)

Breckinridge Long had been raised in rural Missouri, which meant that
it wasn't until he moved to Italy, in adulthood, that his palate was
opened up to sweet vermouth, the Macchiaioli school of painting, and
fascism. Born into a family of Southern aristocrats, his family lore had
it that he had multiple cousins who were generals in the Confederate
army. Long, however, was no soldier. He was a lawyer who joined the
State Department young and spent years toiling away in the dank base-
ments of Seventeenth Street. Thanks to his renowned collection of
racehorses, he'd developed a friendship with a number of gambling
men in Roosevelt's administration. For his prodigious campaign dona-
tions, he was rewarded with an ambassadorship. He arrived in Rome in
'33 and was instantly enthralled by the rich atmosphere of nightly be-
guines and nativist violence.

It wasn't just the trains that ran on time. He found Mussolini's policies toward immigrants and Africans—and especially toward people
who happened to be both—well overdue. Long wrote admiringly of
Mussolini's government and of the ways America might benefit from
something similar. His dispatches back to Washington grew in both
length and radicalism. His friends in the administration chalked his fas-

cist enthusiasm up to a harmless flight of fancy. Ambassadors to France always came home with a hunger for *escargots,* didn't they? But when Mussolini invaded Ethiopia, Long's enthusiasm for the slaughter of Africans became uncomfortable even for his nearest and dearest. Roosevelt's people felt they were doing him a favor when they quietly stripped him of his post and shuttled him back to Washington. They gave him a cushy, somewhat nebulous job as special assistant secretary. How much trouble, they must have figured, could he really cause?

A lot, it turned out. Because the only thing he apparently admired more than Mussolini's treatment of Africans was Hitler's treatment of Jews. And from his lofty sinecure, he'd groomed a tight-knit cadre of like-minded men within the State Department. Together, they pushed for the United States to join the German-Italian axis. And until they could shake FDR from his foolish affinities for the decadent societies of London and Paris, Long and his team pursued their pro-Nazi policies in secret.

"I've been working against Long and his group from inside State for a while," Welles said as the sun began creeping out from behind the European gardens. "Now Harry has kindly offered to help."

"How many other things," Ansel asked his boss, "have been going on that you've elected not to tell me about?"

The cloud of smoke around White's head was impenetrable. "God willing, you won't ever know."

Ansel found this less than reassuring. "What was in the cables? The ones you found?"

"That's the problem." Welles sighed. "There's one missing."

———

THE OPERATIVE WORKED UNDER the code name Verity. His real name was unknown even to his routine handlers in the State Department. All they knew was his nationality—Swiss—and that for some reason he lived in Warsaw. He was there when the German tanks encircled the city.

Verity sent frequent cables to Washington via a relay in London about what he was seeing on the ground. None of it was pretty. His handlers received his reports and summarized them for the secretary and the White House, as per protocol. A week earlier, Verity had sent the State Department an urgent cable: number 631. His handler had received it and replied tersely: "No action to be taken. Do not send reports of this nature."

This handler, Welles explained, was Breckinridge Long. Who had promptly seen to burying the entire exchange. Verity's report was not summarized and sent up the flagpole. Rather, Long destroyed it. Cable number 631 was lost.

However, Long had made one crucial mistake. Or rather, his secretary had. She'd filed carbon copies of the entire exchange between Verity and Long in the State Department's records library. Welles had managed to intercept cable numbers 632, 633, 634, and 635 on their way to being filed. These follow-up cables contained references to the initial report in 631, and to Verity's continued insistence on its importance. But the later cables did not, unfortunately, provide any clues as to what number 631 said.

"Our man saw something big," Welles said to Ansel after making coffee and delivering it to his late-night guests. "By the tone of his follow-up messages, it was so big that he felt he needed to warn the American government about it right away. And you don't need to take my hunch for it. Long clearly thought that whatever was in 631 was lit dynamite. Otherwise, why stick his neck out by burying it?"

"The follow-up cables," Ansel said, gesturing to the pile of papers he'd stolen from White's study. "Those are the carbons?"

"He can add two and two," White said to Welles. "We should at least give him that."

Ansel went over to the messages. He couldn't read a word of Polish. "How do we figure out what Verity saw?"

"We?" White sounded amused.

"If you think I'm going to sit back and do nothing about a conspiracy of Nazi enthusiasts at the State Department . . ."

Welles was more receptive. "We could use another set of hands," he said to White before turning back to Ansel. "The only way to figure out what was in cable 631 is to get the last remaining copy. Which currently sits on the fourth floor of the State Department records library."

"Harry has security clearance. He can quietly put in an inter-agency request. They have to send it to him."

White seemed to take this as confirmation that Ansel was not equipped for the subterfuge that would be required of them. "Think it through. If I put in an official request for cable 631, what will Long do?"

"Long will learn of the carbon in the library," Welles said. "And then he'll destroy it. Our only advantage at the moment is that he doesn't know it's there. Or that I'm working with Harry. Or, now, with you."

White groaned. "Ansel couldn't even snatch a couple of papers from *me*. You really think he can do better against Long and his people?"

"Snatch?" Ansel said.

"If I can prove to the White House that Long is carrying water for the Germans," White said, "then Roosevelt's people will have to face up to the fact that he can no longer be quietly contained. But if that rat stays where he is, then the Research Department is never going to make an inch of headway, no matter what clever schemes we think up."

White stood and stretched. "So we've got to steal the damned thing."

35

ONE VILLAIN
AT A TIME

"The first thing a man will do for his ideals is lie."

—JOSEPH A. SCHUMPETER,
TWENTIETH-CENTURY
AUSTRIAN-AMERICAN ECONOMIST

October 18, 1939

Angela understood that there were important secrets her husband was obligated to keep from her, but this whole story sounded a lot like nonsense.

"You spent all night at Harry's place," she said that morning after Ansel finally returned to a house full of people curious about where he'd been. "And something happened, though you can't tell me what, that left you proof positive that there is no Soviet spy in the Research Department."

Ansel took off his shirt and then his undershirt, flinging both onto the bed. He didn't have time for a shower, but at least he could put on some fresh clothes. "Yes."

Angela was already dressed for the day. She had to be at the office before he did. "You think I was mistaken? What I overheard?"

"No." Ansel shimmied off his pants. "I think that we're swimming in water that's a lot deeper than either of us realized."

Angela took his dirty clothes and set them carefully in the hamper. "I've been at the FBI for no time at all and I can't tell you what I've seen, but . . . the things coming through about Stalin and his government— it's worse there than we think."

"We have bigger problems right now than whatever intrigue is going on in Moscow." Ansel shucked off his socks.

"No we don't." Angela plucked the damp socks from the floor and placed them with his shirts. "It's not in vogue to say it, but Hoover is no fool. He's got his eyes open wide. The Soviets are more aligned with the Nazis than they're letting on, and they've got more people in the District than should make any of us comfortable."

Ansel slipped off his underwear. These he thoughtfully placed in the hamper himself.

He heard a familiar fervor churning in his wife's voice.

"One villain at a time." He stood before her naked.

She found a freshly pressed white shirt in the closet and started pulling out the laundry pins. "You say that there's no spy in your department. And maybe you're right. But there are plenty of spies to go around. And if I've learned anything in Washington . . . there are always more villains than the one."

November 4, 1939

Roosevelt wanted American weapons in British hands and he wanted them there yesterday. So given White and Keynes's continued impasse as to the matter of payment, Morgenthau took it upon himself to cut them both out of the negotiations. He contacted Downing Street and the Exchequer directly. Keynes might be powerful within his government, but he was not all-powerful, and Morgenthau deftly achieved a brief, tenuous financial compromise.

Contra Keynes, the British would not receive their arms for free. Contra White, they would not have to pay in dollars. They would pay in good old-fashioned gold. Since both dollars and sterling were nominally gold convertible, the deal would give neither side a conceptual victory. And since the Exchequer already kept a substantial percentage of its gold reserves at the Federal Reserve Bank of New York, all that would be required for the British to pay for their weapons was for them to instruct their representatives in Manhattan to load up a few tons of gold bars and cart them down a stone hallway, deep beneath the earth, from one of their vaults to one of the Americans'.

Ansel still wasn't sure what to make of Keynes's grand vision for the postwar economy. But while White distrusted anything that came from Keynes out of hand, Morgenthau seemed more willing to meet the man halfway. Perhaps Morgenthau shared Ansel's concerns that White was overreacting on account of personal animosity. Or perhaps Morgenthau was also the type to view the world from high up in the air: a vantage point from which an imperfect deal was far preferable to none at all.

White was as frustrated by the compromise forced upon him, Ansel imagined, as Keynes must have been. But perhaps both could take consolation in the knowledge that the deal would be short-lived. Britain had enough gold in Manhattan to pay for this first round of weaponry but not much more. If Ansel's calculations were correct, the Exchequer would run out of gold in a few months' time. And then the war between White and Keynes would explode anew.

———

AT THE VERY MOMENT that Roosevelt signed his Cash and Carry bill into law, two Federal Reserve workers loaded hundreds of pounds of gold bullion onto a wheeled palette in a subterranean vault beneath Liberty Street. Simultaneously, in Brooklyn, a half-dozen Hudson bombers were loaded into port.

Morgenthau posed with the president and a handful of congressional leaders in the Oval Office. The reporters snapped their photos. The president gave a speech recommitting the country to a policy of pure neutrality in Europe, as evidenced by the eminently neutral Cash and Carry bill he'd just signed. *The New York Times*, Ansel would be pleased to note the following morning, even printed its A-1 article under the headline "President Signs Arms Embargo Repeal Bill and Acts to Guard Our Neutrality." Everyone, it seemed, had bought it.

Meanwhile, above a furniture store on Twelfth Street, Ansel informed his fellow members of the Research Department about a cabal of Nazi sympathizers who'd been conspiring against them from senior positions in the State Department. While Ansel spoke, White sat on a makeshift desk and smoked in silence.

Over the past three weeks, they had debated what to tell the others. Ansel had argued for transparency, White for secrecy. He was spinning a lot of plates in the air at once, and his job was only made harder when more people knew more things about which they had no business. But eventually, and to his surprise, Ansel won out. His reasoning was simple: Stealing the carbon of cable number 631 from the State Department library would require a complicated operation involving multiple players. And none of them could be White. Enough people under Breckinridge Long's command knew him and would be instantly alarmed by his presence in their building. While the rest of the Research Department possessed a singular advantage: Nobody had any idea who they were.

Oliphant wheezed as Ansel detailed the vile conspiracy. Theorizing about how they might hamper Nazi trade was one thing, but exposing a covert plot within the State Department? This was not what he'd signed up for.

The Professor seemed to have a hard time wrapping her consummately logical mind around the idea that any Americans—much less high-ranking State Department officers—could harbor an affinity for the Nazi cause. DuBois was aghast: Nowhere was safe from the devil's tricks. Saxon looked as if he had a mind to dash the few blocks over to the State, War, and Navy building and sock this Breckinridge Long right in the jaw himself.

Pehle seemed the least surprised of the group. He'd been in Washington for enough years to have had dealings with Long, plus plenty of men of his ilk. Pehle was no stranger to hearing snide comments about Jews at cocktail parties, and he'd been privy to plenty of admiring words about Mussolini among the old money diplomatic class.

"Men like Long are a dime a dozen," he said disdainfully. "Aristocratic heirs with a few prestigious degrees after their names, not much to do with themselves but join the foreign service. They typically bounce around the globe for a few years, kissing up to dictators, before coming back home and hosting charity balls. Usually they're harmless."

Ansel wondered whether Pehle might almost as easily have been describing himself, had he joined State instead of Treasury.

"This doesn't sound harmless," Saxon said.

"The only surviving carbon of cable 631," Ansel said, "sits at this moment in a filing cabinet on the fourth floor of the State, War, and Navy building, all of two hundred feet from the White House."

"And you're suggesting that we steal it?" the Professor asked.

Ansel had prepared himself to deliver a lengthy monologue on the moral necessity of the crime in which he wanted them to participate. He certainly didn't want to talk them into it. That wouldn't be fair. But he could explain the stakes of their failure. He could reassure them of the precautions they could take; though of course, he'd have to make clear, treason was treason. Jail was a possibility. But, he would say, if they all worked together—if every man and woman participated—he and White had a plan to pull this off.

Saxon spoke before Ansel could say a word. "Obviously Harry can't be the one to sneak in there. Too recognizable."

DuBois tapped his fingers together thoughtfully. "The key will be a pair of teams working in unison. One group can make sure Long and his people are distracted while the other goes into the library."

"Not distracted," Oliphant added, taking a deep breath and girding himself up. "Too risky. Let's get them out of the building entirely. Perhaps to a meeting somewhere."

"It can't appear to come from us," Pehle advised.

"I should be the one in the library," the Professor said boldly.

"Why you?" Saxon asked.

"Look at me. Who'd be suspicious of a kooky old lady?"

As the group plotted, Ansel caught the faintest hint of a grin on White's face. They hadn't had to talk anyone into doing this.

Hell, they didn't even have to *ask*.

36

STATE, WAR,
AND NAVY

*"The bad economist pursues a small present good, which will be
followed by a great evil to come, while the true economist pursues a
great good to come, at the risk of a small present evil."*

—FRÉDÉRIC BASTIAT

December 4, 1939

Professor Newcomer arrived at the State, War, and Navy building
with two colleagues in tow. Their Treasury badges got them past the
security in the lobby. Given the rapid expansion of these departments
over the past years, there were new faces entering the building's double
doors every day and plenty of officials from other departments dropping by on all manner of routine tasks. The place was swarmed with
visitors in the late morning, so the addition of three wandering mid-
level Treasury nobodies aroused little attention.

The records library occupied suites of adjoining rooms on the third
and fourth floors of the north wing. There, the group was greeted by
an energetic young librarian whom the Professor bombarded with an
impenetrable volley of questions. There was a set of records she needed
urgently. She'd filed all the proper inter-agency document request
forms and everything, so where were they already? What had happened to this place? Used to be she'd fill out a form and voilà! the documents would be on her desk by the next morning. Nowadays? She
didn't even know a one of these new girls. Who'd taught them so
poorly? What was the world coming to and wherever in it might these
records be hiding?

The librarian struggled to make sense of the Professor's rambling. There was something about British financial disclosures that had arrived four years previous and would now be misfiled because of a bureaucratic mix-up in the London embassy, but honestly not even Ansel, standing right behind her, could make heads or tails of what she was saying. Which was, of course, the point. Her dense prattle gave Ansel and DuBois ample opportunity to put on bored faces and idly back away.

The Professor leaned over the librarian's desk to display the smudged and illegible document requisition forms she'd helpfully brought with her. The Dewey decimal entries would fail to match the numbering system employed by the State Department file rooms, thus necessitating a long and tedious process of relocating the record numbers. If, that is, the poor girl could even read them in the first place. The whole mess would take half an hour, easily.

Ansel and DuBois slipped down one of the corridors. They tried to step quietly on the black-and-white granite tiles.

Welles had told them which row of filing cabinets contained the missing cable's carbon copy.

Breckinridge Long, meanwhile, was scheduled to be in a lengthy meeting at the White House. White had petitioned the Oval Office to host a chin-waggle about French Cash and Carry payments. Unlike their British counterparts, the French had plenty of gold in Fort Knox and arguably the world's most well-equipped military, next to the Germans. Surely they wouldn't need as much American help as the Brits did; plus, *les economists* at the Trésor public were professionals. They were able to negotiate like properly dispassionate bureaucrats, unstained by either blue-sky ideology or mystical ponderings about the history of money. Long and his men had seemed, White reported, unsure about why they were being roped into this pointless meeting on matters largely settled. But they were happy to be consulted on all matters European and to have an excuse to whisper in the ears of Roosevelt's closest confidants. The meeting, with White and Saxon speaking for Treasury, was to take place in Roosevelt's prestigious fish room, where he kept his aquarium. Pehle was manning the fort back at the

Research Department, while Oliphant attended to his day job at Treasury counsel. If anyone ended up in a jam, it was Oliphant they were supposed to call.

The State Department officers milling around didn't pay Ansel and DuBois much mind as the two men ascended the granite spiral staircase to the fourth floor. The filing rooms were a two-story space within the acres-wide complex. The ledges of the fourth floor looked down, through the open center, onto the third.

"Can I help you gentlemen?" came a man's voice. Ansel and DuBois stopped to find a short man in a black three-piece suit standing attentively behind them. His waist and his wire-framed glasses were both perfect circles.

Ansel felt it best to act as if he knew what he was doing. "No, thank you."

The man waited for Ansel to continue. But when he received nothing more, he said, "If you show me your requisition form, I can help you find what you're looking for."

Welles hadn't told them that there would be a fourth-floor librarian.

"We're just fine," DuBois said. "Thank you."

The round librarian did not appear satisfied. "Why don't you tell me the record number, and I'll help you locate the files?"

DuBois glanced at Ansel with a flash of panic.

Ansel turned disdainfully toward his colleague. "Well, Joe, give the man the paper."

DuBois looked back at him pleadingly. What was Ansel doing?

Ansel shook his head in exaggerated disappointment. "Joe, the record number? That sheet of paper? You didn't leave it downstairs with Miss Newcomer, did you?"

DuBois got what Ansel was doing. "I'm sorry, sir." He patted his pockets. "I must have."

"Damn it. If I've told you once—"

"I know, sir, I know."

The librarian did not appear eager to get involved in their squabble. "You have the record number downstairs?"

"I left it with our girl," DuBois pleaded. "We'll go get it."

Ansel snapped at him. "*You'll* go get it. I am not traipsing all over this damned maze. I will be waiting right here until you get back, do you understand?"

DuBois nodded. Then looked around, as if confused by where he was headed.

"Could you give me a hand?" he pleaded to the librarian.

The man took pity on poor DuBois and led him down the spiral staircase.

The instant they vanished, Ansel dashed down the hall. He followed Welles's instructions from room to room until he arrived at a bank of file cabinets. They were all labeled with departmental codes. Ansel found the one that was to be filled with Polish cables.

Inside, he found thousands of carbon copies of messages between American and Polish diplomats. All of them were in Polish. Ansel couldn't make out a word.

He could only go by the cable numbers. And those, he found, were not in any sort of order.

He flipped through the mess. A pair of State secretaries, their arms full of documents, chatted down the corridor. They hadn't yet noticed how maniacally he searched the cable numbers, trying to locate number 631.

There.

He grabbed the carbon and was about to stuff it into his jacket pocket when he stopped. He held it in front of his face. One word— *żydowski* for Jewish—he did recognize.

He stood there silently, trying to make sense of what he held, fearful that he already knew.

37

OUR FINGERPRINTS CAN'T BE ON IT

"Imagine if gold turned to lead when stolen."

—SATOSHI NAKAMOTO

December 4, 1939 (cont'd)

The gaswagen was an all-wheel-drive Saurer van with a four-cylinder engine and a modified chassis. The rear exhaust pipe was elongated and attached via hose to the main cabin. When the engine was running, the fumes that would normally be expelled out of the exhaust were instead rerouted back into the body of the wagon, which was separated and sealed from the driver's compartment. The modifications appeared to have been made by hand. The machine had the ungainly look of a prototype.

The wagon could fit ten men at a time in its chamber, probably closer to fifteen if the occupants were women or children. Once the engine was going, it took fewer than thirty minutes for the people inside the chassis to asphyxiate.

A group of enterprising SS officers made the modifications on the military wagon themselves. They tested it by driving it through a set of small towns in western Poland within the newly Nazi-controlled area. They stopped at mental hospitals, loaded patients into the van ten at a time, and measured how long it took them to die.

Two months prior, the same SS unit had been going into hospitals and shooting the patients one by one before tossing the bodies in hastily dug mass graves. But apparently the military brass were concerned about their supply of bullets—perhaps because of Hitler's own experiences in the Great War, where he'd seen how an ammunition supply crisis had precipitated Germany's defeat. This time, Hitler had personally seen to it that the Wehrmacht would be amply stocked—thanks to all the metals being refined in the work camps—and the SS had been additionally instructed not to overuse their pistols. Which led this unit to experiment with gas.

The Professor spoke the most Polish, so she was the one to read aloud the secret cable from the Swiss spy in Warsaw reporting that he'd seen this prototype gaswagen. After she finished, she excused herself to the powder room. She didn't return for a full twenty minutes. DuBois went over to the curtained windows, bowed his head, and whispered what sounded like a prayer. Pehle went out for liquor, and he wasn't the only one who needed a drink. Saxon produced a flask from a file cabinet.

Ansel had been fighting the urge to vomit since he'd first scanned the stolen carbon. He'd known from the papers how difficult things had gotten for the Jews and other "undesirables" of Germany and western Poland. Yet all he'd read up until now felt airily abstract in comparison to the brutal reality of what one SS unit was doing to mental patients in Poznań and Warta. The apocalypse that Ansel had felt nearing was a mere sensation, an intimation of worry. Cable 631 detailed the actual murder of specific human beings. The thousands of lives shattered on Kristallnacht were hard to envisage. The image of a young woman with brain trouble being led by an orderly into the back of a wagon where she'd be suffocated to death while the soldiers timed it—that, Ansel could picture.

White read the Professor's translation of the cable himself when he returned from the president's fish room. He showed no reaction at all. Ansel hadn't expected tears, but he had imagined something more than the usual reach for his Luckys.

Ansel asked a few questions about how things had gone with Breckinridge Long in their intentionally pointless meeting. White just kept his eyes on the carbon, seeming to read it over and over again.

White's smoke plumed. "We have to get this cable to the White House. And we have to do it carefully."

They'd already broken any number of federal laws to get their hands on this carbon. But Ansel knew that if he asked anyone in that room to break all ten of the Bible's commandments in order to put an end to what it described, he would be met with no hesitation.

Saxon stood. "Hell, I'll walk this over there right now."

White shook his head. "Think it through, kid."

Ansel realized White was correct. "How'd we get this cable?"

White nodded. "If we go to the Oval and say that we stole it, what will happen?"

Saxon was indignant. "They'll fire us? Who cares? People need to know that this is happening. If Roosevelt needs to put somebody in jail for the theft, I volunteer."

"I appreciate the offer. But that isn't the problem."

Pehle, who had returned with vodka, appeared to work it through as well. "Damn it."

"What?" Saxon looked to Pehle as if suddenly betrayed from another end.

Ansel approached Saxon and put a friendly hand on the boy's shoulder. "If we show the White House this carbon copy of a stolen cable, they'll go to State to confirm its authenticity. Wouldn't you?"

He indicated that it would be the reasonable thing to do.

"Then," Ansel continued, "Long will say it's forged. There's no original. And because we stole the copy, we can't prove that it's genuine. Moreover, we can't tell anyone it exists without alerting Long to the fact that we're on to him. We have the upper hand right now. We know that he's burying evidence of Nazi atrocities in Poland. And so long as no one puts in a request for this cable, he'll remain in the dark about what we know."

It was only months ago that Saxon had been in cap and gown at his college graduation. "So what do we do?"

White took control. "We get this information to the White House another way. They need to discover this as part of their routine business—and they need to discover it without Long's realizing they've done so. Our fingerprints can't be anywhere near the crime scene."

"We get someone *else* to request the cables." The Professor stood at the door. She wore a look of sternness the likes of which Ansel had not seen on her before.

"But this is the only copy," Saxon said. "Unless we slip it back in the library—which puts it right back within Long's clutches—an inter-agency request for this cable will come up empty."

"We don't get someone to request *this* cable." The Professor's voice was cold. "We get someone to request an unrelated cable. And then we see to it that they receive this one instead. It'll look like a clerical error—some batty secretary sent over the wrong papers. But if the person we trick into making the request is smart, observant, and not a monster, they'll read it—or the handy translation we clip beneath it—and they'll understand exactly what they've got in their hands. They'll think *they've* discovered it. And they'll take it to the White House."

She looked at her boss for confirmation: The plan was smart, and she knew it.

Though this did leave them, Ansel thought, with one more problem. "Who can we trick into requesting State Department documents? Who we know is in the habit of requesting papers like these? And who has the security clearance to file the request? And who we know for sure isn't secretly a Nazi sympathizer?"

White turned to him. "You don't happen to know anyone working with a unit of senior FBI agents conducting extensive surveillance on government officials, do you?"

38

THE STENCH OF
A MARSH

*"The only antidote to dangerous ideas is strong
alternatives vigorously advocated."*

—LARRY SUMMERS

December 12, 1939

Ansel insisted that he was perfectly capable of selling their scheme to
his wife on his own. But White was adamant about coming along and
making the case to her personally. Ansel thought that perhaps he
wanted to observe her reaction himself so that he could gauge her
trustworthiness.

Angela was officially on her lunch break as she walked beneath the
shadow of the Washington Monument listening to White describe
two elaborate conspiracies. The first concerned a coterie of high-
ranking Nazi sympathizers inside the State Department. The second
concerned what would be required to expose them. Angela didn't interrupt as he spoke, and neither did Ansel. They strolled together as a
threesome, Angela in the middle. Her hands remained fixed in her
pockets, tugging her only winter coat tight.

"Lying in the service of a good cause," she said when he'd finished,
"is still lying."

"We're not asking you to lie," White explained gently. "We're asking you to assist in the telling of the truth."

The park wasn't crowded, given the cold. A few bureaucrats sat
alone with brown-paper lunches on the wooden benches. In the dis-

tance, a crew of workers swarmed the half-built Jefferson Memorial. The bones of the stone structure had taken shape, a wide foundation in the dirt and cornerstones lofted high into the air, but the building didn't yet have walls. From this distance, it looked like a toy model, made from balsa wood and Elmer's glue.

"You want me to forge an inter-agency document request on behalf of one of my agents," Angela said, "requesting a ream of random, unimportant State Department cables."

"Yes," White said.

"And then, when those cables arrive, you want me to intercept them and insert this carbon, your cable number 631, into the stack. Such that the inclusion looks to have been a clerical error. And then, somehow, you want me to get one of the agents to look over this stack of cables that he never requested, thereby 'discovering' 631."

"You work alongside these fellas. You must know which one is most likely to make a ruckus if he sees something like this."

"The document request forms, the classified ones . . . They have to be signed."

"You're telling me that none of those agents has ever asked you to sign something for him while he was out?"

Angela made it clear that what he was asking her to do was significantly more dangerous than scribbling an agent's name on some meaningless memorandum.

"I'm not saying it's going to be easy. If it was, I wouldn't need to ask you."

Ansel had never seen White play the salesman before. He'd never used honey to get what he'd needed out of his recruits, had he? Ansel was surprised to discover that he had such a silver tongue in his mouth. It felt particularly strange to stand there listening to him sweet-talk his wife.

"It's important, Angela. You don't need me reminding you what the stakes are here. The way Ansel tells it to me, you know all of that better than anybody. You've been reading your papers every morning, worried sick about the state of the world. You've got this sweet girl and you want her to have a life as good as or better than the one the world's afforded you. I want that for my own girls. Only, the world around us is not so obliging as it was when we were young, is it? It's falling apart. Because of men like Adolf Hitler. And because of men like Breckinridge Long. Fighting back against those bastards is why you've been writing letters to the editor, why you joined your charities back in Minnesota. Heck, that's why you joined up with the FBI, isn't it? So that you could *do something*. Well? The pitcher has put the ball in the air. You're in the batter's box. And the only question you need to answer today is: Are you gonna take a swing?"

Ansel barely remembered telling White those details about her. Perhaps White had been paying more attention than he'd realized.

She turned to her husband. "This is the only way?"

He imagined what would happen if the FBI caught her forging a signature on a classified document. Would she be assured time in prison? He pictured himself raising their daughter alone. Telling Angie that her mother would not be home for a while, but that she'd gone away in the service of something more than good. Only months ago, he'd imagined sacrificing his own life for their cause. Now, here he was, asking her to potentially sacrifice hers.

"Yes," he said. "I wish it wasn't, but we just can't come up with any other way than this."

"All right. Then I'll take my swing."

They spent a few more minutes finishing their loop around the monument. They went over the details of her operation: the procedures involved in inter-agency document requests, where the envelopes were kept, what floor of the stone Department of Justice building on Pennsylvania Avenue housed the mail room.

Delving into the specifics, all three of them seemed to be able to talk themselves into a confidence that this would work.

Then she was bidding the men goodbye. Before she disappeared into the crowd of bureaucrats, she gave White a hearty handshake. Ansel leaned in for a reassuring kiss.

On her lips, he felt her quivering excitement.

39

HAMMER

"If economists wished to study the horse, they wouldn't go and look at horses. They would sit in their studies and say to themselves, 'What would I do if I were a horse?'"

—RONALD COASE,
NOBEL PRIZE—WINNING BRITISH ECONOMIST

December 20, 1939

The other members of the Research Department had all sorts of admiring words for Ansel's marriage. "Now that's a good woman," was how Saxon put it, a touch of wistfulness in his voice, after Ansel told them what she'd agreed to do. "That sort of trust the two of you have . . . A real belief in each other . . . It's not so easy to find."

Ansel hadn't ever gotten the impression that "trust," exactly, was what Saxon had been looking for in a girl. But whatever he was after, he sure seemed to have a hard time finding it.

"I knew I liked her," the Professor declared. "I didn't think you'd marry somebody who was afraid of getting her hands dirty."

Oliphant said he couldn't imagine even telling his wife about half the things they'd been doing here, much less asking her to participate. Julia, he said, demanded they unwrap the Christmas presents early because she couldn't bear the anticipation.

Pehle had known Angela socially for a long time. He'd always sensed she was a good egg.

DuBois asked if she had a sister.

Their admiration was followed by an endless cavalcade of questions. Ansel had never felt his marriage to be under such scrutiny. Was his wife the anxious type, they wanted to know? How had she reacted to the grim contents of cable number 631? Did the Luxfords have any Jewish friends? How was it that they both came to care about their cause so much as to take such risks?

Was he sure she was up to the challenge?

The day Angela was set to file the forged document request, Ansel was a nervous wreck. He'd never felt so useless as his wife put on a dark green dress of heavy wool—something that wouldn't stick out. She went to work like it was any other day. He started in on Saxon's stash of whiskey by nine A.M. He couldn't focus on anything else, so he just sat there like a chump, scratching at his temples, fending off questions from the others who were clearly unable to focus on anything else either.

Ansel rushed back to Bloomingdale early. She wasn't there, which was no surprise.

He told Lucretia that he'd look after Angie. While his wife handled the family espionage, he painted watercolor flowers with their daughter. What a gift! He'd been working so much in these past few months, he'd barely seen her. He realized he hadn't been alone with her for a single minute since they'd moved.

He taped the paintings to the fridge. He showed Angie the letters of their common name: L-U-X-F-O-R-D.

Angela was late getting home. It was long past dark by the time he heard the sound of her key in the lock. She hadn't even gotten her coat off yet when he wrapped her in his arms. She'd made it back in one piece. That, at least, was something.

"I did it," she whispered. Angie's little stomps approached. She tromped headfirst toward her mother, colliding with her knees.

He picked Angie up and held them both close. "You did it?"

Angela smiled, clearly proud. "The request is in. I saw the messenger take it out of the building. We should get a batch of cables back in a few days."

The hammer was cocked.

40

AN UNLOCKED CABINET IN THE THIRD-FLOOR MAIL ROOM

"In the war services . . . the best security for an early conclusion is a plan for long endurance."

—JOHN MAYNARD KEYNES,
HOW TO PAY FOR THE WAR

January 19, 1940

Nearly a month went by.

The problem, Angela explained, was that things at the FBI had gotten awfully busy. First, a Nazi diplomat who worked at the German consulate in New York was found murdered in his Queens apartment. Berlin was livid, and Hitler himself accused the American government of potential involvement. The United States and Germany were not at war; how dare the American government sit by idly while a German citizen—and an official, at that—was killed on its soil! Unless, rumors suggested, the American government had played some part in this murder . . .

Ansel figured that one dead Nazi was a decent start, and he suspected the FBI probably *had* been in on the hit. But Roosevelt did not take kindly to the accusation, so J. Edgar Hoover was forced to trot out in front of the cameras and vow to solve the case personally. This mess, Angela reported, was taking quite a lot of energy from the FBI.

What's more, weeks later, the Bureau successfully arrested eighteen members of the Christian Front, a known anti-Semitic organization, who'd stolen cordite, rifles, and 3,500 rounds of ammunition from a New York National Guard storehouse. The theft was made possible by the fact that most of the criminals were themselves National Guardsmen. They planned to use the weapons to stage simultaneous assaults on Jewish newspapers, Jewish movie theaters, and the American League for Peace and Democracy in Brooklyn. The organization's manifesto advocated for the "eradication" of all Jews in the United States, and assuredly more members remained at large, planning further attacks. It fell to Hoover's FBI to stop them.

Which meant they had bigger things to worry about than some batch of State Department cables that no one had actually requested. The papers sat untouched in an unlocked cabinet in the third-floor mail room. Angela reported that she was able to slip the copy of cable number 631 into the stack with ease. The hard part was getting anyone to notice it.

The weeks seeped away. Lost time. Lost lives.

The news from abroad grew as dark as the short winter days. The Soviet army took Finland, or most of it—another morsel they'd found ripe for the taking. Meanwhile, British ships were sunk daily as the country contemplated a coming food shortage. Within Germany, Hitler's power grew with his popularity: He'd promised war. He'd delivered. And they weren't just winning; they were winning faster than anyone had predicted.

The British army made further use of Cash and Carry at the start of the new year by ordering more aircraft—twelve thousand of them.

But British gold reserves were falling to near zero and the dollar reserves they spent on the international markets were dwindling. Keynes not only sent insistent letters to Morgenthau and Roosevelt, but he also wrote up his concerns in a book and had the thing published. *How to Pay for the War,* which concerned not only how the UK should pay for her share but how the United States should pay for a larger one, became, somehow, an international bestseller.

White blew a gasket. Their dispute should be far too technical and arcane for *The Wall Street Journal,* and yet now, thanks to Keynes, the method by which the UK paid America for weapons had become a matter of public concern. Moreover, the Oval Office had to assure anyone who asked that while Keynes was asking for American assistance—demanding it, in fact—America was not actually "assisting" the British in any meaningful sense. "We are but a neutral arms dealer," et cetera. The argument was growing more ridiculous by the day, but thankfully the White House had no compunction about sticking to it. If hypocrisy was the price that virtue paid to vice, as they said, then how much would out-and-out fraud cost?

White suggested to Downing Street that they could get the dollars required to pay for these twelve thousand planes by selling the *Queen Mary*. He was being provocative, but he had a point. The eighty-thousand-ton ocean liner was the pride of the Cunard-White Star Line, the most elegant of passenger ships on which to cross the Atlantic. The White Star company had famously spent about seventeen million pounds sterling on its construction—but it was now secondhand, so how about ten million? The Treasury would be happy to buy it, and to pay in dollars—which conveniently could be applied directly to the war debt the UK was racking up.

Keynes did not deign to respond personally to the offer. The Exchequer declined politely.

The point, White insisted, was the precedent. If Roosevelt insisted on sending weaponry to our allies, and Keynes obstinately refused to pay for them, then we would simply send them bills until they came to their senses. Ansel worked with Pehle and Oliphant to calculate these bills, which Morgenthau dutifully passed along. By the end of February, the UK owed America just under five hundred million dollars. The British were on their way to running up the largest bar tab in human history. And it was unclear when—or how—or even if—they might pay.

Which suggested certain lines of inquiry for the group's efforts on postwar planning. Whatever the future of the global economy looked like, if it did not involve German victory then—as Keynes had feared—it would likely involve British penury. They set aside Wednesday breakfasts for their meetings on the subject. When they needed a break from their work escalating America's involvement in this war, they would spend a few hours working to prevent the next one.

They didn't know precisely what Keynes's vision for his new global currency was, nor did they know much about his design for the world economy other than that it evidently featured a significant role for sterling: Why else would Keynes be working to expand his sterling bloc, much less to insert sterling into the Cash and Carry deal? But White instructed them not to burden themselves trying to figure out Keynes. "Whatever he's doing, you can be sure it'll be entirely self-serving. If we want an enduring peace, we need a plan that actually does what it says on the tin."

DuBois took to this mission with unexpected enthusiasm. Ansel should have seen it coming: DuBois's fervent pacifism was being tested daily as he made arrangements for the financing of Thompson sub-machine guns. So to take part in designing a global economic order that could stop potential wars before they started? That must have sounded like heaven.

One morning he bounded into the office brandishing his worn Bible. "I've been praying on currency."

Ansel felt himself instinctively recoiling at the sight of the book. He didn't appreciate proselytizing, and he had far too much on his mind to concern himself with another man's prayers.

"And wouldn't you know it?" DuBois's face was flush. "It came to me! A stroke of inspiration. Matthew 22:21."

Saxon scratched his head. White lit a smoke.

"Can you remind us," Ansel asked, "which verse that is again? It's been a while since Sunday school."

" 'Render unto Caesar what is Caesar's . . .' You know the rest. The idea is so simple: What is of the Lord's purview should remain so. What is the purview of man, of our grubby governments and dirty money—it's the humdrum stuff of the here and now."

"Which suggests?" Pehle led him along.

"Keynes has the right idea. But he's trying too hard."

White nodded approvingly. Any criticism of Keynes was good enough for him.

"Keynes is right," DuBois continued, "that the way to stop the next war is to knit economic bonds between countries so tight that war becomes too unwieldy to pursue. Economic interdependence: Any thread in the spider's web breaks, the whole thing crashes. No nation can afford to go to war with another without crashing their own economy."

Ansel remembered his own barroom analysis. "The Reich was able to do what they've done because they spent five years severing Germany from the world economy."

"So we need a system that prevents that kind of severing. Or, at least, hugely disincentivizes it. You want to wage war? Fine. It'll make you broke."

"Keynes seems to want to accomplish that by way of his new currency," the Professor said.

"It's the right aim," DuBois said. "But the wrong medium. We don't need a new currency to tie every nation on earth together. We already have one that'll do just fine."

A moment of silence. The flick of lighters.

"Can we have a hint?" Pehle was doing his best to tolerate DuBois's eccentricities.

"You each have a few in your pockets right now."

White ashed vigorously. "American dollars are already becoming a common global reserve currency. Ecuadorian sucre pegs to it; Cuban, Dominican, and Swiss public debt is denominated in it. Meantime, Keynes's sterling bloc is shaky. The gold bloc is no more, and nobody who lived through the Depression wants it back. When Greece exports olives to France, their central bank ends up holding francs, or the French have to keep all these drachmas around, both of which are constantly changing in value—it's a mess. It's cumbersome. And it's fragile."

The Professor said, "If we made American dollars the standard reserve currency all across the globe—the chits by which every nation could settle their foreign trade—then it would function as a de facto world currency."

"We wouldn't have to invent anything new," DuBois said. "We

needn't overturn the heavens. Or even push against the rising tide. We could simply wash the world clean in an endless sea of dollars."

"Which," White added, "we control. We make 'em. We ship 'em. They're ours."

Pehle responded as if the suggestion were rather gauche. "Isn't that a concern? We'd be signing every country in the world up to a system in which we're in control."

"Exactly!" White had never before seemed so enthusiastic. "*Some-one* has to be in charge. I'm thinking it'll either be Adolf Hitler, Maynard Keynes, or us. Who would you gents prefer?"

Ansel hesitated. The dollar idea had merit, without a doubt. But was White advocating for it because it was the best path to a future peace? Or because it had come from someone, anyone, besides Keynes?

"You say that Keynes's plans won't work because they'll only serve to place him in charge," Ansel humbly ventured. "But isn't placing ourselves in charge the prime merit of this dollars idea?"

White raised an eyebrow in Ansel's direction. "I do sometimes forget that you're only an attorney."

Saxon cleared his throat and spoke for the first time. "We don't know what Keynes's plan really is, do we? But we do know that we need a global reserve currency and sterling won't do. Inventing something new is . . . Well, how could we have any assurance that it would work?"

Ansel didn't have an answer.

Saxon had always taken to efficiency above philosophy.

White was certainly gung ho, that much was obvious. And DuBois was proud of his breakthrough.

But Ansel caught Pehle giving him a look: a fellow doubting Thomas. Perhaps Pehle valued diplomacy more than the others, especially when it came to theoretical plans to prevent hypothetical wars.

From the Professor's silence, Ansel gathered that she harbored her own misgivings. The global economy assuredly had more moving parts than the used car she'd recently purchased, and building one from scratch would require detailed schematics. Dollars might serve well as its fuel. But that didn't explain how the carburetor was going to work.

Her eyes looked cloudy, as if she were already deep into a host of technical details.

Ansel remembered something Keynes had asked him: In what does one need to believe in order to grant money its power? The power White was soon to seek for the dollar would be supreme.

If they were to build an empire of dollars, then in what, precisely, would they be asking people to believe?

41

SUPPLY AND DEMAND

*"MMT [Modern Monetary Theory] says that
the government's deficit is always someone else's surplus."*

—STEPHANIE KELTON,
TWENTY-FIRST-CENTURY AMERICAN ECONOMIST

March 6, 1940

Washington grew like a mosquito engorged on fresh blood. It puffed full of the new bodies who moved to the District each week. They arrived in the big city by the thousands to find jobs in FDR's rapidly expanding government. No one who came, it seemed, had any trouble landing work.

Dry cleaners were becoming millionaires. All these new government workers wore shirts, and those shirts needed washing and pressing. The demand was so great that the shop owners were obliged to raise prices accordingly. Ansel spilled coffee on himself one day and went to the place on Adams Street. Eight dollars, they'd charged him. For a single suit.

He was taking in his own dry cleaning these days: Angela had significantly more important things to do. He imagined that the life of a double agent would be hard on her. Maybe lying to the FBI while working every day inside it would cause her as many sleepless nights as his own secret-keeping had caused him.

It did, though not in the way he'd guessed. He'd never seen her with so much energy. It was as if she'd waited for this moment her entire life, and now that it had arrived, she didn't want to miss a single second. Finally, her beliefs—her politics and her deepest convictions—had a productive outlet. Thought and action were at last unified. She was able to support FDR publicly as a typist in his Department of Justice while simultaneously doing so in secret by aiding the schemes of his Treasury. She even found time for biweekly meetings of the Catholic Daughters of the Americas. The war in Europe was producing Jewish refugees by the thousands, and Angela felt that the Catholic Daughters was the ideal organization to advocate for them. Every moment of her waking hours was spent in the service of her ideals. Even Angie benefited; suddenly her mother was reading her four books every night instead of two.

Ansel had feared for the worst. But Angela, it seemed, found meaning in doing her best.

She was in boom times, just like the city around her. Finding a place to live that wasn't under her parents' roof became near impossible. She spotted an ad for a three-bedroom house for rent in Adams Morgan that, by the time she arrived, had already been let out as four separate apartments to four young typists from who knew where. The girls were ready with their suitcases and portable Underwoods and whatever money they'd brought with them for their first month's rent.

Finally, in February, the Luxfords had been able to buy two stories of weather-beaten old wood in McLean, Virginia. The place had been a farm up until the previous year, though as Ansel took in the cracks along the icicle-sharp eave and the torn mosquito netting around the porch, he didn't think it could have been much of one. But McLean was just over the river from the District, and it was still mostly sheep farms out here, save for the few families that grew blackberries or corn.

The house needed more than a few repairs. Helpfully, Ansel was good with a handsaw. So while his weeks were spent above a furniture store on Twelfth Street, his weekends were spent cutting and sanding acacia in the farmhouse's garage, which he turned into his workshop so he could make as much noise as he needed without disturbing Angie's afternoon naps. It felt good to do something with his hands. At work, all he'd managed to accomplish was the sending of fretful memoranda. He proposed scheme after scheme to collapse the Mefo bill market,

knowing full well that while Breckinridge Long was around to conspire against the Research Department, none of his plans could ever
come to pass.

The memorandum that could end this nightmare was sitting in an
FBI mail room. And all that needed to happen for the dawn to break
was for someone, anyone, to find it.

Ansel was growing to resent his suits. Knotting his bow tie every
morning felt like putting on a costume so that he could playact that
they were making progress. He filled page after page with ink that no
one would read. He analyzed data sets in order to tell his colleagues
what they already knew: They were losing. And they were losing
faster and faster.

He ordered a couple of pairs of green canvas coveralls from the
Sears catalog. Every day, when he got home from the office, he flung
off his jacket and tie as fast as he could and put on the baggy work
clothes. The first time she saw them, Angela said they looked like fa-
tigues. Was he planning on volunteering for the army?

He wished he could. Instead, he retired to the garage most nights
after dinner. The house's staircase needed fresh boards; the rain gutters
around the roof required repair; the plumbing in the kitchen sink was
desperate for overhaul.

He was in the garage one Sunday afternoon, dreading the idea of
returning to the office for another fruitless week, when Angela poked
her head in the door. He had a call.

"Morgenthau wants to see us," were White's first words after Ansel
picked up the receiver.

"When? Why?"

"Now. And we'll find out when we get there, won't we?"

———

ANSEL ONLY HAD TIME to toss a few things into his overnight bag.
Morgenthau was at his Hudson Valley estate in East Fishkill, and he
wanted White and Ansel there by nightfall.

They just barely made the next train to New York, then transferred
at Grand Central to the commuter line upstate. Morgenthau's driver

collected them from the station at Hopewell Junction and took them down the dark country roads, through quiet acres of what the driver said were the biggest squash in the whole valley. "They put the president's to shame." He gestured into the darkness at what Ansel had to assume was Roosevelt's summer estate.

The acres of apple orchards were dark when they arrived, but lights glowed from inside Morgenthau's main farmhouse. Their warmth poured from the windows, illuminating the red paint on the wood slats as the car pulled to a stop.

Ansel carried his overnight bag inside. The driver said that Mr. Morgenthau was waiting, and that they should go up directly. They'd be shown to their rooms after he had finished with them.

Morgenthau's second-floor study was small and without bookshelves. There was a desk and a telephone in the center, and it seemed that these tools—pens and long-distance lines—were the ones Morgenthau most employed. He was no scholar, Ansel reasoned, and he had no need to prove his erudition.

Morgenthau looked up from the letter he was handwriting.

"There's been some turmoil at the State Department," he said after a perfunctory greeting. "Investigations into the staff."

Neither Ansel nor White said a word.

"Suggestions," Morgenthau continued, "of providing aid to the Nazis."

Ansel did his best not to react. Morgenthau let the silence hang, heavy and hot, for what felt like an eternity.

"You gentlemen wouldn't know anything about that, would you?"

White matched the length of his boss's pause. "No."

Morgenthau looked to Ansel for confirmation. He simply shook his head.

Morgenthau gazed at his half-written letter pensively, tapping his pen against the desk. "You don't know anything about messages to Breckinridge Long? Or an inquiry into Polish cables by the FBI?"

White took a step forward, as if blocking Ansel from incoming fire. "What's Roosevelt going to do?"

It seemed that White felt an obligation to his boss and friend not to lie to his face. Ansel watched something pass between the two men. He thought it just might be respect.

"It's a tricky situation." Morgenthau leaned back in his chair. "Long has many allies. Not only in the White House. Old friends, you know, have a way of forgiving each other's incurable sins."

He looked pointedly at White.

"Aiding the enemy?" White said. "Sounds to me like treason."

"Perhaps your attorney can educate you on the subject. Mr. Luxford, are we at war with anyone right now?"

"No, sir." Ansel felt that he'd best serve White with brevity.

"So we don't have enemies to aid, do we?"

"No."

Morgenthau made a show of throwing up his hands in defeat.

White grew indignant. "So Roosevelt is going to let a man like Breckinridge Long remain at the State Department?"

"The politics of removing him are too delicate. He knows where the bodies are buried, and he has powerful benefactors who, at the first sign of his distress, would start shining extremely bright lights into all those darkened tombs. I'd imagine you two might understand better than anyone that at the moment, Long isn't the only one with schemes to hide."

White huffed in silence. They hadn't even achieved anything of note in these past months. It was shameful to think that all they had to hide was a lengthy string of failures.

"Long is not out," Morgenthau continued. "But he can, with pressure, be held at bay."

White perked up. "He doesn't know about this, does he? What you're telling us, what the FBI told the president?"

Morgenthau shook his head. "Let's say that keeping him on a leash will be my job." He smiled, as if relishing the task. "You have far too much to do."

"Such as?"

Morgenthau stood, drawing their brief meeting to a close. "Over the past months, you've proposed a number of schemes for crippling the German economy: cutting off their supply of cotton from Brazil;

confiscating their supply of dollars held in American financial institutions; isolating their currency so the Ponzi scheme at the heart of the
Nazi system reaches a breaking point. Each time, Long has quietly
stuck a thorn in your side."

"And now?"

"Now, my friends, the White House has given me permission to
box Long out, and given you permission to do . . . well, whatever it is
you want to do. No one will stand in your way. Whatever actions you
deem appropriate to take to stem the Nazi threat are preemptively approved."

Morgenthau turned to the windows. As if, perhaps, hiding a proud
smile. "So how far do you want to go?"

42

ALL YOU ARE
IS RICH

*"The only good reason to have money is this:
So that you can tell any SOB in the world to go to hell."*

—HUMPHREY BOGART

May 8, 1940

When the most powerful men on Wall Street issued their most danger-ous threats, their voices grew soft and their smiles grew wide. The more senior the banker, the more he seemed intent on letting Ansel know that he only wanted to be helpful. The most sinister advice was presented through toothy grins: He was a family man, wasn't he? Surely he had ambitions beyond serving as Harry Dexter White's amanuensis. It wasn't too late to turn back and settle this reasonably.

The first time the managing partner of a major New York invest-ment bank implied that he had the power to send the Luxfords into generational poverty, Ansel was intimidated. By the tenth such threat, he had become inured.

"One should be careful in choosing one's enemies," J. P. Morgan Jr. told him on what must have been the twelfth of these meetings. "It's a good thing for a man to have a few. But pick the wrong one . . ." His reedy voice trailed off. Well into his seventies, Morgan's gray mustache had attained roughly the same curvature as his portly belly. He spoke to Ansel with the hoarse condescension of experience.

Ansel gazed around the room at the half-dozen bankers and lawyers Morgan had brought with him. On Ansel's side of the long conference table, he was alone. Outside the window, a gentle spring rain fell across Manhattan. He could just make out the tops of a few umbrellas bobbing down Wall Street past the triangle-shaped, limestone House of Morgan.

"I was at your son's firm yesterday," he replied. "Did he tell you?"

"Our businesses are run independently."

"Of course, of course. But he's just down the street." Ansel pointed in the direction of Number 1 Wall Street, home of the investment bank Morgan Stanley. It was only a block away from J.P. Morgan and Co., the commercial bank from which it had been split off. "Must be nice, you two working so close by. Meeting for lunch in the middle of the day."

The elder Morgan appeared to register Ansel's veiled threat. He'd likely heard it before. After the two Morgans were forced to separate their companies, a sharp line drawn between the investment side and the commercial one, improper communication—or coordination— between father and son could prove criminal. Ansel was, after all, from the government.

"I haven't spoken to my son recently. But do pass along my regards. Something tells me he doesn't appreciate goons from the Treasury Department sticking their necks where they don't belong any more than I do." Morgan sighed wistfully. "Not that I'm privy to his thoughts."

"I'll be sure to share your insights with my colleagues at the SEC."

"Mr. Luxford," Randolph Paul interjected from beside his client, J. P. Morgan, "I think I can be of assistance here."

Paul was around fifty. He wore a baggy pinstripe suit and thick black eyeglasses. His wispy hair was combed—poorly—over his bald spot. He looked, Ansel could not help thinking, like a turtle.

He was also inarguably the most esteemed finance attorney in the country. His genial demeanor and slight country accent disguised the rapier-sharp mind of a man whose firm guided taxation and regulatory efforts for all of the largest companies on Wall Street.

Paul leaned in. "From one tax attorney to another, what you've proposed here is a sledgehammer of a solution to a problem we can resolve with a scalpel."

To describe Randolph Paul as a "tax attorney" was like describing King Kong as a monkey. He was the preeminent star in a field within which Ansel was but a middling nobody. Though to be fair, to describe what Ansel was doing to the most powerful financial institutions in the country as a "sledgehammer" would constitute a similar understatement.

Ansel leaned in to match him. "It's not a sledgehammer, it's a grenade. And I'm not proposing. I'm telling you what's about to happen."

Morgan started to speak, but Paul jumped in before he could. "You and your colleagues at Treasury have expressed a desire to stem the flow of dollars into Germany."

"We've explained that we're going to halt it entirely."

"To do so, you've suggested requiring us to file disclosures on each of our customers' accounts whenever they might want to transact in Germany."

It was Ansel's turn to feign helpfulness. "Oh no, you misunderstand."

"Good."

"It's much more restrictive than that."

Paul scowled.

Ansel felt it his duty to speak plainly. "If anyone with an account at your institution wants to move dollars—or any dollar-denominated security—to a financial institution or company in Germany, they must first get our permission. They'll fill out a disclosure form explaining why the money is being moved, and then, at our leisure, we'll let you know whether you're permitted to make the transaction."

"Mr. Luxford, filling out all these forms and sending them to D.C. for a response will slow our clients' transactions to an untenable crawl. No one can do business under those conditions."

"I agree. Which is why we're going to bring our regulators to you." Ansel tapped his toes against the marble floor for emphasis. "We're going to install a Treasury Department employee in every branch of your bank."

Morgan did not appear able to contain himself any longer. "Son, this won't do. This institution will not be—"

"Don't worry. We're going to install our men in the branches of all of your competitors as well."

A hush fell across the room. The audacity of Ansel's plan was finally landing on the Wall Street men.

"That would require," Paul said, "what? A thousand new Treasury accountants? Two thousand?"

Ansel nodded. "Ten thousand. We'll supply their salaries. You'll supply their office space."

Morgan grumbled. A few of the others whispered to one another. Ansel imagined that their murmurs were likely curses, aimed at him.

The scheme had been worked out by the team over the past few months, though its basic form had been the one suggested by Ansel the previous autumn: plucking the German-owned gold from the nests of American financial institutions. But now Oliphant—who'd been exploring the practicalities for over a year—had developed a more elegant solution: They wouldn't need to confiscate anything. They could simply preclude the banks from transferring it. If the SS forced a Czech citizen to turn over the contents of his savings at an American bank? All Treasury had to do was forbid the bank from moving the money. It wouldn't matter how much the SS stole—what good was money if you couldn't use it?

The idea had been so simple in its audacity that neither Oliphant nor White thought they'd be allowed to do it. But once Roosevelt had fired the starter pistol, they were off to the races. And in a strangely helpful way, the Germans had provided them with political cover by invading Norway, Sweden, and finally northern France. The rapid expansion of German territorial ambitions had come as no surprise to the Research Department—they'd predicted it the previous year—but the sudden display of imperial ambition erupted in bold type across every newspaper in the world. If anyone had thought that Germany would stop after Czechoslovakia and Poland, they now understood otherwise. Ansel had long known that the Nazis could not afford to stop their killing—and as the Seventh Panzer Division marched across the River Meuse, everyone else seemed finally to realize that he'd been right.

The sheer scale of the violence spreading across Europe gave Roosevelt the excuse he needed to push against the edges of his promised neutrality. Officially, America remained an indiscriminate arms dealer, even though in practice she only sold to the British and French. And FDR could now pursue financial sanctions against Germany by the same logic: By stemming the quantity of dollars used in war-making, wasn't he in fact performing a feat of pacifism? America was not involving herself in the war militarily—she was extricating herself from it economically. Hearing Roosevelt announce these policies in a radio address, Ansel was sure he could detect the sly smile that must have been on the president's face as he spoke.

J. P. Morgan Jr. was not taking this development well. He leaned back in his chair, his face hardening, as if he were imagining all the horrible things he might do to this Treasury nobody.

Poor old Randolph Paul was still acting like a lawyer. "This proposal is, as I'm sure you know, plainly unconstitutional."

Ansel shrugged. "Let's find out. Sue us. Your lawsuits will take years to wind their way through the courts. In the meantime, start clearing space for my agents."

Paul said nothing. He'd have to know that Ansel was right.

"This used to be my father's office," Morgan said. "Before we converted it into a conference room. His desk was just over there, beneath the window."

Morgan gestured. Gray light came through the high window and fell on a bust of the great man himself: J. P. Morgan Sr. "This is the room in which my father ruined Thomas Edison. He'd built the fellow up, and then, when the inventor had outlived his usefulness, my father took everything he had with a few strokes of his pen." Morgan sighed regretfully. "You think you're so smart, Mr. Luxford? You might be. But you're not Thomas Edison. What do you think we're going to do to you?"

It occurred to Ansel in that moment that only months before, he would have been petrified by a threat from men such as these.

He packed his notebook and papers back into his black leather case. "You know why you don't frighten me, Mr. Morgan? Because all you are is rich." Ansel snapped the clasp of the case. "You, like your father, like your son, have managed to accumulate a great many dollars. But you forget: We made them. We at the Treasury Department are so pleased that you find our products useful. But they are ours. And we will do with them as we please."

Paul gestured as if preparing to respond, but Ansel did not wait for further argument. He marched out, down the stairs of the venerable House of Morgan, and onto the wet pavement.

The storm was kicking up, and all of Wall Street was drenched in the downpour.

43

HOW TO FIGHT
NAZISM WITH
DOUBLE-ENTRY
BOOKKEEPING

"Hell hath no fury like a bureaucrat scorned."

—MILTON FRIEDMAN

May 14, 1940

By the time Ansel returned to Washington, a trail of livid titans in his wake, the Nazis had overtaken Luxembourg, Neville Chamberlain had resigned the prime ministership, and Winston Churchill was recruited to inherit the unfolding disaster. His promise? To keep the UK fighting. Everyone presumed he was leaving it to Keynes to keep them solvent.

The Treasury Department to which Ansel returned was a new one, literally speaking. While he was in New York, the Research Department split into two teams. Ansel and Saxon moved into offices in the main Treasury building, just down the hall from White. On Twelfth Street, above the furniture store, Pehle would run a new division, no longer secret: Foreign Funds Control. DuBois would help him oversee the hiring of at least ten thousand accountants to ferret out every transaction from an American bank to a German one. But this proved only the beginning. As the Nazis swept across Europe, FFC issued fresh freezing orders for the banks of each country the Nazis conquered. They'd started with Poland. Last week, they added Belgium. On Monday, it was Luxembourg and the Netherlands. The very moment that FFC received word that the Germans had taken control of an area, DuBois would hastily write up an order freezing all transactions to any bank therein. He suggested, given the unbelievable pace of the Nazi victories, that they ought to start freezing assets in anticipation of the German advance. But Pehle astutely noted that they were obligated to do precisely the opposite. Any country that was engaged in fighting the Germans needed *more* dollars, not fewer. Treasury should get them all the dollars they needed. And then yank them away the moment the blitzkrieg made rubble of the local resistance.

The Professor, who was still commuting back and forth from Vassar each week and so found herself borrowing whoever's office was most convenient that day, voiced concerns that in their haste to restrict the flow of dollars, they'd end up mistakenly crashing the economies of friendly nations. French companies needed dollars too. But White was insistent, and Ansel agreed: If the Nazis won, the French economy would face bigger problems than a balance-of-payments crisis. One couldn't make an omelet without breaking a few *oeufs*.

Ansel was proud to enter his new third-floor office for the first time. The fact that they were engaged in wartime planning was no longer a secret, though as Treasury and its Foreign Funds Control division expanded, the need for secrecy about their sharpest anti-Nazi schemes was even greater. There were more ears around to overhear whispers.

The Research Department was officially no more. But then, it had never officially existed in the first place.

In its stead was a tight-knit group of like-minded Treasury agents engaged in a benevolent conspiracy to kneecap the German economy, bolster the British one, and prepare America for the war they were making sure that she entered. Their weekly meetings to hammer out the fine print of the postwar global economy moved to lunchtime at the stool-and-counter on Constitution. Over corned beef on rye and soggy coleslaw, they hashed out White's scheme for a dollar-powered organization to police international trade. He was calling it the "World Bank."

After returning from New York, Ansel spent the morning with Saxon conniving a solution to a new brainteaser that the West Wing sent their way. The president wanted to provide the French with much-needed aerial warcraft. Conveniently, his War Department had dug up 150 fighter planes that would do perfectly. He wanted them in France yesterday. The trick of it was that France lacked both a single ship docked in the United States that was big enough to ferry the planes across and the dollars on hand to pay for them. How, then, to get the planes over without violating the text of Cash and Carry?

It sounded to Ansel like a law school exercise.

The answer he suggested did not, however, dwell upon the legalities. "The War Department says the French have some kind of great big boat in Quebec."

"It'll take at least a week for them to get the thing down here." Saxon was spending as much time on logistics these days as he was on finance.

"Other way around: Fly the planes to Canada. Put 150 American pilots at the wheels."

"That's expedient. But I don't think it's legal. Plus, what about the money?"

"We'll figure out the money somehow. And we won't be *transporting* airplanes to France. We'd be flying them, and they'd happen to land in Quebec. Where the French will provide for their transport."

Saxon rolled his eyes. "You really think anybody will buy that?"

Ansel shrugged. "Put the planes in the air. By the time they're in France, we'll have worked out how it's legal."

They walked down G Street together. Neither had spoken to Pehle or DuBois in a few days and wanted to check on their progress.

"You've started reminding me of someone," Saxon said.

"Who?"

"Harry."

Ansel opened the doors to W&J Sloane. "I appreciate that."

"I'm not sure it's a compliment."

Ansel thought—as he often did—of the woman in the pillbox hat, her eyes on her Perry Mason novel, while beyond the windows of her trolley car a line of Nazis marched into St. Paul. He thought of the way the morning sun had reflected off his own polished shoes as he'd stared at them uselessly.

Harry Dexter White had his faults. But Ansel far preferred being a doer to a worrier.

The Department of Internal Revenue was clearing out the fourth floor to make room for Pehle and DuBois's growing regulatory empire. Ansel and Saxon pressed past uniformed moving men on the staircase before braving a line of potential FFC recruits on the fifth. Ansel didn't think he'd ever seen so many accountants in one place.

"John's getting more popular," Saxon said as they entered what used to be their offices.

Ansel gazed down the line at the applicants. The men—and occasional woman—ranged in age from twenty to probably seventy. Ansel got the impression that they'd come here from all parts of the country; from all the corners of the country's political parties and all its houses of worship. The variety gave him a burst of hope.

"Or maybe," he said, "we're no longer the only ones trying to stop the apocalypse."

They made their way past a pair of new secretaries to find DuBois scratching animatedly at his scalp. His jacket was off. He was deep in conversation with a middle-aged man of some poise.

Ansel didn't see the man's face until he got close.

Randolph Paul smiled beneath his thick black eyeglasses.

"Ansel," said DuBois. "You've met Mr. Paul?"

"Hope you didn't travel all this way just to intimidate the kid," Ansel said to the Wall Street man, gesturing with his chin to DuBois. "You'll find he doesn't scare any easier than I do."

Saxon extended a hand to offer Paul a proper greeting. Ansel thought he might just be starstruck.

"I'm here," Paul said, "because in the span of approximately one week you've managed to make enemies of nearly all the richest men in America."

Ansel considered that an understatement. "Who'd I forget?"

"You're in over your head."

"Send us your lawsuits. We'll hash it out in front of a judge."

DuBois frowned. "Are you suing us?"

Paul shook his head. "Morgan might. But you misunderstand, Mr. Luxford. I'm not here to stop you."

Paul looked at the line of Americans prepared to fight Nazism with double-entry bookkeeping. "I went to Wall Street to get rich. And I did. Now I have more important things on my mind. You've made some powerful enemies, and if you want to keep what you're doing here from being dismantled by men like Morgan, you're going to need all the help you can get.

"I'm here," Paul continued, "for a job."

44

HAVANA

"If we have money,
we shall have friends."

—MENANDER,
ANCIENT GREEK DRAMATIST

July 14, 1940

The war in the Atlantic grew so hot by the summer that only a single shipping route remained between South America and Europe. The volume of exports from everywhere south of Mexico shriveled like dry leaves over a fire. Panic over the economic disaster was setting in. Meanwhile, Germany's territorial ambitions could no longer be denied, not even by their most avid trading partners in Argentina, though the latter's government did take pains to try. Another hemispherical conference was called. This time, the delegates would meet in Cuba.

White sent Ansel and Randolph Paul to Havana a week before the conference was to start. They settled in to a row of adjacent suites in the art deco Hotel Nacional where, from their fourth-floor rooms, they could see Taganana Hill and the sea beyond. Sumner Welles of all people recommended the digs. He'd lived in this hotel for six months back in '33, after the coup, and maintained a warm friendship with the manager. Ansel and Paul spent the week on a tour of the city's best hotel bars making friends.

Word around Havana was that the Americans were coming en masse, and they were coming with money. They were in a mood to spend. Sure, the Americans had some requests, the rumors suggested.

But anyone willing to oblige them would find themselves compensated swiftly and generously.

Ansel would know: He was the one making sure the word got out.

July 21, 1940

"It's a pleasure to make your acquaintance, Mr. White," said Jacome Baggi de Berenger César. A few listless photographers snapped their cameras as the men shook hands. The steps of El Capitolio were filling with diplomats, but White and Jacome went largely unnoticed.

Across from the high Italianate cupola, the sparkling pastels of Havana stretched into the distance. Not even the Cuban summer was humid enough to dampen Ansel's energy as he and Paul, each laden with armfuls of documents, stood behind White. To think that a few months before, Paul had been one of the most powerful lawyers on Wall Street. Now he carried the bags of a mid-level Treasury director. He didn't seem to mind. If anything, he gave the impression that he relished the demotion. Perhaps he harbored secret nostalgias for the life of the young and unproven.

Jacome, Ansel could not fail to notice, had a new aide at his side. She looked eerily similar to the previous one. What, he wondered, had become of the woman who'd slipped him the note in Panama City?

"Jacome," said White, gripping the Brazilian's hand and staring into his dark eyes. "I've heard such great things about you."

———

"SAY, YOU LOOK AMERICAN." A tall, gaunt man of around sixty approached Ansel a few minutes later, once the group had gone off on separate tasks within the cavernous building. "Do you know the way to the east gallery? I'm afraid I've gotten all turned around." The poor guy looked it: bags under his eyes, sweat dampening his shirt collar above a dark, unsuitably heavy jacket.

Ansel pointed to a staircase. "Second floor. Turn left."

The man looked relieved. He offered his thanks and extended a hand. "Breckinridge Long. State Department."

Ansel was confident that he succeeded in hiding his surprise.

"Luxford. Treasury."

Long's palm was sticky. It took a moment of friendly handshaking for Ansel to realize that Long had no idea who he was.

"I sure hope you boys are better organized than we are. They keep giving me the wrong room numbers, bum flight times; would you believe the hotel didn't have my reservation?" Long *harumph*ed. "I don't even know who I'm meeting with now, if anybody."

It occurred to Ansel that he'd never met a Nazi in person before. What had he expected—the devil himself?

Surely they didn't all look so . . . pathetic?

Apparently Morgenthau's operation to box Long out was working. He was the walking wounded and he didn't even know it, wandering aimlessly through a bureaucracy that was conspiring to keep him enfeebled.

Ansel shrugged amiably before bidding Long goodbye. "I wouldn't say Treasury runs like a well-oiled machine or anything, but you know, we get the job done."

———

WITHOUT INTERFERENCE FROM THE State Department, bribing the Brazilians to cut ties with Germany took less than an afternoon. The formal conference was scheduled to kick off at four P.M. with a set of speeches, but Ansel, Paul, and White managed to sketch out a deal with Jacome by three. In the wood-lined library, they sipped sweet café Cubano from porcelain demitasses as the Americans offered to give Brazil what no one else could: dollars. Through some artful changes to the tariff system based on some conceptual work the Professor had suggested back home, American investment capital was going to rush into São Paulo like a biblical flood. Cotton would be just the beginning. U.S. companies would be incentivized to finance massive new steel plants, cocoa farming, and iron drilling—all to be conducted by Brazilian companies supplying jobs exclusively to Brazilian citizens.

Before they shook hands, Paul did have a request: Various Brazilian banks held a bit of German gold, not to mention some German-owned dollars and reais. The U.S. Treasury's Foreign Funds Control had seen fit to block the trading of all such holdings from American banks; surely the Brazilians wouldn't mind blocking the same trades from theirs? They could consider it a show of goodwill toward their new American trading partners.

Jacome was astounded by the size of the ask. Politically, he pointed out, his President Vargas was inclined to support Hitler. Surely Mr. Paul would understand that there was a mutual respect to be found among dictators. It was one thing to sell the Americans some cotton. But was the Brazilian president really expected to commandeer the holdings of private citizens on nothing but the word of the American Treasury?

"Yes," Paul offered. "Because at the end of the day, friend . . . money is money."

Jacome's laughter rang off the crystal chandeliers. "And there is simply no money like American money."

———

WHILE THE DIPLOMATS ON the Committee for the Preservation of Peace assembled in the grand hall for speeches, Ansel and his colleagues returned to the Hotel Nacional and awaited their next customers. The deal they'd given Jacome was more than generous for a reason: Word of their dollar-denominated largesse was spreading through the limestone palaces of central Havana. Other takers were soon to come knocking: The Paraguayans needed money for petroleum, the Ecuadorians for wheat. Even the Argentinean delegation, whose financial arrangements with Germany ran two generations deep, would come by to see what all the fuss was about.

In Panama City, Ansel had moved in secrecy. Here in Havana, he hosted tables of sixteen at the hotel restaurant. Ansel had never in his life dined out with so many people. Back in St. Paul they mostly ate at home. In Harlan? There weren't more than two spots in the whole town, and the Luxfords hadn't patronized either.

Paul rented the rooftop hall of the Ambos Mundos, where Ernest

Hemingway had perfected his recipe for daiquiris. (He added grapefruit juice.) They were on a mission to be loud: as profligate and carefree and heedlessly tipsy as could be.

The nations of South America eagerly negotiated once-in-a-lifetime deals with Americans who seemed too drunk, on both power and rum, to realize what they were doing.

But Ansel knew exactly what he was doing. The diplomats could be depended upon to strike a toothless proclamation of mutual defense and strategic deterrence. Sure, the treaties being hammered out in El Capitolio would say that an attack on any nation of the Americas by a nation from a faraway continent—a long-winded way of saying "Germany or Japan"—was to be treated as an attack on them all. But everyone knew that signing a piece of paper was one thing; drafting young men into war was quite another. Would the United States *really* commit herself to an unpopular one if an errant torpedo happened to strike a Dominican freighter? And would the Dominicans really do likewise, were the United States to decide one day that she ought to come to the defense of her British allies and declare war on Germany?

Ansel wouldn't bet on it.

The State Department did the barking, but it was left to Treasury to produce some bite. By the week's end, all the nations of South and Central America had made lucrative trade deals with the United States. And most had agreed to freeze any German money held within their borders.

This was, at last, the economic warfare that Ansel had long sought to wage. The German economy would not crash overnight. But soon, the Nazis would find themselves plagued by certain deprivations. First cotton . . . then iron . . . And without trading partners or even the currency with which to pay one, their scarcities would grow more and more acute.

While Ansel and his colleagues were in Havana to fight the present war, there could be no mistaking the fruits of their boozy labors: The more dollars the United States plowed into the Americas, the more those nearby nations would hold their foreign exchange reserves in dollars. Gold was unpredictable, its price fluctuating with the haphazard discoveries of some metallurgical mine halfway around the world. Sterling was shriveling as London smoldered. So it wouldn't take long for all the nations of South America to begin trading among one another using the one currency in which they were all newly flush.

July 31, 1940

At the end of their three weeks in Havana, they hauled their hungover bodies onto a brand-new Pan Am Stratoliner bound for Miami. Paul set his hat on the window hook and hunched over the four-seat table as the plane took off with a stomach-churning burst of speed. The Pan Am playing cards rattled in their tabletop case.

"I feel like the French," Paul groaned. "I hadn't expected to win my fight with the rums of Cuba, but I certainly expected I'd stand rather more of a beating before I fell."

Paris had surrendered not long before. The most unnerving part of the French military collapse was not its occurrence, but its speed. The German blitzkrieg bested the French army in a few weeks' time. And *l'armée de terre,* over two million men strong, was substantially better equipped than either the British or the Americans. How long would it take the Wehrmacht to make it to London once it crossed the channel?

It was easy, Ansel felt, when talking about tariffs and currency reserves, to fall into the pleasant comfort of the abstraction finance provided: Money was fiction. The body count, though, was not only real, it was growing.

White ordered three bottles of seltzer and then removed a telegram from the pocket of his ill-fitting linen jacket. "This arrived at the hotel. It came through the military wire."

That meant, Ansel figured, that it had been encrypted.

White continued: "Your friend Mr. Keynes"—he was Ansel's friend now, apparently—"would like to talk."

"Good," Ansel said.

Paul glanced at Ansel. "You're friends with John Maynard Keynes?"

"Harry is giving me a hard time."

"No," White suggested. "I'm giving Keynes a hard time. And you're going to help me do it."

Paul did not let this deter him from being impressed.

Ansel did not know why he'd been elected to serve as middleman. But he certainly agreed they'd need one. "When are we going?"

"According to the Exchequer, who I believe has actually given Keynes some kind of official position again on account of how badly they're losing, he's come to his senses. He wants to talk arms, and he wants to talk dollars. And in a show of goodwill, he's coming to us."

"To Washington?"

"For a *month*." White shivered, as if the dread was already settling in. "But before he makes my life a living hell, he wants to know if you and Angela might be free for dinner."

45

THE AMERICANS WILL
BE SCANDALIZED

"Consider finding a mate. . . . It is indeed a sort of market problem
in that the issue is not just finding a satisfactory person but also
finding someone confronted with the same search problem who
is willing to consider you as his or her best choice."

—ROBERT J. SHILLER,
NOBEL PRIZE—WINNING AMERICAN ECONOMIST

August 20, 1940

The Occidental Grill was far from the most elegant restaurant in the District, but it was the nicest one to which Ansel could convince White to invite Keynes. "I'm not taking John Maynard Keynes to a stool-and-counter for the blue plate special," Ansel exclaimed once White had made clear his intentions. For White, it was a point of defiance: He was not some highfalutin fancy-pants. He was not going to take the trouble to put on a dinner jacket and wings just because *the esteemed Mr. Keynes* had deigned to join the Americans for some grub. Ansel was forced to ask Angela to phone Anne Terry to talk some sense into her obstinate husband.

The Luxfords arrived first, Angela having absconded from the FBI in the afternoon for a visit to the hairdresser. The idea that her husband was conducting business with John Maynard Keynes was interesting and strange, and yet Ansel got the distinct impression that the extra care she took, with curlers and a blue dress he'd never seen before, was for the benefit of another guest: Keynes's wife, Lydia Lopokova.

The ballerina entered the restaurant only moments after they did, her doting husband trailing in her wake. She was barely five feet tall.

She conveyed an aura that was equal parts child and crone, despite being a woman of forty. She wore layers of wispy dark embroidery, a black shawl around her narrow shoulders, and a scarf over her head, tied at the neck, exactly the color of the gray hairs peeking out from underneath it. From a distance, Ansel could be forgiven for thinking she might be Keynes's mother, or a Russian peasant lost in the big city. And yet she moved with the effortless grace of one of the century's leading dancers, which she was.

Ansel greeted Keynes with a stiff, formal handshake. They were supposed to be adversaries, weren't they? Keynes didn't seem too sure about it either.

When the two couples sat to champagne cocktails, Lydia hopped on her chair with youthful vigor, swinging her legs beneath her as a young girl might. She spoke in boldly collapsing English. Her accent was unplaceable, somewhere between St. Petersburg and London. She'd evidently lived in New York for a time in her youth, dancing in Manhattan, which she told the group first thing: "I tell you, a bouncing to be home, back in America."

Ansel got the impression that for a woman like Lydia, everywhere was home. She was no more Russian than she was American or English. She belonged instead to the country of high art that was currently falling under the hard crunch of Nazi jackboots. Borders, for her, were as porous as fresh acrylic. Her references came at a dizzying pace: Picasso and Matisse had never seen eye to eye when they took turns designing her sets back when she'd danced for Diaghilev; her first husband had been an Italian who spoke no English, her first fiancé an American who spoke no Russian, and she was at least three anecdotes deep into this mess before Ansel figured out that neither man was Stravinsky, who by Ansel's count had been her third fiancé, before Keynes became her second husband.

Angela was tickled. She tried valiantly to get Lydia to finish one story before veering off on the tangent of another—"Wait, why had Debussy been so angry with Nijinsky?"—but there was no use in trying to contain the spirit of such a conversationalist. "No no, Vaslav was the man in anger, funny though, because I abide with him in delicious flat over la Seine . . ."

White arrived late and annoyed. He groaned audibly every time Lydia let slip another famous name, and kept trying to needle Keynes with comments about Britain's unbroken stretch of military disasters. Anne Terry seemed entertained as much by her husband's irritation as by Lydia's unabashed glamour. She was not awed by the high-brow characters of whom Lydia spoke, but neither did she find the display an affront.

The sextet drained their champagne cocktails. Oysters were served with two bottles of Sauternes. If it was a surprise that there remained French wine in D.C., such miracles were perhaps to be expected from sommeliers who saw reservations made under names like Keynes and Lopokova.

Ansel was pleased to find Keynes in better health than he had seemed in Sussex. Perhaps the thick, humid air of Washington was doing his constitution some good.

Lydia said she'd heard that Anne Terry had an interest in Shakespeare. Angela offered that Anne Terry was a bit of an expert, and Lydia said that she'd recently tried reading *King Lear* for the first time "at advice of Virginia," which Ansel figured probably meant Keynes's old friend and housemate Mrs. Woolfe. This was confirmed when Keynes commented regretfully about Leonard and Virginia having just lost their home in the blitz. "She hid under a tree in the yard while the German bombs incinerated her house. And all the books within it."

White took this as an opportune moment to lay into him on the subject of sterling. "You can't expect," he said with as little warning as a German bomber, "to prop up your currency via your captive export markets while simultaneously paying for our arms in IOUs. Either your money is as good as ours, or it isn't."

Led by Anne Terry, the ladies turned away to compare notes on various productions of *Lear*.

"I've an appointment to discuss the subject on Thursday," Keynes said. "With Mr. Morgenthau."

If Keynes had hoped that the suggestion of going over White's head would put him in his place, his comment had precisely the opposite effect.

"My friend Henry will follow my advice. And my advice to you is, if you want to survive the nightly bombing of your capital, you better pay up."

"You sound like a gangster. Al Capone. *Pow, pow!*"

"Says the man who's come begging for hard pistols while refusing to pay in hard currency."

"Hard pistols?" Lydia interjected, catching hold of a stray phrase. "They were always, you know, the favorite for Maynard." She said it to him pointedly and he laughed.

"My sweet," responded Keynes, as if chastising her only in jest. "The Americans will be scandalized."

Ansel shared a look with Angela. He wanted to be sure that she was not offended by what seemed to be blue conversation. She appeared, instead, intrigued.

"I'm not the bashful type," White huffed. "Though maybe I am old-fashioned. Ladies being present."

Lydia found this hilarious. "The heart of the matter! Yes!"

A look passed between Lydia and Keynes. It felt as if they were each daring the other to explain. Like their worldly, sophisticated domestic arrangements were too adult for the impressionable ears of these prudish Americans.

Keynes seemed to be conducting an experiment: Might he be able to scandalize Harry into a reaction? "Lydia was my first woman lover."

White's face conveyed nothing so much as boredom.

"If anyone might inspire a change of heart," Anne Terry said, "I imagine it'd be Lydia."

"Or a change of loin," Angela added.

Ansel couldn't believe the bon mot had come from his wife. She scolded him whenever he said *hell* in the house. He didn't mind; he just hadn't known she'd had it in her.

White shot an angry look to Anne Terry. Keynes noticed.

"One spends one's life playing badminton," Keynes said, "one develops a familiarity, indeed, an aptitude. Switching to squash . . . Well, it required some adjustment."

"I'd played all sorts of racket sports," Lydia said. "Never learned any rules. But it's like my husband: All the way one direction, and then all the way another."

White refused to be shocked. "Hard to learn a new sport late in life. Your muscles just haven't built up the strength required."

"I managed," Keynes said. "The rackets may be different, but it's only a matter of mastering the fingering."

Ansel nearly choked on his Sauternes. He was relieved to see Angela finally blush.

White went on the offensive. "You ever miss the company of men?"

Keynes sounded disappointed in his sparring partner for abandoning their playful euphemisms. "I don't miss anyone who is not my wife."

Lydia swooned theatrically. White looked like he'd lost this round.

Thankfully the waiter arrived with soups before anyone was tempted to descend from the euphemistic to the pornographic.

The sniping between White and Keynes simmered through dessert, until the waiter tactfully slid the bill toward the center of the table.

They reached for it simultaneously. Their fingers met above the leather sleeve. Neither man pulled away.

"Please," Keynes said. "It's my treat."

"You're our guests. Don't be silly."

A hush fell across the table as they stared each other down.

"It's the very least I can offer," Keynes said. "After all you're doing for my countrymen."

"What am I doing for your countrymen?"

"Why, supplying our armaments, of course! Such generosity should not go unrewarded."

Ansel reached for the bill himself. Honestly, one ritz dinner was a small price to pay for preventing a transatlantic economic crisis.

White slapped his hand away, then spoke to Keynes: "We'll find plenty of reward in the dollars with which you'll compensate us."

Keynes gestured to his pocket as if he were going to turn it inside out. "Dollars? I'm afraid we're plum out."

White tugged harder at the bill. "You can't pay for our meal in sterling, now can you?"

"Not here. But surely an establishment such as this one will not be troubled by sending the bill to my rooms at the Mayflower."

Lydia stretched like a sinuous cat. "Now that you say the hotel, shall we go for our nightcap?"

"We might be headed straight to bed." Anne Terry eyed a path to the door.

"My mother is with the baby," Angela said, breaking ranks, "so I can speak for Ansel when I say that we're not nearly ready to call it a night."

Keynes tugged again at the bill, but White held on. "You cannot charge a war to your rooms at the Mayflower."

"What else would you have Britain do? We've exhausted our supply of dollars, and what few gold reserves we still possess we require for trade with our other allies. We cannot purchase everything our country needs from America, much as we appreciate that unmistakable Yankee craftsmanship."

"Ansel makes our family furniture himself," Angela offered.

Was she drunk?

"It's quality," she added.

"Henri Matisse tried to make once this chair for me," Lydia said. "What disaster, you know he was not ever any good with the ruler. Shall we?"

"Britain," White said, ignoring everyone but Keynes, "can do precisely what my dad told me to do when I wanted a new pack of Breisch baseball cards: Get a job. Or perhaps hold a yard sale. The UK has ample items of value that can be sold. For *dollars*."

"We are not some town boozer," Keynes replied, "mortgaging the family heirlooms to buy gin. I've seen the proposals. You've asked my government to take ownership of private corporations' holdings—"

"Whose owners could be compensated in sterling," White interjected.

"So that we might sell them to companies in the United States—"

"Who could compensate you in dollars—"

"Purely so that the Exchequer could then turn around and hand all those dollars—"

"Many millions of them—"

"To your government."

White seemed pleased, perhaps, that Keynes had actually read the lengthy proposals he'd been sending to Whitehall. "And in exchange, you get enough planes to stop London from getting bombed to smithereens."

"I see them." Lydia's simple comment halted the overlapping conversations.

"See who?" Angela asked.

"Luftwaffe. Every night, we see them in the air. Tell the Americans, Maynard. They are so close to see the swastikas on the tail. They drop their bombs and the sound . . ."

Ansel tried to imagine what it would be like were bombs dropping nightly in Georgetown. How would he feel about flying halfway across the world to beg for the bullets with which to fight back?

The waiter reappeared. With a flourish, White fished his wallet from his jacket and thrust as many bills as he could at the waiter with no regard for their denomination. The man carried the paper away with pleasure.

White wore a look of victory.

"That's our cue." Anne Terry stood. No arguments would be resolved this evening. Not after a bottle of champagne and four of Sauternes.

White accepted her unspoken plea for a quick and, for him, uncharacteristically gracious exit. He returned his empty wallet to his pocket.

Ansel wasn't sure whether to rise or sit as Keynes remained immobile.

White leaned over and whispered loudly in Keynes's ear. "You want to survive this war? You want to snuff out the next one? We're all going to have to make sacrifices. Yours will have to be the dominance of sterling. Sorry, pal. Let it go. Or else I've got to do it for you."

White took his wife's hand and led her to the door.

Lydia adjusted her scarf.

"Well then," Angela said after an appropriate pause. "How about that nightcap?"

46

LADIES' HOSIERY AND A NEW WORLD CURRENCY

"To be radical is to grasp things at their root."

—KARL MARX

August 20, 1940 (cont'd)

Ansel and Angela entered Keynes's five-room suite at the Mayflower to find the sitting room liberally festooned with silk stockings. Fortunately, the undergarments were unworn. They were folded, some wrapped in paper and others tied with string. They looked to have been flung across the beige davenport and Georgian armchairs with abandon.

"Pardon the sight of my underthings!" Lydia exclaimed without any real note of embarrassment. She half-heartedly cleared seats for her guests, brushing the stockings into shambolic piles on the carpet.

"Been shopping?" Angela asked.

Lydia removed her scarf but not her shawl and draped the former over the arm of a chair. She didn't seem to notice as it promptly slid off. "Do you know, we can get none of this in England? *Les oeufs*, my sunrise café, are difficult enough. But stockings? Nylon? Do not think upon it."

Keynes went straight to the bar. "I am not the only one who's come to America for supplies."

He fixed four Scotch-and-sodas. Evidently Lydia's shopping expedition had not stopped at stockings. There were shoes, raincoats, jewels, Mainbochers, and "but a half-dozen hats" that she wanted to show Angela. She went to the rear bedroom and returned with an armful of boxes.

Ansel sat beside Keynes on the plush davenport as Lydia showed off her haul. Ansel had wondered whether Angela would have much to talk about with the most esteemed dancer of the Ballets Russes, but he needn't have worried. The two had been chatting away merrily not just through the arduous meal but likewise over the half-mile walk to the hotel. Ansel had caught mention of his own name a few times and tried to disregard the paranoid fear that what Angela and Lydia most shared in common were bookish snoozes for husbands.

"Had you imagined yourself ending up like this?" Keynes whispered, bringing the Scotch to his lips. "A happily married man?"

Ansel pondered: Was his what they meant by a happy marriage? And was this, the state that he and Angela were in, where they'd "ended"? It seemed, on the contrary, that his marriage insisted on changing. The expansion of the baby. The contraction of the war. The secrets they'd promised to keep from each other and the truths they'd been compelled to share.

"I'll take it as a compliment," Ansel replied, "that that's how you see us."

"A marriage can be hard enough under normal circumstances. But at wartime, with you both working for your government . . ."

"I only wish we could do more," Angela chimed in from the floor, where she was delicately peeling tissue paper off a feathered fascinator. Lydia had likely bought more headwear this week than Angela had owned in her life.

"Do you?" Keynes asked.

"It's why we're all here, isn't it? To do as much as we can?"

Keynes took in Angela as he might one of his ancient artifacts: What is this new curiosity? In what classification did she fall?

"A feeling," Lydia said to her husband. "I told you that you could trust them."

Angela seemed emboldened by the scrutiny. "Why do you and Harry hate each other?"

Keynes laughed. He might not admire Americans, generally speaking, but he did seem to appreciate their bluntness. "I'll spare you the diplomacy of pretending that we don't. Harry mistakes plainspokenness for wisdom. And perhaps I mistake wisdom for efficacy."

Angela rolled her eyes. "You're on the same side. For the good of the cause, stop being such stubborn dolts and get on with it."

The only person Ansel had previously heard her speak to in such a manner was him.

Keynes seemed impressed. Something was communicated between him and Lydia, though it was too fast and too silent for Ansel to tell what it might be.

"Why do you think that I came to Washington?" Keynes said.

Ansel suggested that he was here to negotiate Cash and Carry payments. But of course, Keynes pointed out, he could do that from Sussex.

Ansel recognized a glint in Keynes's eye. He'd seen it once before. "This trip is about your plan for a lasting peace."

"I hope that I can trust you both," Keynes said. "I am in need of assistance. Harry isn't going to give it to me, even though it would be in his own best interest. So here we are. I come to you on bended knee, bearing an offer: Allow me to make my case for my dastardly scheme to prevent the next Great War. And in return, I'll help you with this one."

What sort of help could Keynes provide Ansel in regard to a war that his country hadn't yet joined?

Keynes smiled, seeming to follow his thoughts. "Money. At some point, and I'd hope sooner rather than later, America will find herself taking up arms. When she does, you'll need more tanks and aircraft carriers and planes for yourselves, won't you, than even what you've sent to us. How do you intend on paying for all of it?"

The question, of course, had come up. So far Treasury lacked a good answer. Simultaneously financing Britain's war on credit and America's war with cash would be a tall order.

"If you like," Keynes offered, "I can show you how."

Ansel did not need reminding that no man alive knew more about wartime financing than the one presently sipping Scotch beside him. Nor, for that matter, did he need reminding of White's suspicions: Was Keynes really a snake, looking out only for himself?

"And in return," Ansel said hesitantly, "you ask what? Only that we listen?"

Keynes nodded.

What harm could there be in simply listening to one of the smartest men in the world expound upon subjects of pressing importance? Especially if it meant possibly breaking this impasse and getting more weapons, more quickly, into the hands of more soldiers who might point them in the direction of Nazis?

Angela used her forefinger to trace the brim of a purple cloche. Then she looked up at her husband: Why not?

Ansel found his tin in his jacket pocket and lit a cigarillo.

Keynes seemed to take in the looks between the Luxfords.

"Perhaps they are alike," he said after a while. "Money and marriage. For example, you tell your wife that you love her."

"Not as often as he should," Angela said.

"You tell him," Keynes spoke to her, "that you love him as well."

Ansel smoked. "Despite her better judgment."

"Do you both mean the same thing, when you use the word *love*?"

Lydia unfurled a scarlet raincoat. "*L'amour. Lyublyu. Liebe.* I hear it all."

Angela seemed to consider the question deeply. "Why should it matter?"

"Don't you think that you and Ansel should feel the same about each other?"

"No," she replied quickly. "We don't need to feel the same. Only complimentarily. What matters is not what I believe he feels or what he believes that I feel but instead our actions. Do I do what I've said I would? Does he? Do I treat him right, does he do likewise?"

Keynes lit up. "Precisely! Actions, not beliefs, are in the end all that truly matters. So it is with money. Would you indulge me in a bit of a thought experiment?"

The Luxfords assented. Ansel noted that Lydia's husband had not seen fit to ask for her permission to lecture. She seemed used to it.

Keynes fished in his pockets for coins before coming up empty-handed. "Do either of you have any?"

Ansel produced a few quarter dollars from his pocket.

Keynes held them up to the light. "What are these worth?"

"Looks like a dollar twenty-five."

"No, I meant what is the *value* of these coins?"

Angela lifted up a pair of blue checkerboard stockings. "I'm no economist, but I bet for a dollar twenty-five you could get a pair of these at Woodies."

"What is this 'Woodies'?" Lydia said. "My spending was much more."

"If I went to the store," Keynes said, "I could hand a man those coins and he'd give me a pair of these checkerboard stockings."

"Woodies usually hires ladies to staff the women's undergarments counter," Angela said, "but yes."

"Why?"

"To save a lady from having to ask a strange man for—"

"No, why will the shopgirl give me a pair of these stockings in exchange for those coins?"

"Because after you give the shopgirl the coins, she can give them to the store's owner, and he can take those coins down the road and use them to buy something else. A chicken dinner, a gallon of gas."

"The crux of the matter!" Keynes seemed to have found in Angela an ideal pupil. "These coins are not worth a pair of stockings because *I* believe that they are, or because you do, or even because the shopgirl who sold these to my wife does. It has this value because the shopgirl, and her employer, believe that *other* people believe the same thing. It does not matter, in the moment of transaction, whether the restaurant down the street will actually accept these coins in exchange for a roast chicken. What matters is that the shopgirl had faith today that the chicken roaster will have the same faith tomorrow."

Ansel suddenly pictured a coin he'd seen in Sussex: the face of a long-forgotten emperor on one side, the image of a Greek god performing a Buddhist ritual on the other. "Your point is that for something to function as money, it must be thought of as having a future."

"Like marriage!" Angela sounded pleased to have returned to her home turf. "If you don't think there's a future, it's not much of a marriage."

"Whether or not it actually lasts isn't the point," Keynes agreed, "so long as both parties believed, at that critical moment of transaction, that it would."

Ansel thought of all those decaying coins and pots and arrowheads: mementos of civilizations whose citizens once believed would last for eternity. "To create a new global currency, you'd need to create something that everyone believes will last forever."

Lydia ventured to the bar to refill everyone's tumbler. Perhaps after a decade of marriage her husband's lectures comforted her, like a well-trod bedtime story.

"When I was young," Keynes said, "one of the Sunday papers had this wretched contest in which they'd print photographs of pretty girls. Did you have this in America?"

"Not where I was raised," Ansel said.

"I'm envious. So the paper would print a hundred images, maybe, of all these girls. And the game was, the reader had to guess which six girls would be voted most pretty by the most readers. You'd send in your predictions and get a prize."

Ansel thought of Keynes's indiscreet provocations at dinner. "Is your point that you weren't very good at this game?"

"Just the opposite! I was tremendous at it. This game is exactly like money. It perfectly describes our entire financial system."

Angela laughed. "Pretty girls?"

"The trick of the game is to disregard whom *you* find pretty. What matters is whom you believe *other people* will find pretty. You want to get rich on the stock market? Buy stocks that you believe *other people* believe will go up. You want to trade currencies? Buy the one that you think the *most people* in the *most places* around the world will want to use. You want to make a fortune on art? Buy the paintings that you believe *other collectors* will . . . Well, you understand."

"Unless I'm mistaken," Ansel said, "you have personally made fortunes on stocks, currencies, and art."

"I know whereof I speak."

"You're talking about the mob," Angela said. "No face is inherently prettier than another; no coin more valuable. It's just the mentality of the mob that makes it so."

Keynes stood and plucked a red polka-dotted stocking from the carpet. "And yet, the real value of these stockings is that they will keep my wife's legs warm on a cold evening."

"*Avec brio,*" Lydia offered.

Ansel thought of the fascist marchers he'd seen on a St. Paul bridge: a mob united in their beliefs, a currency of horrors between them.

"Like guns," Ansel said. "What they *cost* is a question of money. But their *value* . . . It's in the Nazis they can kill."

Keynes nodded. " 'In the lives they might defend,' is how I would put it. But yes. This is precisely why the gold standard was always so absurd. The idea was that our currencies should be tied to something 'real,' such as gold or silver. But what makes gold or silver any more 'real' than our paper money? One cannot make a pair of stockings from a bar of gold, no matter how delicately one tries to sew it."

"Or a gun," Angela offered from the floor.

"If one intended to create a new currency," Keynes said, "that was not tethered to any government, what would one need?"

"You'd need to convince as many people as possible that it had value." Angela looked to the stockings. "No. *That it would have value in the future.*"

"What's the old line about currencies, Ansel? For something to be a currency, it must be—"

"A store of value," he answered. "As Angela just described. But also a unit of account. That is, it must be countable. Numerical. For example, oil makes a great commodity but a terrible currency. How do you measure it? Weight, volume, purity? It's too messy."

"Making a currency out of something countable doesn't sound like a great challenge," Angela suggested. "I can count rocks. Sticks. Pencils."

"It's the third qualification that's tricky," Ansel said. "A currency also has to be a medium of exchange. Lydia needs to be able to hand it to the girl behind the counter at Woodies. The shopgirl needs then to be able to hand it to somebody else. Elaborately engraved coins work well, as do bills. Counterfeiters don't just create fake money; they devalue real money. Mr. Keynes, if your currency isn't tied to any nation, who would handle the coinage? The engraving, the printing?"

"The cuneiform tablets at Tilton House are money, but no one ever traded them. They *record* trades. Information can be exchanged without a physical object moving from one place to another, can it not? Like the marks on the ledgers of your banks? Or like the lines on that five-thousand-year-old tablet?"

"You're saying your new currency could be . . ."

"Virtual. Numbers on a ledger. Not bullion in a vault or paper in a drawer. But the ticks of current on transatlantic wires."

"Someone would still need to maintain the ledger."

"A clearinghouse, such as you describe, might be maintained by a small team of experts. Engineers. The rules by which they did so could be public. Agreed to by all parties. National treasuries are run by self-interested politicians, present company excluded. They're subject to the shifting whims of politics. Our currency needn't be."

"You put a lot of faith in small teams of experts."

"I put very little faith in the mobs who read newspapers only to look at pretty girls. It's those fools who elect the politicians."

"But what about the first qualification?" Angela said. "Value? How do you convince everyone that this new whatever has value? That it will have value in the future?"

Keynes nodded. "My suggestion: Start small."

"How small?"

"Every government in the world."

Only for Keynes would such a thing be considered "small."

He smiled as if recognizing how grand he must sound. "I'm not so gimlet-eyed as to believe that within my lifetime I can convince the United States to part with its dollars, or even my country to part with its sterling. One day. But first, we start with something more technical. A currency for use exclusively in trade *among* countries. You have your currency, we have ours, but when we want to trade with each other, we must exchange our individual currencies for this supranational one."

Ansel tried to think through the implications. "Individuals, corporations, couldn't possess it? Only nations could?"

"If first the world's governments start using it, the mob will soon enough see its value."

"What would you call it?" Angela's concerns were practical.

"Bancor."

Ansel frowned.

"Pronounced," Keynes said, "like the French."

Angela did not seem any more taken with the nomenclature than was her husband.

Keynes acknowledged that titles had never been his strong suit—he'd always been more of an idea man than a salesman. "We can do some more work on the name. But look: Germany fell to fascism because its citizens faced a crushing deflationary spiral and chose as a solution perhaps the most evil one imaginable. But if we had a global reserve currency that was set up to stabilize international trade . . ."

This part of the plan, Ansel could not fail to notice, was quite similar to White's. "Then Germany never would have gotten caught in a deflationary spiral in the first place."

"Stability," Keynes said, pleased. "With bancor—or what have you—we could put an end to the political turmoil caused by inflation, deflation, and the balance-of-payments crises that keep felling the South American nations. At this moment, you're trying to stem Germany's capability to wage war by cutting off its ability to trade in gold and dollars with certain foreign exporters. My point is, if we had a truly supranational reserve currency . . ."

He seemed to be waiting for Ansel to finish his thought.

"None of what I've spent the past year doing would ever be necessary again. Any country that tried to wage war as Germany has could be cut off from international trade with the snap of your fingers." The magnitude of what Keynes was doing finally started to become clear. "You really could end war."

"Not all war. Civil wars, coups, those I don't yet have a solution for. But the larger conflicts, between nations?" Keynes's eyes sparkled in the lamplight. "Ansel, last week Lydia watched a bomb explode across the street from our house."

She shuddered. She was a woman who'd seen a lot in her life, but this, Ansel could see, was among the worst of it.

Keynes returned to the window and gazed out at the dim nighttime of Washington. For a moment, Ansel thought that he might actually be able to see the future from the fourth-floor window of his May-flower suite. His aims were grander, bolder, and riskier than White's. They were honestly bigger than anything Ansel had imagined. To gaze up at Keynes was to feel small. Ansel's concerns—his fears, his greatest, most optimistic hopes for the future of civilization—were petite rumbles incommensurate with the earthquake happening before him.

If ever there was a moment to think bigger, wasn't this it?

"I'd imagine," Keynes continued, "that by now Harry is well into devising his own postwar plan. He's going to make the global reserve currency American dollars." The way Keynes spoke, this sounded about as ambitious as an afternoon nap. "Don't bother denying it. I've seen the financing details of his Cash and Carry proposals and I can read between the lines. Of course Harry would cling to dollars—like a child squeezing a teddy bear. Such a paucity of imagination." He sighed with pity. "But look. I'm not asking you to turn your back on him, or to betray his plans. If you really think his designs are better? So be it. May the best man win. But if you're curious, at all, about this alternative proposal? Well, I'd be pleased to tell you a bit more."

Ansel had so many questions, even just getting them out would take hours. Days.

Angela had always been a shrewder negotiator. "You said you'd tell us what Treasury can do to fund the war."

"I just did." Keynes rattled the last chunk of melted ice around in his otherwise empty tumbler. "Anything you can actually do, you can afford. If you understand what money is, and where money comes from, then you can make as much of it as you need to do whatever it is you want to do. Including, but not limited to, building armies of such magnitude that the Wehrmacht will be dwarfed."

"You're suggesting that the Treasury create more dollars?"

"I'm suggesting that every dollar in existence was created by the Treasury. My country does not lack sterling. Nor dollars. What we lack is bullets. I'm suggesting that if you're committed to making the shells, then I'm quite happy to show you how to make all the dollars you'll ever need."

47

A MAGIC TRICK

"Money isn't a material reality—it is a psychological construct. . . . Trust is the raw material from which all types of money are minted."

—YUVAL NOAH HARARI

September 22, 1940

Over the next month, Ansel met with Keynes first twice, then three times a week. Always in secret. Always somewhere they would not fear being observed. Sometimes in Keynes's rooms at the Mayflower, sometimes in an unpopular Chinese restaurant on Q Street. Every time Keynes spoke, Ansel felt as if he were being let in on mysteries of creation known only to pagan priests and rare men of the occult. He remembered lying on a dorm room bed reading Keynes's first book until he was disturbed by morning birdsong. Now he sat opposite the man, making notebook sketches of supply-demand curves beside half-eaten plates of chop suey.

Ansel had never talked before with anyone the way he did with Keynes. Though perhaps that was because no one talked like Keynes. From Ottoman poetry to German expressionism, Keynes knew something about everything. Economics for him was a social science, not a mathematical one. He seemed to have more in common with Freud than with Leibniz.

Ansel did not tell White about these dinners and late-night conversations. He did not have to lie, exactly. His sins were of omission. Which presented an irony for him as he bid good night to Angela on these evenings to meet with Keynes, only to sometimes hear that she was off to walk or shop with Lydia the following morning: Now it was his wife with whom he was honest and his boss with whom he practiced intermittent deceit.

Angela delighted in the company of Lydia while simultaneously tightening the familial bonds between the Luxfords and the Whites. She invited Anne Terry and her girls to Angie's third birthday party, held in the rec room of her parents' church. She went to the Phillips Collection with Lydia to see the Renoirs. If she passed a Saturday with Anne Terry, she'd then plan an outing with Lydia on the Sunday. She sensed a rupture was on the way. She just couldn't tell the exact shape the crack would take.

It was the Germans that finally did it, as far as Ansel was concerned. Tensions between the U.S. and the UK over financial terms had not gone unnoticed in Berlin, and this was precisely the sort of conflict that the Reich could turn to its advantage. The German Foreign Ministry began blaring its propaganda through the mouths of its American sympathizers: What a chump FDR was, breaking open Uncle Sam's piggy bank just so his friends across the pond could pick up the change. Didn't the president know the value of a dollar?

The Brits were taking us Americans for a ride.

It was when Ansel heard that one over the wireless that he knew: All this squabbling between White and Keynes over preventing the wars of the future would have to wait. Today, all it was doing was helping the Nazis.

Ansel had the Professor and Pehle over that weekend. He made the sweet tea himself. They sat on the porch as he laid it out plain: John Maynard Keynes had a way for the United States to pay for all the weapons the UK needed, plus as many as she'd need herself. It was, to nobody's surprise, whip-smart. Yes, it would give Keynes's postwar plan an initial, conceptual leg up on White's: The sterling bloc would be spared; there would be no postwar deluge of dollars into Europe or Asia. But White would have one significant point to smile about: The Brits would agree to pay in dollars.

They could sit around debating the merits of their paper weapons forever. Defeating the Nazis would require real ones. *Now.*

He closely watched the look that passed between Pehle and the Professor. They knew what he was asking of them. They could well imagine the terrible shocks that would erupt along G Street if they went around White.

Pehle spoke first. "You're asking us to betray Harry. And Joe. Our team has depended upon mutual trust."

"No," Ansel said. "I'm asking you to do what you know is right for the country—for the world—and damn the consequences. I'm asking you to ask yourselves: If the shoe were on the other foot . . . what would Harry Dexter White do?"

———

OF THE HUNDREDS OF dignitaries crowded into the Soviet embassy for the annual autumn reception, not a single one wanted to be there. Still, representatives from nearly every country in the world packed tightly into the gilt-lined grand salon of the Soviets' five-story French villa on Sixteenth Street. Grumblings in every language of Babel echoed through the marble corridors. Bowls of untouched caviar sat tepidly on long buffet tables; waiters circulated with trays of cold boiled shrimp. A band somewhere played what Ansel thought were lively Russian folk songs, but it was hard to hear, and frankly no one much cared to listen. The theme of the party was "obligation."

Nobody talked to the Vichy ambassador. An obsequious Frenchman with a square mustache, he roamed the party in search of a conversation to join. But not even the Japanese ambassador engaged him. The issue, so far as Ansel could understand it, was that he was obviously a Nazi spy. He was letting a team of French-speaking Nazi agents live with him in his palatial embassy on Kalorama Road, and the group went out every night to cocktail parties and governmental receptions in the hopes of overhearing gossip they could report back to Berlin. The impediment they faced was that it was so obvious this was what they were doing—Vichy agents being well-known for their cunning but not for their competence—that it had become a favorite joke within the clubs of Georgetown. At the slightest blue joke or slip of indiscretion, the common retort was now: "I hope the Vichy didn't hear that one!"

Ansel watched the lonely Frenchman fail to find a friendly face. The Italian ambassador, a stern-looking general in a medal-drenched military uniform, pretended not to see him.

Ansel was reminded of the only high school dance he'd been to.

Helpfully, the presence of easily identifiable Nazi spies in the capital helped take the FBI's attention away from what they believed to be a Soviet spy in Treasury. Their defector, Angela divulged, had not gotten his hands on any other secret Treasury memoranda; nor had he produced any other information about the double agent's identity. Since Ansel and Angela knew that no such spy existed, they were relieved to see the Bureau moving on.

Plus, as the guest list of this party would indicate, hopeful cracks were beginning to form in the Soviets' neutrality. Stalin's nonaggression pact with Hitler was still in place, but over the past year it had become clear that "nonaggression" was not the same as "support"— especially given the hassle of jointly ministering a crudely divided Poland. There were rumors that Moscow's allegiance might be in play, so when the Soviets announced the resurrection of their yearly gala, all the ambassadors of Europe, Asia, Africa, and the Americas were quick to accept their invitations.

Ansel pressed his way through the crowd. Lord Lothian, the dapper, round-faced British ambassador, gave a nod. He must know he'd met Ansel before, but a mid-level Treasury bureaucrat was just another face at the table in what had been recent weeks of fruitless meetings. The White House wanted the deal to produce and finance British arms to be done already, and Lothian had shown up expecting American cooperation. Instead, he'd gotten a full dose of Harry Dexter White.

Under White's direction, Treasury had seen to it that the dealmaking process was as painstaking and altogether painful as possible. Keynes took the verbal abuse with sangfroid but did not budge an inch on his commitment to preserve the global reach of sterling.

When Ansel attended these meetings, he tried to avoid eye contact with Keynes. He felt less like a co-conspirator that way.

He found Morgenthau in the Soviet embassy's south wing. The secretary leaned against a mahogany doorframe half-heartedly chatting with a pair of bored Swedes. He was happy to follow Ansel to a private nook where they might speak without being overheard.

"War bonds," Ansel said. "I have an idea about how we can sell them."

In response to Morgenthau's raised eyebrow, Ansel explained: In order to produce the quantity of arms the British required, much less those the United States would need whenever she finally joined the fighting, domestic production would have to expand. And it would need to expand a lot faster than the executives at Ford and Boeing were currently moving. The War Department was well aware of this—why else were they breaking ground on that pentagon-shaped office complex in Virginia if not to handle the overflow of staff?—but they lacked the funding to finance more production. Even if the British paid America back in dollars, it was unclear whether they'd be able to get enough—or if enough even existed.

The subject of war bonds wasn't new—Treasury had sold some to pay for the Great War. Morgenthau had been discussing various plans for new bonds with the White House for months, but the Oval Office doubted its ability to convince a suspicious public to directly finance a manifestly unpopular war. Who would buy?

"Well," Ansel offered, "there is one novel wrinkle I'd like to propose. Government-backed bank loans to help people afford the bonds."

Morgenthau appeared confused. Was there not circular logic to such a proposal?

Yes. And the tautology was the point. Ansel proposed that Treasury offer a new series of bonds that would return to the purchaser 2.9 percent per year for ten years. He'd been working on the math with the Professor and Pehle. They didn't want to offer too much, for fear of crowding out investment in other bonds, but they needed to offer enough return to make it enticing. Simultaneously, Treasury could issue a rule change to the banks—that would not need to go through

Congress—requiring the banks to offer loans to customers who wanted to buy these bonds and *only* these bonds. Treasury would back the loans at a rate of 2.6 percent per year.

Morgenthau did not need to perform any complex mental calculation to determine that one of those percentages was larger than the other. Which meant that . . .

"We'd be creating hundreds of millions of dollars," Ansel said, unafraid to put this plainly. "Just to start. And we'd be doing it by using a bit of trickery in the banking system. A family, let's say, takes out a bank loan—that we guarantee—for one hundred dollars at 2.6 percent interest. They use the hundred dollars to purchase a bond—that we also guarantee—that returns 2.9 percent interest. The family makes thirty cents a year, risk-free."

"Not exactly a windfall."

"Remember, they didn't put in any of their own capital. It's just free money. Thirty cents a year in a few years when the bond matures. And we get the hundred dollars. Now. To spend as we see fit."

"I'm guessing you see fit to spend it on bullets and mortars?"

Ansel shook his head. "On factories that *make* bullets and mortars. Rifles and grenades. Tanks and bombers. And on the salaries of the men in those factories crafting those weapons."

Morgenthau swirled the ice in his glass. "The hundred dollars—where does it come from?"

Ansel thought of the markings on two-hundred-year-old barman's chips. Of a cuneiform tablet etched with unreadable symbols. "Where all money comes from: trust. It comes from our guarantee, to both the bank and the family, in which they share a belief."

Morgenthau looked dubious. This was perhaps a bit metaphysical for his taste. "What about inflation? If one day Americans wake up to find this extra money sloshing around the economy, which you've conjured from thin air . . ."

If the secretary was thinking it through, that meant he was taking it seriously.

"That's the best part," Ansel offered. "The price of something—say, the caviar in that saucer—inflates when the demand for it exceeds the supply. Too many people are trying to buy the same caviar, so the caviar salesman charges more. But with our bonds, the family doesn't have the extra thirty cents for a few years. And our hundred dollars? We're spending it on material that we're producing and buying now. We're both buyer and seller. The supply-demand curve isn't thrown out of whack."

Ansel worried he was now erring on the side of technicality.

"Anything we can *actually* do, we can afford. That's the big insight."

Morgenthau searched his face. "That sounds like something John Maynard Keynes would say."

Ansel refrained from admitting that Keynes had. "Our constraints are not fiscal or monetary. They're physical. If there exists, in the *real* world, not the money world, something we are able to build, and if there are presently idle hands to build it, then we can create the money to do so without raising inflation."

Morgenthau looked at the vaulted ceiling. "That sounds less like a theory and more like a prayer."

"It was good enough for Hjalmar Schacht."

"The Dark Wizard?"

"Sure, this scheme owes a conceptual debt to Keynes. It also owes one to Schacht. But what he achieved dictatorially with forced savings under the watchful eyes of the SS, we can achieve capitalistically through simple incentives. We don't have to bully Americans into supporting our allies, but we can help them turn a profit if they do."

"By conjuring this money like a rabbit from a hat?"

Ansel shrugged. "It might be a magic trick. But don't you want the rabbit?"

Across the room, the Vichy ambassador set in on a trio of Chinese bankers in all-white suits, lighting their cigars with a ceremonial flick.

"Why are you here?" Morgenthau said.

"Because I knew you would be."

"No, why are *you* here? Why am I not having this conversation with Harry?"

Ansel had prepared for some version of this question. "Harry isn't going to like this idea. And he isn't going to like where it's coming from."

"So you're going over his head?"

"Harry is so distrustful of Keynes that he'd rather put the whole war effort at risk than listen to a smart idea. I'm doing what is required so that we might win the war we have not yet entered. For which, when it's all said and done, he'll be grateful."

Morgenthau peered down at Ansel from behind his thin, round glasses. "This might be the first time I've ever heard anybody use the words *Harry* and *grateful* in the same sentence."

The secretary looked back to the grand salon, checking on the locations of all the Nazi spies. "The president wants a deal with the British done."

"I have some ideas about that, too. Building off these bonds."

"I'll bet you do."

"Let's say there was a way to construct the deal that would satisfy Churchill, Roosevelt, the Exchequer, and both of us. Would you go for it?"

"That is, it would satisfy everyone but Harry?"

Ansel had not imagined it would be easy for Morgenthau to accept the betrayal of his most trusted aide. But the secretary had so far been willing to do what victory required of him.

Back in the salon, the Vichy ambassador appeared rudderless again, roaming alone through the indifferent crowd.

"You don't strike me as the type accustomed to making enemies." Morgenthau sighed. "Are you sure you've prepared for making one of Harry Dexter White?"

48

150 MILLION BULLETS

*"Man is an animal that makes bargains: No other animal
does this—no dog exchanges bones with another."*

—ADAM SMITH

November 2, 1940

"Harry stopped speaking to you?" Angela stood in the doorway to
Ansel's workshop.

He paused sanding the edge of a spindle-back chair and set down
his tools. "It's not as if he says *nothing* to me. I mean, we must be in two
meetings a day together. He's cordial."

Angela accused him of splitting hairs.

"Perhaps 'cordial' is an overstatement. He speaks in my presence."

"But not to you?"

"Look, he's not speaking much to the Professor either. Or John."
The two had been regular visitors to the Luxfords' farm these past
months as they'd hashed out the details. Angela had watched them
cover the breakfast table in crumpled notebook paper.

"He stopped speaking to you after you presented him with the plan."

"Morgenthau presented him with the plan. I stayed quiet."

"But he knew it came from you."

"It came from the president."

Angela rubbed her temple with the thumb and middle finger of the
same hand. "You're sure Roosevelt is in favor?"

"The president named the program! 'Lend-Lease.' It will replace Cash and Carry. Next week, Roosevelt is going to give this big speech all about how if your neighbor's house is on fire and you have a hose, you don't try to sell him the hose and haggle over the price. You just put it in his hand and wait until the fire is out to figure out what he owes you."

"I do see his point: London is largely ablaze."

Only weeks before, the president had announced the first peacetime draft in American history. It would be small, he'd assured the country. And no one would be thrust into combat anytime soon. The government was still doing anything and everything possible to avoid war. But since roughly half the world was already fighting, America was obliged to prepare its defenses. God willing, they would never be needed.

Ansel said, "We're going to manufacture a lot of new equipment for our own army and then we're going to 'lend' or 'lease' most of it to the British."

"What are we going to lend them?"

"To start? A hundred and fifty million bullets."

"Pardon?"

"And then guns, planes . . . We have a list."

"A hundred and fifty million bullets? How many German soldiers are there?"

"The British have been known, on occasion, to miss."

"How do you *lend* someone a bullet? Are you going to fly over to Europe and remove them from the soldiers they've killed?"

Ansel conceded that some parts of this plan were more worked out than others. "We can figure out what happens after the Nazis fall when we get there."

"Is this really legal? Lending out military equipment?"

"That was my job!" Ansel swelled with pride. "Figuring out how it might be. Saxon helped. We found a statute. It's been on the books since 1892. Everybody plum forgot it existed. It was written to allow army bases to lend their horses to nearby farms. But it says, plain as day, that the U.S. military may *lend* its equipment to appropriate parties if doing so is in the public interest."

"You're going to use an obscure statute about horses to lend out one hundred and fifty million bullets."

"This was the part that I presented to Harry. The legal solution."

"I can see why he stopped talking to you."

"First of all, he hasn't, and second of all, that's not the part that he's angry about. Harry's concerns are about the leasing."

"Leasing?"

"Some of the larger items—aircraft carriers and the like—will not be lent. They'll be leased."

Angela clearly saw where this was headed. "*Leased* implies the recipient is paying for it."

"Harry *should* be pleased. The British have agreed to pay in dollars."

"But he's not?"

"No. They don't have the dollars. So we're allowing them to pay in debt."

"You mean IOUs?"

"They're going to rack up a considerable dollar-denominated debt, and we're giving them a long time to pay it off."

"Till when?"

"Around 1992."

Angela said nothing.

"It's going to be quite a large debt," Ansel added. "They'll need the time."

"Won't we, I don't know, need our money back?"

"Not really."

"Is the U.S. so rich that we have that much money lying around?"

"No. But we can make as much as we need."

This was probably too conceptually bizarre to get into with her on a Sunday afternoon.

"I'm going over to Anne Terry's when Angie is up from her nap," she said. "Harry may have stopped speaking to you, but she hasn't frozen me out yet."

"I think I can bear a little cold front," Ansel reassured her.

"That's what Edward Smith said."

"Who?"

She turned, leaving him to his woodwork. "The captain of the *Titanic*."

49

SUBTERFUGE AND PROPAGANDA

"Remember that credit is money."

—BENJAMIN FRANKLIN

December 19, 1940

Writing legislation is difficult work under any circumstances, but it is substantially more difficult, Ansel discovered, when your chief co-author is not speaking to you. In the initial weeks of the drafting process for what would become House Resolution 1776—an inspired bit of nomenclature from the Oval Office—Ansel was obliged to scribble out text, hand it off to one of the secretaries for typing, and await corrections from White's red pen.

The notion of providing Britain with a nearly unlimited supply of American goods was not a popular one, even after Roosevelt's speech about the fire hose. The analogy was so evocative that it managed to raise public support for the idea all the way up to thirty-six percent. Congressmen grew wary of supporting legislation that had such a low approval rating, so Ansel was tasked with inserting various limitations into the text. If the bill looked less like charity, perhaps more Americans might support it. He tried to craft these limitations such that they'd be effectively toothless, while White saw this as an opportunity to take a real bite out of Keynes's scheme.

White proposed that the total value of goods lent or leased to the British not exceed a dollar. Ansel proposed a somewhat higher cap:

two billion dollars. The negotiations within the Treasury Department, much less without it, had quite a gap to close.

Ansel understood why White was trying to sabotage Lend-Lease from the inside—it's probably what he would have done in the latter's shoes. But he wished that they could simply scream at each other on the subject rather than duel silently in margin notes to ever-lengthening pages of formal legislation.

The Professor and Pehle were both granted White's forgiveness with surprising speed. To be sure, Pehle was so busy at Foreign Funds Control that he rarely made it over to main Treasury. His chin was rather wide of White's swinging fists. And after dispatching thousands of patriotic accountants to block suspicious transactions, he occupied himself with an even bolder idea: Why not send their men to simply confiscate the cash in suspect accounts and safe-deposit boxes? FFC dispatched Saxon to do just that. The kid became a thin, bespectacled John Dillinger prowling the Midwest for accounts with ties to Germany and simply demanding the cash, gold, or jewelry he found. He didn't even need a pistol. A badge emblazoned with the word *Treasury* sufficed.

At first Ansel wondered whether the Professor had been spared White's vitriol on account of her being a woman. But when Ansel asked her if she thought White's vengeance might come for her soon enough, she pointed out that she was grading Morgenthau's daughter's final essay that very weekend. If White wanted to fire her, he was welcome to take it up with the secretary at the end of the semester.

DuBois was surprisingly unbothered by the subterfuge. Yes, what Ansel and the others had done provided a certain conceptual victory to Keynes's postwar plans over his own: Since the British would not need dollars with which to pay the United States back anytime soon, they could get on just fine with sterling and gold, which would provide a smoother transition to Keynes's bancor system than it would to DuBois's dollar-centric universe. But that war still lay ahead. And DuBois saw the advantage in making a deal with the British in the present to win this one.

He'd never been one to hold grudges, he told Ansel, who attempted an apology. Disagreement in the service of holding evil at bay was no sin.

Paul did not concern himself with office politics, but he liked the look of the Lend-Lease deal. The United States would profit from it eventually. And in the meantime, as a Wall Street man, he placed a value on deal flow: An imperfect deal now was preferable to a slightly better one in six months.

Then, a new challenge: Charles Lindbergh came out against Lend-Lease with a blistering salvo delivered to a crowd of eight thousand Iowans in the Des Moines Coliseum. His speech on behalf of the America First Committee, the organization he'd helped to found months before, was broadcast into American homes from coast to coast on the waves of AM radio.

"These war agitators," he said in a taut and reedy voice, "comprise only a small minority of our people, but they control tremendous influence. Against the determination of the American people to stay out of the war, they have marshaled the power of their propaganda, their money, their patronage." Lindbergh even went so far as to name these groups of agitators who were conspiring, in secret, to bring the United States into the war: "First, the Jews . . . second, the British . . . and the third powerful group . . . the Roosevelt administration."

Ansel dragged the Zenith portable onto the porch so he and Angela could listen while watching the brief, bright flashes of the Virginia fireflies. In point of fact, everything Lindbergh was saying was true. There really was a conspiracy of Brits and Jews within the Roosevelt administration to make the United States a participant in the war while claiming they were doing the opposite. Ansel was one of the conspirators, and honestly he didn't think he'd be able to describe what they were up to as succinctly as Lindbergh had. The speech even went on to explain just how the army had massively increased its budget to build new planes and ships using novel financing schemes on the pretext that what was being built was for American defense, only to turn around and "lease" these planes to the UK . . . only to then say that the UK didn't need to worry about actually paying us back for any of this anytime soon. It was, Ansel felt, quite an insightful summary of his accomplishment.

For a moment, Ansel feared that Lindbergh must have his own spy within Treasury. But no: Lindbergh, or someone working for him, was simply reading his papers every morning, just as Ansel once had, and was possessed of the skill to know when he was being bullshitted. The difference between himself and Lindbergh was that only one of them was rich, famous, and hated Jews.

Lindbergh was coming to D.C. in January to testify to all of this in front of Congress. Morgenthau would need to go to the Hill himself to refute Lindbergh's accusations. He was not, Ansel well knew, the best face for them to put on this new policy. To have the only Jewish member of the cabinet be the one most publicly defending it would be a boon to Lindbergh's argument. And yet Morgenthau was the Treasury Secretary. This was, he would take pains to point out, simply a financial arrangement between the United States and Britain. Indeed, Morgenthau would attest, Lend-Lease had been designed precisely to keep the United States *out* of the war. The surest way to make sure that the United States did not join the fighting was for the fighting to come to a speedy end. And the surest way to achieve that would be for it to conclude in the manner favored by a majority of Americans: a British victory. By selling them arms, Treasury was simply supporting the president's long-stated policy of maximum peace.

This bullshit was hashed out over long sessions in Roosevelt's fish room and shorter ones in Morgenthau's office overlooking it; Harry Dexter White participated begrudgingly. He hated the deal that America was preparing to make with Britain, but even worse, from his perspective, would be no deal at all. And so he had no choice but to aid in the crafting of a bill to secure a deal that he did not like and that had been crafted by his subordinates behind his back.

On the occasions that Ansel passed his silent boss in the halls, he wondered whether this would be the day on which White would either admit the necessity of Ansel's subterfuge . . . or come for his revenge.

50

ASSUME A
CAN OPENER

"A physicist, a chemist, and an economist are stranded on a desert island with a single can of beans—but no can opener. The physicist devises an ingenious method of getting the can open by tossing it from a tree at a precise angle. The chemist devises another method of using the sun's heat to pop it open. The economist says, 'No, I have a better method.' 'What is it?' 'First, assume a can opener.'"

—COMMON ECONOMICS JOKE, SOURCE UNKNOWN

January 6, 1941

The New Year arrived with an unexpected warm front and an even more surprising death toll. Over two hundred Americans were killed in fireworks displays and drunk driving accidents on New Year's Eve alone, a figure that shattered previous records. Inside the District, a twenty-four-year-old undertaker's assistant drove herself into a telephone pole, a rhumba dancer lit her cellophane costume on fire, and nearly a hundred men were admitted to St. Elizabeth's on suspicion of alcohol poisoning. The papers breathlessly reported the mayhem. Perhaps the celebrations had gotten so out of hand because everyone needed to let off a bit of steam. Ansel wouldn't know. The Luxfords spent New Year's at Pehle's family compound in Delaware, where he fell asleep to the chirp of crickets well before midnight.

The following Monday morning, White appeared in the open doorway to Ansel's office for the first time in two months. He didn't bother knocking.

His first words were: "You got a problem."

Ansel set down his cigarillo. "If you're ready to have this out, then let's have it out. I went over your head and behind your back. And I did it because you were too blinded by your irrational hatred for Keynes to do what needed to be done. As was certainly clear to Henry." Ansel had practiced this speech many times in his head.

"You want to be sore with me?" he continued after receiving no response. "Fine. But this was the right thing to do, and one day you'll thank me."

White took his time lighting a Lucky. "That wasn't the problem I was talking about."

"Oh."

"I've been with Cox and the guys from the White House counsel's office. They have some concerns about the Lend-Lease language."

"What concerns?"

"First, that it's plainly unconstitutional. Second, that the justices of the Supreme Court will notice."

Ansel was no constitutional expert. But it had occurred to him that a bill that effectively gave the executive branch the ability to write a blank check to provide military assistance in a conflict to which the United States was not a party might present a few issues.

"What did Morgenthau say?" he asked.

White seemed to be mindfully containing his frustration. "Morgenthau is on the Hill dealing with two hundred Republican congressmen who think, not without cause, that passing Lend-Lease would be tantamount to declaring war on Germany. And before you ask, Randolph and everyone at Treasury counsel are in New York heading off lawsuits from Morgan and all his banking friends. The Professor isn't a lawyer, Joe is buried alive underneath the thousands of accountants he's overseeing, and James . . . Honestly, I haven't seen that kid in a blue moon. I don't have a clue where he is."

Ansel searched his brain for any constitutional law experts he might ask for help. "I'll figure out something."

White sighed. "No you won't, because you're in over your head, and the only things you've put on the table these past six months that weren't dumb as bricks all came from the brilliant but evil mind of your buddy Maynard. Who is probably in London right now celebrating with Churchill over the deal of the damned century that he just talked some numbskull Treasury grunt into giving them. Hell, if I were Maynard I'd be asking for a raise."

He looked at Ansel pointedly. "Not that he needs the money."

Ansel was not going to be cowed. "Feel good? Letting all that out?"

White looked as if he was genuinely taking stock. "Not so much. I was the one that hired you. So your turning into a disloyal rat—it's my own fault for trusting you in the first place."

"I never promised you blind loyalty. I promised you that I would do whatever it took to win. And right now, it'll take working with a man who you happen to hate."

White nodded. "The funny thing is, you're right. Because I hate your guts and yet I'm the only person who can get you out of the hole you've dug for yourself."

"You came down here to help me?"

"I came down here to aid in getting this accursed bill past the Supreme Court. Not because it's what you want. Because it's what Henry and the president want. I came down here to help them." White puffed smoke at Ansel before marching to the door. "If you happen to benefit from the high esteem in which I hold those men—well, consider my good graces to be yours. On loan."

51

PENCILS

*"Surely the plague of lawyers is a worse plague of Egypt
than the pharaohs ever knew."*

—JOHN MAYNARD KEYNES

January 16, 1941

Ansel was transfixed by the cleft in Felix Frankfurter's chin. It moved
up and down as the Supreme Court's newest justice read the pages in
his hand. It seemed to indent further when he arrived at a point of
concern. It waggled side to side as he finished, considered the problem
before him, and then, without saying a word, read through the document again in silence.

The din of the cocktail party downstairs wafted up through the
floorboards. Morgenthau's mansion was just beginning to fill with
guests. Ansel and White had arrived early, before the bulk of the dignitaries, in the hopes of pulling Frankfurter away for this private con-
sultation.

"This section here." Frankfurter directed Ansel's attention to a
paragraph in the middle of the page. "It limits the value of the aid to
Britain at 1.3 billion dollars."

White smoked. "Somewhere between one dollar and two billion
dollars. I suppose it's a compromise."

"But the limit only applies to aid given before the passage of the
bill. The verb tense is past, suggesting the restriction doesn't apply to
future aid. And moreover, the text doesn't specify who assigns a dollar

value to the aid. My read of this is that the army can decide to 'lease' the British a Sherman tank for ten dollars."

"Huh," was all White replied, his tone bone-dry.

Ansel felt it best to stay silent.

"Moreover," Frankfurter said, "two paragraphs later you've included this provision granting Congress oversight and approval of all goods exchanged via Lend-Lease."

"At the behest of our more squeamish Democrats on the Hill."

"But again, the way you've phrased it, the oversight comes *after* the president, or the executive branch, has lent or leased the goods. Effectively, Roosevelt can give the Brits anything he wants, at any price he sets, and Congress has merely reserved for itself the right to tell him afterward that they didn't approve what he's already done. But what's supposed to happen then? The War Department should ask for a battalion of Sherman tanks back from the front?"

White shrugged. "My God, man, you're right. It's almost as if Mr. Luxford here took Congress's complaints and added obtuse language that seemed to address them but in fact gives the president mile-wide loopholes to get around them all."

Ansel confirmed nothing.

"There will be challenges in court," White said.

Frankfurter's cleft made two full circles in the air. "I'd imagine so."

"How many votes will we have on the Supreme Court to let this go through?"

Frankfurter's cleft descended. "Hard to tell. It'll be close."

"Doesn't the executive branch have total authority when it comes to waging war?"

"Are we at war?" Frankfurter flipped the pages again. "I hadn't heard."

Ansel finally stepped in. "Can we alter the text of the bill such that it appears to close those loopholes enough to pass the Supreme Court, but in practice leaves them wide open?"

White shot Ansel a castigating glare. He wanted to keep playing coy with Frankfurter, plying guidance out of him without explicitly asking him to help write the text of legislation that would assuredly end up on his docket.

But Ansel had long ago lost his patience for such pleasantries. They *were* at war, whether the law acknowledged it or not. If the rumors about Frankfurter were true—Communist sympathies, a long-standing rivalry with Hoover from when he was in Roosevelt's administration, and a habit of pursuing the outcomes he favored above the legal analysis he conducted—then he'd either help Treasury or tell them to scram. Either way, what was the point of being coy?

Frankfurter's cleft froze in place.

Then the justice began fishing around Morgenthau's desk. "Do either of you know where Henry keeps his pencils?"

52

AMERICAN IDEALISTS

"I am not afraid of my enemies, but by God,
you must look out when you get among your friends."

—CORNELIUS VANDERBILT

March 11, 1941

The night that Lend-Lease finally passed the Senate by a comfortable vote of 60–31, Harry and Anne Terry White invited the men and women of the one-time Research Department, plus their wives and girlfriends, to an intimate celebration. Angela had visited the Whites frequently over the past six months to socialize with Anne Terry. Ansel had not been over since the fateful night he'd stolen the cables from the study.

They arrived in front of the two-story suburban house to see warm lights glowing inside. Ansel could hear the faint chatter of his victorious colleagues above the rhythmic blasts of the Victrola. He hoped that this would be an evening for reconciliation. If White saw fit to finally welcome his colleagues back into his home, then even though he'd opposed much of the Lend-Lease bill they'd written—his being in favor of neither the "Lend" nor the "Lease" provisions—this invitation was a sign that he at least acknowledged its necessity.

Ansel found Saxon accompanied by a striking blonde. She introduced herself as Lucy, and this time Ansel was prepared to tell her how much he'd heard about her without divulging that he hadn't. Even Saxon seemed impressed with Ansel's gamesmanship.

DuBois attended stag and didn't touch the booze. He stuck to soda water that he pumped himself from the siphon on the bar cart.

Adopting the celebratory spirit, the Professor wore a black silk gown complete with matching gloves. She looked like she was on her way to the opera.

John and Francha Pehle brought chocolate boxes for the host's daughters.

Herman Oliphant was dead. Early one morning a few weeks before, a heart attack had struck him. His wife telephoned White from the hospital. The stress of the past year could not have been easy on him. Ansel felt rotten for having once joked to Pehle that Oliphant seemed perpetually on the verge of a coronary. There was a strange sensation in losing someone around whom he had spent so much time, and yet whom he turned out to know so poorly. Here was a man he'd talked to for hours about the design of German tariffs, yet not for even a minute about the lives for which they'd fought this secret war. Ansel had to learn from his *Times* obituary that he had three grown children.

Oliphant had not lived long enough to see his labors bear fruit, but it would have made him proud, Ansel hoped, to have witnessed the accomplishments wrought by what had once been their small and shadowy trust. Pehle and DuBois oversaw an empire of accountants at FFC, for which Saxon served as a wandering gunslinger. Lend-Lease would be administered by its own special commission, a joint project of Treasury, State, Commerce, and War. Roosevelt chose a man named Harry Hopkins from Commerce to run the show; he seemed to get along better with the British than had anyone at Treasury or State. Meanwhile, the war bonds that Ansel had dreamed up with help from Keynes were going on sale. The Professor bounced with Ansel between these massive new organizations.

Anne Terry took a turn on the piano, slipping into Ukrainian to play a few of the folk songs her grandparents had taught her on their upright back in Kyiv. Lucy turned out to be quite the singer, in English and French. Francha admired Angela's new scarf, which Angela admitted freely had been a gift from Lydia.

After a few hours of drinking, they were all good and relaxed. The ladies sustained themselves on spinach canapés and crackers. Ansel felt the spirit of the occasion when he glimpsed White alone in the kitchen slicing roast beef onto a platter. It was time to bridge their divide magnanimously.

"Thanks for having us." Ansel stood beside him watching the juice drip from the pink meat. "I know Angela and Anne Terry have done a bang-up job of keeping cordial, despite our differences, and I'd like to follow suit. What say we put this all behind us?"

White sliced. "Was that a sideways kind of 'I'm sorry'?"

"Have you been waiting on an apology?" It came out more aggressively than he'd intended.

"No. But I promised Anne Terry we could discuss apologies at the office."

"What's wrong with now?"

"Tomorrow." White said the single word with enough condescension for a dozen.

Ansel had the uneasy feeling there was something he didn't know. "The last time you didn't share information with me when you should have, I ended up with a pistol in my face."

White set down the knife. "Fine."

He led Ansel into the study, then closed the door behind them. He found a memorandum on the desk and dangled it sneeringly.

"Your buddy Maynard did you rotten. Sold you out, exactly like I told you he would. And now, wouldn't you know, he's sitting high on the hog while we—and, more importantly, Morgenthau and the president—pay the price."

The memo bore the stamp of the Commerce Department. It was from the desk of Harry Hopkins, the new Lend-Lease czar.

And Ansel needed only to read the first few sentences to realize how badly he'd been betrayed.

53

TOO MUCH OF A
GOOD THING

*"Concentrated power is not rendered harmless by
the good intentions of those who create it."*

—MILTON FRIEDMAN

March 12, 1941

He had to bang on the Mayflower suite's door for the better part of a minute before Keynes finally opened it, bleary-eyed in his sky-blue pajamas, and Ansel could bark: "You goddamned liar."

Groggily, Keynes waved away the night manager, who was stuck awkwardly behind Ansel in the hallway. It had taken both a lot of yelling and a badge that read *Treasury Agent* to convince the manager to escort him up here at two in the morning.

Keynes led Ansel inside and put a finger to his lips: *Hush.* Lydia was asleep in the next room.

Ansel saw a stack of suitcases. Of course Keynes was headed back to London in the morning. He'd gotten everything he wanted here.

Ansel said, "The whole reason you convinced me to structure Lend-Lease as a loan was because you told me you didn't have the dollars to pay and that we could make as many of them as we needed."

Keynes smoothed the wrinkles in his pajamas. "The second part of that is true."

"At the same time you were working with me, you were conniving to get a loan from Harry Hopkins. We're lending you *billions* of dollars' worth of weapons on credit—now I find out that simultaneously

Commerce is simply lending you billions of dollars. We're not just financing your war, we're financing it twice!"

Keynes scratched at his unkempt hair. "I suppose one can't have too much of a good thing. Do you want a drink? A coffee? What time is it?"

It turned out, Ansel learned from White, that Hopkins controlled an obscure Commerce program called the New Deal Reconstruction Corporation: one of those decades-old government programs where, after Congress approved the budget, they promptly forgot it existed. Apparently, everybody had. Everybody except Maynard. The entire time he was sweet-talking Ansel into Lend-Lease, he was whispering into Hopkins's ear about securing a loan from the NDRC.

Treasury would have noticed, of course, if the NDRC loans went straight to the British government. So Keynes had gotten Hopkins to grant the loans to private British corporations that just so happened to have U.S. holdings. That way, it would look like the American government was simply investing in American manufacturing. But in reality, all the dollars would end up back under the control of the Exchequer.

Keynes had worked the American government inside and out. Back to front and twice around.

He made no attempt to deny it. "You were never going to be able to get me everything I needed. So I got it elsewhere. You're all hot and bothered now because . . . what? I neglected to inform you of what I was doing when you weren't around? How is that any different from the way you treated poor Harry?"

Ansel couldn't tell if he was angrier with Keynes for lying to him or for convincing him to lie to White. "The difference is that this morning, the White House figured out what you did, and they blew a gasket. Only their hands are tied: Hopkins already gave out the NDRC money. It's gone. And Roosevelt can't exactly sit down to his next fireside chat and say 'Oops, never mind, we're not doing Lend-Lease after all!' He's trapped. So is Morgenthau. But they're not even who I need to worry about most. I need to worry about what happens when the Republicans find out how badly you played me. What's Lindbergh

going to say? At best, we're incompetent. At worst, what we did—
what you tricked me into doing—is criminal."

Moreover, what would Angela say? Right now she was probably in
bed after accepting a ride home from the Pehles. Ansel could picture
her face in the morning when he'd have to tell her how badly he'd
botched things up for her president.

He thought of that look she'd given him back in St. Paul as they
packed up for a last-minute move to D.C. to save the world. Was that
the last time she would ever be proud of him?

Ansel forced himself to look Keynes in the eye, which on account
of his mortification and rage took considerable effort. The extent of
Keynes's deception was hard to even calculate: the dinners, the late-
night chin-wags about the history of money, the shopping expeditions
between their wives. Had Lydia known what her husband was keeping
from the husband of her new friend? Of course she had. She'd been in
on the swindle. They'd known exactly how to hoodwink a pair of
American idealists like Ansel and Angela. Keynes had pegged him perfectly back in Sussex and laid the groundwork for his con among the
cuneiform tablets of the ancients.

Keynes went to the bar and found a pair of empty tumblers. "Will
it be water or whiskey? They appear to be our only options." He took
in the look on Ansel's face. "Oh, come on. Be a good sport, won't you?
All's fair in love and . . . well, you're not even at war yet, are you?"

"All that talk of a lasting peace? Of a new currency to stop wars
before they started? My God, White *told* me—it's all about maintaining your own power, isn't it? I should have seen it when you kept in-
sisting on maintaining your sterling bloc. Why would you care about
bolstering sterling if you were going to go create this new 'bancor'—
unless, of course, bancor was just a front."

"A front? You sound like Jimmy Cagney. Sterling will serve us well
as bancor grows in prominence."

"It'll serve *you* well, because *you* control it."

"Just because it happens to be in my interest doesn't make it a bad
idea."

"Do you care at all about the war—this war, the one in which people are dying every day? Or is the only thing that really matters to you preserving your place on the throne?"

Keynes opted for water. "Do you think I don't belong there? Dear boy, if you didn't have me to run things, then who would? Harry? *You?*"

He shuddered: Perish the thought.

Ansel looked up at Keynes, whose boundless erudition he could now see was only eclipsed by his entitlement, and thought, *What am I still doing here?*

He had a lot to do. None of it could be accomplished from a palatial suite on the fourth floor of the Mayflower.

"Maybe bancor really is brilliant. Maybe it's insane. I don't know." Ansel went to the door. "But I know I can't trust you. So what's going to happen now is you're going to get your money. You're going to get your guns. Together we're going to kill a lot of Nazis. And then when this is over . . . Me and Harry are going to build a global economic system of such strength that no great war will ever again darken our skies. And we're going to do it with good old American dollars."

54

MODUS VIVENDI

"Money is a matter of belief, even faith: belief in the person
paying us; belief in the person issuing the money. . . . Money is
not metal. It is trust inscribed. And it does not seem to
matter much where it is inscribed: on silver, on clay,
on paper, on a liquid crystal display."

—NIALL FERGUSON,
SCOTTISH-AMERICAN ECONOMIC HISTORIAN

July 10, 1941

In the spring and summer of 1941, a geyser of dollars burst forth from deep in the earth and surged across America. In Long Beach, Douglas Aircraft expanded its factory to build tens of thousands of B-17 bombers. Outside of Detroit, Chrysler erected the Arsenal Tank Plant from scratch to build the M3 Grant and M4 Sherman models. In the single leafy suburb of Warren, Michigan, American boys were hired to build more tanks than had been built in all of Britain. The soil, damp with investment, sprouted jobs. There had never been a better time to find work. It wasn't simply the government that was doing the hiring: Every factory from coast to coast had manufacturing to do, and every farm under the Midwestern sun had newly flush citizens to feed. The eggheads at the NBER reported that unemployment was set to fall by twenty percent, achieving a level not seen since before the Depression. The Professor suggested that the GNP statistic with which they'd recently been experimenting was going to surge ten percent. *Within the year.* The only country that had pulled off such a miracle in the last two decades? Nazi Germany. Hjalmar Schacht's dark wizardry had taken his country from depleted backwater to ascendant empire in five years; the dollars conjured by the U.S. Treasury would have to build the

Anglo-American war machines into something much larger in only one. The previous year, the U.S. defense budget was two billion dollars. Next year? Ten billion.

By the end of the summer, the UK was on track to receive 130 million of their "borrowed" bullets.

The number of dollars in existence was set to go up sixteen percent by the end of this year and then by at least as much the following. The Professor made a bet with Pehle on precisely when the money supply would double.

Not everyone enjoyed the flood. The Wall Street men—who'd been blessed with so very many dollars before Ansel's geyser erupted—feared the excess. *The Wall Street Journal* shrieked with terror, as if its editors were personally being drowned by the rising tide of capital. Surely this would capsize the American economy on a wave of inflation!

It didn't.

Thanks to the ingenuity of Keynes's design—and with the assistance of Ansel's pen in composing the legislation—the purchasing power of each individual dollar was barely affected. Keynes had argued that the financial system was at heart a fiction, an elaborate narrative of numerals that we tell ourselves to obscure the truth that it's all just a barman scratching symbols on wood pellets so that his patrons might close their working day with an extra pint. As he predicted, America spent the summer drinking well—and she bought rounds for her mates across the pond.

Ansel wondered whether Keynes was appreciating his triumph. No one at Treasury exchanged transatlantic messages with him anymore, and the White House had practically cut off all ties as well. Harry Hopkins and his staff at Lend-Lease were instructed to deal with other Exchequer bureaucrats. Meanwhile, Ansel found himself grateful for the perfection of the ruse by which he'd been deceived: He was no longer burdened by doubts about whose side he was on. Now he could devote himself fully to aiding White in plotting Keynes's comeuppance.

They penciled in their postwar planning meetings for Monday

lunchtimes. The gatherings became more official: sandwiches in An-sel's office, and everyone was hungry. Pehle had not found Keynes's deceptions sporting and so paid no further mind to whatever "bancor" was supposed to be. The Professor's analysis was practical: Her days were not infinite, and she was not going to waste her time hunting for subtle tricks buried in the proposals of a man she now knew could not be trusted. Better she disregard Keynes's schemes entirely.

DuBois, bless him, didn't bother saying I told you so. He was too busy working on plans for this World Bank, which would need to be joined by another entity, some kind of international monetary fund. He made his motivations plain: This wasn't about revenge—it was about peace.

———

THAT JUNE, PEHLE AND DuBois found a way to press harder against the Axis: Their team at Foreign Funds Control instituted a rule declaring that *all* foreign ownership of *all* U.S. assets must be declared to the government. Which meant that any American who owned any asset that also had foreign investment had to submit a detailed disclosure form to Treasury. They quickly received 560,000 reports of foreign-owned property to investigate. How were they supposed to do all that with only ten thousand new accountants?

FFC began requisitioning agents from Customs. Then from the Se-cret Service. Then from the Bureau of Narcotics, and finally even from the Bureau of Alcohol. An army of gumshoes whose fountain pens could, with a single stroke, obliterate entire corporations.

On the twenty-second of June, Germany invaded the Soviet Union with a wave of violence stretching from the Arctic to the Baltic Sea. Hitler declared that his attack was a defensive maneuver rendered nec-essary by unspecified Soviet collaboration with Britain to "prolong" the war. Riding the trolley down H Street the following morning, Ansel heard anxious chattering from every passenger. But if the mood in Washington was grim, he was elated. He knew that the German in-vasion of the USSR was not a sign of strength; it was a sign of weak-ness. Schacht and the Nazi economic team had not failed to notice the terrifying extent of American mobilization. Now they would be doing the same math as Ansel—math that Keynes and White had done long before. Germany could defeat Britain and the Soviet Union. She could defeat Britain and America. What she could simply not create enough reichsmarks to do, now that she was without trading partners in South America, was defeat Britain, the Soviet Union, and America simultaneously. By the analysis Ansel had done nearly two years before, it was clear that Germany could never stop fighting. The moment Germany had no more territory to conquer, her economy would collapse. What other moves did she have, Ansel reasoned, besides trying to conquer the Soviet Union before the United States began to fight?

This, it became increasingly clear to Ansel and White that summer, was the one real advantage the Germans still possessed: The United States had not yet taken the trouble of going to war. She was financing a war. She was supplying a war. She was building enough firepower for all the war on earth. But she was not actually at war. The brief peacetime draft had lasted only a few months, and many of the men quit as soon as they were allowed. The German invasion of the Soviet Union was conducted in the hope that a *Panzergruppe* might make it to Moscow before the First Infantry made it to Europe. This was a race. Germany had a head start.

At the end of July, Japanese troops moved south into what had, before the fall of Paris, been French Indochina. The peninsula was now technically Vichy territory, so in a magnanimous act of allyship, they granted Emperor Hirohito permission to station his troops in Cam Ranh so the Japanese could use it as a regrouping station on their way to invading more of China. But neither Downing Street nor the White House failed to notice that the new Japanese naval base was a hop, skip, and a jump from the British outpost in Singapore. And the small American force nearby.

Morgenthau and White used this provocation as an excuse to freeze *all* Japanese assets within the United States. Ansel had been working with DuBois on the language of such a resolution for a while, and now FDR had a perfect excuse to justify pulling the trigger. They cut Japan off from all the world's dollar-denominated trade—including the increasingly dollar-orientated economies of South America. But Treasury didn't stop there: They worked with State to embargo all oil sales from the United States to Japan.

Hirohito—and his economists—were clearly unprepared for the battlefields of economic warfare on which Treasury had become skilled. By Ansel's calculations, Japan imported eighty percent of its oil from the United States. Tokyo panicked, suddenly unable to buy oil from America, Chile, or even Argentina. How would they keep the lights on? In response, they sent a group of tankers to San Francisco Bay. It was as if the Japanese hoped that once the tankers arrived, the captains might talk *someone* into selling them oil. They did not. For weeks, the ships sat empty in the bay before returning, bellies full of only air, to the open ocean.

November 22, 1941

When White said the word *peace,* he spat it with a vitriol that Ansel had only ever heard before in reference to English bureaucrats and Brazilian spies. He had a way of turning the word into an expulsion of nearly two syllables, a powerful pop at the start and then a sinister slink, drawn out as if on the tongue of a snake. "There is," he told Ansel from the confines of his wood-paneled Treasury office, "a back-channel negotiation with Japan for"—he loaded up the cannon before firing—"peace."

"This is coming from Roosevelt?" With the oil maneuvers, Ansel had been prodding the Japanese into further bellicosity. If they couldn't get their oil from either North or South America they would have to look elsewhere. Their best option—hell, their only option—was so glaringly obvious that the army even dragged General MacArthur out of retirement and stationed him outside Singapore to whip the small Filipino forces into shape: Japan would almost certainly have to invade the Philippines. The idea that the White House was considering, or advocating, some kind of *peace* was absurd.

"The president," White said with disdain, "is engaged in quiet talks with the Japanese ambassadors to avoid a war in the Pacific."

"Do they intend on joining the Allies and supporting the Soviets from the East, then? Because the Germans have to keep fighting and will get to the U.S. eventually. There is no possibility for peace until the Germans are finished. So either the Japanese join our side, or else we'll end up at war with them. It's just a question of when."

"I agree."

White hadn't said those two words to Ansel in a year.

"Any peace with Japan," White continued, "would be temporary. And any delay will only give them time—time to acquire oil from the Philippines, time for the Germans to acquire Moscow."

"What are the conditions they're asking for?"

"Ambassador Nomura has evidently supplied the White House with a six-point modus vivendi. They'll agree to organize a withdrawal from Indochina, and they'll promise nonaggression toward the United States."

"What do they want in exchange?"

"What does everybody want? Dollars." White huffed. It was hard to tell if he was bitter or proud. Here they were making dollars the lingua franca of foreign trade while decrying Japan's efforts to get ahold of them. One way of looking at it: Whatever they were doing, it was working. "They want Japanese assets in the U.S. unfrozen, and they want to use them to purchase oil. At a discount."

"What's Roosevelt's counteroffer?"

White made his way to the windows. "The White House hasn't countered yet. Before they do, they've solicited lists of potential demands from State, from War . . . and from us."

"On behalf of Treasury, we should demand quite a bit."

"You think?" White's tone made plain that he already knew exactly what he wanted to do. He hadn't asked Ansel here for advice; he wanted to know if Ansel was willing to go in on this with him.

"Ask for enough," White continued, "and we might even slip a demand into the counteroffer to which we *know* that the Japanese could not possibly agree." Whatever White was planning, it was going to be devious and it was going to be dangerous.

"Are you suggesting that we sabotage this final attempt at peace such that it cannot succeed?" Ansel had developed a willingness to make enemies over these past two years—most notably White himself. But if they did what White seemed to be proposing, then their next enemies could be in the Oval Office.

"What do you think?" White kept his face pointed toward the gloomy skies outside.

"I think," Ansel said, "that the only way this would work is if we did it using such arcane and technical economics that the White House never even realizes what we've done. To the naked eye, our counter-offer would need to look plum. The White House, War, and State, they all have to think we're offering a solid deal. So do the ambassadors, on both sides. But when the economists in Tokyo get their eyes on the fine print, our counteroffer would need to send them into such a hot rage that they toss the thing out the window."

White turned. Only now could Ansel see the delight in his eyes. If this had been a test, Ansel had passed.

55

THIS IS HOW THE APOCALYPSE ENDS

"In economics, things take longer to happen than you think they will, and then they happen faster than you thought they could."

—RÜDIGER DORNBUSCH,
GERMAN-AMERICAN ECONOMIST

December 7, 1941

"The most common mistake is people make the pens too small," he said to Angie. "Sheep like to stay together but they don't appreciate being crowded." He shook the wooden post to demonstrate its sturdiness. Sure enough, it didn't budge. "You see that silver bracket right there? Bring it here."

Angie, in canvas overalls and leather boots, looked across the array of tools lying in the dirt.

"The silver bracket there." He pointed encouragingly. "Can you hand it to me?" The tools were only a few feet away, and he could just as easily have gone and gotten it himself. But she liked having a job to do, and Sunday afternoons were the only time he really got to spend with her. A lot of people might have said that building a sheep pen was hardly an appropriate activity for a four-year-old girl. But that was what Ansel was doing today, and he'd rather do it with her than not see her at all. It wasn't like she was slowing the process down *that* much.

"That's it," he said as she continued staring at the tools. She hadn't moved. "The silver one there."

Hesitantly, Angie knelt and picked up the silver bracket. "This?" The way she made the *th* sound was more like a *d*. It was awfully cute.

"That's the one. Can you hand it to me?"

Angie cautiously stepped the few paces to her father and placed the bracket in his outstretched palm.

"There you go!"

Maybe he should have started with a dog. He'd come to the realization, watching Angie stare wide-eyed at the passing starlings and squeal at the water bugs that snuck into her bed, that she was growing up without any animals around. Weren't they living on a farm? So when he saw a classified ad from a guy selling a dozen merinos, he jumped.

If only he could get this pen squared away.

"Poppa? What's he say?" She made a concerned face.

"He?"

Ansel realized she was talking about a voice on the radio. He'd brought the Zenith portable out here to play a little something while they worked, but he hadn't been listening. The music, he now noticed, had been replaced by a man's urgent voice.

". . . attacked from the air," the announcer said. "Hostilities have opened up across the Southwest Pacific. Ambassador Nomura has gone to the State Department to meet with Secretary Hull . . ."

Ansel hustled to the radio and turned up the volume.

"President Roosevelt's statement says that the Japanese have attacked American Army and Navy bases on the island of Oahu. Additionally, CBS News has received a report from Singapore that Japanese ships have entered the Bay of Siam and are headed to Thailand. Our reporters have attempted to confirm additional reports of an attack in Manila, but the lines are dead and we are at this time unable to say with certainty . . ."

"Poppa?"

Ansel faced her. He wasn't sure how many of these words she'd understand. But evidently she'd grasped enough of the announcer's tone to know that something was going on.

Ansel felt himself overcome with joy.

A warmth spread through his chest.

"Sweetheart." Only as he heard the shake in his own voice did he realize that his eyes were watering. "Sweetheart. It's over."

He scooped her up in his arms. She gave a small yell of surprise, but when she felt the strength of her father's giddy grip, she couldn't help but squeal.

"It's over!" he yelled.

She giggled as he carried her into the house. He opened the door with one hand and swung her around in the other. "Angela?"

His wife appeared at the top of the stairs. "What happened?"

"It over!" Angie said to her mother.

Poor Angela couldn't have any idea what she was talking about. "Over?"

"Turn on the radio," he said. "The Japanese just bombed an island in Hawaii."

"Oh my . . ." Angela appeared frozen.

His gambit with White had worked. In exchange for peace, they'd offered the Japanese two billion dollars. Plus another five hundred million for a joint project to rebuild the areas of China they'd already invaded. The White House had been more than a little shocked at Treasury's sudden largesse. How could the Japanese say no to that?

But in fact, they'd absolutely had to. The exchange was structured like a loan, and this loan—unlike the ones to the British—had extensive terms and conditions. The Japanese wouldn't be able to use their dollars to buy oil directly from U.S. producers; the money wouldn't become available until *after* they'd left Indochina; and the interest rate on the twenty-year note would be enough to hobble Tokyo for decades to come.

For two weeks, Ansel had woken up each morning with the terrible fear that this would be the day their counteroffer would be accepted.

But all the lies he'd told and all the subterfuge he'd employed had been for this moment. The United States would declare war on Japan within the hour; Germany would declare war on the United States in response; and then, soon enough, the Allies would prevail. The outcome of the brutal fighting to come was laid out, plain as day, in the balance sheets on his desk. There was simply no way, now that the full weight of the U.S. military machine would be brought to bear, that Germany and Japan could win. The Japanese didn't have the oil, and the Germans didn't have enough cotton to make clothes to survive winters of frigid combat. All that would be left now was the shooting, a violent formality, a ringing up on the cash register of a price already agreed. The scale would be unprecedented in human history. But the surety of this tragedy had begun years ago, the gears thrown into horrific motion in a moonlit castle outside Berlin. The United States couldn't have avoided this bloodshed any more than the sky could avoid the setting sun.

Angela came down the stairs and flipped on the den radio: "The president has called for a meeting with the cabinet this evening, which will be followed by a meeting with congressional leaders of both political parties."

Ansel tossed Angie a few inches into the air and caught her in a soft puff of laughter. "It's over!"

Angela still did not seem to see what a happy occasion this was. "Oh my God."

Had White heard the news yet? Ansel should call him. But not now. The only place Ansel wanted to be was here, and the only people he wanted to be around he was already with.

"Do you need to go into the office?" Angela asked.

Ansel danced around the den with his daughter. "No, no. Not today."

He knew that the next morning he'd march straight into postwar meetings. The shooting would last a few years. Hopefully no longer than that. At which point Europe would be littered with smoldering rubble. The global economy would be in tatters. And the world would need rebuilding. The coming death toll was impossible to calculate, hard even to comprehend, and its likely magnitude spoke to the stakes of getting the postwar order done right. Rebuild the global economy poorly and they would be back here again in twenty years. When Angie would be a young woman.

But right now, for a few hours on this singular Sunday, a victory.

He set his dizzy girl on the floor and grabbed his wife's arms. She seemed uncertain, as if unable to trust this one moment of relief. He pulled her to his chest. "This is how the apocalypse ends."

She reached up and touched his cheek. He noticed that her fingers came away wet—those must be his tears.

This was what she'd worked for, too. What she'd lied for. What she'd believed in. Her faith had not been misplaced.

In the kitchen he found wine. He poured two glasses plus a tall orange juice for Angie. The three of them sat on the floor listening to the updates. Every half hour they'd flip the station so they could hear a different voice tell them all the same things they'd just heard. The CBS station brought on military analysts, a parade of retired generals to describe what must hypothetically be going on in the White House. The NBC station reported that Japanese soldiers had landed by parachute on Oahu, then retracted it forty-five minutes later. Some expert got on the line to opine about whether the Japanese government even knew about the attack; perhaps saboteurs within their navy had been responsible, so lunatic was the strategy. By five o'clock, the chairman of NBC had sent a personal telegram to President Roosevelt, which the 980 AM station read on the air. He pledged the full support of his network to the war operation. The man on CBS News read a statement from Churchill promising that whenever the United States declared war on Japan—and his assumption seemed to be that the United States would do so imminently—the UK would follow suit within the hour.

The telephone rang a few times, but Ansel didn't want to speak to anyone. Angela answered: Her parents were terrified. Would there be another draft? Angela had four brothers. Strong boys without fancy degrees to spare them. Of what consolation was it to Dominick and Lucretia that the coming violence had long been an inevitability?

Ansel thought he heard Angela hold back from crying, just for a moment, as she tried to calm her mother down.

Then it was one of the girls from the FBI on the line. She didn't know who else she could call. She'd heard that Washington would have an air raid drill that night after sunset. Every light in the city would have to be turned off. Bombers might be headed to California from Japan; to Washington from Vichy France.

Was it helpful to tell a worried kid, alone in the city without family, that the rumors sounded far-fetched? Or was it better to let her fret, to listen patiently, to say you understood?

Night came, and the air did not fill with bombs. It filled with dread.

How many people that he knew personally would die? How many that he was related to?

He thought of his sisters in Harlan. He hadn't written them in a year.

They let Angie stay up late, well past eight. They weren't sure why. She was clearly tuckered. Ansel was the one with this strange energy in him, a spark of joy slowly getting doused by the reality of the coming horrors.

Once Angie was down, Ansel and Angela returned to the den, and this time they sat on the davenport. Angela opened the third bottle of wine. She'd been preparing for this for as many years as he had— begging for it, pleading for it; even, he imagined, praying for it.

A pair of idealists no longer living in a world of wishful theory: This was here. This was now. Something terrible hung in the crisp night air.

"We did the right thing," he said.

"Even though it doesn't feel that way." Was it a question?

"If doing the right thing felt good all the time, everybody would do it." He truly believed that.

She folded her palms over her lap, nervously digging into one with the opposing thumb.

He placed an arm gently around her shoulders and his other hand in between hers.

Over the din of the radio man announcing something about bombers, he could just hear the clink of their wedding rings.

PART
III

EXCHANGES

56

A TRIP TO
NEW HAMPSHIRE

*"When I was young, I thought money was the most important
thing in life. Now that I am old, I know that it is."*

—OSCAR WILDE

June 29, 1944

Ansel tried to comfort his crying son by quantifying the strangeness of
time. He explained that Momma and Poppa were going out of town
for three weeks. That was twenty-one sleeps. Ansel Jr.'s nonna would
put him in his crib on each of those nights and sing him "La Vispa
Teresa." She promised to sing at least two rounds per bedtime, just like
Momma did. That was eighty-four verses. He would wake up on
twenty-one mornings to find his nonna there to play with him before
the nanny arrived.

The poor boy had been in tears since he first glimpsed his parents
with their suitcases at the front door. Ansel's math wasn't helping. Angela tried taking him into her arms, but he swatted her hand away. His
big sister, Angie, had already retreated to her room with her Judy Gar-
land dolls.

Ansel understood where he was coming from. Could Ansel claim
to fathom the passage of time himself? His son had been born two
years ago, but that time had vanished behind them both into a distant
point, like the sunlit entrance to a long tunnel that he was now nearly
through. How long was two years? A flash of light that was gone be-

fore he knew it was there. How long would three weeks be? Perhaps eighty-four verses; perhaps a lifetime. It depended on your perspective.

It was mere seconds ago that the shy boy wailing before him, thick tears dripping down his red cheeks, had not existed. It was only yesterday that Ansel stumbled into a law school lecture hall and first saw a pale girl with hair the color of moonless night. Where had these children and houses and careers and sinks full of dishes come from?

Maybe Junior was right to cry. By the time they returned in three weeks, the earth itself might have shifted.

"Poppa and I are going to New Hampshire." Angela knelt down to look at him eye to eye. "We're going to a conference."

Ansel wondered whether he would understand the concept of "New Hampshire," much less "conference." But Angela never dumbed things down for the kids. She told it to them like it was.

A few weeks ago, 150,000 American boys had stormed the beaches at Normandy, and now a million Allied troops were liberating France, inch by blood-drenched inch. Angela's four brothers were among them. Her parents hadn't heard from their sons in a month.

How long was that?

Ansel had barely noticed the shifting headlines over the past years. He'd never before read the morning paper with such disinterest. He thought of the Agatha Christie stories he loved—there wasn't much point in reading carefully once you knew the ending. The American war effort had been built well. Its operation proceeded with few hitches. Ansel knew the figures by heart, because his job was to calculate them. In the entirety of 1939, the United States had produced two thousand airplanes. Last year? Eighty-six thousand. By the end of this year, they'd build nearly a hundred thousand. The Germans, at the height of their powers, were producing less than half of that. All the dollars Ansel had generated had been put to productive use. And neither Mefo bills nor reichsmarks stood a chance when confronted with the full force of the unshackled dollar.

Angela had left her job at the FBI when Junior was born. The collection of grandmothers, cousins, and part-time nannies they'd employed had sufficed for one child but proved to be more challenging for two.

Finding nannies had become near impossible anyway—government work paid better. Ansel should know: He'd created the money with which they paid.

Ansel had been relieved when Angela left the FBI, though he hadn't said so to her. They'd discussed it as a matter of pure practicality. But he slept better knowing she was out.

Or perhaps not entirely out: White insisted that she join them in New Hampshire. Anne Terry was coming too. Wives were permitted and conveniently not included among the conference's official head count. Which meant that in Angela and Anne Terry, they had the advantage of unofficial reinforcements.

Ansel had been preparing for this moment for nearly three years. While the soldiers danced to a tune written long before, the choreography improvised but the denouement preordained, he and White had worked on barely anything besides this conference. Over the coming days, more than seven hundred delegates from over forty nations would converge on the small town of Bretton Woods. There, in a sprawling hotel tucked beneath Mount Washington, they had three weeks to agree on an economic system to govern the postwar world. Every country in existence—save Germany, Japan, and Italy, who no longer got a say—was to send her sharpest economic minds to stake a claim on the new world order. The Axis would surrender soon, and by now it wasn't only the economists who knew it. The Old World was rubble; with what money would they build the next one?

The phantasmagorical bancor of Keynes? Or the all-too-real dollars of White?

Both promised peace. But only one, Ansel knew, was capable of delivering it.

Time: Three years had gone by in the flap of a butterfly's wings. The next three weeks would wind the clock for generations to come.

If Ansel had learned anything these past years, it was that peace, like money, depended on trust. The safety of Ansel's children, not to mention billions of others, could not be trusted to the devious and self-interested machinations of bancor's brilliant but power-hungry author.

And yet another danger lingered: What if they could not get each and every country to agree? Neither system would work if instituted only partially. One couldn't knit together *half* the economies of the world and expect the fabric not to tear. This game would be all-or-nothing.

Which meant, Ansel reminded himself as he kissed the head of his crying son, that he had exactly three weeks in which to outplay John Maynard Keynes.

57

HOME FIELD
ADVANTAGE

"Rule number one is never lose money.
Rule number two is never forget rule number one."

—WARREN BUFFETT

June 29, 1944 (cont'd)

An army bus brought Ansel and Angela, along with Harry and Anne
Terry, from the Fabyan train station through the mountains. The couples arrived at the Mount Washington Hotel to discover that it had
been painted white. Not just the Spanish-style stucco façade, nor simply the five-story towers, nor merely every wall of its four hundred
guest rooms. No, apparently when a military advance team had arrived
weeks before, they'd found it shabby from years of wartime disuse. So
they'd hired a local painting company to spruce it up. Only the town
craftsmen had taken their instructions literally and painted everything
in the hotel that was not on wheels in the exact same shade of pure-
white acrylic. Every golden light fixture; every dark wood door trim;
the candy cane pole of the barbershop and the slick floor of the bowl-
ing alley; even the marquees of both movie theaters. Anne Terry
laughed when she entered the sweeping lobby, its ornate bannisters
still pungent with the odor of paint. Her husband did not find it
funny—this sort of hideousness made America look bad—so the first
thing he did upon arriving, after years of rigorous economic planning,
was to order a team of newly drafted army boys to stay up all night
chipping acrylic from the light fixtures.

The foreign guests—all seven hundred of them—would arrive over the next two days. Which gave the conference's hosts in the Treasury Department one night to prepare. The Professor showed up with a single suitcase, Randolph Paul, inexplicably, with six. DuBois brought his portable Smith-Corona so he could continue hammering out the fiendishly complex trade agreements, a task he'd taken to with relish. He seemed to enjoy it a lot more than dealing with a staff of what now numbered fifteen thousand accountants at Foreign Funds Control. Pehle remained in Washington to mind their regulatory army.

Nobody had a clue where Saxon was. Last Ansel had heard, he was somewhere in North Africa, having spent a few months traveling around Ethiopia, finding every last dollar bill he could get his hands on and burning them. The kid had proven himself gifted at tactical arson: He'd spent the better part of three years searching the globe for American currency and lighting it all on fire. The scheme started the day after the attack on Pearl Harbor, when White dispatched him on a navy submarine to the Philippines to fetch as much gold bullion as he could and ferret it away before the Japanese invaded. If DuBois and Pehle were using pen and paper to freeze dollar and gold assets of enemy nations—with gold, the Japanese might have been able to buy oil on some international market—then Saxon was to accomplish the same thing with submarines and matches. The gold they tried to salvage, but when it came to paper money, it was simplest to have Saxon just incinerate all the bills he could find. Treasury could always make more. They'd never know for sure, but as of his last letter from Ethiopia, he reckoned he'd torched a few hundred million dollars that might have fallen under Axis control. Not bad for a kid making 3,600 dollars a year.

White took Ansel on a tour through the hotel. Keynes and his wife were booked into room 219. The Ecuadorians could be placed in 217, on one side, and the Nigerians in 221, on the other. That way Keynes might have a sense of security when he placed his phone calls. No one who might be listening was among the people he feared held a dagger to his back.

Morgenthau and his wife would be in 119. The floorboards were thin. Perhaps the secretary might overhear something useful.

"Isn't OSS or FBI tapping everyone's phone calls?" Ansel gazed out the window from what was to be Keynes's room at the million acres of national forest beyond. The army had barricaded all the roads leading to the hotel. He was pretty sure they had patrol boats on the Ammonoosuc River, whose rushing waters he could make out beneath the mountain. He searched for snipers in the pine trees.

White shrugged. "You think they'd tell me?"

He had a point.

"Let's assume they're tapping ours too." White knocked on the walls: They seemed thin enough to let pass even the most casual conversations. "Not much of a home field advantage. But I'd hate to be playing an away game."

————

THE RULES WERE SIMPLE and had been agreed upon by all parties at a series of pre-conferences. Two global organizations would be formed to administer the world's economy: The International Monetary Fund would lend to countries in dire financial straits to aid in resolving currency crises, while the World Bank would essentially be a massive pile of capital to be deployed to promote growth, most pressingly for the reconstruction of Europe's war-torn capitals. In principle, all seven hundred delegates agreed that both institutions would be crucial to global harmony. The IMF could make it difficult for any country to ever again do what Schacht had done in Germany; the WB could make sure that no country ever wanted to.

But the devil, as ever, was in the details. How would these massively powerful organizations be run? Who would lead them? Could they really get every nation on earth to agree to this system? And most crucially: By whose currency would they be powered?

Keynes and White had been sending bellicose letters across the war-torn Atlantic on the subject for years. Ansel was certain there did not exist an economist in the world who was unaware of both their antipathy and their dispute:

Would it be bancor . . . or dollars?

From the great river of this fundamental disagreement gushed a thousand small streams of discord: the size of the IMF's capitalization, the location of the World Bank's headquarters, the granting of veto privileges to certain nations over loans whose recipients were not trading in good faith—each a point of verbose contention, each following in turn from the two men's single central divergence.

Just as White had predicted, Keynes's proposals turned out, in their intricate details, to place control of bancor in the hands of a small team of experts who looked suspiciously like him. An unnamed group of academic economists would run the world from offices in London. Of course they would need government experience. Oh, and connections around the globe. Ansel was surprised that Keynes hadn't attached an actual self-portrait to his financial schematics.

But the tool with which White would force Keynes's hand was plain as day: The United Kingdom was in an unfathomable amount of debt. Ansel had put the calculations together: From their Lend-Lease purchases, even at steep discounts, they were on the cuff for 26.9 billion dollars. And the fighting wasn't even over. The terms of the American loan, however, did not wait for the German surrender. Merely servicing the debt and avoiding default would require a payment from the Exchequer to the Treasury of nine billion dollars.

By August.

Calculating the number of dollars the Exchequer had on hand with which to make this payment was easy: They had none.

Thanks in part to the great success of the Lend-Lease program, they'd spent all they had. Even the greenbacks Harry Hopkins had so generously provided were long gone. Britain was a train speeding toward a cliff. In only four weeks she would hurtle off, into sovereign default and incalculable economic disaster, unless somehow she was able to conjure a payment of nine billion dollars—not sterling, not gold, not silver, but *dollars*—from thin air.

Or Keynes could swallow his pride, give up his bancor, and make a deal with Harry Dexter White.

———

ANSEL AND ANGELA'S ROOM had no hot water. No one answered at the desk on each of the dozen times they rang down for assistance. But the kitchen did manage some biscuits in the morning and laid out brown coffee-like liquid in silver carafes in the main dining hall.

There was an eeriness to the massive, empty hotel. There were no more than ten guests in its four hundred rooms. But there was a constant din from the army boys chipping paint and tightening faucets, the hotel staff laundering thousands of bedsheets. Ansel felt a haunted sensation of standing on an empty stage awaiting the cast, the costumes, and the audience.

They decided that he and DuBois would handle the daily press briefings. They'd invited over seventy reporters, representing papers from San Francisco to St. Petersburg. Whatever deals were agreed to in New Hampshire would need to be ratified by the legislatures of each signatory nation. Which meant that what they accomplished here needed to be not merely effective but also popular. Pehle had been the one to venture that putting White in front of a line of newspapermen every afternoon was a recipe for disaster. Their boss wasn't offended. The Professor, they agreed, might be able to put a pleasant face to the proceedings, but she was by her own admission an odd duck. Process of elimination: Ansel and DuBois were the storytellers.

When the Professor joined Ansel and White at the breakfast table, she slapped a copy of the *Chicago Tribune* on the linen. The front page carried an article about the conference and its unquestionable star. There was a three-column portrait of a man with thick lips whose face Ansel knew well. The headline read: "The Englishman Who Rules America."

Ansel winced. White flicked cigarette ash toward the newsprint.

"It's a good portrait of Maynard," Angela said.

The Professor checked her wristwatch. "I do believe His Royal Highness is arriving."

58

THERE'S A MAN IN SWEDEN WHO HAS ACCESS TO A BOAT

"Keynes was one of the most intelligent people I knew, but he understood very little economics."

—FRIEDRICH AUGUST VON HAYEK

July 1, 1944

John Maynard Keynes brought along a dozen-man retinue and a persistent cough. Lydia, by his side, doted on him with a handkerchief. He waved it away. The aides and advisers who trailed behind seemed an uncharacteristic appendage for a man who, in Ansel's experience, preferred to work alone. Ansel nodded at him from across the lobby. Angela went over to kiss Lydia on each cheek. White was nowhere to be found.

A fleet of porters descended and reached out for Keynes's bags only to find their entreaties rejected. Ansel noticed one black leather bag in Keynes's hand that not even his countrymen were allowed to touch.

That afternoon, all seven hundred delegates assembled in rows of wicker chairs in the central ballroom. Keynes and White took turns inaugurating the conference with speeches that reached new pinnacles of vacuousness. They seemed to be having a competition of sorts to determine who might say the least. They honestly both laid it on so heavily that Ansel caught a few reporters giving each other incredulous looks.

Angela took the opportunity for a mountain hike with Lydia.

Many of the delegates brought their wives—and in the cases of the few women delegates, their husbands. Such was the spirit of the event as so long-windedly described by Keynes and White: a family of nations meeting at the kitchen table to go over their finances. Who'd rung up the largest bill down at the grocer's? Could they afford a new wireless this Christmas? Would one of the boys need to get an after-school job?

At the podium, Keynes rambled on about the great victory that their transatlantic collaboration had achieved. That it had not actually yet been achieved, technically speaking, went unmentioned: The blood was on the wall. Ansel gazed across the rows of delegates and noticed H. H. Kung, the Chinese representative, breaking into a wide smile. A short, balding man in his sixties, he insisted that everyone call him Daddy. He wore black round glasses that seemed too small for his face, making him look like he was perpetually peering through the lenses of a microscope. Supposedly he was a seventy-fifth-generation descendant of Confucius; but then all the Republic of China bankers whom Ansel had met claimed similar lineage.

Kung turned to an aide and whispered something that made the junior man laugh. What was he hoping to get from the British, Ansel wondered? For that matter, what were the other 699 delegates hoping to get from the Americans?

At the close of the speeches, the doors were flung open and the attendees spilled out onto the cocktail veranda. The mountains ahead gleamed in the afternoon sun. One of the military aides tapped Ansel on his shoulder.

"Mr. Luxford? There's a message from a John Pehle. From Washington."

———

ANSEL TOOK THE CALL in his room. It was unseasonably cold, so he kept his jacket on as he lifted the receiver.

Pehle didn't bother with a greeting. "I need fifty thousand dollars."

"This hotel is guarded by the military." Ansel accented the final word.

"Thank you for reminding me. Would anyone from the army who might be on the line be able to get me fifty thousand dollars?"

Ansel listened to the silence.

"Sounds as if that's a no." Pehle was upset, that much was clear. "Ansel? How about you?"

For over a year now, Pehle had run a division within Treasury called the War Refugee Board. White had taken Pehle with him to the Oval Office to plead for permission to help the persecuted Jews of Europe get to safety. Pehle was granted his own small unit to perform this refugee work. Ansel enjoyed watching the most refined patrician he knew become their resident firebrand. The rising tide of atrocity was more than even Pehle—born to the manor and raised on the financial pages—could bear.

"Where does the money need to go?" Ansel asked.

"Sweden," Pehle said. "In kronor."

"Do I want to ask you what it's for?"

Pehle paused. "Let's say there's a man in Sweden who has access to a boat."

"I would imagine there are a few."

"This one can get that boat to Lithuania. Squeeze a couple hundred passengers on board. And then set sail for faraway lands."

This wasn't the first time that Pehle had found a bribable ship's captain to ferry Jewish refugees out of Nazi-controlled territory. A few months back he'd concocted a wild scheme with a group of Spanish pirates. A cruel irony: Throughout the hotel, the war was being discussed purely in the past tense. But Pehle's own son, Ansel well knew, was fighting somewhere in France. For the soldiers in the field, not to mention the Jews of Europe, the difference between the theoretical end of the war and the actual end of the fighting was a matter of life and death. The undeniability of the Nazi defeat had only magnified their brutality. The concentration camp at Auschwitz was no longer putting its captives to work making synthetic rubber. Reports had come through that the Germans had moved on to wholesale slaughter.

"I'm going to assume," Ansel said, "that you've tried Joe already?" The easiest way to sneak Treasury funds in and out of Europe, they'd found, was through Foreign Funds Control. DuBois had fingers in every interbank transaction that went across the transatlantic wires.

"He has not returned my calls all day."

"I think he's downstairs. . . . And he may be a little overwhelmed at the moment."

Pehle was unsympathetic. "Bully for him. I still need fifty thousand dollars' worth of Swedish kronor in a particular bank account in forty-eight hours or else these people are going to die." The line crackled as if breaking under the weight of Pehle's frustration. "And it can't look like the money came from the U.S. I can't use Treasury dollars."

"I'll handle it."

Pehle did not say thank you. Ansel could hear the rustle of papers on his desk. He was already fishing around for the next crisis.

"How's the New York situation?" Ansel asked, anticipating his friend's next headache.

"I'm getting strange and unexplained resistance from Customs."

Ansel frowned. Pehle had spent months working on a plan to bring a thousand Jewish refugees out of Italy to a disused army barracks in the town of Oswego, New York. The total number of Jewish refugees thus far taken in by the United States over three years of war was zero. So for Pehle and Ansel, this first thousand amounted to far too little, far too late—but it was better than nothing. And it would hopefully be the first ship of many.

"State?" Ansel didn't even know why he bothered to ask.

"Long's old people, I'd venture to guess. The ones we can't get rid of, gumming up the paperwork."

Ansel considered. "Would you like me to get involved?"

"Is that your way of saying that you are, as ever, overcome with bright ideas?"

Ansel considered the massive hotel full of economists, spies, and reporters. "I have a couple things at my disposal here that you don't back in D.C. Among them are ideas, though I suppose only time will tell whether or not they're bright."

59

MERCHANT
OF VENICE

*"The economy is a very sensitive organism.
Every disturbance, from whatever direction it may come,
acts as sand in the machine."*

—HJALMAR SCHACHT

July 2, 1944

For the conference's first full day of meetings, the delegates split into two committees. The first concerned the World Bank and was chaired by Keynes. The second, concerning the International Monetary Fund, was chaired by White. Neither accomplished a single thing.

Ansel and the Professor sat as the American representatives in Keynes's committee, while Sir Dennis Robertson, a tall, broad-shouldered bulldog, served as Keynes's representative in White's. All the surrogates saw to it that everything proposed by the other side was either shot down or footnoted to death with technical objections.

Keynes and White had long agreed on the conceptual uses of having something like a World Bank and something like an IMF, and among the oddities of their pre–Bretton Woods agreements was that the names of the two organizations had migrated around a bit and no longer accurately represented their functions. In point of fact, the International Monetary Fund worked like a bank, and the World Bank was really a fund. Ansel had tried bringing this up to White the previous week but had been shot down with the argument that it didn't matter what they called the things; what mattered, in fact the only thing that mattered, was what currency they traded in.

Helpfully, the two institutions would have to use the same one. A given country would "buy in" to each with identical sums. If, say, the Republic of China were to buy in to the IMF with three hundred million dollars—and it was—then it would have to buy in to the WB for the same amount. Each organization was to sit on a pool of about eight billion dollars. The WB would use its pool to make long-term loans to the nations most in need of rebuilding. The IMF would use its pool to stem potential currency crises before they got out of hand. If a country needed a particular currency for its foreign trade, it needn't resort to subterfuge to get it: The IMF would lend it some. In Keynes's vision, a country would use gold to buy the IMF's bancor, which it could then use for its foreign trade. But notably, a country would be allowed to buy bancor with gold, but not buy gold with bancor. So the IMF would end up sitting on huge pools of gold that it could not sell. Thus would Keynes slowly remove gold from the practice of international trade, to be replaced—in its entirety—by his purely digital bancor.

In White's plan, gold would play a similarly temporary role, as a country's ante into the system. But since the WB and IMF would do their lending in dollars, according to White, greenbacks would then constitute the material of more and more transactions. Soon enough, all of them.

Ansel spent the day playing defense in the WB meetings while imagining the bludgeoning offense that White would be playing in the IMF committee: endlessly, insistently making the same point over and over again—the UK was in debt.

The UK was in debt.

The UK was in a *gargantuan* amount of debt.

Surely allowing the empire to default on its sovereign debt would be a calamity that might further blanche even a complexion as pasty as Sir Dennis's.

At the close of the day's session, Ansel and the Professor ran to White's room. They found him ranting and raving to Anne Terry so loudly that they could hear him through the door.

". . . 'without our participation'! Those were his words! What does he even mean by something like that?"

Ansel knocked.

White opened the door in a huff. "Look at this!"

White handed over a freshly typed copy of the IMF committee's meeting minutes. How did he even have these so quickly?

"The typists are all American," White said, anticipating Ansel's question as he shut the door.

"I hired them myself," the Professor added. "Harry, what happened?"

"The Brits are threatening to back out."

Ansel scanned the pages. Sir Dennis, according to this transcript, had done more than threaten. He'd flatly told White that the UK was more than happy to let the new global financial system march forward without their participation.

"They can't walk away," Ansel said, confused. "They owe us nine billion dollars in four weeks that they don't have. We have a knife at their throats."

The Professor tapped her long nails against her teeth. "Keynes wouldn't dare risk defaulting. Sterling would collapse."

"If thou wilt lend this money," came the voice of Anne Terry, who was seated on the beige davenport. "Lend it rather to thine enemy, who, if he break, thou mayst with better face exact the penalty."

They turned to look at her and found her making a thoughtful expression. *"Merchant of Venice,"* she said.

Ansel hadn't read it.

"I'm no economist," she continued, "but I do believe Shakespeare had a good point. Better to lend to, or borrow from, an enemy. Because when things get ugly, you'll face no compunction about doing what's necessary to collect."

Ansel did not understand how that timeworn wisdom applied to the present predicament.

The Professor ran ahead of him. "Keynes found a way to get the dollars from someone else."

White shook his head. "Nobody has that kind of money."

Ansel searched his memory for any country on earth, other than the United States, that had dollar reserves of such magnitude. The Brazilians probably had a few billion, but nothing of the scale required. "No nation has nine billion dollars they can part with at all, much less in a month's time."

The Professor put her head in her hands, as if confronting an awful truth. "I didn't say 'country.' I said 'someone.' Because I can think of exactly one person who has that kind of money."

60

THE ROAD
TO SERFDOM

"If you have to ask how much it costs, you can't afford it."

—APOCRYPHALLY ATTRIBUTED TO
J. P. MORGAN

July 5, 1944

"MORGAN NOT WORKING ALONE," began the urgent telegram from Randolph Paul, who'd been dispatched back to New York. "FOUR OTHER BANKS INVOLVED. CAN DELAY BUT NOT PREVENT."

Ansel rang up to White's room. Not finding him, he searched the various bars and restaurants of the hotel, finally locating him in the Tiffany glass conservatory. Dozens of sparkling lamps glowed inside display cases, casting a crystal shimmer onto White as he sat with a table of Chinese bankers, a half-empty bottle of whiskey between them.

Daddy Kung greeted Ansel with a nod before Ansel pulled White away to a quiet corner.

"J. P. Morgan Jr. put together a multibillion-dollar loan at a lower interest rate than Treasury can offer," White said bitterly after reading Paul's telegram.

Ansel felt foolish for not having anticipated Morgan's maneuver. The financier might have wanted revenge, but not as much as he wanted money. By inserting his bank right into the center of the Lend-Lease loans, he could get both—removing all of Ansel's leverage against Keynes while simultaneously making another couple of fortunes. He was unencumbered by idealism for the future of the global economy.

He didn't care whose money the world ran on, so long as nobody else had more of it than he did.

"If the British pull out . . ." Ansel did not see a need to finish the thought. Of course if they pulled out, an avalanche of other countries would do similarly. The new global financial system would be dead, and the dog-eat-dog system of commerce that had thus far produced two world wars would continue unchecked.

White muttered obscenities under his breath.

"On the bright side," Ansel offered, "at least our choice of enemies remains impeccable."

———

ANSEL RETURNED TO HIS room to find Angela sipping port with Lydia Lopokova.

"Mr. Luxford!" Lydia kissed him once, twice, a third time, on alternating cheeks. "Just the man who is the look for me."

Ansel glanced at Angela, who shrugged.

"Lydia said she had a message for you. I said there was a bottle of port if she didn't mind waiting."

"Isn't it deliciousness? The hotel?"

"It seems we made a good decision to host the conference in America," Ansel said petulantly.

Lydia shivered. "It is three months in London without the pipe's hot water."

"I wouldn't say," Angela confessed, "that the plumbing in Mount Washington has been entirely smooth sailing."

Ansel gestured to the envelope in Lydia's hand. "Is that for me?"

It was. And to Ansel's surprise, the message inside was not from Keynes. It was from the Soviet delegation. It was typed in Cyrillic characters with a handwritten translation beneath. But the English was nearly as indecipherable as the Russian.

"I enjoy to make me of use," Lydia said. "Maynard found the work for me with Soviet delegation. I do translate for them."

Ansel couldn't help but be impressed. By way of Lydia, Keynes had established a back-channel communication with the men from Moscow. If Ansel was reading this message accurately—which to be fair was not a given—then the Soviets were threatening to join the British in pulling out.

"How kind of you to deliver their message," Ansel said. "Has your husband by any chance seen this?"

Lydia appeared surprised. "Why?"

"I should find Mr. White." Ansel let it go.

Lydia took her cue.

She opened the door. "My sister is killed in Leningrad. Last winter. The last family, of mine, in Russia."

"I'm sorry to hear that."

She seemed as if she'd shed her final tears some time ago. "My Russia is dead. I think then that now, after all this, I am English."

———

"YOU'RE TELLING ME," WHITE grumbled as he stood on the wooden veranda, "that the Soviets are willing to kill an eighteen-billion-dollar deal to remake the global economy over ten million in German marks?"

The stars above were bright. It was nearly midnight, but they illuminated every wrinkle on his face.

"Honestly?" Ansel said. "It's hard to tell. But the marks aren't German, they're ours." As Allied troops swept across Europe, freeing town after town from German control, they were also distributing money. This had always been a war not just of armies but of currencies. The reichsmarks held by civilians were worthless as soon as the men and women holding them were back under Allied control. As were the Vichy francs in newly liberated France, or the gunpyō in islands freed from Japan. In their place, the advancing Allied soldiers handed out a temporary new currency until an appropriate government could get back up and running. The money was printed by Treasury agents embedded with army units. They called it Allied Military currency— "AM-francs" in France, "AM-marks" in Germany.

Ansel gestured to Lydia's colorfully translated message. "The Soviets want to be able to print AM-marks themselves. They want us to give them a set of printing plates."

"This is a question for the military," White said. "Not us. The Soviets will go into Germany from the east, so of course they'll want to control the currency in the areas they cleave off."

"The problem is that all the AM currencies are backed by U.S. dollars. Fixed conversion rates. If we give them the plates, they can essentially print as many dollars as they want."

"It sounds like they want ten million of them. Hell, if that's all, they can have them."

"How confident are you that the Soviets even want into our system in the first place? This could be a scam. Keynes would happily serve as the devil on their shoulder, egging them on."

"Why wouldn't the Soviets want to join the IMF?"

Ansel occasionally got the feeling that when his boss encountered arguments with which he disagreed, he simply pretended they did not exist. "Because they're Communists."

White's disdain was withering. "Point being?"

"The global financial system we're proposing is . . . well, capitalist."

"You don't say."

"Maybe Moscow is looking at it and thinking it's AC versus D.C. Communism and capitalism are two incompatible systems."

"They're not."

"I know *you* don't think so. But if I were at Narkomfin, I might take one look at what we're building here and conclude that signing on would be a tacit admission that capitalism will form the core of future international trade. Commissioners have been executed for less."

White waved a hand in the air. "First of all, communism and capitalism are merely ranges on a sliding scale. Central planning over yonder, laissez-faire right here. Maybe the U.S. is a six, the UK a seven, the USSR a three. Maybe the right answer is a five, and none of us are there yet. But second, and more importantly: This is a debate for freshman dormitories. The Soviets are here. They're here because the whole point of an international monetary system is that all the nations are in on the money. They want peace as much as we do."

"Peace enforced by the heavy stick of the U.S. dollar?"

The faint chirp of summer crickets came from the endless acres of forest.

White made a decision. "I want you to go to Keynes's room and deliver a message."

———

LYDIA OPENED THE DOOR to room 219 wearing a thin silk nightgown. But she did not appear to have been roused from bed, despite the hour.

She led Ansel inside. She told him that her husband was in bed, and as if suspecting that he might doubt her, she flung open the French doors. Maynard sat up against the pillows, a writing pad on his lap. Ice packs covered his legs. An additional ice pack hung from each shoulder. A manuscript covered in pencil notations was strewn across the blanket.

He did not appear embarrassed to be seen in this condition. "Is there something you want to say to me that cannot wait for our morning committee?"

"Are you ill?"

"Bacteria, the doctors said. In one of my heart valves."

Ansel wasn't sure he could believe a single word that came from Keynes. But the man did look frail—even weaker than he had when they'd first met.

Ansel gestured to the manuscript. "Is that about Harry's intellectual failings?"

"No. It's about mine." Keynes held up the title page. It was called *The Road to Serfdom,* by someone named Friedrich Hayek.

"Bright young man," Keynes continued. "At the University of Chicago. Have you read him?"

Ansel hadn't even heard of him.

"He's a friend. Once, even something like a protégé. And now, when he publishes this manuscript, he hopes to make a name for himself by tearing me down."

"You do have a way of alienating protégés, don't you? And inspiring apostates?"

Keynes tapped *The Road to Serfdom* approvingly. "Some apostates are more gifted than others."

"Harry wants to talk. Privately. Just you and him."

"And you?"

Ansel nodded. "Worried you'll be ganged up on?"

"Not particularly."

"Two A.M."

Keynes checked his watch. That was less than an hour away. "Where?"

61

A PHILOSOPHICAL DUEL CONCERNING THE PAST, PRESENT, AND FUTURE OF MONEY

"So you think that money is the root of all evil.
Have you ever asked what is the root of all money?"

—AYN RAND

July 5, 1944 (cont'd)

The atrium was lined with palm trees. There must have been over a hundred of them tucked into clay planters. At one end, the trees led to an empty orchestra pit. Ansel could practically hear the soirees that once filled the grand space. Now the atrium was quiet and still, save for the two angry economists sizing each other up.

It occurred to Ansel that if anyone had told him, as a young man, that one day he'd mediate a debate between Harry Dexter White and John Maynard Keynes, he'd have fallen out of his chair. Yet he'd somehow become a prospective disciple of both men, before failing to amount to what either had hoped for. He'd turned on them both when he'd thought it had been the right thing to do.

"You and I agree about a whole lot of things." White spoke first, with unexpected charm.

Perhaps Keynes was pleased to begin with gentility. "We always have."

"We agree that at the close of this war, the world faces exactly three great crises. First, we must furnish the capital required to rebuild civilization."

"And that will take quite a bit of money."

"Second, we agree that we must restore cordial trading relations among nations that have for years been bombing each other to rubble. And we must knot these bonds of trade together so tightly that another war of this magnitude will become impossible."

"Ideally, another war of any magnitude." It was just like Keynes to aim higher.

White pressed on. "Third, and more subtly, we need to tie these economic knots even tighter still, such that no nation ever faces a time when it seeks to cut the cord. This war happened because the reichsmark collapsed under the twin pressures of Great War reparations and the Depression. Once the monetary system failed, the people of Germany were desperate. The solution they chose was to separate themselves from the rest of the world economy and begin a campaign of systemic murder, theft, and conquest."

"If only someone had predicted this back in '19."

"Damn it, I'm *giving* you credit for predicting this! I'm saying you were right!" White composed himself. "Point is, if we fail to make a deal, you'll be right again. Neither of us is naive about human nature. We have not seen the last of evil men with large microphones and larger audiences. We need to be sure that there exists no soil in which such poisonous plants can lay roots."

Keynes smiled approvingly. "This is precisely why my system is superior. Having a common currency that is under no nation's control will allow it to spread more widely. Tighter bonds, stronger sinews, more trade. Which means fewer bombs. Not to mention a more widely shared prosperity."

"Well, some people might have a bit more control of bancor than others, mightn't they?"

Keynes waved a hand in the air. "As opposed to dollars, which I've no doubt are managed by benevolent angels sent straight from God's right hand to watch over us?"

"Well you figured me out. I'm no angel, and I make no appeals to such. Just the opposite. Unlike bancor, dollars are of the here and now. They're *real*."

Keynes shot a glance at Ansel, perhaps hoping to remind him of their talks at the Mayflower. "And what makes dollars any more real than bancor?"

"I have some in my wallet. If I take them to the bar, the man will pour me a glass."

"Another point of agreement! But we can make bancor just as real, if only you'll listen to reason."

Unreasonableness was perhaps one of White's core virtues. "You are never going to get people to believe in bancor."

"And why not? People believed in *gold,* didn't they? Less useful than iron, less transportable than quartz. It's just this dumb rock."

"Dollars have something behind it that gold never did: the U.S. military. We don't back our currency with rocks, we back them with guns. Any stretch of land that's under the protection of our weapons is bound by law to accept our paper. Why on earth would anyone believe in bancor?"

Keynes smiled. "Because everyone else does."

White seemed momentarily flummoxed.

Ansel felt the heavenly tug of Keynes's visions: He wanted to believe that something like that was possible. But he wasn't even sure if Keynes did, or if it wasn't all just pretty words hiding another dirty trick.

"Surely you won't walk away without a deal," White said. "So let's end this. Right now. You say your system is superior; I say mine is. Fine. That's why the good Lord gave us negotiation. Surely we can agree that having *no system at all* would be infinitely worse than adopting either one of ours."

Keynes sighed pityingly. "I know you believe that. You once asked me about leverage. Well, I'll tell you mine: You cannot bring yourself to walk away, Harry. You never could. So faced with the prospect of accepting my bancor or allowing civilization to tumble into another Great War? I'm confident you'll make the smart decision."

"You cannot play a game of chicken with the fate of the world."

Keynes shrugged. "What game would you prefer we play?"

Ansel watched the two men stare at each other, wondering when either would finally blink.

An ominous sign: White caved first.

He turned to Ansel: Can you believe this guy? The unmitigated gall.

The Englishman finally allowed himself to blink. "I think you would be well served by a lesson in values."

"Oh dear God," White groaned, "not another lesson."

"Your beloved Adam Smith argued for what we now call the utility theory of value. He believed that the value of a given object came entirely from its utility. For example . . ." Keynes searched the room, finding an abandoned set of cutlery and tea cups on a side table that the overworked hotel staff must have failed to clean up. "That knife."

Keynes picked up the steak knife, displaying its serrated edge to Ansel. "I can cut meat with this. I can cut other things, too. Its price, if I wanted to buy it, would be based on how much use I thought I'd get out of it. And use can mean appeal as well. Is the wood of the hilt pleasing to the eye? According to utility theory, value is subjective. You might not enjoy steak. You may not like the look of the blade. If it has less utility for you, then for you it is worth less. Now for Smith, if I'm willing to pay two dollars for this knife, and you only one—that is to say, if I value it twice as much as you do—then which of us is correct?"

Ansel vaguely recalled this point from some long-ago undergraduate course. "We both are? Right?"

"Neither of you is," White grumbled. "This whole conversation has achieved negative utility."

"Correct, Ansel, and in a way, correct, Harry. There is no such thing as inherent value for our friend Adam Smith. To the man willing to pay two dollars for the blade, it really is worth two dollars. For the man willing to pay only one, it's actually worth only one."

"Can we get on with this?" White found a pack of Luckys in his jacket and took his time lighting one, as if he were trying to keep himself entertained over the course of what he gathered would be a long and tedious lecture.

"Karl Marx, however, argued against Smith by saying that all value derived from labor. This knife really does have an inherent value, he would say. The value of this knife is *objectively* the sum total of all the work that went into making it. The hours workers spent fashioning the steel. Carving the wood. Packaging it and selling it and even bringing it here, to this hotel, where it can be used. Life is sadly finite. Our days on earth are numbered. And the time that those men who made this knife spent crafting it, the portions of their brief time alive they devoted to providing me, here, tonight, with its use, that is worth something, whether one dollar, two dollars, or something else."

Keynes ran his fingers slowly over the serrated edge, as if feeling the worth of every sharp bump. "The thing of it is, Smith and Marx are both wrong."

White blew smoke. "Thank God for giving us Baron Keynes to correct Misters Smith and Marx."

Two years earlier, Keynes had been gazetted into the peerage. White had read reports of the ceremony aloud to the office on more than one occasion.

"I know such theorizing bores you. But this matters! Don't you see? The German 'National Socialists' got their *national* part from Smith and their *socialist* part from Marx, so these ideas matter. They have consequences, these airy philosophies, as you can well see upon the blood-soaked mud of France. You cannot hope to rid the world of fascism if you remain incurious about its intellectual origins."

White smoked angrily. "Enlighten us."

"Smith was right that utility is the source of value. But Marx was right that value is not wholly subjective. Some uses really are more valuable than others. If I buy this knife in order to murder you—and I won't pretend that the thought hasn't crossed my mind—that is wrong. The utility I get from committing murder and the utility Ansel might get from slicing up a ribeye are not of equal value. Because some things are simply wrong, and others simply right. The problem with Smith's system is that it allows for no morality. No differentiation in value between pain and joy, cruelty and kindness. Marx was correct that *core* values are objective—it's not a matter of opinion that employing the knife to kill is a poorer use than employing the knife to dine. But where Marx erred, fundamentally, is in thinking that the labor that went into making something was the primary source of its value. A painting that required a hundred hours to compose is not a hundred times more valuable than a painting that required only one. It isn't even necessarily more valuable at all."

"If value is at root objective," Ansel asked, "contra Smith, and if value is also not the same as labor, contra Marx . . . then what is it?"

Ansel couldn't help but feel the pull of Keynes's arguments. He must be saying all of this in the hopes of talking Ansel and White into doing precisely what was in his own best interests. But that didn't mean what he was saying was wrong.

White dropped the burnt nub of his cigarette and stomped on it. "I cannot believe he's suckering you in again with this nonsense."

Keynes seemed as if he needed someone, anyone, to understand why this was so important to him. Even if it was only Ansel.

Keynes spoke to him alone. "I'll tell you . . ."

62

THE DISMAL SCIENCE

"The misery of life was having to persuade people."

—JOHN MAYNARD KEYNES

July 5, 1944 (cont'd)

"Good." Keynes uttered that single word as if it contained the holiness of divine prophecy.

Ansel wasn't sure what that was supposed to mean.

"You asked what value really is," Keynes continued. "And I am telling you: It is Good. The Good life. Good health. A Good time. Happiness and human flourishing—that is value. Our lives are so short." He paused for a moment, as if pondering the frailty of his body. The state of the bacteria that he'd said was filling his heart. "Immortality is unattainable and God is, at best, indifferent to our suffering. We have these few days above the ground, and how we spend them—in joy or pain, in miserable toil or in the fulfillment of meaningful work, surrounded by people we loathe"—he glanced to White—"or enveloped in the warmth of people who love us"—he glanced in the direction of Lydia's bedroom—"is the only thing that matters. That's value. The function of the economy is not to make a bunch of numbers add up to x or to y, to make some line on some graph achieve a neat curve. It is to produce as much Good as possible. The job of economists—we dismal scientists, as they say—is to study how we might create the most Good."

For some reason Ansel thought of his children playing jacks on a porch step he'd built himself.

Keynes seemed to listen to his own voice echo into silence in the empty atrium. "Do you know where that phrase originated? 'The dismal science' of economics? It was coined by an American slaver. A line of economists, in an intellectual tradition I'm proud to carry on, was arguing that the enslavement of human souls, such as they were doing in the American South, was not merely immoral but poor economics. So this slaver called economics the dismal science because its theories were so dreary as to oppose a little something like chattel slavery. Well. If economics is to be dismal for that, then a scientist of the dismal is something I am quite proud to be."

Ansel saw his point. But it did not fully clarify the question at hand. "Some things may be clearly evil, and others clearly good. But day to day, the line gets blurry."

Keynes raised a thick eyebrow. Was Ansel speaking from experience about the well-meaning lies he'd told over the years? His earnest, honest subterfuges? "Not so much as you might think, if you do things a certain way."

"But who is to be the judge of this Good? You?"

Keynes nodded. "Our visions of the Good—like our visions of value—are actually not so different. When you look upon a Cézanne— say, the one in my country house that you admired—are you telling me that you cannot see its beauty? Of course you can. The beauty is real. It exists."

White seemed unable to bear any more of this gibberish. "As always, Baron Keynes comes back around to Baron Keynes. Something is good because you say it is. Something works because you say it will."

"Because I'm right!" Now it was Keynes who seemed unable to contain his exasperation. "For God's sake, man, it's only *money*! It can be anything we want it to be. It can do anything we want it to do. A more equitable world? A fairer one? We can do it! Money is paper and ink; value is real. If we, the three of us, draw the money up correctly? We can create a world in which everyone can have enough of it. In which anyone might spend some of his few living days engaged by his labors, enveloped by his loving family, and occasionally gazing up in wonder upon the still lifes of Cézanne."

Ansel and White were both silent as Keynes's words faded.

Then White made a snoring noise, as if he'd been asleep for hours. "That it?"

Keynes sighed: What more could he say?

"You ever work in a hardware store, Baron?"

"I have not."

"I did. Ansel knows. I had this regular customer once upon a time. Teddy Allen. Hands as calloused as barnacles. Always fixing up this and that for his missus. Like clockwork, every week he was back in the shop. But then, Teddy switched from beer to whiskey. You know the story. He was playing the ponies. Honest work dried up. He didn't. A real shame. But the new roof he was fixing wasn't done. So still, even in that condition, Teddy would come down for this, that, and the other. Sometimes he had a few bills with him. Then, more and more, he didn't. One Saturday, I'm in the shop with my dad, before he passed. Teddy comes in. Whiskey on the breath. Needs a box of nails. What do they cost?"

A silence hung in the atrium.

"What does a box of nails cost, Maynard? You don't even know, do you? You've never bought one. It's about twenty-five cents. But Teddy didn't have a single coin in his pocket. Asked if he could put it on the cuff. And that was the moment that my dad and me, we looked into Teddy's eyes and we *knew* he wasn't ever going to pay us back. So, what does my dad do?"

Keynes did not disturb the story by speaking.

"My dad hands him the nails. 'I'll see you next week.' And that's that. No, actually, it wasn't. Because the next week it was insulation, and the week after it was something else. I can't remember what. But all those items went on Teddy's tab. And a while later, when Teddy finally drank himself to death, at least his wife could cry herself to sleep underneath a roof that didn't leak."

White lit himself another smoke.

Keynes finally responded, "Is this some kind of homespun folk wisdom about the value of debt forgiveness? If so, I have 26.9 billion points to add in agreement."

"No. The thing I always wonder is, what if somebody else besides my dad had been running that shop? If it was anybody else—hell, honestly, if it had been *me*—then Teddy's wife would have suffered her grief in a house soggy with rainwater. You go on and on about your philosophy of money, history of whatever, Mesopotamia and Cézanne. The only thing that counts in this world is who's standing behind the cash register when a customer comes in. It's power. All there ever was, all there will ever be. Who has it? Who doesn't? This isn't complicated. It isn't deep. It's barely even interesting. You're saying you should be the one manning the shop; I'm saying we should. We're going to win, because London is half ashes right now and Washington has never been bigger. Sorry it worked out this way. If we were the ones that got blitzed and you were the ones that made all our guns? Probably would have gone down different. But here we are. You'll never get all these delegates to sign on to bancor. I can get them to sign on to dollars. *Ka-ching!* Next customer. That's all this is and all that matters: Who has the nails? And who's getting screwed?"

63

HOW MUCH OF THIS DO YOU WANT TO BE ABLE TO DENY?

"Anytime you have change, it costs somebody.
Somebody is a loser."

—ROBERT SHILLER,
NOBEL PRIZE—WINNING AMERICAN ECONOMIST

July 6, 1944

Henry Morgenthau sipped blearily from his coffee cup. He hadn't slept a wink all night, he told the others over breakfast, on account of Lydia's all-hours dancing from the room above. "I finally threw a shoe at the ceiling. She just stomped harder."

White sliced open the yolk of his over-easy eggs, then spread it on his toast. "That would be Lydia's way of telling you to suck gasoline on behalf of her far-too-elegant husband."

None of them turned out to have gotten much rest. Ansel and White had stewed for a while after failing to reach any kind of compromise with Keynes. The Professor and DuBois had been trying to charm various delegations into staying, should the British and Soviets back out. The Professor had organized a small-hour meeting with the Ethiopian and Icelandic delegations in the basement Blue Room after the Peruvian dancers had finished their nightly show. But even the Ethiopians and Icelanders, she reported, were ready to bolt.

"My question is: What are we doing about it?" Morgenthau spooned more sugar into his cup.

Ansel and the others exchanged brief glances.

Ansel spoke first. "We have an idea."

"Why does that not sound reassuring?"

"It's risky," DuBois admitted.

"Define *risky*."

"Ansel has spent some time with Baron Keynes," White offered. "To my consternation. But it's afforded us a couple of insights."

The Professor sliced the stem off a strawberry. "Am I the only one who doesn't get to spend time with John Maynard Keynes and Lydia Lopokova?"

Ansel ignored her. "He's an idealist. He really believes that his pie-in-the-sky bancor idea is the only way to achieve world peace."

Morgenthau sighed. "*Bancor*. It even sounds stupid."

"Agreed," White said. "But Keynes thinks he's genius, and that if only we—or anybody—were as smart as him, we'd see it. Which is how we might be able to beat him."

Morgenthau did not seem to immediately see how this would constitute their victory.

"Let's give him what he wants," Ansel said. "Let's allow him to talk us into agreeing with him."

"And how," Morgenthau said, "does that help us?"

Ansel paused. They'd all been up till dawn discussing the plan that he was about to propose, and he wasn't even sure it made sense.

He leaned in to the secretary. "How much of this do you want to know before it happens? And how much do you want to be able to deny you knew about later?"

64

UNITAS

"Finance is the art of passing money from hand to hand
until it finally disappears."

—ROBERT SARNOFF, CHAIRMAN OF RCA

July 10, 1944

"Unitas," announced White to the committee, "will be the name of our new global currency." This was met with confused looks from the other delegates. Daddy Kung leaned closer, as if sure he must have misheard.

He hadn't. "On behalf of the whole American delegation," White continued, "I'd like to propose that the answer to the divisions that plague us can be found in the aptly named unitas."

"You are suggesting a uniform global trade currency?" This was Shanmukham Chetty, who represented India. A handsome man of fifty, he had a politician's charm and a gambler's knack for spotting the weak hand at the table.

"That's right. I'd suggest that countries can buy their allotments of unitas from the IMF with gold, which would then fade from the system as unitas becomes the sole means of foreign exchange."

There was a long moment of confused silence.

"Isn't this exactly like Mr. Keynes's bancor?" Kung asked.

"No, no," White responded. "Unitas will be completely different."

Ansel was not present for what followed, as he was with Keynes in the WB meeting. But according to the Professor—who gleefully showed Ansel the minutes over their brief lunch break—White then launched into an utterly incomprehensible monologue about all the technical differences between unitas and bancor. These purported differences were, by Ansel's design, gibberish. Unitas and bancor were identical. The Professor reported that watching experts as savvy as Kung and Chetty try to make any sense out of White's authoritatively spoken nonsense had been like watching chess grandmasters trying their hands at checkers: This was really all there was to it?

"Do they like the unitas idea?" Ansel asked her as they stood on the veranda, away from prying eyes.

"I think they don't really care," she replied. "I think the practical difference between a trading system powered by dollars and one powered by some new currency is less pressing to a nation in possession of neither, such as China or India. They're more concerned about their allotments. If they get into trouble down the line, how much leeway will they have with the IMF to bail them out? You can measure your trade in rocks for all they care, as long as they get enough voting rights in the institutions."

Ansel was pleased. So far so good.

He checked his wristwatch. Their greatest enemy was time. "Can you sit in on the World Bank committee for me this afternoon? Keynes should be finding out about unitas any minute now. I need a read on his reaction."

The Professor nodded. "Where are you going to be?"

———

THE LAST OF THE morning fog was fading from the base of the mountain when Ansel found Russell Porter, the wide-bodied *New York Times* financial reporter, in his sporting attire.

"Luxford? Didn't expect you'd have time for a hike."

"I don't," Ansel responded. "I'm here to make a deal."

He explained the bargain: He needed a big, splashy *Times* piece about the Jewish refugees soon to land in Oswego. The nobility of America's largesse in taking them in—and of the State Department's particular role therein—should be extensively complimented. "And before you tell me that the Jewish question isn't your beat, I will remind you that your paper printed a front-pager last week about the 1.7 million Jews who died in the death camps. It's somebody's beat, and you can feed the story to him if you'd prefer."

Porter was a man well versed in complicated finance, which meant that he was no stranger to the artfully composed deal. "And what do I get in return?"

Ansel handed him a ream of papers. "These are the minutes from this morning's IMF committee meetings."

Porter looked over them curiously. An edited version would be available to him in a few hours. What Ansel was offering was a head start on his competitors—and an unfiltered feed.

"A leg up every day?" he asked.

Ansel nodded.

He appeared satisfied by the trade. He wasn't being asked to embellish a story or to withhold a scoop; merely to print some additional truths that might otherwise have gone unreported. Only Ansel and his colleagues knew that the bit about the State Department's being anything other than an obstacle to the refugees' arrival was bunk; but it shouldn't matter much to Porter. And hopefully it would box Breckinridge Long's people in. After being praised for their charity, they couldn't very easily announce to the world that they were actually misers.

"What about Keynes?" Porter asked. "Can I get a statement from Harry about him?"

"What do you want to know about Keynes?"

Porter frowned. It seemed that he had information that Ansel did not. "My colleague is camped outside his room. One of the UK papers is saying he's dead."

———

KEYNES HAD SUFFERED A heart attack during the afternoon, Ansel learned when he returned to the hotel. It would have been difficult to avoid learning this: No one was talking about anything else. Doctors were supposedly up in his room, which was closely guarded by Sir Dennis and the rest of the British delegation. They weren't saying a thing, but his obituary had already gone to print.

The afternoon WB session was canceled, which gave Ansel and the Professor a lot of time to sit in the hotel bar waiting for news. They weren't the only ones. Two generations of economists poured in to share their memories of the legend who'd inspired them to take up this line of work in the first place. Ansel had no idea what the wakes of Adam Smith or Karl Marx might have been like, but Keynes's swilled with gin and tears. Ansel caught more than one man removing spectacles to dry his eyes. Hours before, any of them would have swiped Keynes's wallet from his pocket if it would have helped their home countries secure a place of prominence in the future of global trade. They'd arrived at this hotel as Keynes's opponents. But now that most of them figured he was dead, he was on his way to sainthood.

"All the first-year girls read his *General Theory*," the Professor said, sipping a soda water. "I assign it every autumn."

Ansel had a hard time softening into sentimentality. "It's kind of tough to follow, don't you think? He argues for more government spending to alleviate social problems. Fantastic. But he never really says how much. It's all theory, no practice."

"He had his faults. But a confinement to small ideas was not one of them."

Across the bar, the Ecuadorians burst into a round of toasts.

"If you knew him," Ansel said, perhaps indelicately, "you wouldn't be quite so mournful of his passing."

She seemed surprised by Ansel's coldheartedness. "I suppose I'll never have the pleasure."

A rousing song came from the Philippine delegation across the bar.

"Best not to meet your heroes," Ansel said.

She didn't look up from her glass. "Or let them meet you?"

White joined them at the dinner hour. The IMF meeting had dissolved hours before, but he said he'd been off trying to get information as to Keynes's condition. He hadn't been successful. "One bit of good news: As far as I can tell, the whole of the British delegation—including Sir Dennis—is holed up in room 219. Hard to imagine they'd still be in there with a corpse under the bedsheets."

"Good news?" Ansel lowered his voice. "If Keynes is dead, that could buy us time."

White disagreed. "If he's dead, the conference is a bust. You think the Exchequer is going to let Sir Dennis make a deal in his place?"

The Professor nodded. "The British will postpone, and everyone else will fly home."

White ordered a drink. "God help me for saying so . . . But I actually hope the bastard lives."

65

A FAVOR, A BRIBE, AND A BETRAYAL

"When I was a kid, I reckoned things in Hershey bars.
Is this worth three Hershey bars to me?"

—PAUL SAMUELSON,
THE FIRST AMERICAN TO WIN THE
NOBEL PRIZE IN ECONOMICS

July 12, 1944

"Have you seen him yourself?" asked Shanmukham Chetty. He stood at the short end of the placid indoor pool, which at this evening hour was empty of swimmers. The ceiling lamps reflected a strange green color in the murky water. "The Exchequer men assure me that Keynes is alive. But you know, they have not always provided me with the most accurate information."

Ansel joined him in gazing into the greenish water. "I haven't laid eyes on him. But I've been similarly assured."

Ansel tried to gauge how Chetty felt about Keynes's survival. But the Indian kept his feelings concealed.

"If so," Chetty said, "then meetings will resume early in the morning. It's past time we were asleep ourselves. Unless you brought me here for a swim?"

"I brought you here so I could do you a favor."

Chetty was not an idiot. "In my experience, there is no more expensive favor than one from Americans."

"What if you were able to pay this expense using someone else's money?"

"Unitas?" Chetty seemed unable to say the word without smiling.

"Sterling."

Now Ansel had his interest.

"Thanks to Keynes's beloved system of imperial preference," Ansel continued, "you're obligated to buy your imports from England. And you're obligated to pay in sterling."

Chetty shrugged: So it had been for a long time. What could be done about it?

"Keynes uses imperial preference to bolster his sterling bloc," Ansel said. "The demand for sterling is artificially inflated. Which just rubs me the wrong way, because it crowds out other currencies."

"Such as?"

Ansel stepped forward, his feet inches from the long pool of murky water. "Now that's a good question. Maybe you like doing all your business in sterling. But if you don't . . . I wonder, just between you and me: What if there was another currency you could use for your foreign trade? One in which you might be able to get a better deal? Something . . . I don't know, greener?"

July 17, 1944

The Professor turned out to be even better at bribery than Ansel was. The trick to it, she explained, was not to make the recipient feel like a rat for taking it. The man had to feel like what he was doing was just routine business, the natural outcome of a difficult but lucrative negotiation. "You've got to leave him feeling classy."

She spent the next four days bribing nearly every non-British delegate in New Hampshire. What she had to offer was something even sweeter than money: influence. Voting power in the IMF and WB would be, by long-standing agreement, doled out according to the amount each member nation put into it. The United States had helpfully offered to lay its marker down with a billion dollars. This would be the largest share, so naturally the United States would have the most votes, and thus certain additional approvals and unique rights. Now: How much would other countries like to contribute?

This made the Professor's bribery a curious sort, in that she was bribing the delegates with their own money. How much of their reserves would they be able—or allowed—to put into the system? The Chinese wanted three hundred million dollars. The French wanted five hundred million dollars. The currency in which these quantities would eventually be paid remained for the moment undetermined.

The Professor raised the Liberian quota. She raised the Argentinean quota. She raised the quotas of Colombia, Egypt, and Iceland. She doled out massive quantities of each nation's own money in exchange for the same promise: participation. The more they put in now, the more they'd be able to easily withdraw later, as needed. It was as if they were buying insurance against their own economic crises. Or, perhaps, protection.

No one wanted to end up like the Germans, did they?

———

THE SOVIETS REQUIRED A more elaborate means of bribery suitable just for them. White and the Professor worked out a three-way deal in which the Chinese and Canadians would be allowed to put extra money into the IMF on the Soviets' behalf, and the Soviets would be allowed to put up less than the twenty-five percent up-front collateral that all other nations did to secure their place. No need to give them the AM-mark plates—disproportionate voting power at the IMF would do the trick.

For some reason, DuBois was the one sent to the wine cellars for a secret midday rendezvous with the Soviet delegation to seal the deal.

He returned to Ansel's room with a proud smile on his face. "I think I'm going to miss being a spy when this is all over."

The comment surprised Ansel: Is that what they were?

If not, what were they?

July 18, 1944

Keynes's reappearance at his committee on Tuesday morning was met with a round of applause. Ansel found himself standing to lead the cheer. Keynes's hair seemed whiter, his gait more stooped. But here he was, using what strength he had left to rant on and on about the need for bancor. Or unitas, which even in his diminished state he could tell was exactly the same thing. If White needed to change the name in order to feel like it'd been his idea, Keynes seemed to think, then fine. Keynes didn't care about the nomenclature. His ideals were as lofty as the heaven he'd nearly entered a few nights before.

Keynes seemed surprised when Ansel stopped objecting. He'd been the one whose heart had weakened—and yet here were his opponents giving up. But Ansel could see the smug satisfaction returning to his cheeks: He believed he'd won. He believed that his brilliant oration the night before had finally convinced these dimwitted Americans of the need to trust his judgment, to trust his money—or at least to design one identical to it.

Keynes had bought it.

July 19, 1944

"MORGAN AND CO OFFER FIXED. DOUBTS SEEDED IN OTHER BANKS. OFFER EXPIRES ON 24TH."

Ansel shared Paul's telegram with White and the Professor when it arrived. But they spared Morgenthau its contents.

July 20, 1944

Ansel's conversation with Sir Dennis would be the most difficult and would necessarily need to be the most secret. No other member of the British delegation could know he was even speaking to the Americans. So Angela was enlisted to make contact at the restaurant, offering a private meeting with her husband that he would not want to miss.

Ansel and White were waiting for them when they arrived at the riverbank. The air was unseasonably cold, and all the men kept their arms crossed for warmth. None of them had thought to pack scarves or coats in July.

Sir Dennis was smart enough to know a viper's nest when he saw one teeming beside a river's edge. "And what is it you think you can offer me to betray my country?" he said without introduction.

"Not your country," White offered. "Just Keynes."

"I don't believe Downing Street would acknowledge a difference."

"But you know better."

He didn't deny the point. If the information White had gathered was true, then Sir Dennis and Baron Keynes had come to significant strategic disagreements. And not just in New Hampshire. The way White had heard it, they'd been at each other's throats since Churchill had conscripted Keynes back into government service above Sir Dennis back in '40.

Sir Dennis turned to Angela, seemingly curious for the first time about her role here. "This isn't about replacing bancor with its identical twin unitas, is it?"

Angela shrugged.

"Convince Keynes to abandon bancor at the World Bank," Ansel said, "and White will abandon unitas at the IMF."

"Why would I do that?"

"First, because they're both stupid, and you know it."

"The great system of the world must run on something." His allegiance to bancor—much less unitas—sounded as weak as Ansel had hoped. Sir Dennis would be a sterling man through and through. But if he couldn't have the sterling of old, at least not right now, then the Americans were prepared to offer him something with which he was just as comfortable.

"How about gold?" White said. "It has served humanity well for the last thousand years; we can settle for a thousand more."

"Says the man sitting on eighty percent of the world's monetary gold supply."

"What's your point? That I'm selling you on a sneaky deal that's in my own interest? I sure am. But you're going to take it, because you know what I'm selling you is in your interest too."

Gold, Sir Dennis knew. Gold, Sir Dennis could understand.

"I don't trust you," he said to White.

"You shouldn't. But when I stab you, it'll be in the belly. Where and when do you think J. P. Morgan is going to bury his blade?"

White's bet was simple enough: Why would Sir Dennis risk a deal with a snake like J. P. Morgan purely to allow Keynes time to institute bancor when he could make a deal for gold with the Americans right here and now?

Even the sound of the river seemed to hush as Sir Dennis thought it over.

66

GOOD LUCK

*"Different constraints are decisive for different situations,
but the most fundamental constraint is limited time."*

—GARY BECKER,
NOBEL PRIZE—WINNING AMERICAN ECONOMIST

July 22, 1944, 6:14 A.M.

The sun had just risen when Ansel, halfway through knotting his neck-tie, gazed out the window and spotted Lydia swimming naked in the pond. For a second he thought he must be dreaming, that his subconscious had conjured up this image of the nude wife of the man he was out to destroy for reasons only Freud might comprehend. Then, he wondered whether it might be some other small, lithe woman of middle age dunking her gray hair up and down in what must be water from a frigid mountain stream. But no, it was Lydia. Swimming naked beside a hotel full of her husband's enemies, she seemed as gay as if she were all alone. Or perhaps she was most free only when she suspected that everyone was watching.

Ansel turned at the sound of a key in the lock.

Angela entered. She seemed in such a daze that for a moment he wondered whether she'd seen the same thing he had.

He asked whether everything was all right.

She held up two telegrams, one open. "Tom is alive. Somewhere in France, he can't say where."

Ansel wrapped her in his arms, relieved. But she felt unsteady.

"No word on the others."

He squeezed. "Just because you haven't heard, doesn't mean . . . It doesn't mean anything."

He didn't think she believed it, but she was trying to. Did notices of death take longer to receive than letters of correspondence?

The partial silence, and its suggestion of a horrible truth known but not yet committed to letters, seemed tougher than a full one.

She pulled away and handed him the other telegram. His name was on the sleeve. The message came from Randolph Paul:

"KEYNES REJECTED OFFER. MORGAN LIVID. GOOD LUCK."

8:02 A.M.

The first indication that the Soviets had come back to the table was that the delegates had literally returned to the table. The pair of quiet, dour Russian economists were the first two in their chairs at the start of the day's IMF meeting. Their presence did not go unnoticed by the others. Even Sir Dennis, not usually known for being impressed by either Soviet or American planning, gave Ansel an approving nod. Not bad.

As the day's negotiations began, the Professor joined Keynes in the WB session, while Ansel went to sit beside White at the IMF session. Chetty and Sir Dennis were both in the IMF meeting as well.

The pieces were all in place.

12:10 P.M.

The Professor ran down the hall toward Ansel and White at the start of the lunch hour. "He agreed to drop bancor," she said between breaths, "if we agree to drop unitas."

"Sir Dennis must have been persuasive," Ansel said approvingly.

"He thinks we'll make a deal," White said. "To compromise on gold. Nobody wins, we both lose, but at least there's an agreement. And gold will provide a better foundation on which to build his bancor in the coming years than dollars would."

He placed a hand on Ansel's shoulder. "You're up to the plate."

1:11 P.M.

Soon after the IMF meeting resumed, White began a lengthy and tedious remembrance for the dearly departed unitas. All present had seen
the WB meeting minutes thanks to the quick work of White's army of
hand-picked secretaries. Since few of the delegates cared about either
bancor or unitas one way or another, to be rid of both nuisances was
freeing. Working with good old gold again would be a pleasure.

But White played his part with enthusiasm, acting as if unitas had
been his great dream for as long as bancor had been Keynes's. Its demise
pained him as would the loss of one of his own children. But he would
give it up for now to get an agreement done. Such was the importance
of the deal that was within their grasp. Gold would be an imperfect
compromise, but for the moment it would do.

The next time White mentioned the word *gold,* Ansel gave a telling
nod to Chetty. He nodded back, as they'd agreed days before. And then
Chetty raised a hand in objection: "Mr. White, you talk about gold
this and gold that, but surely it has not escaped your attention that
your nation possesses much of it, and we who do not—most of us
present—will lack the reserves to buy into these institutions. Let's just
put an asterisk on the word *gold,* here in paragraph nine, and say that
throughout the document, *gold* can equally be understood as *gold-
convertible currency* as of today's date."

White frowned. But Daddy Kung and the Soviets were pleased—
they didn't have much gold either, so buying into the IMF with gold-
convertible currency would make their lives easier.

White begrudgingly accepted. "Very well . . ." And then moved on
to a discussion of other seemingly mundane technical details.

Ansel tried to glance at Sir Dennis without moving his head. This
was the most dangerous moment of their plan. If the British delegate
took undue notice of the precise language that Chetty had just inserted
into a footnote, he might bring it to Keynes's attention. And the game
would be over. But Sir Dennis did not seem to realize the importance
of the phrase that Chetty had appended to an asterisk over White's

seeming annoyance. If White was annoyed, Sir Dennis must have felt, then all was well.

Ansel reminded himself to breathe as he glanced at the typist in the corner. He gave her the same nod he'd given Chetty, but she seemed to be ahead of him. He heard the briefest of pauses from her stenograph. And then its faint clacking resumed.

The exchange between Chetty and White would be rendered in the official transcript as a lost garble concerning a "footnote to paragraph nine." Which was the only reference that Keynes, or anyone else who looked over the transcript this evening, would find to this stray asterisk.

The meeting droned along.

And that was it. By the time the conference adjourned, the IMF agreement would come to ninety-six excruciatingly detailed pages, and the most important point in the biggest deal in the history of international finance would be buried within an obscure footnote.

Because the only fully "gold-convertible currency" on today's date, July 22, 1944, was the U.S. dollar. Every one of these nations would buy into the Bretton Woods system with the easiest payment method at their disposal. And thus would the American dollar become the crude oil that powered all of global commerce.

Keynes would have what he wanted: a world currency. Only it would be one that was manufactured in Philadelphia.

The empire to come would not be ruled by the barrel of a gun, but by the gravity of coins. The future of the world belonged to greenbacks. And to the man who could make them.

And that man was sitting at Ansel's side, scratching at his chin while using his hand to cover the first stirrings of a sly smile.

Now all they had to do was make it another thirty-six hours without Keynes's seeing that footnote.

67

DEAD DROP

"History is written by the victors . . .
except on Wikipedia haha."

—ELON MUSK

July 22, 1944 (cont'd)

After the delegates agreed by verbal assent to the lengthy text establishing the WB and the IMF, they all went straight to the bar. Ansel and the Professor, however, went to the ballroom. There they aided the legion of secretaries in preparing forty-four identical copies of the agreements. Before checkout the following morning, each nation's head delegate would have to sign.

By the time the papers were ready—every sheet meticulously proofread, including the footnotes, which were rendered in smaller-than-usual type—the bulk of the delegates were so drunk that their signatures had been reduced to abstract scribbles. DuBois demonstrated the patience of Job as he slid ballpoint pens between their fingers.

Keynes, Ansel realized, had gone back to his room. Ansel decided to let him rest up. In the morning, at the last possible moment, he would casually slide the agreement in front of him and collect the final signature.

Ansel was leaving the Ethiopians' room on the third floor when he saw a figure rushing toward him down the hall: a woman in a yellow patterned dress, her black hair rustling behind her.

It was Angela.

Was that panic on her face?

He thought of her three unaccounted-for brothers.

"There you are!" She pulled him close and spoke in a breathy whisper. "I saw someone. In the hotel. Someone who shouldn't be here."

What was she saying in between huffs?

"When you gave the press briefings," Angela whispered, "who were the Soviet journalists?"

Ansel didn't remember their names. "What's going on?"

"The journalist from Soviet TASS. Dark hair, rectangle glasses?"

Ansel vaguely recalled the man in question.

"He's not a journalist," Angela said. "His name is Vladimir Pravdin. The FBI had a tail on him when he was based in San Francisco. The photos of him and his spies, they were all over the desk of the agent I was working for . . . Ansel, he's GRU. He's Soviet intelligence."

"What's he doing here? How'd he even get in?"

"I have no idea." She glanced up and down the hallway making sure they weren't being observed. "I saw him in the lobby. Just minutes ago. The second I saw his face—I knew I recognized him. I went up close, walked by, saw his press badge . . . It's Pravdin, I know it. He's a handler."

"What does that mean?"

"He runs GRU double agents." The next breath caught in her throat. "The ones with positions in the U.S. government."

———

PRAVDIN WAS JUST LEAVING the hotel when Ansel and Angela made it back to the lobby. He was holding a brown leather case, soft and worn. They followed him through the double doors into the summer night.

The twinkle of fireflies in the fresh cut grass.

The front steps were crowded with tippled economists. Ansel and Angela were careful to stay a ways behind Pravdin as they trailed him into the woods.

Ansel had never given someone a tail before. Everything he knew about the process came from *Dick Tracy*. Was this an appropriate distance to maintain?

68

AM I A
GOOD PERSON?

*"Virtue is more to be feared than vice, because its excesses
are not subject to the regulation of conscience."*

—ADAM SMITH

uly 22, 1944 (cont'd)

Harry and **A**nne Terry White had been selling information to Moscow
ince '35. They'd first met Pravdin at the home of a junior Treasury
man named **N**athan Silvermaster at a Sunday afternoon cocktail party
ull of like-minded young bureaucrats nurturing ambitious plans.
'ravdin's English was poor, but Anne Terry's Russian was good; White
uselessly contributed his French. They all, their host included, had
ound themselves frustrated by Washington's culture of secrecy, especially in regard to the United States's allies in the Soviet Union. Surely
at a time of mounting dangers to both nations, chiefly from Germany,
ome cooperation would be to the benefit of all!

It wasn't about the money. Anne Terry was adamant on that point
as she began explaining the situation to Ansel and Angela after they
confronted the couple in the clearing. It was never about money, she
assured the Luxfords, not for an instant. Even though, yes, Harry had
been compensated for his efforts.

At first the secret information, her husband interjected, had in fact
traveled *toward* Washington. A week after cocktails, Pravdin had offered to share some mildly interesting GRU intelligence with White
via Silvermaster. They had men in London with information on

Either Angela *had* done this before, or she had an instinct for
had a great many questions he wanted to ask her, but as they cre
the nighttime forest, sliding behind the sugar maples, he could
saying a word.

He didn't remember making the decision to follow Pravdin
had both just started doing it. Perhaps the war had left its m;
them. Or was it that every morning they'd sat at their St. Paul b1
table and decried the coming apocalypse, wishing they could d(
thing, this was secretly what they'd both always had in mind: sl
through the bare moonlight on the trail of villains.

Ansel stepped gingerly over the fallen branches.

He had no idea how long they crept before they came to
clearing. Pravdin placed a hand on a large tree trunk and set his
case beside it.

Then he turned around.

Ansel and Angela crouched. Pravdin didn't seem to see the
went back the way he'd come.

Ansel started to follow again before Angela pressed a han
chest: *Wait*, she mouthed. Then she pointed to the case.

When Pravdin had made it a safe distance away, Angela l
close, her whisper like the hush of wind against dried leave
dead drop. Someone is going to come pick up that case. Or m
something in it. I say we wait here, see who it is."

They didn't have to wait long.

It couldn't have been twenty minutes of crouching silent
the clearing, listening to the static of crickets and the occasio
terings of the summer breeze, before they heard the crunch
steps.

Ansel tried his best not to even breathe.

The footsteps approached from opposite the direction :
Pravdin had left.

And then into the clearing came a pair of faces they kne
well.

Keynes's plans to devalue sterling before a trilateral economic conference between the UK, France, and America. Surely the ongoing war of competitive devaluation that was all the rage in '35—largely at Keynes's instigation—was a one-way ticket to mutual ruin. So Pravdin didn't mind sharing his intel on the Brits, as it would, of course, serve the common good.

It was that leak of internal Exchequer plans that gave White his first major victory at Treasury. And thereafter, his first substantial promotion. Soon he sat at Morgenthau's side.

From which position he began taking copies of classified Treasury documents home in his briefcase. Anne Terry would make copies overnight before delivering them to either Pravdin or Silvermaster. Moscow was grateful for the Whites' assistance and paid them more in information than in currency. Which is to say that with the information White traded to and from Moscow, he could dictate the fate of many more dollars than whatever modest few sat in his checking account at Hamilton National.

They were doing it for patriotic reasons, White emphasized again. He knew exactly what information he could share with Moscow and exactly what he could not. He knew what would help the Soviets against only the Germans. Moscow's tenuous nonaggression pact with Berlin caused only a slight damper in his cooperation. He'd known it wouldn't last. Sure enough, the Soviets eventually realized the error of their ways.

He assured the Luxfords that he never gave the Soviets anything that helped them get the better of Washington. He was smarter than they were; that was how he put it. He could use them while pretending to let them use him.

Was it illegal? Well sure, but wasn't half of what the Research Department did illegal? This was simply another in his noble schemes. And this one worked.

How did he first get all that internal Reich Statistical Office financial data from which the Research Department had worked out Mefo bills? The GRU smuggled it out of Berlin for him.

Who'd broken into Ansel's hotel room back in '39 and accidentally displaced that telltale paper clip? The goon wasn't from the FBI—he was from the GRU. White had asked Pravdin for assistance in vetting his new recruit. Soviet intelligence ascertained that Ansel was clean as a whistle.

How did White know what financial demands to put in Roosevelt's final peace offer to the Japanese back in '41 such that he could be absolutely sure the Japanese would say no? The GRU, of course. Soviet intelligence was more than happy to assist him in detonating, so to speak, peace talks between America and Japan.

How did White get the Soviets to agree to the deal in Bretton Woods? It wasn't DuBois's offer of an extra hundred million in IMF commitments. It was Anne Terry's promise to smuggle the AM-mark printing plates to Pravdin. She'd had no trouble making arrangements with Silvermaster's other Treasury spies to get copies of the plates.

Ansel and Angela watched mutely as White removed the plates from his own briefcase and placed them into Pravdin's. A simple piece of business.

The Soviets would now be able to make as much German currency as they wanted. But that was Germany's problem. Or, as Anne Terry put it, that was the problem of a bunch of German pig farmers who'd been dumb enough to elect Adolf Hitler in the first place.

Ansel wondered what it must feel like to believe that you could outsmart not one but two nations' intelligence services. Perhaps it felt similar to believing that you, and only you, were smart enough to manage the finances of the entire world. Ansel wouldn't know. He'd never, in the whole of his life, felt less smart than he did right then.

"There's no need to make hay here," White said, his face illuminated only by his lighter as he set the flame against a cigarette. "After all, you both helped."

Hadn't Angela forged FBI documents and delivered stolen State Department cables? Hadn't Ansel been committing all manner of treason at White's side for years? Hadn't it been the Luxfords, working in clandestine concert, who'd thrown the FBI off White's scent? The Soviet defector who'd told the FBI that there was a spy inside the Research Department hadn't been a plant from Breckinridge Long—he'd been telling the truth. And when White had convinced both Ansel and Sumner Welles that the defector was part of Long's plot, they'd been only too eager, hadn't they, to delegitimize a genuine source?

Why, it was almost as if Ansel and Angela had been in on it from the start! At least that's how it would look, were any federal investigators to start digging their noses into this pile of lies and carefully nourished half-truths.

Plus, who could argue that the Luxfords hadn't, in the end, served their country well?

Look where it had gotten them! Look where they were, these two couples bound together by betrayal and, at last, victory.

Unless, of course, Ansel and Angela were to run to the FBI. In that case, they'd *all* go to jail. The Luxfords could try to claim that their crimes had been committed out of ignorance. But who'd believe them? To the Department of Justice, would such a distinction even matter?

What would the FBI make of Ansel's insistence that when he'd torpedoed a Japanese peace deal at the instruction of the GRU, he hadn't realized on whose information he was acting?

White reached for another Lucky before crumpling the pack: Wouldn't you know it? Empty.

Anne Terry found a stray smoke in her own case and lit it for her husband.

"So then," she said. "Shall we return to the hotel and get on with the evening?"

Ansel felt an urge to stand between his wife and these traitors. He wanted to protect her. But from what? He had a sickening feeling that the person from whom she most needed protection was him.

He was the one who'd gotten her into this. He was the one who thought he knew what he was doing.

He spoke to White: "You two-faced fraud. You've been lying to me, to her, to all of our colleagues and friends for years."

"You mean, exactly like I told you I would back when we first met?" White did not seem to have the patience for any more lectures. "Didn't I tell you I'd do whatever it took to win? Didn't I tell you I'd lie, cheat, steal, break any laws of our country, not to mention common decency? I did. We won." He puffed smoke toward the stars. "We stopped the Nazis. And so help me, just this week we stopped another Great War from ever starting. You know we did. And you think I'm bound for eternal torment because, what? I told *you* a couple fibs?" He laughed at the tender innocence of such concerns. "Am I a good person? I don't know. I'm the guy who got the job done. You're welcome."

Angela spoke before Ansel could. "You didn't just lie to *us*. Morgenthau? The president?"

"And you two were unfailingly forthcoming with your government, were you?" White's voice had a note of sympathy when he spoke to her. She, after all, hadn't signed up for this. "I did them a favor. They didn't have to do what I had to do to win. Those are great men. Thanks to me, they get to stay that way.

"I know you're sore. But I don't think it's this Soviet business you're really angry about. All the moves we've each made in this game and *this* is the one that crosses the line for you? No, I don't buy it. You're angry because you wanted to help save the world, *and* you wanted to be the good guys. This is the moment when you've got to come to grips with the tough nut that you can't well do both."

Ansel was ready to throw a punch. He hadn't slugged those Silver Shirts in St. Paul. So he'd been saving up this one big swing for a while.

White gave him this little smirk like he just *wanted* him to. But if getting his jaw broken would give White the moral high ground he craved, well, he could have it.

Anne Terry stepped between the two men. She spoke to Ansel: "Think carefully now. Talk to your wife. Because if anybody else finds out what the two of you just did, then the entire deal you put together to preserve a lasting peace goes up in smoke. Everybody pulls out and we're back in 1919 again, twiddling our thumbs until another great wave of violence churns onto the shore. I'm thinking of my girls here. I'm thinking of yours. I'm thinking of Junior."

Angela grabbed her husband's hand. She said nothing as he turned to her. But in her eyes he could see the passing of the headstrong idealist he'd first met in a law school lecture hall. In her place another woman was settling in, picking out curtains, firing up the stove. She was squeezing his hand and she was telling him, silently, that she was still going to love him even after this.

Even after they did what she already knew, in her hardening heart, they'd have to do.

He wondered whom he was married to now, and what it would be like, in the years to come, to get to know her.

"Which'll it be, buddy?" White gestured back to the hotel, where the Professor and DuBois should have finished collecting the last of the delegates' signatures. Only Keynes's would remain. "You want to bring us to justice, whatever that means? Or do you want world peace?"

69

SIGNATURE

*"Whoever becomes a lamb will find
a wolf to eat him."*

—VILFREDO PARETO

July 23, 1944

When Lydia opened the door to room 219, she looked refreshed even though it was barely dawn. "Mr. Luxford! Do come in."

Her bags were packed and neatly lined up for the coming porters. No stranger, she, to fine hotels or the niceties of being properly served.

After calling to the bedroom for her husband, she told Ansel that they were bound that evening for Toronto. She hoped the cooler air might do Maynard's constitution some good.

"How's he feeling?" Ansel asked.

Before she could answer, he appeared in the doorway and did it for her: "Like new."

But Keynes seemed weak as he shuffled to the dining table. He had to place a hand on a chair to help himself to a seat. "Perhaps hearts are like automobiles. Sometimes it helps to turn them off and back on again." He squinted at the stack of documents under Ansel's arm. "Is one of those for me?"

Ansel brought over the contract.

Setting it down, he paused. All he'd have to do is speak a few words in Keynes's ear and White's villainies would be exposed.

He took in the frail genius sitting before him, moments away from signing his name to a paper that he had not read, that in its fine print would give away all hope of achieving his life's work. One stroke of a pen, and his dream of building a new global currency would be over.

Perhaps he would discover the ruse on the way to Toronto, or perhaps not until he'd returned to Tilton House, surrounded by his sun-faded reminders of disbelieved currencies. Either way, his hands would be tied. To be sure, Parliament would have to ratify the agreement, as would Congress in the United States. But that would only magnify Keynes's humiliation: Unless he was willing to let the whole thing collapse, he'd have to go in front of Parliament and passionately advocate for a deal in which he'd been cheated. He'd have to argue to his incredulous countrymen that White's ideas had in fact been the better ones. Or at least were the best they could do under the circumstances. And he'd do it, Ansel knew, because the only alternative to suffering this humiliation would be accepting another war.

This was the sting, the raw cruelty of Ansel's victory: Keynes was the best of them. He'd told the fewest lies to achieve the greatest good. He'd been bested only because Ansel had employed the very loftiness of Keynes's own ideals in engineering his fall.

Would Keynes's vision for the global economy have been the superior one? Could it have produced a more widespread prosperity than the one they were about to put into place?

Ansel would never know. His wife was not the only idealist coming to grips with a world in which morality was not always so simple as decrying Nazism.

He felt a brief longing for his enemies. He missed the clarity that their cruelty had provided.

He thought of White, the crooked architect of what would be their enduring triumph: Rumors were already spreading that he was going to put himself up to be the first director of the IMF. A spider at the center of his vast web of dollars.

Ansel had a plan for that, though. White had let slip that Sumner Welles hadn't been in on the double dealing; and while White was obviously no stranger to the casually dropped lie, the order of events necessary for Welles to have been working in secret for the Soviets simply made no sense. Welles was clean. And moreover, Welles would know people in the intelligence services. The sort of people who could be approached carefully, and who, provided with the identity of an American double agent, would know better than to arrest him. They'd want to keep him in place and control him. Box him out from real influence, just as White had once done to Breckinridge Long, to spend the rest of his sad career wondering why his phone calls went unreturned, why his appointment to lead the institutions he created never materialized, why the Oval Office never again opened for his visits.

In exchange for the gift of Harry Dexter White—their very own Soviet agent through whom they might leak whatever half-truths they found convenient—Ansel would ask for only one thing: Protection for Angela. Safety for his family.

And if they'd give it to him, he could offer more.

Stories already circled around G Street of Treasury men leaving government service to open up private firms that did business abroad. Firms with unknown client lists and frequent travel to Cairo, to Cuba, to Brazil. As the war came to its bloody close, military intelligence was not what it used to be. It was much bigger. And if the rumors were true, they might have use for dismal scientists unafraid of having dirty hands. Numbers men, the kind you'd never glance at twice, who could unseat governments by adjusting decimal points on spreadsheets.

Dollars were going to become so ubiquitous that even the Soviets would have to move mountains of them all around the world. And who knew more about tracking illicit dollars than Ansel and his colleagues? They'd invented the art. They'd created the dollars.

He felt certain he could make a deal. After all, when it came to such shadowy exchanges, he had learned from the best.

He found himself, not only on that day but on many of the days to come, wishing that he lived in a world where Keynes had prevailed. It would be a more beautiful place than this: a drab territory of palatable compromise. But that had always been Keynes's point, hadn't it? Money was ephemeral, candles in a drafty cathedral, prayers to something in which we might all believe. But this table, this chair, this suite; Keynes's loving wife, his weakening body, his remaining days on earth; these coarse papers, this smooth pen, the beating hearts that hung in the balance; these things were real. No: They were the only things that were real.

Ansel flipped through the sheets, straight to the signature page. He pointed Keynes toward the dotted line.

Keynes stared at it for what seemed like ten minutes. In reality, it was probably ten seconds. He tapped his jacket pocket for a pen. Ansel handed him one.

"You see?" Keynes said as he signed his name. "It all worked out in the end."

AUTHOR'S NOTE

"An economic writer requires from his reader
much goodwill and intelligence and a large
measure of cooperation."

—JOHN MAYNARD KEYNES

WHAT YOU'VE JUST READ IS A WORK OF HISTORICAL FICTION THAT—TRUTH in advertising!—contains quite a bit of both history and fiction. It often tumbles back and forth between the two within the span of a single sentence. But it has the word *novel* on its cover for a reason: I'd urge you to think of this first and foremost as fiction, though one that's been sketched upon a canvas of reality.

That said, every major character depicted herein existed; the majority of the incidents described did occur in one way or another, and some lines of dialogue are even direct quotations. The Gordian knot of fact, supposition, conjecture, and dramatization has been tied so tightly that I wanted to include this brief note to help you tease out what's what and to explain, when I've departed from historical record, *why* I've done so. A peek under the hood, so to speak, so that like Professor Newcomer at the car dealership, you know what it is you bought.

The largest single source for this novel is *The Battle of Bretton Woods: John Maynard Keynes, Harry Dexter White, and the Making of a New World Order* by Benn Steil. It features brilliant short biographies of Keynes and White, as well as a detailed recounting of how their profound philosophical disagreements inspired their duel in New Hampshire. Initially I was interested in writing a book about Bretton Woods. Hundreds of delegates from nearly every country in the world met at a hotel over a few weeks to hash out the future economic system of the world? That sounded like a great setting for a spy novel. But as I pored over the full wartime history of the Treasury Department, I noticed that one name kept popping up: Ansel Luxford.

How was it, I wondered, that this person I'd never heard of had come to be in the room for so many pivotal moments in twentieth-century economic history?

All basic biographical information about Ansel Luxford in this book is accurate and was collected principally from interviews with his three children: Angela, Ansel Jr., and Stephen. I'm grateful to them all—and to Angela's husband, Henry Kerfoot—for their time and their memories. (I can only imagine how I'd respond if some stranger called me up one day and said he wanted to write a novel about *my* parents . . .)

All basic biographical information about Angela and her family is likewise accurate and was drawn from the same interviews.

The only official sources we have on Ansel's life are a single oral interview he conducted for the World Bank archives on July 13, 1961, and a brief profile of him printed in the February 15, 1950, issue of *International Bank Notes,* a publication for WB employees. He was not famous. He was not even well-known. Which is exactly why I was excited about telling this story from his perspective. The lives of White and Keynes have been exceptionally well depicted in terrific nonfiction accounts. (More on those shortly.) But it seemed to me that historical fiction would be an excellent form for telling Ansel's story, given its freedom to slip back and forth between factual reportage and novelistic portraiture.

CHAPTER 1: Marches and rallies of the Silver Shirts and affiliated pro-Nazi organizations, such as the one described here, were common in 1939 and have been rendered accurately, though no such march occurred in St. Paul on this specific date. Frequently throughout the novel I've simplified and tweaked the historical timeline for dramatic purposes in precisely the manner I've done here: I've pulled details from a few different pro-Nazi rallies held in 1939, combined them into one event, and placed Ansel within view of it.

CHAPTER 2: All basic biographical information about Harry Dexter and Anne Terry White in this book is accurate. *Treasonable Doubt: The Harry Dexter White Spy Case* by R. Bruce Craig is excellent not only as a biography but as a thorough analysis of the evidence that White was a Soviet spy. And I thank Craig for his time discussing the evidence with me.

I should note that there is some debate about the *extent* of White's espionage—what exactly did he pass along to Moscow?—as well as a few people who've argued that the evidence that he was a spy has been exaggerated. James Boughton's IMF working paper "The Case Against Harry White: Still Not Proven" from 2000 provides as good of a defense as you'll find.

Personally, as this text would indicate, I side with the prosecution.

CHAPTERS 2–3: The economic analysis that Ansel performs here is accurate, if simplified, and is largely based on a pioneering work of scholarship that was utterly foundational to this novel: Adam Tooze's *The Wages of Destruction: The Making and Breaking of the Nazi Economy*. Tooze's book is, in a sense, a mirror image of the one you've just read. It tells the economic story of WWII from the German perspective, and Tooze, unlike me, is one of the most acclaimed economists alive.

On which point, I'd like to thank the economic experts who read early drafts of this novel and provided invaluable corrections, guidance, and much-needed tutorials: Ernie Tedeschi, Liaquat Ahamed, and Austan Goolsbee.

All remaining errors are assuredly my own.

CHAPTER 7: Ansel did not leave his St. Paul practice to return to Washington in order to perform clandestine work on economic warfare for Treasury in September 1939. He did so in April 1940. However, it seems likely that he was in communication with White over that six-month period and was advising Treasury on its work against the German economy. (Which they'd begun even earlier still.) This was an instance of my sliding the historical record around a bit for narrative efficiency.

CHAPTER 8: All quotes from Roosevelt's radio address are verbatim.

Throughout this book, whenever I quote from a public figure's speeches, or from a newspaper report, I've done so word for word.

CHAPTER 9: All biographical information on John Pehle (pronounced "PAY-lee") is accurate and largely comes from another much-utilized source: *Rescue Board: The Untold Story of America's Efforts to Save the Jews of Europe* by Rebecca Erbelding. A resident scholar at the United States Holocaust Memorial Museum, Erbelding brilliantly recounts the work that Pehle, Joe DuBois, James Saxon, and Ansel Luxford did at Foreign Funds Control and then at the War Refugee Board.

Employees of FFC composed their own classified history of their actions during the war, perhaps recording them for a posterity they suspected they may not publicly be able to enjoy. That self-recorded history was recently declassified and to my knowledge was discovered by Erbelding. My thanks to her for sending it my way.

All biographical information about Mabel Newcomer, Joe DuBois, and James Saxon contained here is accurate, though their personalities had to be largely imagined. Much of the portrait of Professor Newcomer comes from a profile published during Bretton Woods ("Monetary Conference Keeps Dr. Newcomer Too Busy for Her Mountain-Climbing Hobby," *New York Times,* July 5, 1940) and the Vassar College Encyclopedia.

A fascinating oral interview with DuBois can be found in the Truman Library archives.

Herman Oliphant was not present for the meetings described here, because in reality he died in January 1939. But because Oliphant did so much important work on the freezing of German-held bank accounts for Treasury, and because after his death his role was filled by a series of rotating characters—including Joe DuBois—I extended Oliphant's life for an extra two years in this novel. That way, new Treasury Counsel characters didn't have to keep coming and going every few months as the narrative moved along. And Oliphant could be given the credit he well deserved.

This set of characters also did not all start working for White on the same day. It was more of a start-and-stop process over several months.

CHAPTER 12: Some early readers expressed surprise that I'd written of Americans' having common knowledge of the existence of German concentration camps as early as 1939, as well as knowing that the conditions therein were horrific. It saddens me to report that both are in fact accurate. "Concentration camp" meant something akin to "POW camp" to an American in 1939, and the phrase was commonly used. As to the German camps and the Jews within them, these were thoroughly reported on by mainstream American newspapers and magazines throughout the late 1930s.

Here are a few (of many) examples, all from *The New York Times*: "Life Inside a Nazi Concentration Camp," published February 14, 1937, which even has photos from inside Dachau; "Punished for Hitler Slur: Six Heidelberg Students Said to Be in Concentration Camp," published July 17, 1935; and most graphically, "Nazi Tortures Detailed by Britain; Concentration Camp Horrors Told," published October 31, 1939.

CHAPTER 13: Angela Luxford did go to work as a typist for the FBI after the family returned to Washington, as described here, though in reality she did not start the job until six months later.

Many of the details of life in the District in this period come from *Washington Goes to War* by David Brinkley, as well as *Washington, D.C.: The World War II Years* by Paul K. Williams.

CHAPTER 14: My description of the Nazi economic system is largely based on the work of Adam Tooze, once again, including his book *Statistics and the German State, 1900–1945: The Making of Modern Economic Knowledge*. Mark Harrison's *The Economics of WWII: Six Great Powers in International Comparison* is a terrific collection of essays on various elements of the wartime economy in different countries.

Henry Morgenthau: The Remarkable Life of FDR's Secretary of the Treasury by Herbert Levy, and *The Jew Who Defeated Hitler: Henry Morgenthau Jr., FDR, and How We Won the War* by Peter Moreira are both tremendous resources on the Treasury Secretary, whom I've tried to capture faithfully.

CHAPTER 18: The description of the Panama Conference here is accurate, though the specific meetings between Ansel, White, and Jacome Baggi de Berenger César have been imagined. In reality, Ansel was not present.

CHAPTER 19: While we know that Angela was working for the FBI in this period, what she might have learned there, and what of that she might have told her husband, are necessarily products of my imagination.

CHAPTER 21: The horrific scheme by which the Gestapo gained access to the bank savings of Jews—not to mention the savings of other people in German-conquered territories—is both accurate and, crucially, was in fact known to Treasury economists at the time. Evidence for the former is uncontroversial; a good description can be found in *The Swiss Banks* by T. R. Fehrenbach, a wide-ranging history of the role of Swiss banks in hiding money throughout the twentieth century that goes into some details about these Nazi schemes. My description of the latter, on the other hand, comes from the newly de-classified Treasury files discovered by Erbelding.

CHAPTER 22: Professor Newcomer's trip to the used car dealership was inspired by George Akerlof's seminal 1970 economics paper "The Market for Lemons."

CHAPTERS 23–24: These specific scenes illustrating the genesis of the Cash and Carry program have been invented, but the gist of both the program and the challenge of enacting it have been rendered accurately. *The Most Unsordid Act: Lend-Lease, 1939–1941* by Warren F. Kimball contains a nearly day-by-day description of the process by which Cash and Carry, and then Lend-Lease, were created.

CHAPTER 25: The voyage to England described here is an amalgamation of several trips Ansel and White took to the UK over the course of a year.

CHAPTER 27: All biographical information about John Maynard Keynes contained here is accurate. As befits a man who was easily among the most influential intellectuals of the century, we have no shortage of excellent biographies of him. Two favorites are *The Price of Peace: Money, Democracy, and the Life of John Maynard Keynes* by Zachary D. Carter, which beautifully takes us through not only Keynes's life and work but also illustrates the ways in which the latter lived on long after the all-too-early end of the former; and *Universal Man: The Seven Lives of John Maynard Keynes* by Richard Davenport-Hines, which teases out the many ironies and contradictions within a mind so complex.

The argument between Keynes and White in this chapter and the next was in reality largely conducted by way of angry letters, though a few in-person meetings did occur, and by all accounts they were explosive. All dialogue here is, of course, my own.

CHAPTER 29: What Keynes referred to as his "Babylonian madness"—his obsession with ancient currencies and the origin of money—reached its nadir in reality about ten years earlier than is described here. By 1939, I'm not sure where he would have kept his collection—it was large—but a special room in Tilton House seemed a reasonable place to put it for novelistic purposes.

My discursions on the history of money lean heavily on David Graeber's *Debt: The First 5,000 Years*. Graeber's views had an even more profound influence on me than Knapp's chartalist theories did on Keynes.

But because argument is always healthy: Niall Ferguson's *The Ascent of Money: A Financial History of the World* provides an excellent counterpoint to Graeber, though Ferguson's topic is less about where money came from and more about how it's changed over the centuries. To describe the political leanings of Graeber and Ferguson as being in total opposition would be to put the matter mildly. Which makes them a great set of paired reading.

CHAPTER 30: All the biographical information about White in this chapter is accurate, though the specific story he tells about the abandoned church in France has been imagined.

CHAPTER 31: The description of the D.C. premiere of *Mr. Smith Goes to Washington* is accurate, though Ansel and Angela did not attend.

CHAPTERS 32–33: All the biographical information about Sumner Welles here is accurate, though my bringing him into White's espionage storyline in this manner is a novelistic conceit. That said, Welles really was a committed anti-fascist embroiled in significant behind-the-scenes conflict with Breckinridge Long and other Nazi sympathizers at State. *Secret City: The Hidden History of Gay Washington* by James Kirchick contains a beautiful portrait of Welles, and of many other gay men and women living in Washington during the war.

CHAPTER 34: All biographical information about Breckinridge Long contained here is accurate. However, he did not secretly bury a cable to the State Department reporting German atrocities against Jews in 1939. He did so in 1943.

This is a section that might benefit from a more detailed explanation of my timeline shifting: Long's pro-Nazi deceptions, as well as the fact that Treasury employees had to literally sneak into the State Department to steal a cable that proved what Long had done, is real and comes from Erbelding's work discussed above. Once I first read about this incident, I knew I had to include it in this novel. But the break-in occurred in 1943, a year that my narrative skips over. What to do? I decided to move the incident to 1939 for novelistic purposes. But that brought up a serious moral issue: Moving around the timeline of State Department skullduggery is one thing, but I do not believe that it would be ethical on my part to play fast and loose with the timeline of the Holocaust. Some horrors are too sacred to be bent to the plotting efficiencies of fiction.

So what I did was change the *contents* of the cable that Long buried—and that Treasury uncovered—to reflect an incident of anti-Jewish atrocity that was accurate to 1939. That way, I was able to preserve the true stomach-churning timeline of the Holocaust, while moving the specifics of our characters' break-in at the State Department building ahead a few years.

In reality Joe DuBois was the one who led the break-in, not Ansel. Though he was involved in the operation.

CHAPTER 35: How aware was Angela of what her husband and his colleagues were up to, and how involved was she, given her role at the FBI? The historical record is blank.

CHAPTER 41: Ansel and Angela moved the family into this farmhouse in McLean, Virginia, in 1947, not 1940.

The White House defanged Breckinridge Long, as depicted here, in 1943—since that was when the cable was actually uncovered—not 1940. However, Morgenthau was given the green light to take the gloves off, so to speak, regarding Germany in April 1940, as shown here. In reality it seems likely that the White House did this in response to the German invasion of Norway, not because of anything having to do with Long.

CHAPTER 42: All biographical information about J. P. Morgan Jr. here is accurate, as is my description of his work to sabotage the Bretton Woods accords. That said, these specific scenes are invented.

Likewise, this description of Randolph Paul is essentially accurate, though he wasn't Morgan's lawyer specifically, just a prominent Wall Street one. And in reality, he joined Treasury a few months before this.

CHAPTER 44: Descriptions of the Havana Conference are accurate, though again, these specific scenes are invented. In reality, White was definitely there, but I have not been able to determine whether Ansel was.

CHAPTER 45: My depiction of the inimitable Lydia Lopokova is based largely on *Bloomsbury Ballerina* by Judith Mackrell. While the dialogue in these scenes is invented, my description of Keynes and his wife's unique marriage is, I believe, accurate.

I'll note that some commentators have argued that Keynes was exclusively homosexual and that his marriage to Lydia was a fiction maintained for social reasons. My feeling, however, is that the truth was more complicated. We have ample evidence that Keynes kept only male lovers for most of his life and that he had many hundreds of them. But likewise, we have letters between Keynes and Lydia after they met that make quite clear they were attempting to have sex, and attempting it frequently, if somewhat fumblingly. We also have evidence that their union became monogamous, after which they both forswore other sexual partners. We have no evidence that they reneged on such promises.

People are complicated.

CHAPTER 46: Not least among them John Maynard Keynes! For further insight into his singular philosophies, I recommend going straight to the horse's mouth: *The General Theory of Employment, Interest and Money* is by far his most accessible book.

CHAPTER 47: In these chapters I portray Keynes as helping Ansel design the system by which the United States would finance the coming war on both sides of the Atlantic. In reality, it was more that his work provided the theoretical underpinnings for what Ansel and Treasury were doing. That said, Keynes did write many letters to his American counterparts providing unsolicited advice on how they ought to manage their economy. (Advice that, needless to say, was conveniently to his own advantage.)

CHAPTER 51: This description of Felix Frankfurter's role in crafting the text of Lend-Lease is, believe it or not, accurate.

CHAPTER 53: Keynes really did betray White and Ansel by simultaneously negotiating these loans with both Treasury and Commerce. White really was livid. I can only presume that Ansel was as well. That said, this specific scene is invented.

CHAPTER 54: My description of White's and Ansel's roles in intentionally sabotaging last-minute peace negotiations with Japan is, I believe, accurate—though in fairness there are significant arguments to the contrary. We know for sure that White presented an offer to Roosevelt for a modus vivendi with Japan, and that when he proposed it, he described it as a huge concession designed to ensure peace. But we also know, obviously, that this offer was rejected. Did White (with Ansel's assistance) *intentionally* craft the offer so that it would be rejected? Their true thoughts will always remain obscure to us, though my opinion on this point comes from Steil, whose evidence I found compelling: both for intentionality and for the role Soviet intelligence played in *prompting* White to sabotage the modus vivendi, as discussed in chapter 67.

CHAPTERS 56–66: All descriptions of the Bretton Woods conference, and of the roles played by Ansel, White, and Keynes therein, are essentially accurate, while all dialogue has been invented. Ed Conway's *The Summit: Bretton Woods, 1944* is a terrifically lyrical and personal account of the proceedings. In reality, Angela and Anne Terry were not present, though Lydia was. But since many of the delegates brought their wives (and husbands), it seemed reasonable to include them.

I will note that most of the strange little details I've included—the white paint, Lydia's swimming naked in the pond, the placement of everyone's rooms, the Chinese and Soviet delegates, Keynes's heart attack, etc.—are all way too good for a writer of my limited abilities to have made up: They are real.

But most importantly: Did Ansel and White conspire to make U.S. dollars the global reserve currency by tricking Keynes into signing an agreement that he had not read, containing a buried footnote of which he was unaware?

They did.

CHAPTER 67: As to how, or whether, or to what extent Angela and Ansel learned of the Whites' espionage? I don't think we'll ever know.

CHAPTER 68: As discussed, I believe that the essentials of my description of both White's Soviet espionage and Anne Terry's knowledge and support of such espionage are accurate. But it's important to note that there are informed parties who would disagree with me here, some on minor points and some on major ones.

In 1945, a defecting Soviet courier named Elizabeth Bentley identified White as a fellow spy in interviews with the FBI. However, there are unquestionably inconsistencies in Bentley's story, and there are other parts of her tale that have since been proven to be untrue. Supporters of White have argued that all of Bentley's testimony needs to be disregarded on account of these problems.

After Bentley spoke to the FBI, J. Edgar Hoover himself was so concerned about White he put the economist under full FBI surveillance. Hoover personally worked to scuttle White's nomination to be the first head of the IMF, preparing a special report on White for President Truman.

In 1948, Bentley repeated her accusations against White under oath while testifying before the House Committee on Un-American Activities. White then publicly refuted these allegations in his own testimony.

Two days later, White died of a heart attack. He was fifty-five.

In 1995, the NSA began declassifying Soviet cables from its Venona project, a forty-year operation begun by the Signal Intelligence Service in 1943 to capture and decrypt secret Soviet communications.

These decrypted cables make frequent references to Soviet intelligence receiving classified information and guidance from someone at the U.S. Treasury—someone who went under the codenames "Richard," "Jurist," and "Lawyer."

As Steil puts it: "Based on the other names, dates, and places referenced in the cables, it is clear that Richard, Jurist, and Lawyer are cover names for Harry Dexter White."

Most historians consider the Venona decrypts to be proof positive of White's deceptions.

JOHN MAYNARD KEYNES DIED in his sleep, Lydia at his side, in 1946.

After the war, Ansel worked at the World Bank for a few years and then opened up a law firm with a few of his former Treasury colleagues, including John Pehle. His son Ansel Jr. believes that he was secretly working for American intelligence, though his other children told me they weren't sure. The historical record offers few clues. I believe that he was, but I cannot prove it.

Ansel Luxford died of complications from throat cancer in 1971.

True to his imaginings in chapter 1, no obituaries of him were published. Not a single newspaper, magazine, or periodical that I can find noted his death. His passing, like his life and work, was spent in quiet anonymity.

GPM

LOS ANGELES, CA

OCTOBER 2023

ACKNOWLEDGMENTS

IN ADDITION TO THOSE MENTIONED ABOVE, SPECIAL THANKS—AND MUCH besides—are due to:

Jennifer Joel, my literary agent of fifteen years, who has nudged this book along since it was a three-sentence email;

Caitlin McKenna, my editor, who has never once failed to ask the hardest questions;

Taylor Holt and Matthew Rusthoeven, my research assistants, who have spent innumerable hours talking with me about both Mefo bills and the Minneapolis trolley system;

And to the team at Random House who brought this book into existence: Noa Shapiro, Caroline Clouse, Vanessa DeJesus, Greg Kubie, Maria Braeckel, Michael Hoak, Windy Dorrestyn, Andy Ward, Ben Greenberg, Rachel Rokicki, Rebecca Berlant, Richard Elman, Dennis Ambrose, and Carlos Beltrán.

GRAHAM MOORE is the *New York Times* bestselling author of *The Holdout, The Last Days of Night,* and *The Sherlockian.* The latter was nominated for an Anthony Award for best first novel, while *The Last Days of Night* was named one of the best books of the year by *The Washington Post* and *The Philadelphia Inquirer.* He is also the Academy Award–winning screenwriter of *The Imitation Game,* for which he additionally won a Writers Guild of America Award and a PEN Award; and director and co-writer of *The Outfit,* which was nominated for a British Independent Film Award. Moore was born in Chicago, received a BA in religious history from Columbia University, and lives in Los Angeles with his wife and their two energetic children.

This book was set in Bembo, a typeface based on an old-style Roman face that was used for Cardinal Pietro Bembo's tract *De Aetna* in 1495. Bembo was cut by Francesco Griffo (1450–1518) in the early sixteenth century for Italian Renaissance printer and publisher Aldus Manutius (1449–1515). The Lanston Monotype Company of Philadelphia brought the well-proportioned letterforms of Bembo to the United States in the 1930s.